THE PENDRAGON WYTCH

THE PENDRAGON CHRONICLES

C. C. DAVIE

For those with a dark little soul, a sharp tongue, and a heart of gold. Morgana is for you.

TO DISTANT EASTERN WATERS
ROOK'S REST
SIREN'S COVE
THE MOORE
WRENSGATE
DEAD MAN'S DROP
SIRINELL
IRLING
THE SPINE
PEN DUBH
KINCONNAL
LOCH CRUINN

EAST
NE
NORTH
NW
KELPIES TEETH
GLENROCK
NAIRN
LALLYMOORE
WINDHAVEN
THE LOWLANDS
VINKIRK
THE HOLLOW
CRAIGEN DUBH
THE GREAT LANDS OF
KAMBRIA
TO UNCHARTED WESTERN WATERS

PRONUNCIATION GUIDE

A lot of the names in The Pendragon Wytch have been taken
from Irish and Gaelic origins which are both beautiful
languages. Some can be a little different to pronounce, so I
have listed those below. I hope you enjoy!

Gods

Ankii —*An-key* (God of death and decay)
Isstar — *Iss-tar* (Goddess of growth and life)
Mardur — *Mar-derr* (God of earth and land)
Nimmet — *Nih-met* (Celestial Goddess)
Tiamet — *Tee-met* (Goddess of the seas)

Names

Cerridwen — *Cer-id-when*
Faolán — *Fay-lan*
Gallin — *Ga-lin*
Gisslain — *Giss-lane*

Kerrich — *Care-rich*
Mads (Madraigh) — *Ma-drey*
Otto — *O-toe*
O'Mordha — *Oh-more-ra*
Rian — *Ree-an*
Saoirse — *Sir-sha*
Tadgh — *Tie-g*
Una — *Oo-na*

Creatures

Bánánach — *Bar-na-nach*
Druka — *Drew-ka*

Races

Drayvn — *Dray-van*
Sylvyn — *Sil-van*

Places

Adairn — *Add-dare-n*
Calibyre — *Cal-i-burr*
Craighen Dubh — *Craig-han Doo*
Endreal — *En-dree-all*
Kambria — *Cam-brie-ah*
Loch Cruin — *Lock Crew-in*
Nairn — *Nair-en*
Pen Dubh — *Pen-Doo*
Rhaore — *Roar*
Sirinelle — *Sih-rin-ell*

CONTENT WARNING

The Pendragon Wytch is an adult fantasy book that contains
content some readers
may find distressing, including;

Misogyny
Degradation
Murder
Physical assault
Gore

Less distressing content includes;

Strong language which may upset delicate sensibilities,
Unusual humor (Trust me, my editor tries to contain it)
(Actually that's a lie, she's as bad as I am)
Incredibly sapphic moments.
Like really sapphic.
Prepare yourself.

On page F/M
Sirin and her smart mouth.

If you would like to view the full, exhaustive list, please head to
my website:
www.ccdavieauthor.com

TRANSLATION GUIDE

A ghrà mo chroì: My love
Cinniúint, a ghrà mo chroì: Destiny, my love.
Nach bhfuil tú réidh, a ghrà mo chroì: You are not ready, my love.
Bhreugan cho milis, mo fhear dorcha: Such sweet lies, my dark one.

PROLOGUE

NIMMET

Thousands of years ago there was no separation of the mortal and immortal races. The five gods created all life equal, to live alongside one another.

Tiamet, Goddess of the seas and waters, Mardur, God of the earth and land, Isstar, Goddess of growth and life, Ankii, God of death and decay, and myself, Nimmet.

I am the celestial Goddess.

They say I dance the line of sanity, but they do not see what I do. My creations are amongst some of the most beautiful in this world we created—and some of the ugliest. Life is not as black and white as they seem to believe. There can be no light without the dark, no good without evil.

I birthed the stars for our creations to dwell within after their mortal bodies expire.

I created the places their minds slip to in moments of peace, both waking and asleep.

I molded the light and dark in their souls, while giving them the ability to choose where they settled on that scale.

There is beauty in both and that was my greatest gift to them, the potential to become unique amongst themselves.

I named our creations humans and watched them flourish, becoming hungry for knowledge, to be more than their baser selves. The more they changed and became their own sentient beings as a result of my gift, the more the other Gods grew angry with me.

Tiamet, Mardur and Isstar blamed me, as our humans began fighting amongst themselves. They did not see the humans learning from these moments. Pain, hunger, even death was teaching them valuable lessons.

They were no longer *ours.* They belonged to themselves, a product of their own hopes and dreams, and their minds are my greatest achievement.

Tiamet, her temper as harsh and unforgiving as the seas she created was the one who convinced the others to banish me, cutting me off from this world I love so much, though their power was only great enough to push me as far as my stars. From here, I have watched for millennia.

As time passed, Ankii grew restless, his yearning for chaos guiding his hand to create beings in his own image.

And so, the Drayvn were born, a race so like humans, but lacking the vital parts that made our humans so special. Vicious, long-lived and bloodthirsty, they do not follow their hearts as our humans do, but their minds, and they crave dominance.

Our humans were nearly wiped from existence, and it was only when Tiamet, Mardur and Isstar stepped in and created the Helix, pooling their magic into a crystal that imbued select humans with a kernel of their power, that our precious creations were saved from extinction. These beings became the Sylvyns, protectors of life. Protectors of our humans, as long-lived and powerful as the Drayvn.

The others have since grown bored of this world, leaving it to begin a new one, leaving our world to fend for itself.

But I'm still here. Still watching from the stars.

The humans are growing unhappy, coveting the power of the immortals and the Sylvyns are distracted by the Drayvn.

I fear what is coming.

I remain banished, whatever power the Gods used to keep me away still holds strong, yet occasionally a soul is born who shines brighter than the rest. A beacon to me, guiding me through their dreams, close enough to brush a fingertip against them and leave them with a gift.

They call these children blessed. Children touched by Nimmet, each so vastly different. Some have the light of my stars, others the whispers of my darkest dreams.

But they are mine.

My assurance that the balance of life will be protected until my legacy returns.

1

MERLIN

In my twenty-six years of life, I can honestly say that the feel of a woman's lips around my cock is amongst my favorite things. I would love to say I'm a simple man, with simple needs. But I'm not.

I am Merlin, a Child of Nimmet. Youngest hand to ever been appointed to the King, and one of the most powerful mages to walk the lands of Kambria... and right now, this kitchen maid, with her chestnut hair and sultry eyes, has me wrapped around her delicate little finger.

Which also happens to be cupping my balls with its companions.

I *can* be simple in this moment, I can almost forget what an absolute clusterfuck this day has been.

Almost.

I grit my teeth against the silken ecstasy that was her mouth, and listened to the sounds of my piercings clink against her teeth as I eased back before I lost myself down her throat too soon. After this day, the only balm to my ragged nerves would be the sweet sound of her moans… and I planned to extract my fill of them.

I should have known luck was not going to be on my side. I guess I should be grateful that whatever God was looking down and giving me the middle finger waited until I flipped her over, burying myself deep within her from behind, and at least prised the first orgasm from her shuddering body before they sent the messenger to knock on my door.

What was that saying? Don't kill the messenger? Right now I'm struggling to see why.

I pushed a hand between her shoulders, muffling her cries into a pillow to better hear the nasal voice that was calling through the thick panes of wood.

"Sir Merlin? His Highness requires your presence in his chambers."

I didn't answer, trying valiantly to focus on my rhythm as I adjusted my grip to wrap my fingers into the sweet girl's hair and pull her up.

"Another," I rasped in her ear, driving her harder into the mattress with every thrust as I slapped her hard across that beautiful arse.

"Sir—Sir Merlin?"

The knock came again just as pleasure built in a wave up my spine. I could feel her beginning to climax too, the delicate flutters of her inner walls as she convulsed and I listened to her gasped cries with satisfaction.

I came with my own groan, collapsing over her boneless body for a moment and resting my forehead against the damp skin between her shoulder blades, taking care not to crush her with my bulk.

"S-Sir?"

The knock was feeble now, almost like a cat scratching to be let in and I sighed, extracting myself from the girl and hastily throwing a blanket over her to cover her modestly. I padded to the door, cock still at half-mast and glistening with her release, and yanked the door open to reveal a ruffled-looking guard with the worst case of acne I have ever seen.

His eyes instantly dropped in respect, then widened in alarm and came snapping straight back up.

I watched the poor lad in amusement as he struggled between looking the infamous Merlin in the eye… or the other option of looking the smaller Merlin… in the eye. He seemed to be about to have an apoplexy, so I threw him a lifeline before I had to explain *why* I had a guard dead at my doorway.

"Did he say what it was regarding?" I asked, as easily as if I was enquiring about the weather.

"N-n-no—I mean—he said he needed to speak with you imm-immediately," the young man stammered, his eyes still pinging around his skull in every direction but toward me as he tried to choose a safe direction.

"Please let his Highness know that I will be down shortly," I replied.

"Yes, Milord," the lad squeaked, turning and racing off down the stairs.

Chuckling, I turned and padded back into the room, moving to the bed and pulling on my discarded pants before lifting the corner of the blanket to peer underneath.

"You still breathing?" I asked gently.

She cracked an eye at me, cheeks flushed as she nodded with a shy smile.

I patted her on the rear, annoyed I hadn't gotten the chance to introduce myself to it more thoroughly, then passed her the jug of water from the ledge next to the bed before running my hands hastily through my dark locks to make myself somewhat presentable.

The streak of silver hair on the left side of my temple was

a stark contrast to the black of the rest, and an unruly lock of it would always flop across the golden brown skin my forehead. It glinted in the sunlight that streamed in the window as—true to form—it escaped my ministrations. I was born with this silver, along with a vivid blue eye on the same side in stark contrast to the hazel of the other. I had hated it as a child, but now in my prime… I quite liked it.

"Do you want me to wait for you?" The girl—I'm ashamed to admit I didn't know her name—asked.

I pulled a clean shirt over my head before answering, giving her a smile that I hoped didn't show my worry about what the next few hours were to bring. "I might be a while."

She nodded, pouting, and I spared the few moments it took to lean across the bed and whisper a kiss against those pretty lips of hers.

Gods damned guards and their shithouse timing.

"Come back tomorrow and I will show you every devious idea I came up with while I had you beneath me. I haven't had nearly enough time to worship your body," I murmured, delighting in the flush that crept up her neck as she blinked at me. I winked at her, grabbed my cloak from the chair by the door and strode out.

The castle was in upheaval as I made my way to Arthur's quarters and I knew what it meant. He had finally found the Helix.

Fuck.

The Sylvyns hid it centuries ago after the humans began desecrating it, carving chips off it in an effort to glean some of the power it held for themselves, and now Arthur coveted it in its entirety.

Millennia ago, the Gods created the Helix crystal, a vessel of immense power that blessed select humans with near-immortal lives who became known as Sylvyn. In some cases a kernel of the God's power was also given, creating Wytchling Sylvyn.

But, the Gods—in their infinite wisdom, forgot about one thing.

Envy.

The humans grew tired of their lot. They wanted to rule as the Sylvyns have done for centuries. The Sylvyns accepted this and created territories that were governed by either race, allowing the humans to preside over themselves. But this was not enough. The humans coveted the Sylvyn's power, and when the Helix did not gift it, they began chipping slices from it.

An echo of Sylvyn magic was forced into their bodies when worn against their skin. A mere taste of what they had missed out on. Longer lives, weak Wytchling powers, a mockery of what they could have been.

The desecration of the Helix resulted in the end of spontaneous Sylvyn births through the humans—whether because the Helix had lost power or was angry is unknown. Even the Sylvyns themselves had begun to lose power. With each generation, fewer Wytchling gifts were passed on to them. The change was slight, but enough to become noticeable… and when Sylvyn and human blood is crossed, it is almost certain the babe will be human.

The Sylvyns are a dying race, and envy is the cause.

"Merlin," Arthur greeted me without looking up as I entered his chambers. He was pouring over a large map, his finger tracing along the intricate artwork of valleys and coastlines.

"Sire," I murmured, bowing to him. "You sent for me."

"Sixty years," he said, shaking his head. "Sixty years I have searched for the Helix, and today I finally learn where it has been resting all this time. A group of Sylvyn were picked up last night and one of them has been very helpful."

I felt like someone had wrapped an icy fist around my heart at his words. "My Lord, the Helix is already weakened, taking more from it could do irreparable damage."

Arthur scoffed, waving a hand at me. "I am just relocating it. I am no fool, the Helix is the last of the God's gifts to us." He looked at the two iron cuffs he wore, the slivers of Helix sunk into the undersides, against his skin. "I feel it, Merlin. I can feel the years creeping over me, slowly sapping my strength. I am not done, I have too many plans, too much to do before death takes me."

"And bringing the Helix back to your estate will stop that?" I asked, trying to keep my voice calm. "The Helix decides who it will gift, if it could be forced, it would have been done years ago before the Sylvyns hid it."

"Perhaps," Arthur said. "But having two slices of that rock has given me over seventy years already, imagine what the Helix in its entirety can give me. With it, I can see this Kingdom through to greatness. The Sylvyns are not the only ones who deserve the time to be great, Merlin."

I bit my tongue. I was only given the position of advisor three years ago, not for my years, nor my knowledge, but for *what* I was. Nimmet blessed. Powerful. My role here was purely ornamental and if I wanted to change that, actively disagreeing with my King was not the way I was going to achieve it.

Arthur rapped his knuckles twice on the table, a habit I have noticed him do when he has come to a decision.

"We ride today. Through the ranges to the south of here and out to the coast. We can reach it within three weeks."

My brows rose. "The Helix is in Wrensgate territory?"

Arthur gave me a smile that was pure wolf. "It's been under my nose all this time."

Rain lashed at us, the horse's heads angled into the rain as they walked, ears flat to their head. We had ridden at a hard pace to get here, Arthur forgoing a proper guard and leaving the carriage long behind us in his haste to get to the coast.

I slid an eye over a beaten and bloodied male strapped to a horse just ahead, it had taken a fair bit of my concentration to keep the male's pain at bay as we traveled, his life slipping from his grasp with every step we took. Better he had died before divulging the location of the Helix.

I didn't blame him, I had seen the lengths the dungeon masters had gone to before when they thought they were close to the Helix. I had even managed to aid the passing of some before they had felt too much pain. I had encountered this one too late and now I bore witness to the consequences.

I smelled the sea before we reached it, the cries of the gulls drifting to us on a salt breeze as we crested the last rise before descending to the coast. Wiping the rain from my eyes, I squinted toward the stormy expanse of the sea ahead of us, just making out the craggy terrain as my horse slipped and skidded on the narrow mud trail.

Arthur wheeled his horse as we leveled out onto flatter land, coming abreast of the bedraggled man who slouched in his saddle, head hanging low.

"Where?" Arthur growled, leaning across to grasp him by his hair, wrenching him upright.

I lightened the hold my power had on the man, letting a bit more of his consciousness filter in.

He raised a hand, more than one finger misshapen and broken on it, gasping with pain as he pointed along the stretch of coast to the right.

"Dead man's drop," I muttered, throwing a look at Arthur. "We should wait for the weather to clear before attempting access to that."

"What do you think I have you for?" Arthur scoffed, kicking his horse ahead with a barked order to the rest of the men.

I leaned cautiously over the cliffs of dead man's drop to the waves crashing on the jagged rocks below.

There was no surviving that fall, and the vicious coastline prevented any ships from coming in to retrieve any bodies unfortunate enough to end up at the bottom.

Soldiers behind me were uncoiling rope, a few knotting it around their waists while others were tied off to boulders along the cliffs edge.

"Merlin, you are with me," Arthur yelled across the wind and the men, tying his own rope and gesturing toward a spare coil with his chin.

I strode to him, passing my hand over the frayed rope around him and sending a whisper of my power into its bonds, strengthening it. "Let us go ahead, my lord. If the Helix is there, we will report back."

Arthur shook his head motioning for me to attend the

other soldier's ropes too. "I have come this far. I will see it myself first."

I set my jaw, turning to the remaining soldiers and seeing to their ropes. The man I currently had my hands on was shaking like a leaf, the knots he had tied useless and loose. I gave him a dark look, yanking them tighter just as he made an involuntary jerk forward, his eyes flying wide.

"Sire!" He yelled, lurching past me.

I turned in time to see Arthur disappear over the edge of the cliff, uncoiling the rope as he went.

"*Fucking* boneheaded imbec—" I cut off as another one of the soldiers threw themselves over the edge next to me, propelling themselves at a breakneck pace down the cliff after our king. Closing my eyes and sending a prayer to Nimmet, I followed.

I had never been a massive fan of heights, but dangling over the edge of one of the roughest sections of coastline in Kambria was definitely one of the lower points of my life. Wind whistled up the rockface as I descended while rain pelted us from every angle, making every handhold treacherous.

I caught up to Arthur quickly and matched his pace, carefully metering out the rope as I went, his armor slowing his descent.

My feet had only just hit the lip of the cave etched into the cliffside when a scream, followed by rubble skittering above had me throwing my body against Arthur, pushing us both out of the path as one of the soldiers lost his grip and fell, his terrorized scream cutting off sharply as he reached the end of his rope. The sound of a dull crack as his spine snapped when the rope—strengthened by my power—jerked him to a sudden stop, is one I know would remain in my dreams for years to come. As would his face, the terror of the moments prior to his death still etched on his face though his eyes were unseeing.

Arthur propelled himself away from the cliff face, using the momentum to swing himself into the opening and perch on the entrance, the rest of us following suit.

The air in here smelled musty and unnaturally still, as if it had been undisturbed for a century. Unease grew at the base of my spine, something deep within me urging me to turn back. But it was too late, Arthur was already striding off into the pitch black of the cavern, toward the whisper of a voice that was calling to me beyond the gloom.

My heart thundered in my ears as we moved through the darkness, lit by an orb of light dancing across my fingertips. I could hear the nervous murmuring of the soldiers at my back, but the deeper we walked, the stronger the voice ahead became. Its whisper echoed through my mind, both young and ancient at once.

"Child of Nimmet, why are you here?"

Light began to glow on the walls around us, and I let the light at my fingers wink out as we stepped into a cavern, light refracting off every glistening wall. In its center, glowing like a newly-born star, the Helix hovered, and holy Gods it was beautiful.

Slightly larger than a man, the crystal pillar glowed with an internal light, shimmering softly as power danced beneath its surface.

I couldn't stop myself from walking toward it, the light dazzling, yet not blinding. I ran a shaking hand over its surface and I *felt* it reach out, a whisper of its power caressing my own as if in greeting.

It flickered, as if faltering slightly and my eyes were drawn to the cracks and grooves along its surface. The marks of human hands stealing from it over the years. Injuring it. *Hurting it.*

I could feel its pain in that moment of connection, how it

yearned for its lost pieces. Even now I could feel it reach past me, toward the chips Arthur wore, beckoning them back to itself.

"Child of Nimmet," The voice was a brush against my mind —a question—and I opened to it, letting it curl into my soul, the tendrils of it reaching into every part of my mind.

"I am sorry, Helix. This was a mistake."

"Darkness gathers here, Child of Nimmet. Long foretold. I have been waiting for you."

I glanced over my shoulder, wondering if anyone else could hear its voice, but they all just stood, Arthur included, staring at the Helix as if transfixed.

"Sundered blood can heal what is broken this day, Child of Nimmet."

My attention snapped back to the Helix.

"She who was banished will guide the hand of her celestial children. Listen to her, Child of Nimmet, her legacy is the key to it all. She who created the wonders of this world. Only when sundered threads of the old ones are reconciled, will its children be worthy of the God's gifts once more."

It flickered again, and a soft sigh brushed past my mind as the Helix drew back into itself once more.

"Wait," I called, mentally lurching after it. This was a mistake. My complacency had caused this. I thought letting Arthur take the Helix would give me the time I desperately needed . Stop him from torturing Sylvyn's while I came up with a way of stopping him altogether from pursuing this obsession with the Helix power.

Dread curled in my stomach. I needed to get him out of here. Even if it resulted in my death, to touch the King… I had to get him away from the Helix.

I spun, power gathering in my hands, ready to unleash it.

Too late.

I caught the glint of metal as Arthurs's sword came down

on the Helix, its point embedding deep in the fissure, into its heart.

Screaming.

That is all I could hear as light exploded in the cavern. The death throes of the Helix echoed into my mind, my own screams mingling with it as I was thrown into a wall, feeling the crunch of bone against rock before I dropped to the ground.

It took a while for the ringing in my ears to abate, longer for the stars to clear from my vision.

Groaning to my right had me peering up to see a soldier painfully pulling himself up, another still motionless beyond him and I struggled to my feet, feeling blood trickling from my nose as I forced myself to look at the Helix.

It lay in ruins. Black rubble surrounded what was left of it and where it had glistened with light it was now as black as the darkest night. Excalibur, Arthurs's sword, still lay embedded in its heart, a lump of black rock the size of a curled child, but the blade had melted—metal rivulets running around the rock and encasing it in a cage, its hilt still grasped by Arthur.

My breath caught in my throat as I reached a hand to a piece of Helix that had come to rest by me. The second I touched it, it sucked at me, drawing my power into it as if trying to regain what had been ripped from it. I hissed, pulling my hand away and turned to Arthur, utter rage burning within me.

He had his eyes closed, a look of pure elation on his face. I took a step toward him, to do what… I don't know. Hurt him? Kill him in the way he had the Helix?

I was stopped short as he turned his head to me, his eyes slowly opening. They danced with the light of the Helix, flaring bright and then dimming to a roiling storm behind his eyes.

"What did you do?" I choke out, horror filtering into me. "The Helix—"

"Is mine," he interrupted, a slow, malicious smile spreading over his face. "I *am* the Helix. And now my kind will rise to their rightful place and the Sylvyn will bow to *us*, Merlin." He let the remnants of his blade go slowly, rolling his shoulders. "And with you at my side, the Sylvyn will know they are not the absolute power anymore."

He snapped a finger at the soldiers, now standing, terrified as they stared at him.

"Take what is left of this rock and bury it in the four corners of this world. I will not have it healed. The heart will come with us."

The men lurched forward and began gathering the shards. They didn't falter as they touched it, it can't affect them as it did myself... or Arthur, from how he flinched back from a soldier as he passed with an armful.

What have I done?

2

MORGANA

A CENTURY LATER

I have always been a restless sleeper; the stars call to me, and darkness is my friend. During the day I can fade into the shadows, but night is where I am truly comfortable. I can move through it like a ghost, unseen unless I will it.

But tonight, there are whispers in the shadowed winds, they are warning me of something, and I can feel that I am not going to like it.

The days are at their longest this time of year, the sun clinging to the sky late into the day, and I watch as it gradually gives way to night's inky fingers as I sit, curled in the window seat of my room. A tenuous, fragile calm descends over the world, and yet I am anything but calm myself. I can feel The Pendragon closing in on us, and now we have no further to run.

I shiver as the cold creeps through the glass, padding across the room to throw the message that had arrived by rook into the unnatural black flames of my fireplace, my power keeping it roaring with the dwindling supply of wood we had left to us now. I glared at the small slip of paper as it crumbled to ash in the dark flames, contemplating its words.

So there go my hopes of getting some of our people out along the Kinconnal coast before the winter storms make a sea crossing too perilous, and with how harshly it was setting in already, this was going to be the worst winter yet. The coastline of the Lowlands was impenetrable, along the west the mountains made access impossible, through the south and east the Kelpies Teeth made only the smallest of crafts able to navigate jagged rocks. Closer to Windhaven, the sheer cliffs with rocky feet meant no ship could get close.

It had kept The Pendragon's forces out all these years, the one time he had risked the Kelpies had cost him many men, their bodies still littered the ocean floor as our archers had easily picked the small vessels off from far away. But it also kept us trapped, the great walls of Windhaven both our protector and our cell walls. I had held a faint hope of getting some of our people out to Kinconnal, the coast there more agreeable, but The Pendragon was always a step ahead and Tadgh had been reluctant at the mention of it.

Everything was in short supply. Food, wood… hope. The people were hungry and had been for a while, which makes the banquet currently going on downstairs even more irritating to me than usual. It was a luxury that we could not afford, and the thought of people in the Lowlands going without because of this frivolity was not something I could forgive. I was expected to be there, but I only needed to show my face briefly and first, my bones were cold.

I set a bath running in my adjoining washroom. Only cold water ran in the castle pipes these days, there wasn't enough fuel to waste on the furnaces below, but it was barely half a thought to have my power heat the water until it steamed invitingly. The one luxury I afforded myself.

I lost my clothes, strewn in a line behind me and padded naked to my bookcase, twisting my long, inky curls into a bun at the back of my head. The bookcase was a solid wooden behemoth that stretched the entire wall behind my four-poster bed. I rested a hand on the generous curve of my hip, contemplating the titles before sliding one out. One of my favorites—a tale of the Goddess Nimmet.

Holding the book above the steam that wafted from the bath I eased myself into it, the water hot enough to redden my pale skin and set it pleasantly stinging as my eyes skimmed across words I could have recited in my sleep.

I leaned my head back against the back of the bath, propping my long legs on the edge of the tub as the words began to blur together. I closed my eyes, sighing as I felt the warmth finally reach my bones and tucked the book onto a shelf above my head, letting myself relax into the water as I trailed my fingers through the water, the ripples caressing my skin.

A tentative knock came at the door, and I groaned.

"What?" I called, raising my voice enough to be heard through the thick wood of my door.

"The Lord O'Mordha sent me to fetch ye' Milady," came the feminine voice from behind it.

"I will be down when I am ready," I called back, losing the battle to keep the irritation from my voice.

A pause. "I will just wait here then, Ma'am."

Swearing under my breath I hauled myself out of the tub, the cool air making me shiver, and wrapped a thick towel around myself before stalking to the door and yanking it open.

The maid took one look at me, towel low around my breasts and water dripping on the floor and paled.

"Unless you want me to come dressed in nothing but my skin, run along and find someone else to harass."

Her eyes darted down the hallway and back. "He said I was to stay until you came, Milady."

This was my fault. I was so careful to hide every trace of my power that the damned servants were more scared of Tadgh fucking O'Mordha than myself. I let some of my control slip, let the beast within me rise and dance behind my eyes.

"Scram," I hissed, huffing in amusement to myself as the girl picked up her skirts and fled.

I retreated into my rooms still laughing under my breath, and dressed reluctantly, choosing a forest green gown the same color as my eyes. I wasn't vain, but I can appreciate the ease my looks have lent me. In many ways a beautiful face can be more powerful than the deadliest of weapons. Men have begged on their knees for my affections without me having to wield a tendril of Nimmet's gift. Foolish creatures.

I studied my reflection for a moment. Pale, flawless skin that didn't see nearly enough sun, high cheekbones, full lips with a perfect cupids bow hiding the darkness in my soul. It was only my eyes that sometimes revealed what truly lay beneath, and even they were staring prettily back at me now beneath thick, dark lashes. I tended to shun the normal fashions, opting to leave my long hair loose around my shoulders rather than twisting it into the intricate designs some of the other women wore here. It seemed like far too much hassle for the headache it seemed to give them. Sighing at my reflection I headed out, making my way down to the great hall and this ridiculous fucking banquet.

The merriment in the hall was a mockery. Music filled the space, echoing off the vaulted ceilings as dancers twirled beneath it dressed in gaudy colors, laughing as if our destruction wasn't lurking beyond the gates of Windhaven. I poured myself a glass of wine and slipped into a seat along the back wall, pulling my face into the most unapproachable mask I could manage, my eyes instantly finding a flash of red hair as I picked Gwen dancing amongst the throng of people.

The middle sibling of the O'Mordha children, she was nothing like her brother… or her younger sister Saoirse. After the death of their parents during one of the countless battles, Tadgh became Lord of Windhaven, but it was Gwen who should be leading our people. A fact that was even more obvious now that she had returned for good from the Lowlands after the loss of Kinconnal, our last foothold beyond the walls. Even now, as I watched her trying to disengage herself from the throng of males surrounding her, she was doing it with grace, her face not portraying the irritation I knew she must be feeling.

"Lady Morgana, would you do me the honor of dan—"

"Fuck off," I growled, not even bothering to look at the male who had sidled up to me, though I saw him stiffen out of my peripheral vision, looking uncertain as to whether to push his luck. It seemed his cock won over his common sense, and he opened his mouth again.

I beat him to it, sliding my gaze to him disdainfully, brow arched. "No, I'm not going to dance with you, I am not hungry, I am most certainly not in need of company, I have no use for your tongue, much less your cock and no I do not need my drink refilled. Does that answer the rest of your questions, Lord…." I drifted off, trying to put a name to the face.

"Declan," he offered, looking as though he was caught between outrage and intrigue.

How is it that even a male that has lived hundreds of years can be this clueless? And given the length of his pointed Sylvyn ears, this male was far too old to be this thick.

"The lady already has a dance partner."

I bit back a groan as Tadgh appeared behind Declan, a smirk on his handsome face. He had his mother's blonde hair and the same whiskey-colored eyes as his father. Both Saoirse and Tadgh had inherited their father's fair complexion that could tan golden with only the barest hint of sun, whereas Gwen had the paleness of their mother, her moonlight skin dusted with the faintest freckles over the bridge of her nose.

Lady Cerridwen and Lord Kerrich O'Mordha were two people I had respected and was grateful for the home they had offered me when they found me all those years ago, wandering alone as a child in the unforgiving spine. They could have turned me into a weapon, wielded me against The Pendragon just as he used The Blood Traitor, Merlin's gifts against us.

Merlin—the Child of Nimmet who had betrayed us all and helped The Pendragon take what was not his—he was a traitor to his kind, shunned by us all. But they hadn't, and instead showed me how to hide my power, giving me an education alongside their own children and letting me have a childhood.

"The Wolf sent word earlier tonight, I was going to update you in the morning," I said dismissively.

"Let politics rest for a night," Tadgh said, his eyes roving over me. "Come dance."

"The Lady Gisslain seems eager for a dance, Tadgh. Why don't you go bother her?" I asked, eyeing up the pretty woman who had been throwing doe eyes at him since I had arrived.

She saw me looking in her direction, and gave me a sour, jealous look, and I leaned back in my chair throwing a casual arm over the back of it and giving her a wink before turning my attention back to Tadgh. "I have wine to drink."

He chuckled, holding his hand out to me. "One dance, Mim."

My lips curled over my teeth at the pet name his parents had given me. "Don't call me that."

He gave me what I'm pretty sure he thought was a charming smile, wiggling his hand at me as if he were coaxing a dog with a treat.

"I'm not dancing at a banquet when our people go hungry," I hissed under my breath.

His eyes hardened. "They need to have fun, Morgana," he said, his tone low. "They have lost much."

His hand hovered in the air between us, and he wiggled his fingers again, giving me a lopsided smile. "Please. Just one and I will leave you be."

Sighing, I placed my glass down, pushed out of my seat and stalked past him into the throng of people. I heard him snort quietly as he followed me, taking my hand and spinning me into his chest as we merged seamlessly into the dancers.

Tadgh's hand slipped around my waist, settling on the curve of my hip, holding me against him with a firm grip as we moved together.

"I missed you at the dinner last night," Tadgh said, executing a flawless lead change and sweeping me around the edge of the dancers.

"I'm sure you had plenty of wonderful company." I raised a brow toward Gisslain, then slid my gaze back to him. "I think she is currently plotting ways to slip some arsenic into my wine."

His lips twitched as he threw a subtle look her direction. "lackluster at best." He dipped his head toward my neck. "How do you always smell so intoxicating?"

I leaned back in his grip slightly, giving him a dark look. "Stop that." I was silent a moment as we moved through an intricate set of steps, ending in Tadgh spinning me out and back before whirling me along with him. "We need to talk about The Wolf. He's not willing to risk the ships."

I caught the exasperation on Tadgh's face before he masked it. "Can we not just enjoy the night?"

"Sure," I snapped, frowning up at him. "I will send word to the men who came pleading for more food for their children last week that they can wait another day because we were taking a break to enjoy ourselves."

I nearly tripped as Tadgh came to a sudden halt, pulling us out of the throng and into the shadows of an alcove.

"Enough," he said, his voice low. "Where is the girl who would dance with me in the halls when we were meant to be in bed? Have you become so cold that you have forgotten how it feels to enjoy life?"

"If I am cold, it is because we have no wood for our fires.

Our homes are cold, and our people's children go to bed hungry," I spat back. "Yet *these* people, who do not even hold the swords that fight for us sit here with full bellies and fine clothes, dancing as if we are not losing this war."

"*My* people, Morgana. Not yours," he snapped. "And we are not losing this war, it has been decades since The Pendragon last attacked, he knows he cannot breach our walls."

I ignored the slight. I had heard it enough times anyway. I was not Sylvyn, nor was I human. My ears would never tip into Sylvyn points, yet I lived an immortal life alongside them. My green eyes glowed with more power than any Sylvyn I had ever met, though I had learned as a child to dim it—to leash it, along with the darkness within me. The only ones alive who knew my secret were a small group who had watched me grow, and they had been ordered under pain of death to remain silent.

It was Tadgh's decision that had brought me into the public eye, and as yet, not enough years had passed for the Sylvyns to openly question why I was not beginning to tip. It was around a female's twenty-seventh year that her body slowed its aging process, and her ears began to tip into points, the only true way to observe the age of an immortal. For males, this began in their early thirties.

It was only a matter of time before it was revealed that I had somehow escaped the slaughter of every Nimmet-touched child born since The Pendragon's rise to power.

My parents had been searched for, yet there was no trace of them, except for a few burned-out cabins high in The Spine, and Lady Cerridwen had surmised they had taken me there as a babe to protect me.

I didn't even have a last name to claim, I was Morgana le

Fay. Morgana of the wild folk. A bastard-born nobody had I not been blessed as a Child of Nimmet.

"We lost the supply chains through Sirinelle, Glenrock and now Kinconnal, Tadgh. Open your eyes," I snarled. "You have allowed them to crumble, there is no way of getting anything in safely anymore and we lose four out of five shipments—not to mention the lives that are lost as well. The Pendragon is nearly knocking on our front gates, he is using hunger to smoke us out and he knows he has you by the balls. We should be out there securing the supply chain again, not filling these useless fools with food we do not have! You should be out there taking back what is keeping our people alive for fucks sake!"

Tadgh's face hardened. "The filth that comes out of your mouth is not your most attractive quality."

I sneered, standing so close that I could feel his breath heat my face.

His pupils flared, his eyes dipping to my mouth.

"Good thing my filthy mouth isn't something you will ever have to worry about then, isn't it?" I murmured, pushing past him and heading for the table of refreshments. I tried to swallow the feeling of hypocrisy as I poured myself another glass, letting the breeze from the open window next to me cool the anger that sizzled in my veins.

"I wondered when you would turn up."

I turned to see Gwen behind me, her cheeks flushed and looking slightly rumpled. She took the glass out of my hand, drinking deeply from it.

"Saoirse has disappeared again, and Tadgh's pride couldn't take both of you not showing up to this," she murmured.

I grunted, poured myself a new glass of wine and eyed the men approaching us over its rim. They were a mix of tradesmen and descendants of once esteemed families that had dotted Kambria. Now just as wretched as the rest of us with no titles to their names.

Gwen followed my line of sight and sighed audibly.

"I have a feeling your brother had ulterior motives for this occasion," I said, tone still short from my simmering anger toward Tadgh.

Her gaze flicked to mine reproachfully. "I'm not a fool, he has not been subtle."

The thought of her, married to one of these soft-handed men that hung on Tadgh's every word turned my stomach. As if a common-born husband would keep her from being a threat to his rule. I almost laughed at the thought. What was there left to rule over? A dying, starving race and lands that had been overcrowded and ravaged by the needs of the desperate.

I raised a brow at the males closing on us. "That one looks decent, he at least walks in a straight line. Quite the selection you have here, Princess."

Princess. The title that would have rightfully been hers had Kerrich not stripped himself of his own crown before the birth of his children in an effort to deter The Pendragon from his obsession to destroy them.

The barely audible growl she gave me had me hiding the corners of my lips twitching in my wine as she turned to greet the men.

"A dance, Milady?" The male held an arm out, looking hopeful.

Gwen smiled in apology, patting his arm. "No, I need a moment's breather, my Lord."

"Just one," he wheedled, crowding her. "I have been trying to catch you all night."

"A bit later," Gwen insisted, her gaze sliding down to where he had laid a possessive hand on her arm.

I bristled. "I believe the Lady said no, which is a short enough word that it shouldn't need explaining to you."

He blinked at me, irritation fading to caution as he looked into my eyes. "Remove your *fucking* hand from her," I said, my voice a low growl.

His hand snapped back as if he had been scorched, muttering his apologies as he backed away. Even Gwen looked at me with a hint of alarm on her face as I struggled to reign in the power that had once again risen in me.

I needed to let some of it off, I had been holding it on such a tight leash these past months that it was restless within me, too easily riled.

"Where is Saoirse tonight?" I asked, trying to distract myself.

Gwen huffed softly, "If I had to guess, I would say she's knee-deep in mud somewhere, handing someone's ego-crushed arse to them, or stripping some poor soul of the clothes off his back with her wagering rather than suffering through this damned idiotic night."

My eyebrows flew to my hairline. I had never heard Gwen openly disagree with any of Tadgh's ideas.

"What?" She asked, defensively.

I stifled the smile that was threatening and shook my head.

She put her glass down, her blue eyes casting across the milling dancers. "Back to it then," she groaned, smoothing her hands down her dress. She glanced at me, resting her hand on my arm for a moment. "Try not to insult too many of them tonight. They barely respect Tadgh as it is, and everyone knows he intends to ask for your hand."

I felt my shoulders stiffen, struggling to keep my face neutral as I nodded stiffly. "Enjoy your night, Princess."

Her hand squeezed my arm before she moved away, swept

up quickly by a waiting male and disappearing into the throng of people.

I watched her go, the warmth of her hand still lingering on my skin as a tendril of my shadows whispered past my ear, murmuring softly.

A hand that he is not worthy of, A ghrà mo chroì.

3

MERLIN

The book I had been studying for hours had begun to blur, a dull ache forming at my temple when the rustle of wings at my window dragged my attention from it.

I gave the rook that flew through it a questioning look as she swooped to her perch next to my desk with a small chirrup of greeting.

"You took your time this trip, Sirin," I scolded her, holding my hand out for the note she was holding in her beak.

I had found myself in possession of Sirin seven years ago, raising her from a scrawny fledgling, near dead after being attacked by her own kind for her unusual coloring. She was stark white in comparison to the black of the wild rooks that inhabited the mountains of Kambria, an oddity amongst her kind. Much like myself.

Rooks were smart. Too smart at times, and Sirin had proven just how deep their intelligence went during our years together. She was my loyal companion, my greatest weapon in the art of secrets, and a total fucking smartass.

"Report," I commanded, running a finger down her

hooked beak, and scratching a pin feather that stuck out from the rest as I deftly uncurled the note with my free hand.

> Tell me how I pluck the eyes from the dragon so that my people have more than snow to eat during winter.
> Enjoy your abundant resources in Irling.
> No rush of course.
> -Black Rook

I chuckled as I read the note a few times before throwing it into the flames of my fire. Of the two people I conversed with in Windhaven, Rook was my favorite. Whomever they were, they had a dark sense of humor that had survived through the poverty the lowlands were falling into.

Sirin ruffled her feathers, blinking at me in silence, and I sighed, reaching for the box of treats I kept on my desk for her and offered her a walnut.

"You want this? Tell me what you have overheard, my sweet."

Sirin cocked her head, her feathers puffing in indignation. *"Oh, pretty bird, pretty bird want some dinner?"* She said in the cracked voice of an older woman.

I gave her a grim look, holding up the walnut pointedly.

"Would you like a muffin?" She continued, this time in the voice of a young girl. *"I burned it, you take it before Cook sees, off you pop now."*

I sighed. "You have been hanging around the damn kitchens haven't you, fiend?"

Sirin cackled, sounding like an old crone as I rolled the walnut between my fingers and reached for my wine—which I promptly choked on as Sirin launched into a perfect rendition of a woman's moan, the owner of the voice very clearly enjoying herself.

Spluttering, I lobbed walnut at the damned bird. She squawked as it hit her, chasing it as it rolled across my desk, cackling again.

"Perverted creature," I muttered, dabbing at the map where I had spilled wine over it.

"Enjoy your night, Princess."

That made me stop. My gaze shot to the rook, now happily breaking into her walnut, the crack and pop as she broke through the shell the only sounds in the room as that voice... that sultry, female voice still echoed in my mind.

"Princess?" I palmed another nut, showing it to Sirin. "Who were you listening to, Sirin?"

"Try not to insult too many of them tonight. They barely respect Tadgh as it is—Enjoy your night, Princess." Sirin's throat worked as she repeated back the two voices, the voice I recognized as the Lady Guinevere of Windhaven... and the other that held my interest, a voice I hadn't heard yet. So, the young Lord wasn't held in high regard? I tucked that morsel away for later, picking through the treat box absently as Sirin continued.

"There's that blasted bird again—" This time it was a rough, older male voice and Sirin cocked her head at me, peering at where my fingers had stilled in the box.

I snagged a few more treats and offered them to her, giving her a cursory scratch.

"Be careful of that one, my sweet," I crooned. "It seems you have been noticed."

My door banged open, making us both startle as Una stalked in, half of her face covered in soot as she flopped onto the chaise lounge in front of my fireplace.

"What, in the name of Nimmet happened to y—" I cut myself off, holding a hand up. "Actually, don't tell me, I already have a headache." I eyed the door. "Where is your brother?"

Una scowled, pushing back a white ringlet of hair from her face, which only served to smear the soot further, her unruly curls flopping back over her eyes again.

"Finishing his chores," she muttered. She pulled up her sleeve, scrubbed at her face and then eyed the black smear across the material.

I shook my head, sighing. "Go wash. Before you make everything as black as your morals. Tell Otto I need to see him when he turns up."

Una grunted, flouncing out of the chair, sticking her tongue out at Sirin as the rook muttered obscenities her way.

How I ended up with this gaggle of irritants I did not know. The twins were thirteen years old, though they could pass for much younger. Semi-feral cretins that had been left on the doorstep of my rooms as babes. Apparently, their mother thought I was responsible for their existence due to their mass of black and white hair, the distinct patterning spreading to cover their skin as well in patches of pale and tan. It was not lost on me *why* this connection was made, given my own odd hair and mismatched eyes. Both twins had vitiligo, and until they turned three, it was only the slightly different patterns on their skin that made it possible for me to differentiate between them.

Had the woman given me a chance to defend my honor, I could have told her I was incapable of siring a child. I was as infertile as a rock, which suited me fine.

And then I was saddled with this pair of twats So, I did what any self-respecting male in his prime would do. Panicked and gave them to one of the kitchen maids.

Problem sorted. Except that trouble seems to be drawn to me like a moth to a flame and these two haven't given me a moment of peace—or respect for my love of a childless existence—since the moment they could move.

The second of these two headaches slunk through my door later that night, only Sirin's croak of greeting as she cracked an eye from her perch alerting me to his presence. The boy was a damned ghost with how quietly he moved.

"You wanted me, Da?"

"Not your Da," I muttered, blowing on the ink I had just written and squinting at the scrawling letters. I rolled it up, sealed it, then broke the seal to look as if it had been read and handed it to Otto with three others. "See this makes it into Sir Gregor's chambers. Somewhere he will not find it before tomorrow's round table meeting."

Otto took them, the scrolls disappearing under his tunic with a flick of his wrist, his eyes alight with interest.

"Yes, you can take whatever you want in there, just don't be stupid about it," I said, knowing exactly what he was about to ask.

Otto's face lit up in a grin, patting his tunic. "You want them there tonight?"

"No," I said, going back to my papers. "Tomorrow is soon enough."

He took that for the dismissal it was, dipping his head before turning to leave.

"Otto," I drawled, holding my hand up, without bothering to look at him.

He paused, one of my sharp letter openers appearing from his sleeve and he placed it down on my desk.

"Sorry, Da."

I huffed, eyeing him sardonically. "No, you're not. What have I taught you about lying?"

His lips twitched. "If you're going to lie, make it believable."

I nodded, shooing him off with a wave of a hand.

"Oh, and Otto."

He paused, looking back over his shoulder.

"Not your Da."

He smirked at me, disappearing into the dark hallway.

"Reports are in from the western legions that they return home within the month."

I tried to keep my face blank as I watched the pompous git, also known as Sir Gregor, address the room at large. I swear they get more arrogant every decade. It almost makes me miss the last Captain of the guard, at least he had a sense of humor.

I try not to dislike humans. I try so hard… but when you have men like these in places of authority, it really sets my teeth on edge.

Arthur rapped his knuckles twice on the table, looking bored. "Send word for them to move north. We lost more men in Endreal than I anticipated. The hive of Drayvn there have allied with a Sylvyn stronghold and they could use the support."

"Sire," Gregor protested cautiously. "These men have not seen our homeland in fourteen months, they have already secured the west and altering their course to Endreal is at least a month of sea travel from their location during storm season. Do you not feel it would be better to send fresh men from here once the spring winds pick up?"

"If I felt that, Gregor, I would have ordered it," Arthur said, his expression cold.

Gregor blanched, sitting back in his seat, but still tried again.

"Wintering the men here in Kambria means we could use them to clear the Lowlands out once and for all, and then they could move fresh into Endreal during spring when the winds are more desirable for sea travel.

"The Lowlands are not currently a threat to us," I interjected. "The Sylvyn there have not strayed past the walls of Windhaven for years."

"Spoken like a man who is sympathetic to the Gods-blessed," Gregor snapped at me.

"Says a man who has a hundred years more experience than you, *Sir Gregor*," I sighed. "Are we really going to do this again? The King is right. The Drayvn hive in Endreal is one of the largest we have found to date, allied as they are with a powerful line of Sylvyn they could end up a very real threat to Kambria. My sources say they have not seen Sylvyn the likes of the house of Morus yet, but hey, if it's the half-starved Sylvyn hiding behind Windhaven's walls that scare you, then don't let me be your judge."

Gregor glared at me. "Windhaven should be kneeling to the rightful King, the fact they have been allowed to carry on this rebellion as long as they have is a stain on the King's reign."

"Why don't you go knock on the gates and inform them of that," I said mildly. "I'm sure they will agree to hand over their lands if you ask nicely."

"Speaking of Windhaven." It was watery-eyed old Bastian that spoke this time. I quite liked this doddery old, retired knight. In his fourties, we had frequented taverns together, sharing drinks—and the occasional woman—on nights I needed to drink myself into a coma.

"We need to discuss this 'Grey Wolf' who has been corresponding with them," he went on.

I leaned back in my chair, picking up my wine and taking a long draft. "Yes, let's do that," I said, a slow smile spreading across my lips.

"Your sources have information?" Arthur asked, his attention on me.

"Names have been given, yes."

A murmur went around the table, a few of them stiffening.

"I have guards searching the quarters of a few named individuals currently," I continued, letting my eyes fall briefly on Gregor. "I expect a report back shortly."

His eyes narrowed on me, his fingers fiddling nervously with the gold edging of his tunic before turning back to Arthur. "We have pushed them back to Windhaven, yet we can't breach their walls. We do not know *what* they have beyond those walls. For all we know, they could be building an army that will take back everything that has been conquered in your name."

Arthur grunted. "Their time will come," he mused, his eyes dancing with the power I so rarely saw these days. It was as if he had drawn it down deep into himself, hoarding it like a Druka on a nest. There were times that I could almost imagine him breathing flames like the great winged beasts themselves. "It is a game of chess, Gregor. Take out the strongest players and then the pawns are yours for the taking. The O'Mordha's *were* a problem. Merlin pulled that threat out at the roots and their offspring are nothing I need concern myself with until I am ready to take the rest of the board, and stronger players have been threatening from across the seas."

"If they are so little of a threat, why have we not been able to breach their defenses?" It was Sir Calgorn this time. I was actually slightly impressed; the weed usually didn't speak at all. He preferred to just agree industriously with whoever had an opinion that day.

"Cerridwen and Kerrich O'Mordha were gifted Elementyls," I said softly. Ignoring the slight pinch that came from deep in my heart and throwing a cautious eye toward Arthur. "They also—if my sources are correct—had a handful of Nimmet-blessed. The wall is woven of both Elementyl and Gods magic, though I have felt it waning over the years. I believe the Blessed they had, have either fallen or abandoned them, and it is only a matter of time before the barricades protecting them weaken enough for me to get through."

"And what of our King?" Bastian asked, "Does the magic of Sylvyn and Blessed truly stand your strength, my Liege?"

Arthur stilled, though his eyes sparked in a way that made the hairs on my arms rise. "The power of the Nimmet-blessed is something I have not yet been able to overcome." He nearly spat the word *Nimmet,* his jaw clenching. "We have reason to believe the Drayvn hold the answers we seek to aid with that. With one success will come another."

The door to the chambers scraped open as a group of guards came in, bowing low to the King.

One approached me, giving me the same low bow. "Your sources were correct, Lord Merlin," he said, producing a handful of scrolls from within his cloak. I took them, unrolling the top one and scanning the writing before handing them across the table to Arthur and nodding to the guards.

Arthur looked over the first one, anger darkening his features just as Gregor began to protest.

"What are you doing?" There was scuffling and the bang of a chair falling as the guards seized Gregor. "Wait—what is this?"

Arthur held up a scroll in his fingers, waving it lazily in the air. "You thought I wouldn't find out, Lord Gregor?"

"What is that?" Gregor snapped.

Arthur tutted, shaking his head. "A poor decision." He jerked his head at the guards. "Take him."

Gregor's voice was still echoing through the hall as he was dragged away, pleading his innocence as I gestured the guard forward.

"The rest?"

"All clean," he said. "Gregor's sons' quarters were searched too. He was questioned and I am confident he knew nothing of what his father was doing."

I nodded. Cedric Gregor was not one of my favorite people, but he had done nothing to deserve being pulled into this and I had made sure he was kept clean in the eyes of the King. It was the least I could do after condemning his father to death. Even if he was working to exterminate every Sylvyn left in Kambria.

Arthur leaned back against his chair with a bored look, sliding has gaze to mine. "Looks like we will need a new Captain of the guard again."

MORGANA

"Morgana!"

I turned to see Saoirse striding toward me, her pale hair whipping in the wind. I took in the blade hung loosely at her waist and the tense look on her face.

"Trouble?"

"An issue in Lallymoore, Gwen rode out at daybreak without taking a guard. I think she is trying to diffuse the situation before it gets out of hand."

I swore under my breath, glancing at the sun. "That was hours ago, why has no one ridden after her already?" I asked, matching her stride for stride as we headed toward the stables.

"Tadgh only just informed me," Saoirse muttered.

"And why haven't you taken guards?" I pushed.

"Tadgh forbade it, I think he assumes it will rectify itself if we ignore it," she bit out. Sliding her hazel eyes to me she gave me a wonky smile. "Assumption, as always, is the mother of all fuck ups. For the record, he forbade me to take you as well, but I figured that would just piss you off."

I growled under my breath, drawing a chuckle from her, even if I could almost feel the worry emanating from her.

"How bad is it?" I asked, as she barked orders for the horses to be readied.

"Starving people were told their already meager rations were being cut, heading into one of the longest stretches of winter," she said. "By the same people who had a banquet in honor of their lost loved ones. If they are not in full riot, they are about to be, and Gwen—in all her pigheaded glory—is going to be caught right in the middle of it."

"Fuck," I breathed, hauling myself into the saddle and hitching my dress up around my calves.

We rode out hard, the horses slipping on the icy ground and breathe curling in the frozen air. Lallymoore was a good half a day's ride ahead of us which meant Gwen would nearly be there already.

Neither of us spoke much, focusing on the treacherous ground underfoot. Snow was thick, and we were taking the shortcut off the main road, which meant the horses occasionally stumbled over hidden roots and dips in the ground. We were forced to slow our pace after Saoirse's mare tripped and went to her knees, Saoirse barely clinging to her neck as the horse stumbled and lurched, though thankfully neither were injured in the process.

The sun had just set as I began to smell the faint scent of woodsmoke from the chimneys of Lallymoore, the air bitterly cold.

"I should have just brought men with us and taken the consequences," Saoirse muttered as raised voices could be heard, even from the distance we were at.

The voices grew louder as we passed a home with the front door caved in, half of the building burned away entirely and still smoking with no sign of the Windhaven representatives that usually inhabited it. The sight made the hairs on my skin rise as my eyes scanned the ruin for any sign of bodies. The houses around were quiet, the windows dark, though a few had fires going inside, the chimneys chugging away slowly.

"The town square?" I asked, alert for any sign of movement. I sent my shadows skittering through the darkness ahead, searching for life, feeling them beckon me forward.

"Sounds like it," Saoirse said, patting at her weapons.

We followed the voices, the hum turning to a clamor, having to dismount as we got to the edge of a small crowd that had formed.

Hitching the horses, I followed Saoirse through the throng of people, shoving and pushing toward where their attention was focused. People were angry, the tension in the air high, and small scuffles were breaking out around us as we fought our way through.

A flare of fire from Saoirse had a group of men backing away from her, golden flames curling around her fingers as she warned them to make way, and then I heard Gwen's voice raised above the rest.

"I hear you, I understand your anger, but this is not the way."

I pushed through the last of the people and into an open space to see Gwen, hair coming loose from her plait, with one hand out to the crowd as flames swirled slowly around it.

"Morgana, Saoirse," she gasped. I didn't miss the relief that flashed over her features, nor the four men cowering behind her. One had vivid burns up one side of his face. Another was clutching a hand to his shoulder.

Saoirse's own flames flickered out as she opted for her physical weapons, drawing her blade instead and planting herself between her sister and the growing crowd. "What was your plan, sis?" She called over her shoulder.

I was struggling to hold in the wave of pressure that was rising in me, whisps of my shadows curling from my fingers as I grabbed Gwen's arm, eyeing a deep cut across it. "Who did that?" I snarled under my breath to her.

"Don't," she whispered, looking alarmed as one of my shadows curled across her wrist. "You are going to give yourself away. Rein it in."

"You brought men with you?" One of the men she protected asked, coming up and pulling at my cloak to get my attention.

My hand snapped to his throat, squeezing until his hand loosened from me. "You are Wytchlings of Windhaven, and yet you cower behind Guinevere, allowing her to be injured?" I hissed, rage overcoming me.

"Morgana, it's ok," Gwen insisted, running a hand over mine and pulling me off him. "Stop, I have it in hand."

"Guinevere," Saoirse called, sounding slightly nervous as the crowd surged forward, coming closer to her outstretched blade.

Gwen moved to flank her sister, letting her flames die out and holding her open hands to the crowd. "I *hear* you," she yelled, her voice carrying across them all. "I am *listening* to you, but I need you to give me the same courtesy."

Voices rose in anger and Saoirse's blade rose in warning.

Gwen rested a hand on her arm with a subtle shake of her head.

"You want us to listen to these men? Let them cut our rations in half while they eat like kings in their guardhouse? You dine in warmth in Windhaven while my son cries himself to sleep every night because his belly is empty," a woman snapped.

Voices rose in agreement, women nodding either side of her.

"My father has been hunting every night this month, and only once has he found game for us to eat," a young man said, stepping out of the crowd. "We are barely surviving. The rations that come through Windhaven were holding us through the worst of it, but if they are cut now people will die."

Gwen grimaced, her eyes squeezing shut briefly.

"I am sorry," she said, and this time there was a lull in the noise. "You are my people, and you deserve better," she called.

There was only a slight murmur this time, silence descending across the square.

"We lost Glenrock. It was the main channel for the supplies we had coming through. Without it, we are having to bring supplies through The Spine, and four out of five of these runs are intercepted and destroyed."

A low murmur went through the people.

"We are trying," Gwen said, her voice heartbroken. "Lallymoore has it the worst, I know. The Hollow still has decent hunting in the mountains, and even though we can't get ships out of the Kelpies Teeth, it's providing adequate fishing for Vinkirk and Nairn. Lallymoore is secluded though, you get the worst of the winter winds through the channel from Windhaven and it has driven game further into the Lowlands." She held a hand to her heart. "But it is our responsibility to help you through this, and we haven't been doing it well enough. Give me a chance to rectify this."

"Give us our rations back then," a voice called from the crowd.

"I can't," Gwen said. "And I know that is hard to hear. I can't give you what isn't coming in, though I swear on my parent's graves I will ensure Windhaven will ration the same as you do. I will do all I can to help facilitate trade with Vinkirk and Nairn to see you through the winter."

"With what?" A long-eared Sylvyn asked. "We have nothing to trade for, and even if we did, we haven't the means of getting it there. We burned everything that could be burned during the blizzard last year."

"Both Vinkirk and Nairn are struggling for fuel. The coastal areas allow for fewer forests and the time it takes them to travel inland to gather it cuts into the time they need to fish," Gwen said. "Give me a group of your strongest once a month to fell trees, and Windhaven will supply the wagons for transport. You can trade fuel for fish. Hopefully, we will only need to do this a few times before we can restore access to Glenrock and our supply chain will increase."

I felt myself relax slightly as the atmosphere calmed around us, people murmuring to one another. Saoirse sheathed her sword, though she remained tense, her hand on the blade's hilt.

"When?" an old woman called. "We are hungry now!"

"Give me time to go back to Windhaven and make arrangements. Men can head out this week to begin felling the trees and I will have the wagons meet them there for transport." She gestured to the men behind her still. "This will not work if you attack Windhaven's representatives. They are here to help you, even if you feel they are doing a poor job of it."

There were hesitant grumbles through the crowd, but it seemed to mollify them, some even beginning to disperse into the dark streets around us.

I tensed as Gwen moved off, talking to individuals in hushed tones, giving her full attention to every person that approached her, and I watched in fascination as they calmed. Small touches of her hand on their arms, the way she angled her body toward them to let them know she was focused on them. She even drew a laugh out of a few of them, a few younger men eyeing her with lingering glances that irked me.

Saoirse called me after a moment, and I turned to see her surveying the man who had sustained burns. He was panting against the pain I knew would be overtaking him, overwhelming agony that he couldn't escape from.

"This one will need healing," she said, her eyes wary as she looked at me.

Healing was one of the gifts Nimmet had blessed me with, though it made it obvious where my power came from when I used it. Windhaven had a few healers that our people went to, however, from the look of him, the trip would be too much.

I pulled him into the shadows of an alcove, his breath coming in gasps of pain now as I turned his head to the moonlight to see. "Be still," I growled, placing my hand over the worst of his burns. Heat radiated from it as my shadows whispered from me, washing over his skin and coating it in a dark layer.

His eyes rolled, a deep sigh coming from him as his whole body relaxed. It only took a moment for healthy, pink skin to cover what had been a deep burn. He opened his eyes as my power drew away from him, falling on the dark tendrils that still floated between us like ash on a breeze. His eyes widened, snapping to mine, then widened further as a blade rested against his throat.

Saoirse leaned into him, her blade grazing his skin as he swallowed. "One word, to anyone, and I will gut you, understand? Don't make us regret healing you, we could have let you suffer."

He nodded once, the whites showing all the way around his eyes. "I won't."

Saoirse stepped back, letting him scurry away into the night as Gwen came toward us, looking utterly exhausted.

"You could have told me," Saoirse snapped.

"I'm sorry," Gwen said, lifting tired eyes to her sister. "I was worried Tadgh would block the gates and I didn't know where you were. I didn't think to leave word."

"He did block the gates after he found out, but you had already gone," Saoirse muttered.

"Thank you," Gwen said quietly, her blue eyes resting on me. "I think I would have lost them if you hadn't have shown."

Saoirse grunted. "We are not riding back tonight. Not with how deep the drifts are. There's an inn further out we will stay at and head back at first light."

"Great," I muttered, glancing down at my dress that was caked in mud at the hem.

"I have spare clothes in my bag," Gwen offered, following my stare. "You didn't pack anything?"

"We were too busy trying to save your neck," Saoirse grumbled, prodding Gwen with her sheathed sword. "Move, before I decide to break it myself."

The inn was small, it only had three rooms, two of which were occupied by the Windhaven representatives whose house had been damaged in the fire. We took the third room, Saoirse claiming the threadbare couch under the window, flopping onto it under her cloak and promptly falling asleep fully clothed.

There was a small fireplace, and I had dark, low flames burning in it the second I walked into the room, the small space warming instantly.

"I wish I could do that," Gwen sighed, gesturing to Saoirse, who was snoring lightly under the arm slung across her face.

I grunted, taking the shirt and pants Gwen handed me and silently thanking the Gods that I wouldn't have to ride in a dress tomorrow. My thighs had nearly rubbed raw on the saddle, and I hadn't yet surveyed the damage. I was not a rider, not like Gwen and Saoirse who had traveled over every inch of the Lowlands. I was already beginning to ache, and I could tell tomorrow was going to be rough. Unlike Wytchling healers, my healing abilities didn't stretch to healing myself.

Clearly, Nimmet was a masochist. Or had a really dark sense of humor.

Moving to the fireplace where it was warmest, my back to Gwen, I dropped my dress and slipped into the fresh clothing, noticing how her eyes flitted away as I turned back. I cocked a brow at her, letting my gaze linger and enjoying the blush that was creeping up her neck.

I gestured to her arm. "Let me see."

"It's not bad, it will be fine," she argued, pulling her sleeve over it.

"Give me your arm, *Princess*," I said, enunciating each word clearly.

She scowled. "I'm not a Princess."

"You would be, had you retained your birthright," I muttered, snapping my fingers and holding my hand out.

She sighed, her eyes glittering with unspoken words before reluctantly holding it out to me.

I sat on the end of the bed next to her, tucking one leg under myself as I carefully pushed the blood-caked sleeve up. A tendril of my shadows curled around her wrist, her skin so pale against it, another danced up her arm to explore the edges of the wound I had exposed.

My teeth ground into each other as I saw how deep it was, the tips of my fingers tinged black as I ran them gently along the wound, shadows flowing from them to knit the wound together.

Her skin was stained black as night for a moment as my power melted into it, fading away after a moment leaving clear flesh behind, untainted by my darkness.

"Thank you," she said quietly, running her hand across it.

"Is that all?" I asked, scanning her over. She hesitated long enough to let me know it wasn't. "Where?"

"It's just a bruise I think," she said, blushing again.

"Show me."

After another pause her hands moved to the lacing of her pants, undoing them, and dropping one side to show the curve of her hip and a deep purple bruise across her hipbone, a graze in the center.

She must have seen the anger flash across my face because she quickly said, "No one did it, the beam in the house fell in the fire and knocked me into the edge of a table."

"You were *in* the house when it was on fire?" I snapped.

"I'm the one who started the fire," she muttered, looking guilty. "I was trying to talk the villagers down when I heard they were going for the Windhaven representative's house. They were barricaded in, and the front door was almost gone so I took out a side wall to get them out, but it got away from me."

Shaking my head, I carefully ran my fingers along it, my other hand grasping her hip to hold her steady, noting the way her breath caught as my fingertips brushed her skin.

"Painful?" I asked, pulling the edge of her pants down further to get to the last of it. Her fingers clutched at the fabric momentarily before letting me.

"Not anymore," she said peering down. "Thank you."

Touching her was affecting me more than I wanted to admit, the tingling in the tips of my fingers had nothing to do with the power that still surged within me. It had been an effort to keep my shadows from surging forward, wrapping their inky tendrils around her possessively.

"I can go and ask if there is any food to be purchased downstairs?" She asked, turning from me as she changed her own clothing.

"I'm not taking food away from these people," I said, groaning as I lay on the side of the bed. "Gods, I'm *not* built for riding."

She huffed softly. "You get used to it. Though you will ache tomorrow."

"Marvelous," I groused as the bed dipped on her side. It was small enough that her arm nearly brushed mine as she nestled into the pillows, her scent filling my senses.

Gods she smelled good.

A mix of jasmine and… Gwen.

"Did you not stop to think that you could have been seriously hurt today, Gwen?" I asked, peering at her in the dim light.

She turned to me, the beautiful green of her eyes glowing softly. "So could of many people in Lallymoore. What makes their lives more important than mine?"

I blinked. "Because you have the chance to do some real good. To help them."

"I am of no use to them if they do not respect me," she murmured. "And you do not gain the respect of your people by hiding from them, by not knowing their pain and trials." She shook her head, a lock of her red hair brushing my arm. "Tadgh is going to lose them, the way he is going. Then panic will set in, they will turn on one another and The Pendragon will win without even drawing blood himself." She rolled her body toward me, settling her hip into the mattress, and I felt her study my face. "But you know all of this."

I returned her gaze, noticing how her eyes kept dipping to my lips. "I do. I just wanted to reassure myself."

"Of?"

"That the Sylvyns still have hope. That all is not lost. The wards are weakening, and I don't know how to fix them. I am only patching up what your parents built, strengthening them where I can, but I don't know what I am doing or how to create my own. The Blood Traitor has been testing it, and unlike him, I have had no one to teach me how to wield Nimmet's gifts anymore."

"There is always hope, Morgana. As long as there is one person still fighting for us, there is hope."

Grunting, I pulled the blanket out from under me, the weight of exhaustion settling over me. "I hope you are right."

5

———

MERLIN

Sirin was stuck on one of the infernal songs the village children sang again. Warbling away to herself sitting on her perch that overlooked the palace gardens, the odd curse word interjected that would have made my mother turn in her grave.

"Would you cease that racket, Sirin," I muttered. "Why don't you go and make yourself useful? You have been loitering here long enough."

She cackled, ruffling her feathers, but made no move to leave her perch.

"Have the twins been through this morning?" I asked, running a hand through my hair to tame it. A wave of my hand had pale flames roaring in my fireplace, heating the air comfortably.

"*G'night, Sirin,*" the rook said in Una's voice.

No then, if that was the last time she had heard the girl. Odd, usually the twins were here first thing to raid my food cache and create chaos in my quarters.

"Go cast an eye over them," I said, shrugging into my overcoat. "I will be in the great hall."

Birds don't tend to have expressive faces, but the look she gave me was pure irritation as she ruffled her wings and took off out the open window, muttering something under her breath that I was sure was less than complimentary.

I snorted, tempering the flames in the fireplace to a dull glow that would have me coming back to a cozy room later even with Sirin's open window, and headed out.

I entered the great hall to murmured greetings and nods of respect, heading to the table I frequented that was already laid out with the usual array of foods I preferred. Light flickered over the food as I sat, my power checking for poisons surreptitiously. It was a habit I had picked up after a few attempts on my life after the death of the O'Mordha's. Whether it had come from Windhaven or within Irling itself, I was yet to find out.

A hand brushed my back as I was pouring myself a cup of steaming tea.

"Want some company with that breakfast?" A soft voice crooned.

"From you, gorgeous woman? Always," I replied, smiling as Vivian slipped into the seat next to me. "I trust your visit home was good?"

She huffed under her breath, holding a cup out for me to fill. "Loch Cruin is as dull as always, but my family fares well, thank you."

I smiled at her over the rim of my mug. "Has your father found you a dashing husband yet?"

She gave me a filthy look. "He is… rather insistent on the blacksmith's son."

"The blacksmith's son does not please you?" I let my finger trail down her arm, a trail of sparks skittering in its wake.

Vivian shivered. "Oh, he is kind enough, handsome and will inherit a good trade…" she leaned into my touch subtly.

"Then what is the problem? I asked, dipping my head to kiss the soft skin of her shoulder, chuckling at the small sound she made.

"It's Loch Cruin," she replied, tilting her neck to grant me better access.

I pulled away, taking a sip of my tea and reached for a bannock, drizzling honey over it one-handed.

"And it's hard to be pleased by another after being pleased by you," she continued, giving me a sultry look over her own cup.

"My sincerest apologies," I murmured, winking.

I inclined my head as two more women joined us, giving me shy smiles before starting to talk animatedly with Vivian. I politely answered questions thrown my way as they tried to drag me into the conversation, but refrained from more than that, content to listen. It was relaxing, in a way, to hear the trifling issues that concerned them and know that this is what life was for some people. Their largest issues were the stitching on a new gown or an argument with a friend.

Raised voices pulled my attention away, turning to see guards rushing after a young man that was storming my way. It took me a moment to recognize him, his face older than when I had met him last.

"You!" Cedric Gregor spat at me. "It was you, wasn't it?"

Guards had reached him, grabbing hold of the young man's arms, but I waved them off.

"Careful what you say boy, it is treason to question the

hand of the King, and it is the King who has ordered your father's imprisonment," I warned.

Cedric lunged for me, fury dark in his eyes.

I had him frozen in the space between us before the guards even had a chance to blink. Light flickered at his wrists and around his neck as his eyes bugged in alarm.

"You forget to whom you speak, boy," I said, holding a hand up to the guards who looked as though they were going to launch onto the suspended boy.

All eyes turned to us, a hush descending across the hall.

"My father is no traitor," Cedric hissed, spittle flying from his lips. He struggled against my power, getting nowhere fast. "Unhand me," he snapped.

I held my hands up, wiggling my fingers. "My hands are nowhere near you." I leaned in, close enough that only he could hear my next words. "Go back to your father's estate, Cedric. Take your mother and your young sisters and stay away from court. Heed my warning, you do not want to be dragged into the trouble your father has started for himself. Your name is clean. Keep it so."

"The King banished us from court," Cedric snarled. "But he has it wrong, *YOU* are the traitor he—" I cut him off with half a thought, his mouth opening and closing in silent accusation, and I jerked my chin at the guard.

"Take him. See his family are treated with care but escort them from the castle and set them on the road to Wrensgate before he says something that will earn him the same fate as his sire."

The guards pulled a struggling Cedric away, his eyes burning into mine as I retook my seat and pulled my breakfast toward me. The food tasted like ash now, sticking in my throat and threatening to choke me.

Vivian and her friends had stayed silent through the

altercation, throwing me furtive glances. I had all but forgotten they still sat beside me until all three jumped suddenly, Vivian spilling her drink as Sirin landed on my shoulder in a flurry of wings.

"Found them, my sweet?" I asked, craning my neck to see her and offering a lump of bannock.

Sirin ignored the treat. *"Let me out of here you filthy, flea-infested son-of-a—"* I closed my hand around her beak, muffling the rest of whatever she was repeating back from Una.

"Where are they?" I sighed, downing the rest of my drink.

Sirin took off with a chirrup, swooping low over a group of young girls and making them shriek loudly.

I slid my gaze to Vivian and her friends, smiling apologetically. "It appears I am to have one of those days. Enjoy the rest of yours, ladies."

I gave the pock-faced guard a hard look. "Where are they?"

"Dunno who you be on about," he said sullenly, though his eyes watched my every move.

"I think you do," I said, flicking my eyes over his shoulder to the open door behind him where Una's voice could be heard snapping at someone. "And unless I am hearing things, I believe that is one of my irritants abusing one of your men."

"They be going in the stockade for the day. Boy was caught with coin on 'im that clearly don't belong to 'im."

I felt Sirin shift on my shoulder, sending a shimmering tendril of power to hold her beak shut in case she decided to join the conversation and turn my already trying day, rapidly worse.

"So why, pray tell, do you have the girl in there as well if it was just Otto with the coin?"

The guard shifted on his feet, scowling harder. "She bit me." He held up his arm, an angry double crescent on his forearm.

I snorted, pushed past him and strode into the guardhouse, ignoring his outraged protests and instantly picked Otto and Una out in the gloom.

Una was leaning against the bars of the cell they were in, her eye an interesting shade of purple and rapidly closing as she glowered at a guard. Otto sat against the far wall, cradling his wrist, an equally dark look on his own face.

I gave them a hard look, then transferred my attention to the guard who was cowering behind the desk, and pointed at the door to their cell. "Release them."

He ducked his head, looking conflicted. "I can't Milord. Boss will have my balls if I do."

"What balls?" Una hissed. "Certainly wasn't anything there when I stuck my knee in 'em."

"Una," I warned, closing in on the limit of my tolerance.

She went silent, sullenly crossing her arms.

"The coin was mine, they are both under my employ, so you had no right to detain them," I said, raising a brow at the guard. "I only ask nicely once. Do you want to see what happens the second time?"

He visibly swallowed, his fingers fiddling nervously with the keys at his belt. "The girl still attacked one of the men and tried to damage me'self." He was already moving to the cell door though, giving me a wide berth.

I grabbed Una's shoulder as they both slunk out, turning her chin into the weak shaft of light coming through the window so I could see her face better. The black eye was a beauty, the deep reds and purples coming through already and her eye watered. I cupped the side of it with my palm, her face glowing with flickering light as it skittered across her skin before melting into it, the bruising fading, and swelling disappearing before my eyes.

"Thanks," she muttered, rubbing at it with her sleeve after I released her.

Otto held his wrist out and I gave him the same treatment, falling into step with me as I strode back out.

Sirin abandoned my shoulder promptly for him, who gave her a scratch.

"Thanks, Rin," I heard him murmur to the bird as I stood back to let them pass and into the sunlight.

"You could have at least waited until after breakfast," I muttered as I slammed the door behind me. "Not like you to get caught, Otto."

He frowned up at me. "Didn't."

"One of the kitchen maids sent me to fetch eggs and I got in a scuffle with one of the stable boys." Una interjected. "Otto decked him, but he told his Da on us and he's the son of one of the Dragon Guard. Filthy prick shook Otto down looking for something to lock 'im up for."

"I see," I muttered, eyeing the guard from before who was glaring across the yard at us with obvious disappointment as he oiled the hinges on the stockade. A subtle wave of my hand had the stockade slamming closed on his fingers and I smirked as he buckled and yelped, curses that I just *knew* Sirin would blurt out at some inopportune moment filling the air.

I eyed the back of Otto's head. "Why were you there in the first place? You were meant to be sending a rook for me this morning."

"Sent it first thing," Otto replied, shrugging his shoulder. "Kitchen girls been pickin' on Una, so I been hangin' about to make sure they don't trouble her none."

I couldn't even reprimand him for that. The two of them

were fiercely loyal to one another and considering they were the only family each of them had, I couldn't fault them for it.

"You're lucky I didn't leave you in the stockade," I muttered.

"Una saw Sirin at the window. We knew you would come," Otto said cheerily, patting the bird affectionately.

The little hussy was puffed up like a feather duster on his shoulder, contorting herself into odd angles so he could hit her favorite scratch spots.

"Glad I'm becoming predictable," I said darkly. "Next time, I will take my time." I snapped my fingers at Sirin. "The Gregors have been sent back to Wrensgate. Follow them as far as The Moore Sirin, let me know if they try to return to Irling."

She took off with a last nuzzle against Otto's ear, disappearing quickly against the glare of the sun.

"As for you two," I said, glaring at them. "Do you think you can stay out of trouble for the rest of the day?"

6

MORGANA

Saoirse was singing. She had a beautiful voice, but the birds had only just begun chirping and I was ready to shove a handful of snow down her throat. Even Gwen looked less than impressed. She didn't sleep well last night, tossing and turning against the sheets and today was the closest I had ever seen her to being short-tempered.

I ached. My thighs were killing me from yesterday's riding and spending the night next to the woman I was aching to touch was not improving my mood. Everything about her was alluring to me and she was nothing like those I was usually attracted to. I am drawn to fire—crave the excitement of coming up against someone who can match my temperament and give it back to me. My flings are usually short, intense, and rare. I never form an attachment to one person, and I prefer it that way.

Gwen is sweet and kind with a calmness to her that tempers the storm in my soul. I would corrupt her, and that… in truth, is why I'm ignoring the glances she keeps giving me. The lingering looks from underneath her lashes and the way she seems to track me whenever I am near her, like prey wary of a predator.

I made myself look at Saoirse's ramrod straight back, blonde curls tipping back as she took a great lungful of frostbitten air and began the next infernal song.

A wave of my hand had the snow that had been resting on the bow of a tree slamming into the back of her head, her horse startling and nearly unseating her as she whooped in alarm.

"The fuck was that for?" She snapped, eyes flashing as she twisted in the saddle to stare at me accusingly.

"There is only so much of that I can take," I muttered. "Would you please shut up for a bit and let the birds get a look in?"

She narrowed her eyes at me, but twisted back, leading her horse over a particularly rocky patch carefully. "Have you figured out how you are going to get Tadgh to agree to you taking the wagons, Sis?" She called over her shoulder.

There was a moment's silence as Gwen urged her horse up further, drawing abreast of me. "I haven't stopped working on that since I promised it," she said, her eyes scanning the trees for anyone who could overhear.

"No one follows us," I assured her, seeing the tenseness of her features.

"Any bright ideas?" Saoirse asked.

"Yes, actually. Morgana will request it."

"What!?" I spluttered as Saoirse twisted back to look at us, then promptly started laughing as she caught sight of my face.

"I can assure you I am not!"

"I need you to," Gwen said, looking at me pleadingly. "You are the only one Tadgh has the slightest bit of respect for. Saoirse is a thorn in his side, and he wishes I had disappeared into the Lowlands and not come back. What I did yesterday is only going to irritate him further, but if you were to ask, say you had set this up… he will see it as a move to strengthen his position with our people… as… as his future wife."

I didn't miss how she faltered on those words, though it didn't stop the wave of anger that flooded me.

"I am not going to be marrying your brother," I snapped.

"Not what he seems to think," Saoirse called over her shoulder, still chuckling. "He's as good as announced it, and you haven't exactly spoken against it."

"Shall I announce to all of Windhaven I plan to take *you* to my bed then, Saoirse? Or do I need a dick to swing around to be able to do that? I didn't realize I needed to defend my right to choose who I want to bind myself to."

Saoirse twisted in the saddle to wink at me. "Announce it all you like. You wouldn't be able to handle me *Child of Nimmet.* Even with those flirty shadows of yours."

I snorted, reigning my mare back for Gwen to move ahead as the trail narrowed. Her eyes caught mine a moment, a flush high on her face which I knew had nothing to do with the brisk air we traveled in, and I couldn't help the wink I gave her.

Stop it. Not her.

We were silent for a moment, listening to the horses' hooves crunch against the snow.

"So, are you just going to ask him for the wagons then? Or is the almighty Morgana going to get on her knees and use that sharp tongue for good for once?" Saoirse called back.

"Saoirse!" Gwen snapped.

This time, Saoirse was knocked clean off her horse from the snow I sent hurtling her way.

"Absolutely not," Tadgh roared, blue eyes burning into his sisters. "You put her up to this didn't you, Guinevere?"

"Lower your fucking voice, Tadgh," I snapped, turning his attention back to me. "Gwen stopped Lallymoore from going into full revolt yesterday. Something *you* should have been doing, so don't you dare speak to her like that. The trade between the townships will keep them sustained through winter while we try to get Glenrock back under us and restart the supply chains. Can't you see that? We can't fight back with dead men."

"I don't have the men to send with you," he snapped back, raking his hand through his hair in an old habit that I knew meant he was losing control of his temper. "Every spare horse I have is about to move to secure the pass between Kinconnal and Glenrock and try to bring back the supplies headed through The Spine. We are desperate for those supplies and they are the last that will make it through the mountains before the snow sets in. Even if I wanted to, I can't."

"We don't need the warhorses," Gwen said. "The old mares, the mules. Anything harness trained that can pull wagons will do."

"I still don't have the men to send with you!" He argued.

"We didn't have men with us yesterday and we were fine," Gwen shot back.

"You were *lucky*," he hissed. "Next time your pretty words might not be enough to calm them and then I will have to bury you next to Moth——"

"Do not forget what I am, Tadgh." I snarled, letting my shadows loose to curl toward him. One wrapped itself around his throat as the light in the room dimmed, the candles guttering and dancing. "I may be untrained. I may be the last of my kind to stand with the Sylvyn, but don't forget I can still end you with half a thought. Just because I choose to hide my power, does not mean it does not exist. I swore an oath to your parents to protect you all, even though I was but a child myself. You think I would have allowed Gwen or Saoirse to be hurt yesterday if it had come to it?" I tightened my grip on his throat a fraction, seeing his eyes widen. "We don't need men. I will accompany them myself."

Fire curled around my wrist, not burning, but a warning that it could if he wanted it to, and it took everything in me not to cringe from those flames. I released my grip on him, reeling them back to me like threads.

"You can take the mules," he said, his tone short and clipped. "And Saoirse, the Gods know it will keep her out of my hair. Take some of the stable boys to control the mules but no others."

"Thank you," Gwen said, heaving a sigh of relief.

The room descended into frozen silence as Tadgh and I glared at each other. Gwen's gaze flitted between us, looking as if she would move between us for a moment and I wondered offhandedly if Tadgh and I lost our tempers over this, who she would side with. I glanced at her, my eye catching on where she chewed the side of her lip uncertainly and she avoided my gaze.

"I will leave you two to talk," she murmured, turning and disappearing quickly.

Tadgh watched her go, a small frown on his face before turning his attention back to me. "You are right," he murmured to me, anger still written across his features. "You swore an oath to my parents to protect and serve us for the life they granted you here in safety. Don't ever raise your power to me again Morgana. We are on the same side."

"I swore to protect, Tadgh. I serve no one," I replied, letting my voice show just how angry I was.

"And when you are my wife?' He asked. "Will you refuse to

serve me then too?"

I glared at him. "I am not a commodity to be claimed, Tadgh. Just because I owe your family a life debt, does not give you rights to my body. How dare you presume who I will give myself to!"

"I do not claim you because of your debt to my family, I claim you because you are the only one I want to stand with me as my equal. You *know* my feelings for you."

"You think I would only be equal to you as your wife?" I said, my voice rising. "Because I am a woman? You may be the Lord of Windhaven, but you could learn a lot from your sister. She's out there doing more for your people than you have in years. Then you demean her by making her feel she must go through me to ask for the tools to do it. Not to mention your complete disregard for Saoirse who has defended you since she was a child. You want me to respect you? Learn *to* respect, Tadgh."

"I do respect you!" he roared.

"You don't know the meaning of the word," I said, anger boiling in my veins. "And until you do, the only thing you can claim from me is my protection. I owe you nothing else."

I spun on my heel, stalking after Gwen, his final words reaching me as I passed through his doors.

"You're mine, Morgana. You always have been."

"This is going to be fun!" Saoirse laughed, whacking my mare on the rump to encourage the reluctant animal forward. We had taken the night to rest and pack. I had made a quick trip to the healers to heal my raw thighs and purchase some thick, fur-lined riding pants that would hopefully save me from the same fate again.

"You have an absurd notion of fun," I grumbled, casting an eye over the eleven mule-drawn carts that trailed us. Gwen was driving the lead mule, our supplies sitting in the bed of her cart.

"You can always go bump around in the back of the cart if you hate riding that much," Saoirse teased.

"You just need to build the muscle up," Gwen laughed, her mule ambling between the pair of us. "It gets easier."

I ignored them both, tipping my face up to let the sun soak into my skin as I listened to the pair of them bicker good-naturedly. Saoirse was younger, but only by a year. It was almost unheard of for Sylvyn pregnancies to be so close together. There were five years between Tadgh and Gwen and that had been considered unusually close until Saoirse had been born.

I was three years younger than Tadgh, though I had come to Windhaven at about two years old, my true age and birthdate unknown. I did not have many memories of those early years.

Where Gwen had been a quiet, sweet-natured child, Saoirse had been fiery from the moment she was born.

The O'Mordha's had gone from one child to three and one ward within a handful of years and it had taken a toll on them. I had heard they were a loving couple before, but that had changed, and even I could feel the coldness between them at times. It was even worse when Gwen and Saoirse had come into their power at seven, Lord Kerrich had been at his wits end putting out all the fires his offspring had started, all three of them inheriting his fire gifts and not his mate's healing.

We traveled until dusk, finding a spot next to a small creek to camp. The stable lads saw to the beasts, hobbling them and throwing out some of the hay one of the carts had carried for them.

Gwen unrolled our sleeping mats in the bed of her cart, not bothering to set the tents up on such a clear night, while I set fires to burn around the outside of the camp and another in the middle for cooking. Wolves were not common in this more open ground, but it did not mean they wouldn't pick off an easy dinner given the chance and hobbled mules were as easy as they came.

The stable boys kept to themselves, choosing to relax around the fire closest to the beasts while they cooked their food and left us to our own.

"You behave as though I have served you raw meat," Gwen grumbled, eyeing Saoirse who was holding a drumstick from one of the pheasants she had shot during the day, flames rippling from her finger as she passed it along the underside.

"Ignore her, the heathen likes it black, she chars everything she is served in the castle too," I muttered, rolling a potato out of the embers with a stick and gingerly spiking it to eat before moving away from the heat of the fire.

"It tastes better when it's burned," Saoirse shot back, raising a brow at me over the rapidly blackening drumstick. "Plus, if you had spent as much time as we have traipsing all over the Lowlands, *Morgana*, you would know how utterly abysmal it is to get food poisoning while sleeping rough. I would take eating charred food over bubble-gut any day."

"Do you ever listen to what comes out your mouth?" Gwen asked, giving her sister an exasperated look.

"Don't act like you don't know what it's like. Remember that bad shellfish you had last time we were in Vinkirk? I've never seen someone come so close to throwing up a lung before."

Gwen gave her sister a dark look as she tucked into her own food.

A yipping wail in the distance made the hair on my arms rise.

Gwen peered out into the gloom. Past the light of the fires it was pitch black, just the gurgle of the small creek breaking the stillness around us.

"Bánánach down this low?" She murmured, her brow furrowing as she looked at her sister.

Saoirse wrinkled her nose. "It sounds like a loner. I saw one last winter too, it was following a pack of wolves and picking at their kills after they were done with it. Food must be getting scarce for them as well."

"A lone bánánach is no threat to us," I murmured. "They won't come near the fire."

"A pack of them were coming down from the mountains in The Hollow and terrorizing the people there," Gwen said, shivering. "Hunger creates desperation, and bánánach are vicious if they have kits to feed. It was all we could do to keep them away from stock."

I huffed softly. "I will go and check the perimeter now before I turn in."

I got up, brushing my clothes off, but was stopped short as a warm hand enclosed around my wrist.

"Father always warned us never to stray past the fires at night," Gwen said, eyes flicking to the gloom beyond.

A tendril of shadow whispered across her fingers, twining around her like a cat. I smiled at her, letting a bit of the beast that lurked within me show. "I *am* the thing in the dark your father warned you of, Princess."

Even in the dim light, I saw the color rise in her cheeks, her hand slipping from my wrist as I melted into the shadows, making sure I was well out of sight of the stableboys before I released the hold I had on the roiling darkness inside of me.

I moved like a wraith through the darkness, my body a

mere shadow itself as I glided through the trees, leaving no trace that I had passed. I sent tendrils out, testing the air, searching for any signs of life lurking around the camp, coming back empty-handed and whispering that all was well. It was only after I had completed two passes that I was satisfied, finding only old bánánach tracks that led away from us, though, I had paused to look closer, the size of the four-toed print, and the deep gouges its claws had left behind larger than any I had seen before.

Gwen was already tucked in her sleeping roll when I returned, Saoirse just returning from relieving herself at the edge of the camp. I emerged next to her in a flurry of shadows, making her jump and curse at me under her breath, her eyes snapping to the huddled forms of the stable lads, sleeping under one of the carts. "Careful," she breathed, jutting her chin at them. "All clear out there?"

I nodded, waving a hand at her. "Go, sleep. I will stay up a while longer and keep an eye on the fires. I will wake you later when I need to rest."

I settled against a tree as Saoirse found her bedroll, my gaze falling on the small mound of blankets that was Gwen. I watched the slow rise and fall of her even breaths, curious as to what it was that entranced me. She was an unnatural beauty to be sure, and I had appreciated this for many, many years. But I had been with beautiful women before and none seemed to capture my attention like this.

She had changed, I realized. The years she had spent away in the Lowlands gave her something I hadn't noticed before. A glimmer of something that she seemed to be holding onto deep within her that was calling to me.

I cocked my head, listening as a shadow brushed my ear but it was not in warning, and I relaxed slightly, listening to the voice both young and old that had been my constant companion my entire life.

Cinniúint, a ghrà mo chroì.

7

MERLIN

> *I have men ready to receive the shipment*
> *coming through the spine. Tell your people we*
> *will be waiting on the new moon.*
> *— Red Jox*

I glanced over the note once more before throwing it into the flames, pocketing the second note that had come tucked into the first.

> *A ship is due into Glenrock on the new moon.*
> *— Red Jox.*

Clicking my fingers at Sirin I waited for her to fly to my shoulder before heading to the council chambers. I had been avoiding it like the plague all week, the reminder of yet another of my failures was hanging on the wall and I had to pass directly by it to get there.

I had been on one of my weekly trips to the city when Gregor's questioning and execution had been brought forward a full two days. Patience was not something Arthur had mastered over the years, though I had expected Gregor to be at the bottom of a very long list that required his attention.

By the time Una had found me, I had been too late to prevent Gregor from feeling the pain of my betrayal. He was not a good man, no man who advocates for the death of innocents is, yet it still weighed heavily upon me this past week.

I looked up at his body, still hanging from the wall—a warning to those considering treason—his body broken to near unrecognizable levels. Fingers and an ear missing. His face was swollen from torture and decay, and a wave of nausea overcame me at the sight. Even Sirin remained silent on my shoulder.

At this point, I fear my soul is beyond redemption. At what point does sacrifice for good become the evil I fight against? I have strayed too far into the grey to see clearly anymore. Even Nimmet seems to have pulled away from me, the voice that once whispered to me since birth becoming fainter with every year that passes.

Pushing through the heavy wooden doors into the chambers I was greeted by the sight of Arthur looking less than enthusiastic as he listened to one of his lower advisors drone on about some insignificant issue in Pen Dubh.

His eyes met mine as I approached him, a smile twitching the corner of his lips.

"Ah, Merlin. Come and save me from this tedium."

I flourish a bow, Sirin flapping as I nearly unseat her, scolding me under her breath with a string of filthy insults that I remind myself to reprimand her for later. "Of course, Sire, though first, I have intercepted word of another shipment coming through to The Lowlands." I pass the note off to one of the men as Arthur waves a finger at me to do so.

"Any word from Endreal?"

"The Drayvn there are proving difficult to eliminate," he said, eyeing me with a calculating look. "I think you may be right about it being their seat of power."

I nod, keeping my face impassive and turn to help myself to the tankard of ale sitting on the table. "There is still time for me to make the crossing and aid them," I said, pouring myself a wine.

Arthur huffed, gesturing for me to pour him one too. "You think that little of our men?"

"If there is one thing I have learned over the years, my King, if you want a job done well, you need to do it yourself."

Arthur laughed under his breath. "I have ordered any scrolls or libraries uncovered to be untouched. I'm not sure how civilized the Drayvn are, but if the information you wanted about the wards is there, it will be untouched until you retrieve it, as you requested."

I inclined my head, raising my glass to him.

"Inform the Dragon guard of the shipment," he said, pushing out of his chair. "The Sylvyns grow bold it seems. This is the second attempt this quarter." His forehead furrowed as he gazed at the line of men looking at him expectantly and clasping their notes. "I'm done, Merlin. You can carry on with this, if I hear about one more property line dispute, I will go mad."

He clapped me on the shoulder as he strode past, and I held in my sigh as I turned to the group of men.

"Right then, who was first?"

The streets of Irling were bustling, even with the icy nip to the air, the smell of unwashed bodies mingling with cooking street food and chimney smoke. Men and women alike shrank from me as I passed, either lowering their eyes in respect or making the superstitious sign against evil surreptitiously beneath cloaks and shawls. I ignored them, I couldn't blame them for the reputation I had a hand in spreading.

I paused at a corner baker as I passed, purchasing a few steaming meat pies before heading toward my destination, a little shop I knew as well as the back of my own hand.

A small bell tinkled on the door as I opened it, Emmie smiling at me from behind the counter as I walked in, her eyes holding more than just friendliness as they raked over me.

"Merlin," she purred, coming around the counter with a sultry sway of her hips. "We haven't seen you in a long while."

"Emmie," I greeted her casually, turning my attention to the old crone sitting in a patch of light that was streaming in from the window. "Hello Ameena, how are you feeling today, beautiful?"

Ameena's watery eyes turned toward my voice, a smile creasing her weathered face.

"Merlin? Is that you?"

"It is," I said, smiling at her warmly. I clasped her hands in my free one, letting a tendril of light flow through her thin skin, feeling for the aches of old age and soothing them. I saw her face relax, her eyes focusing on mine with a bit more clarity.

"Have you come to take me dancing again?" She asked, one bony hand patting mine.

"Not today," I murmured, "Though I did bring you your favorites." I placed the bundle of pies on her lap, and she blinked down at them, before giving me another soft smile. "Always looking after me."

I gave her shoulder a gentle squeeze, trying to hide my shock at how frail she was under her shawl. It was something I had never gotten used to, living amongst the humans. How fleeting their lives were, and the gaping holes they could leave behind.

I turned back to Emmie. It was still a surprise how closely she resembled her grandmother, or at least, resembled the woman I had met sixty years ago, and it didn't escape me how she held the same flirtatious look in her eye whenever I came here. She was beautiful, with long dark hair, a figure that was curved in all the right places and an ass that had tempted me for years... but there is something about having had her grandmother—in her younger years—bent over the very counter Emmie now leaned on, twisted into every position known while screaming my name, that just wouldn't let me look at her granddaughter the same way.

Ameena and I had spent many years in each other's company, and even after she had been married to a good man, birthed her children and was widowed, I had kept an eye out for her and her family.

"What brings you here?" Emmie asked, fingers playing with one of the many delicate earrings that pierced her ear. "I have some new jewelry if you want to take a look?" She gestured toward the racks of beautiful necklaces and earrings. "I sourced some gold from a traveling merchant last month, it's been fantastic to work into this finer stuff. It's so easy to work with." She reached under the counter, pulled out a handful of small gold-colored rods with little balls on each end and gave me a wink. "I made some of these too if you wanted another?"

I chuckled. "No, I'm not here for myself today." I pulled out three small gemstones from a hidden pocket, the clear glass-like stones glowing softly with an inner light from the small piece of my power that I had imbued each stone with. "I need these to be made wearable. Bracelets, if you can."

Emmie squinted at the stones. "You know I can—how pretty do you want them?"

"Strength over beauty," I replied. "Something sturdy for the larger two that can survive a rough life, the smaller is for Ameena, so make something she can wear comfortably. It will help her with her joint pain through… this last bit."

"Oh—" her eyes softened. "Thank you. It's been troubling her a lot in this colder weather." Her fingers curled around the stones as she smiled across at her grandmother. "Is next week soon enough?"

I dropped a heavy purse on the counter and pushed it toward her. "This is yours if you can halve that time."

She eyed the bag with incredulity, trying to push it back toward me. "I can't take this, it's three times the cost."

Ignoring her protests, I stepped back over to Ameena who was now absently eating one of the pies as she looked out the window.

"Bye, beautiful," I murmured, leaning down so she could hear me.

"Oh, Merlin," she beamed at me. "Are you here to take me dancing?"

"Next time," I said gently, patting her knee. "I will see you soon, Ameena."

She stroked my hand absently, her eyes glassy and distant

again as she nodded cheerily, eyes drifting back out the window as I headed back into the busy streets of Irling with a nod of farewell to Emmie.

8

———

MORGANA

Vinkirk was gorgeous, though it had been ravaged by poverty like the rest of the Lowlands. It had taken two weeks to get through to where the men of Lallymoore had felled and chopped the wood, then load it onto the wagons and continue through to Vinkirk.

Gwen had overseen the trade of wood and food and Saoirse and the carts had already turned back for Lallymoore, loaded with barrels of salted fish and baskets of dried seaweed for their people… minus one cart that had blown an axle from the weight of the wood.

We had barely made it to the outskirts of town before it had snapped entirely.

"Is it repairable?" Gwen's voice came from under the deck of the cart. The town's blacksmith was peering at her from under the other side, rubbing at the back of his neck.

"I can patch it up enough to make the trip back, but it won't take a load, Milady," he said, frowning. "I don't have the metal to spare for it at the moment."

Gwen shook her head. "Save the metal then, I will leave it here with the mule and send an extra driver for it on the next run. If you can look after them for me, I will bring back metal for its repairs on our next trip and extra for payment for the inconvenience, does that suit you?"

"Aye, it does," he said, beaming at her. "I thank ye kindly, Lady Guinevere, and for the wood, we had enough to just make it through the winter, but it was gonna be tight. This has taken the burden off my family."

"I'm glad," she said, the smile that lit her face turning her from beautiful to exquisite. "Though there are still many families without. There will be another shipment through next month, it's going on four-week cycles between Vinkirk and Nairn once Lallymoore have organized a workforce to take over."

"Our people will always be in debt to you, Milady," the blacksmith said, his soot-smeared face earnest. "Ye have always put the people first. None of us forget it. Nor everything else you and the Lady Saoirse have done for us."

Gwen just patted his arm, passing him the reins to the mule who had already been unhitched. She turned to me, looking apologetic. "I'm going to have to ride with you until we catch up to Saoirse. It's late though, we can stay here tonight and ride out early, it won't take long to catch them."

"I'm not going to argue with a real bed for the night," I said, glancing at the sun that was already beginning to set. "And food that isn't Saoirse's chargrilled pheasant."

Vinkirk offered a few larger taverns, being greater in size than Lallymoore—Gwen knew the owners of one and secured us two rooms on the top floor. Both looked out over the rocky coast of the Kelpies Teeth and while simple, they were clean. Food here wasn't quite as scarce as in Lallymoore and we purchased bowls of fish stew and crusty bread for dinner.

Coin was near worthless in the Lowlands when no one had anything to buy, so Gwen had handed over two thick blankets for the food, far more than the thin stew was worth, but the look in the innkeeper's eyes had been so grateful it was hard to fault her actions.

"This used to be so full of life," Gwen said, her eyes scanning the near-empty tavern. Only one other table had a customer seated at it, the shelves behind the bar as bare as the rest of the place. "I spent a lot of time here after I left home," she went on, leaning back in her seat. "There were a few elderly Sylvyns that resided here, and with Mother and Father so caught up in the war, it was here that I really learned how to control my gift."

"You never said why you left?" I asked, genuinely curious. "You just vanished one day."

She smiled grimly; her eyes fixed on the cup in her hand. "There were a few reasons, but the main one was that Father and I never got along. Saoirse is a free spirit and would always keep to herself, and she was too young to leave Mother, but I was always dragged into the middle of Mother and Father's issues. Don't get me wrong, I loved them dearly, but they were flawed rulers and Tadgh was being raised to lead in their image. The older we got, the more I disagreed with their ways," she raised her eyes to mine. "They allowed our people to be pushed here, knowing we would be trapped in the Lowlands if The Pendragon kept advancing. It was a risk they should never have taken and one I argued with them about a lot. If I could have left Kambria then I would have, but that wasn't an option for me, and I was so young. I hadn't been gone long before they died, and it's time I wish I had not wasted. I was so numb for so long, and it was the Lowlands that pulled me out of my grief. I fell in love with our people, and the more I learned about them, the more I realized I could never be happy living in Windhaven."

I tried to hide the surprise coursing through me. "So why did you come back?"

"For the people," she said softly. "I owed it to them to try to help Tadgh become the leader they needed. Even if it is too late. Seeing what was becoming of them here as more and more of our supply chains providing desperately needed resources fell." She glanced around. "We are mere ghosts of what we were. So many lost to the war. Mothers raising children, not knowing if they will live long enough to see what wonders await out there in the world, all because of that monster's greed polluting Kambria." Her beautiful face pulled into a snarl. "I hate him, Morgana. I hate him so much and there is nothing I can do but watch him close in on us. He toys with us like a cat with a mouse. He knows we are cornered, yet he leaves us here to slowly starve, to become weaker and weaker until he can simply walk in and take the final scraps for himself. I thought we were lucky, years ago. That we were safe behind our walls. I see it for what it is now. He is torturing us, breaking us down until we beg him to end our suffering."

I didn't know what to say, staring at her as she wiped angrily at her eyes with her sleeve.

"I'm sorry, I don't know why I'm telling you all this," she said, making to stand up.

I grabbed her arm. "Do not apologize. Not for being passionate about your people." I let her go as my shadows reached for her again, needing the physical distance to regain control of them as I tried to think of what else to say. "What were the other reasons you left?"

She stiffened slightly, "It doesn't matter," she muttered.

I raised a brow. "It clearly does to you?"

She looked as if she were about to say something, indecision written clearly across her features, but then she shook her head, frowning. "I'm going to bed. We need to be up early to catch Saoirse. Goodnight, Morgana."

She was gone before I could answer her, up the small staircase that led to the higher levels, leaving me completely bewildered.

When I followed her up a while later, no sound came from behind her door as I passed and slipped into mine, our conversation turning over and over in my mind.

Restless thoughts became restless dreams as images of Cerridwen and Kerrich's death plagued them; Saoirse's face when their bodies had been dumped outside Windhaven's walls, mutilated and defiled.

The Blood Traitor had taken out so many of ours in that battle. Not only had we lost the Lord and Lady O'Mordha, but we had also lost our last Child of Nimmet, the last person who could have taught me how to harness my power. I could still smell the funeral pyres in my nightmares, choking me, mocking me about what was to come.

"Morgana."

It was his face I could see. The Blood Traitor. Smirking at me, knowing my power was never going to be enough to hold him back. I had only seen him once. I was in Sirinelle with Gallin, the last Child of Nimmet to wield for the Sylvyns.

Cerridwen had finally relented on her wish for me to have

a normal childhood once my power began growing more than I could handle and had agreed for me to begin training. I was eighteen when Gallin began teaching me in the moments he could spare, showing me how to tame and mold the well of power within me to do what I commanded, how to shadow walk in the shade and through the night. It was during one of these lessons in Sirinelle when horns began to sound.

Gallin had ordered me to stay in my tent, slipping out into the night to investigate.

That was the last time I had seen him alive.

I had stayed in that tent like a coward, listening to the sounds of screaming coming closer, the crash of swords and rush of flames, and then I had heard Cerridwen, the terror in her voice filling me with dread. It had taken a moment for her words to sink in, struggling to hear past my shadows that were screaming the same message to me.

"Run, Morgana!"

She had screamed the words again and again as the sounds of fighting grew louder outside.

I will never forget the wild look of her as I pushed out of the tent and our eyes met, the grief and anger as her flames raged around her, fighting her way toward me across what had become a battlefield. Nor will I forget my glimpse of The Blood Traitor, his own power a deadly inferno around him as people fell, screaming in pain. He and I had locked gazes for the briefest of moments before he roared something, the words lost in the screams of dying men.

I had turned and fled, but not fast enough. I heard Cerridwen's broken voice as she yelled a warning to Kerrich seconds before flames had engulfed me, the pain of them not registering at first.

I had fallen, curled in a tight ball against the earth, my shadows lashing at the flames, trying to smother them.

Multiple people stood on me as the fight raged around my curled form, the faint pain of a bone snapping nothing compared to the pain of the fire that was consuming me alive.

Suddenly, a cool blanket had covered me, the flames hissing out as quickly as they had engulfed me, and I had been dragged away, hauled into strong arms that had carried me from the noise. I can only remember the relief I had felt, and the faintest scent of cedarwood lingering in my senses before I had passed out from the pain.

The flames hadn't touched my face, but the pain of the healer pulling the fabric from the melted skin under my dress in the days that followed was something I would never be able to forget.

It had taken me days to get back to Windhaven, travelling only at night when I felt safe, and by the time I got there—half delirious with pain and infection—the burns had fused to my clothing and the healers had needed to rip them off to get to my injuries as I screamed until my voice had given out.

I was one of the few who had survived him that day, a betrayal I had no words for. The Traitor owed me nothing. We were not kin, yet we were both of Nimmet.

"Morgana." He was calling my name. Calling it as if he knew me.

"No," I snarled, lashing out. My dark power clashed with light, forcing him back.

"Morgana!" His voice changed, merging with another I knew well. Feminine and—*Shit.*

My eyes flew open, and I struggled to center myself, seeing the walls of the small bedroom I had fallen asleep in. The room was clouded in dark shadows that had escaped me in the throes of my nightmare. A small sound dragged my gaze to the side, to where Gwen was crumpled against the far wall.

"Oh Gods!" I rushed to her, grabbing her shoulders and hauling her upright. "Did I hurt you?"

She flapped a hand at me, wheezing. "Just winded."

I cupped her face, making her look at me. "Are you sure? I'm so sorry."

"Yes, I didn't mean to startle you, I… something woke me, and your shadows, they were everywhere… all through my room and down the hall. I came to see if you were oka—" she broke off suddenly and I saw her face flame, even in the dim light.

"What?" I ask alarmed.

"You—you um. I'm sorry, I shouldn't have come in like this."

I glanced down, realizing the source of her embarrassment, the corners of my lips twitching as I realized the only thing covering me were the tattoos inked across my skin, usually hidden from view.

"It's just skin," I said, crossing an arm over my breasts and standing up. I offered her a hand, my amusement fading as she stood up with obvious discomfort.

"Where are you hurt?" I asked, guilt descending over me like a thick cloud.

She grimaced. "I think my back hit the wall a bit harder than I realized," she replied, her gaze flitting to my nakedness and seeming to catch on the intricate linework that curled over one of my hips.

I grabbed a sheet from my bed, wrapping myself in it before a wave of my hand made candles flare to light around us so I could see her better. Another wave of my hand had the door shutting with a click. "Show me," I ordered.

She looked as if she would, hesitating a moment before shaking her head. "I'm fine, honestly." She ran a hand up her arm. "What were you dreaming about?"

I stiffened. "I'd rather not say."

"Oh."

I watched how her full lips molded around the word, tightening my grip on the sheet at my breast to give my hands something to do.

"Do you have nightmares often?"

There was an edge of sympathy in her tone that I didn't like.

"More than I would like, less than I deserve," I murmured, letting my gaze rove down her body. *Gods I wanted to touch her. To see if her skin was as soft as it looked.*

"What do you mean by that?"

Her question drew my eyes back to hers.

"Hmm?"

She drew in a breath, her eyes searching mine. "What do you mean, 'less than you deserve'?"

"It doesn't matter." I stepped closer to her, unable to help myself as I reached to tuck her hair back, noticing how she turned her head the slightest fraction toward my touch, the rest of her body frozen in place.

"Let me see where I hurt you," I said, my voice husky. Gods, at this point I wasn't sure what my intentions were. I *needed* to get my hands on her. *Fuck. I shouldn't be doing this. Stop. Now, Morgana.*

She swallowed and took a step back, her breath coming faster as I gave her a wicked smile, seeing how flustered she was this close to me.

"You can't look at me like that," she said, her voice sounding strained.

"Look at you like what, Princess?" I murmured.

"Like you want me." She breathed.

"Can't I?" The words were out before I even realized what I was saying.

"Morgana." The words were barely a whisper from her lips, her eyes dropping suddenly downwards.

Mine followed, seeing a tendril of my shadows curl around her wrist possessively.

"I—" she took another step back, the shadow immediately dissipating. "I can't." She turned and fled back out the door, leaving me staring after her.

9

___

MORGANA

I was up the next morning before the sun. I hadn't slept much, part of me not wanting to slip back into the nightmare that had gripped me, and the other caught up in images of Gwen, the way she had looked at me with what I could only describe as longing.

I was still lost in my thoughts when I heard her footsteps coming down the hall.

"We can't fit the tent *and* the bedrolls on the horse," she said, popping her head into my room as I was struggling with the buckles of my pack. "I would rather sleep warm than under cover if we don't catch Saoirse today."

I spared a moment to look at her before answering. She looked as if nothing had happened last night, though she was studiously avoiding my eyes.

"I can give us cover if we get caught out," I said, grabbing my cloak from the back of a chair and following her out the door.

My mare was a sturdy one, and took both of our weights easily, even with our packs strapped to the back of the saddle.

Gwen was seated in front of me, controlling the horse easily one-handed, her other hand shielding her eyes from the rising sun as she peered ahead.

I had one hand on her waist to steady myself, feeling her muscles move beneath my fingers with the gait of the horse as the silence stretched between us.

"Can we talk about last night?" I asked when the hours stretched past, and it was clear she wasn't going to bring it up.

She stiffened, sucking in a deep breath and holding it for a moment. "Do we need to?"

I huffed, watching her breath mist the air and adjusting my grip. I felt her wince as my hand brushed her back and leveled a hard gaze on the back of her head.

"How bad is it?"

"It's just bruised, it's nothing terrible," she said after a moment. "I shouldn't have startled you like that."

I snorted, pulled my glove off with my teeth and fumbled with her cloak that was caught between us.

"What are you doing?" She hissed, twisting in the saddle.

"Doing what I should have done last night," I mouthed around my glove and gave her a dark look. "Sit straight."

She turned hesitantly as I managed to get my hand under the folds of the cloak, fumbling with her tunic next until I brushed against the warmth of her skin.

"Where?" I asked, flatting my hand against her lower back. "Here?"

"Lower," she said, her voice tight.

I shuffled back on the horse a bit, trying to get more space between our bodies.

"It can wait until tonight," she protested.

"Shuuuut uuuup," I muttered through my glove, repositioning my hand. "Here?"

She nodded and I closed my eyes, focusing on the spot,

keenly aware that the curve of her ass rested just under my fingers. I felt my shadows flow eagerly and melt against her skin, feeling for the deep bruising I had caused and drew it out.

She shifted in the saddle as I finished, testing for stiffness. "Thank you."

I grunted, not trusting my voice as I smoothed her clothes back down and tugged my glove back on before sliding my arm back around her waist. "It was the least I could do."

She shook her head, loose strands of her hair brushing over my face in the wind. "It was my fault."

We rode in silence a moment longer.

"Why did you run from me last night?' I asked.

I thought she was going to ignore my question until I heard her exhale softly. "Because I wanted to stay."

"Running seems counterproductive then," I teased softly.

Shut up, Morgana.

My shadows on the other hand seemed almost gleeful, at total odds with my mind and I had to focus for a moment, reeling them back to me as they seemed intent on reaching out to brush against her. I had a mental image of what she would look like, covered only in my shadows stretched out on my bed and had to shut my eyes for a moment to regain a modicum of composure.

I could almost hear the cogs turning in her mind as I mentally argued with myself, lust winning over common sense.

"Talk to me, Princess. Does the thought of being in my bed scare you?"

She made a small noise of embarrassment. "We can't... I can't... it's not... I mean." She seemed to struggle to string a sentence together and I chuckled softly, waiting for her to regain control of herself.

She glanced at me over her shoulder. "I saw how you were

looking at me last night, and I am too weak to stop myself from doing something I shouldn't."

I tried to unpick what she was trying to say, confused. "Gwen, you have lost me here…"

"You are to be my brother's wife," she said shortly. "The future of our people. I can't—we can't—"

It dawned on me what she was insinuating, and all amusement vanished in seconds.

"Stop the horse," I snapped, making her jump as sudden, hot anger flooded me. I needed to get off this damned creature. I didn't want her to see how much it tore at me that *she* of all people viewed me like Tadgh's fucking possession too.

"What?" She asked, looking surprised as she reigned up.

I slid off the back of the horse, not waiting for her to say anything further and stalked toward the stream, grappling with my *far* too quick temper as I knelt next to the small stream we followed, splashing the frigid water over my face and neck. Not anger at her. Never her, just this fucking situation that seemed to be constantly slapping me in the face.

"Morgana…"

"I am going to say this once more, Gwen." I stood to face her, trying to keep my voice steady. "I am not marrying your brother. I don't care if it is expected, I don't care if he grovels on his knees for my hand. I don't care that we were childhood friends. I don't even care if he has told the entire Kingdom that it is happening. I don't *want* Tadgh, not in that way, and I will not spend a lifetime pretending to love someone that I do not. I thought you of all people would respect that."

"I didn't mean to assume… I just—" she cut off, looking miserable. "You are my last hope that he will be anything other than a failure. You are the only one he will listen to."

Her words felt like a punch to the gut. "You want me to

play whore to your brother, to have a say in how he will lead our people?" I asked incredulously.

"I don't *want* that," she breathed, reaching for me "I want —" she trailed off as she looked at my face, seeing my anger.

"I can see what you want," I said, my voice low as I stepped close enough to her to feel her breath caress my face. Her eyes flared, dipping to my mouth and up again. "It's written across your face as clear as words on a page." I reached out, running my thumb in the slightest caress across her lower lip, leaning in as if I were going to kiss her.

Her breath caught, her pupils flaring, looking both completely enthralled and terrified at once.

I stopped, inches from her face, my fingers gripping her chin. "I decide who I give myself to," I breathed. "I thought you were the same."

I stepped past her, leaving her swaying in the snow, gathering my shadows around me.

"Morgana, wait. Don't go," she called, sounding breathless.

I ignored her, melting into the shadows of the trees, needing the solitude to catch my breath. To rid myself of the feel of her skin under my fingers.

The canopy of the thick forest we had been skirting was dark enough that I could shadow walk through them, and I trailed her for the rest of the day, out of her sight as she rode —a lot faster now with just her weight burdening the horse. I barely expended any energy in this form, flitting from shadow to shadow, my figure a mere ghost of smoky darkness. I could see her searching the trees for me as she rode, knowing I was out here somewhere.

She arrived at Saoirse's camp just before dark, calling out to them as the smoke of their fires became visible, and I left her trail once I knew she was safely within their boundary to go and check the perimeter of the camp.

It was well past nightfall when I finally stepped from the darkness and into the light of the fire, taking a moment to regain my bearings as the world tilted. It was always an effort to do this after shadow walking for so long, it was blissfully easy to let my body melt into the world, free to flow wherever I wanted it to.

Saoirse startled as she saw me, nearly dropping the skewer of meat she had been holding, and across the fire Gwen's gaze locked on me, her expression unreadable.

I picked up one of the skins of water from a pile by the carts as I passed and took one of the meat skewers Saoirse held out to me.

"Glad you could join us," she said darkly, her gaze flitting between me and Gwen.

"Saoirse," Gwen murmured in a warning tone.

Saoirse rolled her eyes. "Well, you go and fight and then don't explain why," she muttered. She jabbed a finger at a tent across the camp. "That's yours," she said to me. "Gwen can squeeze in with me."

"Thank you," I said, my voice husky from a day of disuse. "I found fresh bánánach tracks over on the far side," I nodded in the direction I meant. "I will keep watch for the night and sleep in the cart tomorrow while we travel."

"We can take turns, get some rest at least, Morgana," Gwen argued.

"I'm here to protect you both," I said, deliberately not looking at her and hating myself for the hard edge in my voice. "I'm just doing my job, Princess."

I took the remainder of the water skin and the meat to the

outskirts of the camp, settling myself in a spot where I was hidden by shadows, but could still see the camp clearly, releasing my shadows to prowl around the outskirts.

"What did you do?" I heard Saoirse hiss at Gwen, the words almost lost in the murmuring from the stable boys as they settled the beasts by their own fire.

"Leave it be," Gwen snapped back, heading for her tent, though I could see the misery etched into her face as the firelight caught the side of her face as she ducked inside.

10

MERLIN

"You *will* wear it, and be grateful," I snapped, holding the delicate metal cuff out to Una, the gem glowing softly in its middle.

"I won't," she snapped back, glaring at the jewelry as if I had asked her to smear drain sludge across her wrist.

Otto peered at the one on his own wrist, poking at the gem. "What is this?"

"I can't watch you two idiots all the time," I said, shoving Una's into her hands. "This will give you a bit more protection since you are intent on getting yourself killed." I did a double take at Otto who was touching the tip of his tongue to the crystal. "Don't lick it! What is wrong with you?"

"It crackles when I touch it with my tongue," Otto snorted, ignoring me, and doing it again anyway.

Una squinted at hers, sticking her own tongue out gingerly.

"Nimmet save me," I muttered, wiping a tired hand over my face as I watched the two fools *licking* the incredibly expensive jewelry I had just given them. I eyed the ceiling darkly. "You live to test me, don't you?" I muttered to the distant Goddess.

"First sign of madness is talking to yourself," Una quipped, slipping the bracelet onto her arm.

"First sign of madness was not drowning the pair of you when you were dumped on my doorstep," I shot back. "I am most certainly a lost cause now." I smacked her across the head gently with my rolled-up scroll and she flounced out of my chair, climbing up onto the seat next to her brother and leaning into him.

"Keep them on, you hear me? They won't save you from getting *into* trouble, but they will heal any injuries until the magic in them runs out. The more you draw from it, the faster it goes. Tell me when it dulls, and I can push more into them—and for the love of the Gods don't show them to anyone." I fixed them both with a hard stare and they nodded.

"Thanks, Da," Otto said, his face lighting up as Sirin sailed in the window.

"Not your D—" I was interrupted as Sirin hopped across my desk to me, opening her beak and launching into a panicked young male voice.

"Tell him to come, Sirin!"

My stomach dropped at the terror laced into the message, and I leveled an eye at the twins. "Stay here until I get back, understand?"

"That's Henry!" Otto said, looking alarmed as he jumped out of his seat. "I'm coming."

"You are not," I snapped, giving him as menacing a look as I could manage. "Stay. Here."

Both twins were looking at me with identically stubborn looks that I knew meant trouble. "I don't have time for this, do what I say for once," I warned, pointing at the pair of them in turn as I grabbed my cloak and strode for the door, ordering Sirin to stay on her perch.

The streets of Irling were strangely quiet as I strode through them, and my skin prickled as I walked. The street lamps remained unlit, casting long shadows along the ground as night crept across the sky. Light danced at my fingertips, illuminating my way as I felt familiar whispers coming from them, urging me to hurry.

I could hear faint crying coming from a few of the houses as I made my way into The Grotto—the slums of Irling. The sense of wrongness was heavier here, and I broke into a jog as more voices rose in grief.

It was as if The Grotto itself had taken a deep breath, the sound of wailing from one house rising just as more joined in, then suddenly a young woman stumbled out of her home on unsteady legs before crashing to her knees and vomiting blood. I paused, my eyes searching the houses around us as an old woman came after the girl, sobbing as she tried to pull her upright.

"Help us," she croaked at me, before she too began to bleed from her mouth.

I swore under my breath, lurching forward and catching hold of the girl, my power instantly feeling the damage going on inside her. It was as if every one of her organs were shutting down at once and I faltered for a moment, overwhelmed at where to start while the whispers were beginning to scream at me to keep moving.

I sent a wave of light through her body, burning away the sickness within it and heard her gasp, her body stiffening under my hands. In the next breath, I grabbed the old woman's hand to find she wasn't nearly as bad, and flushed light through her body too. I left them at a run, still kneeling outside their home but no longer dying as I sprinted through the last of the street, not as careful as I usually was to hide my course.

I burst through the door of the Chitam's home, not bothering to knock. No light lit the house, no fire burned in the stone fireplace of the kitchen, and I could feel death hovering in the air around me.

"Henry!" I yelled, sending a wave of light skittering into the air around me and lighting up the ramshackle house.

There was nothing. No noise, no voices, not even a breath came from a house that usually teemed with life.

"Enid? Martin?" I called, striding into the living area, then swore, rushing across to the still form of Martin, who was face down on the floor. I knew the second I touched him he was gone; his body cool to the touch and stiffening. When I pushed the large man's body over, blood coated his chest and face, a large pool of it on the ground beneath him.

I swore under my breath and turned, sprinting up the narrow stairs to the upper levels. I found Enid next, as dead as her husband on the floor of her children's bedroom, and with a heavy heart I found her two young daughters had also passed. It would look as if they were just sleeping in the small bed they shared if it wasn't for the blood that coated all of them.

"Henry!" I called again, searching the rest of the rooms. I had ever been up here before, my quick visits usually late at night had been as far as the kitchen below.

The next room appeared to be Enid and Martin's room, the bed made and the room neat. Another empty room held a single bed, also neatly made... but no Henry.

I was coming back down the stairs, wracking my brain for

where the boy could be when the sound of the front door crashing open was followed by Otto's shouts.

"Da! Are you here?"

"Nimmet strike me the fuck down," I muttered, vaulting down the last of the steps and bursting into the kitchen to see both twins shuffling into the kitchen. Sirin was flapping and cursing to herself on Otto's shoulder as they half dragged Henry between them, the younger boy's head hanging limp as he struggled to walk.

"Quick!" Una begged, her eyes wild.

I had my hands on the boy immediately, pushing threads of light into every corner of his body, feeling the same organ shutdown that I had with the women… and then paused as I felt him already healing. Henry stirred, looking up at me with dazed, pain-filled eyes, his light brown hair stuck to his clammy forehead and a dried dribble of blood at the side of his mouth.

"We put our bracelets on him," Otto said, just as my eyes caught the glint of metal on each of the boy's wrists. "He was barely breathing… and then he started moving again," Una added.

I sighed in relief, lifting the boy's chin to look into eyes that were slowly starting to sharpen into focus. Reassuring myself as I began to feel him grow stronger, I turned my attention to the twins. I grabbed Una's chin, fear lancing through me as I peered at her face, then Otto's, dragging him closer by his grubby shirt to look at his eyes, still bright and sharp as always.

"Do you feel okay?" I asked urgently, shaking him gently. "Does anything hurt?"

"No?" Otto said, squinting at his sister in alarm. "What is happening?"

"I don't know but it's too fast and too localized to be sickness," I muttered, slipping the bracelets off Henry and handing them back to the twins after checking the stones still shone brightly. "Put these back on."

They did—immediately, watching intently as I began working on Henry again, the boy still barely lucid. I could feel the damage that had been wrought on him, the boy must have been barely alive when the twins found him… something I would have to reprimand them for later, though it didn't escape me that Henry would already be dead if not for them.

Henry coughed, bringing up old blood that had been caught in his throat, heaving and rasping as my power chased the last of the vileness from his body.

"Are they dead?" Henry croaked when he had caught his breath enough to speak.

I clasped his shoulder gently. "I'm sorry, lad. They were gone before I got here."

Henry's brows drew together, his face scrunching and then smoothing again as he fought to keep his emotions at bay. He nodded, scrubbing at his eyes with his sleeve and swallowing hard a few times. "I was coming back from old Nan's house, then everyone was screaming, and people were dying in the streets down there. I saw Sirin fly past and yelled at her to get you," he paused to cough again, and I handed him a cloth from the kitchen bench as he choked and hacked. "I'm sorry," he croaked, "I know you said never to mention your name."

"It's fine," I reassured him, taking the cloth to wipe at a smear of blood on his chin. "Do you have any idea what happened?"

Henry shook his head, took the mug of water Una handed him and drank deeply.

"No, I started feeling bad just after I saw Sirin and then I was throwing up… then Una and Otto were dragging me here."

"Has there been anyone with this before today?" I pushed, "any illness in The Grotto?"

"No," Henry shook his head, his normally pale skin a deathly shade of white, making the smatter of freckles across his cheeks stand out starkly in contrast.

My eye caught sight of a pot of soup sitting on the table next to a stack of dirty bowls. I frowned, getting up and walking toward it, light dancing at my fingers so I could see clearly. Little sparks of light detached themselves from my fingers as I approached, hovering near me, their whispers warning me of the dangers within. I sniffed at the cold soup cautiously. It smelled fine, and it couldn't be the cause of the greater area all getting sick at once. "Do you know where Enid got this meat?" I asked, glancing at Henry who was wiping silent tears away with his shirt. Una was patting his back gently looking close to tears herself.

"No, I—ah" Henry's face contorted in pain, and he pushed a hand to his stomach.

"Henry?" I asked, moving toward him again.

He dropped the cup he had been holding, the contents splashing to the ground as he pushed a second hand to his stomach.

"It hurts again," he gasped, just as realization hit me.

I whirled, smacking the cup from Otto's hand that had been halfway to his own lips. "It's the water," I snapped, "Do not eat or drink anything here!" I quickly grabbed Henry, flooding him with light, pushing out the poison that had been quickly ravaging his already weakened body.

"The water?" Una said, looking alarmed. "What's in the water?"

"Poison," I muttered, as Henry grimaced again. "We need to warn everyone not to touch the w—" The sound of hooves on cobblestone interrupted me... many hooves.

Otto swore, getting up and peering out of the small, dirty window.

"What is it?" I asked as he whirled to look at me, his face tight as screaming rose in the distance.

"It's the Dragon guard," he said, his voice shaking. "They are setting fire to the houses."

"Of course they are," I muttered, "How far away?"

"End of the street," Otto said, glancing through the window, his hand going to his shoulder to rest on Sirin's foot, who was silent and watchful for once.

"Take Henry out the back," I said, getting to my feet and peering out over his head. Far down the end I could see a large group of the King's Dragon guard—some mounted, others on foot, their emerald green cloaks visible—all with white cloths tied around their faces as they darted into houses with burning torches. Smoke was billowing from the houses behind them. "Now!"

"Where to?" Una asked, the quiver in her voice the only indication of how scared she truly was.

"The shop, Ameena—uh, Emmie's shop," I replied. "Stay there until I come for you, make sure they don't touch the water until I can check it."

Otto nodded, hauling Henry up between them. Henry was only nine, but he was big for his age, so it took both Una and Otto to secure him between them.

I heard Una give a little shriek as they moved through the house and cursed myself for not warning them that Martin's body was in there, hearing Otto reassure both his sister and Henry as they thudded through the back door. I waited until I heard the tell-tale sound of the glass rattling in the frame as it thudded into the wall before striding out the front door.

"What are you doing?" I roared at the soldier closest to me

as I approached them. They turned, one of them bowing low as he recognized me.

"Lord Merlin," he said. "You shouldn't be here, there's a sickness spreading."

"It's not a sickness, the water has been poisoned," I snapped, anger washing over me as I saw a woman pleading with a soldier who was advancing on her home with a burning torch.

"Call your men in!"

"My lord, it's a direct order from the King," the soldier said, looking around nervously. "The Grotto is to be purged before it spreads."

"It's in *the damned* water here," I spat. I stepped around him, yelling at the soldier who was now brandishing his torch at the stricken woman who was on her knees, hands clasped as she begged for her home. "Stand down!" I snarled, reaching the woman's side and helping her up. "There is *no* sickness here. The waterways have been compromised."

He ducked his head, looking at the woman and then at me, ducking his head. "Forgive me," he said under his breath. If I disobey a direct order, it's my neck. Get out of here, I didn't see you. The King ordered the plagued to be burned with their homes." He met my stare, his eyes haunted. "Dead or alive." He lobbed the burning torch over our heads and straight into the open doorway of the home, the threadbare mat at the door instantly catching on fire. I grabbed the woman as she lurched toward her home. "Is anyone in there?" I asked urgently.

She dragged her eyes from the house to me, tears running down her stricken face. "M-my husband," she stammered, a sob wracking her body. "But h-he's dead."

I squeezed her shoulders. "Do you have anyone you can go to outside of The Grotto?" I asked, shaking her slightly when she didn't answer me. "Y-yes," she croaked, beginning to shake as behind us, her house ignited fully. "Go," I said, giving her a gentle shove. "Get out of here and tell anyone you see not to touch the water and to get out of The Grotto. The King has ordered this, and I cannot get back to the castle in time to stop it."

She nodded, looking half-dazed as she turned and ran, disappearing quickly into the plumes of smoke that choked the cobbled streets.

I ran, trying to keep ahead of the guard and yelling to everyone I saw about the danger of the water, to take their children and get out of The Grotto. My power lit the streets as I went, fingers of light reaching out, guiding me to the houses where I found the living huddling in their houses, terrified. I had them out and moving, warning others as they ran, like a wave of rats running from a sinking ship.

I don't know what made me look up as I passed the well that ran to the waterways through The Grotto, even the whispers that guided me couldn't be heard over the frantic hammering of my heart, but I caught a black smudge from the corner of my eye and paused.

Above the well, stretched with its wings wide, the outline of a huge bird was painted in charcoal on the side of a burning building. A calling card from whoever had condemned these people to die. A black rook.

Swearing under my breath I pushed on, running past bleeding bodies in the street, past burning homes and grieving families. I ran until the smoke cleared and people were standing in the streets, peering at the plumes of smoke behind me in concern, no tears of lost loved ones marring their cheeks. The citizens of The Grotto dispersed through the crowds into safety—where exactly I did not know—but even an alleyway was safer than their homes. I kept moving, for what felt like an age as the ramshackle houses of the poor gave way to stone buildings closer to the castle. My heart only began to slow its frantic hammering when I saw light coming from the living area above Emmie's shop and her figure peering out of the window and into the gloom.

Emmie must have seen me coming up the street because she had the front door open for me as I clattered up the steps, ushering me inside.

"The twins and Henry?" I panted.

"Safe," she said, shutting and deadbolting the door behind me. "What is happening?"

"An attack on The Grotto," I said, fighting to catch my breath and placing my hands on her shoulders. There was no echo of sickness in her body, and I sagged in relief. "None of you have touched the water?"

She shook her head, frowning, "No, the twins warned me not to. Merlin, are we not safe here?"

"It seems to only be The Grotto," I muttered, pushing past her to the kitchen. I ran some water from her copper taps, letting the water slide through my fingers, feeling for the poison. It was as clear as normal, with no taint or darkness coming from it.

"Do you have any spare barrels? Any kegs?"

"Yes?" Emmy said, looking confused.

"Fill everything you can now. Only use the stored water if there is another attack. If you need to refill them, take Ameena's bracelet and let it sit in the water before you do. If it glows, the water is tainted, don't touch it."

She nodded, moving to a closet and coming out with a keg under one arm and another in her hand. I pushed through into the living area, seeing Henry sprawled out on a low couch with Una watching over him while Otto talked to Ameena who was in her rocking chair. I crossed to Ameena, running a gentle hand down her cheek. Nothing except the effects of age affected her body and I felt another small weight lift from my shoulders.

"Merlin," she smiled at me, her eyes clearer than I had seen in years. I noticed the delicate bracelet around her wrist, the gemstone flickering softly. "There seems to be some kerfuffle this eve."

I smiled at the term I had heard so often from her, crouching so she could see me better. "There is bad news in The Grotto. I need to ask you for a favor, beautiful."

She wrinkled her nose at me, a glint in her eye. "Stop with that silver tongue, Merlin," she laughed softly, her old voice creaking. "Tell me what you need, and it is done."

"The boy, Henry. He needs somewhere safe to stay, he is important."

Ameena turned to look at Henry, a calculating look in her eye. "Well, I know he isn't yours. Is he another of your strays?"

I squeezed her hand gently, smiling. "Not quite, but I have ensured his survival since his birth." I felt Emmie enter the room, waiting for her to get near before I gave her a look that I hoped showed my apology for what I had just stashed under her roof. "He is the King's son.

Emmie gasped, her hand flying to her mouth. She looked at Henry again, and I knew she was trying to gauge his age.

"He is nine," I said quietly. "He looks a lot older than his years, something that has helped him survive."

Ameena was eyeing the boy. "The boy that should never have been," she murmured softly. "I wondered if you had a hand in his disappearance." She turned back to me, her eyes sad. "So many innocent babes were massacred when they were looking for him. He is the reason my Emmie had no children, should the *King* order another execution of newborns." She spat the word King as if it were a foul taste in her mouth.

"I know," I choked, guilt wracking me. I looked at Emmie, her mouth was set in a hard line and her face pale. "I wouldn't ask if I had any other choice. His mother hid her pregnancy until the last minute. It was all I could do to get the child out the castle and hide him where he wouldn't be found. By the time I got back, it had already happened. I have paid for those deaths with my soul."

"One child for hundreds," Emmie said, quietly enough that only I could hear her. "Why? Even if he is the King's spawn."

"The actions of the sire do not taint the child," I said, "and even if his life alone was not worth it, his blood could be the key to the King's downfall, maybe even the salvation of thousands."

Both women's eyes snapped to Henry, shock plastered on both of their faces.

"I need you to trust me," I said urgently. "You know I would never willingly put your family in harm's way, Ameena, but Henry is part of a larger plan I have been working on for decades. If I lose him, we all lose, and The Pendragon's tyranny will continue."

Ameena turned her pale eyes on me, staring at me for a long moment. Then she patted my hand, nodding as if to herself. "I have always trusted you, Merlin. That will not change now. The child will be safe under my roof." She looked at Emmie, "And my daughter's roof, once I am no longer here."

Emmie let out a long breath but nodded curtly. "So be it."

11

MORGANA

The bánánach that had been following us trailed us on the way back to Lallymoore, becoming more and more curious about our camp every night. I had kept up my routine of guarding the camp at night and sleeping through the day, bundled in one of the sleeping rolls and my cloak, wedged between sacks of dried seaweed on one of the carts. It wasn't comfortable by any stretch, but I got used to the bumping, jolting movements of the cart. That and I was so exhausted I could have slept through anything.

It was overkill. Gwen and Saoirse had survived the Lowlands for decades without my help, but I used it as an excuse to create distance between myself and Gwen, determined not to push something she was clearly conflicted about.

Gwen had barely spoken to me, not that there had been a chance for us to speak alone, though I felt her eyes on me, her good-natured bickering with her sister slightly muted.

It was on the fifth night that I felt her presence at my back as I looked out over the near-silent woods, keeping tabs on a pair of bánánach that were lurking in the darkness.

"I don't want to be someone you avoid," Gwen said, moving silently up to my side.

I tilted my head in her direction, surveying her. She wasn't looking at me and radiated anxiety, though was trying to mask it.

"I was not avoiding you."

A tendril of shadow whispered past my ear. *Bhreugan cho milis, mo fhear dorcha.*

Her gaze slid to mine in the dark, and I could see the faintest echo of amusement on her face.

"At least not for the reason you probably think I was," I amended, dispersing the shadow with a wave of my hand.

She hummed softly, casting an eye back into the camp where Saoirse was curled in her sleeping roll, reassuring herself her sister slept before turning her attention back to me.

"Enlighten me?"

I laughed softly, pausing for a moment as one of the bánánach moved and I tracked it as it prowled away before I gave Gwen my full attention again. "There is a darkness in me that I do not want to corrupt you with," I said, keeping my voice low. "My anger the other day was at the situation, not at you, Gwen."

"Corrupt me?" There was a dry note in her voice that made me look at her. She had a brow cocked, a slight curve to her lips that were begging to be kissed.

Fuuuuckkk.

I pulled my gaze away again, focusing back on the lone bánánach that seemed to have hunkered down for the night.

She hummed softly, sounding amused. "Please come and sleep. The bánánach have never come close when the fires are lit, and I am tired of being the only one subjected to Saoirse's terrible jokes all day.

I laughed softly. "There is always a first time, and I swore to Tadgh that I would keep you both safe."

Light flared next to me, and I narrowed my eyes against it as flames shimmered along Gwen's fingers. She waggled them slowly, giving me a small smile. "I may not be a Child of Nimmet, Morgana. I may prefer to use reason over brute force, but please do not think that I am not capable of defending myself. I have always been safe out here, and Saoirse is safe with me."

I watched her flames, unable to help the prickle of unease they gave me. "Sorry," I conceded. "Force of habit."

She hummed again, the flames dying out as she dropped her hand and turned back to the camp, pausing with a look over her shoulder.

I huffed under my breath, sending a few more shadows to lurk around the perimeter, and then turned to follow her back to the bedrolls.

We rolled back into Lallymoore six days later, travel-stained and exhausted. Saoirse disappeared to learn if any word had come from Windhaven while Gwen and I oversaw the supplies being distributed amongst the grateful townsfolk.

Gwen was whisked away to organize the group of men that would be taking over the continued trips between Nairn and Vinkirk while I grabbed our packs and trudged toward the inn we had stayed at last time.

This time we had the whole upper level, so I threw my bags into one room and Gwen and Saoirse's into the other two before asking for bathing water to be brought up to the rooms.

A large, battered copper tub was brought up and filled with cold water that I promptly heated to near scalding, washing my dusty, lank hair in it first before stripping off to scrub at my travel-stained skin until it was glowing pink, groaning at the ecstasy of being properly clean for the first time in weeks.

The innkeeper's daughter knocked on the door after a while, adding my filthy clothes to the pile of Gwen and Saoirse's already in her arms and leaving some fresh ones behind that I slipped into gratefully.

They were slightly large; a men's cotton shirt, the dark blue dye faded in patches, and pants of sturdy material that—from how firmly they gripped my hips and thighs—must have belonged to one of the teen boys I had seen working below. I didn't care, they smelled fresh and clean, and I tucked the corner of the shirt into the waist of the pants to stop it billowing when I moved, running my fingers through my damp hair loose around my shoulders, and headed below to look for food.

We had brought a small goat with us that Saoirse had shot and skinned the night before and I could smell it cooking below, the scent of stew wafting invitingly up the stairs.

Mouth watering, I ordered a bowl of it and asked them to put some aside for Gwen and Saoirse too, then found a seat for myself near one of the windows. It was already so different here, villagers arriving with smiles on their faces to order a share of the huge cauldron of stew that was bubbling over the fire pit.

I watched a group of children sitting around the large fireplace, bowls in their laps and sharing some of the strips of dried seaweed between them as they devoured their dinner, mopping up the dregs with their fingers and smacking their lips loudly in appreciation. They giggled amongst themselves, socked feet stretched toward the fire, threadbare with their little toes poking through them… but they looked so content. Warm, with full bellies—most likely for the first time all winter.

I was so engrossed as I watched them that I didn't notice Gwen and Saoirse slipping into seats next to me until Gwen pushed a hot roll in front of me, her own tucked under her chin as she balanced two bowls in her hands, Saoirse holding a jug of mead with some dented pewter mugs.

"It's a beautiful sight, isn't it?" Gwen said softly, her eyes following where mine had been.

"It is," I agreed, breaking my roll open and dipping it into the rich stew.

Saoirse shovelled the food into her mouth, letting out an erotic moan and rolled her eyes back into her skull. "My gods this is good," she muttered around a mouthful.

"Can you not?" Gwen sighed, giving Saoirse an exasperated look.

Saoirse just held up her stew-covered spoon, running her tongue up it with another long, low moan before putting the entire thing down her throat and pulling it slowly back out of her lips.

"That explains why the men love you so much, Saoirse," I chuckled, mopping up some of the gravy that was running down the side of my bowl with a heel of bread.

She turned her gaze on me, giving me a sultry look. "Want to find out exactly what they love so much?" She waggled her brows at me, a wide grin on her face. "It's been a while, I'm getting desperate enough to even entertain the thought of you, you cranky bitch."

I made a show of looking her up and down, sucking on a tooth as I leaned back in my seat. I studiously ignored the glare I could feel coming from Gwen. "I think I would rather stick pins in my eyes."

"You know you want me," Saoirse purred, popping small bits of bread into her mouth and giving me a wink.

"My hand doesn't talk incessantly. I'm good. Plus, I'm sure I could get myself off faster than your fumbled attempts."

Saoirse chuckled, throwing a rude gesture my way just as Gwen knocked her cup, tipping the water across the table, swearing under her breath as it splashed down her leg. "I can do it," she snapped as Saoirse jumped to grab her bowl before that went flying too.

Saoirse raised a brow at her, handing the bowl of stew slowly back to her. "Oookay," she said. "You ok, Gwen?"

"Yes," Gwen said shortly, taking the bowl off her and ripping aggressively into her bread roll.

"No word from Tadgh?" I asked.

Saoirse shook her head, eyes watering from the heat of her food. "No, but The Hollow sent word a week ago that they were having issues with the bánánach you mentioned, Gwen. I'm thinking of going there to see for myself."

"I'm coming if you do," Gwen stated. "I haven't checked in on the school in months, I would like to see how they are doing and by the time we get back, the next run will be ready to go through to Nairn and we can see them off before we go back to Windhaven." She turned to me, her eyes wary. "You don't have to come with us if you don't want to."

"Tadgh is fine without my help," I replied. I hadn't meant it as a dig, but Gwen flinched so I added, "If there are bánánach in the area, I'm coming," to soften the blow.

"We still don't have enough horses so you will have to ride with one of us," Saoirse said, running her finger around the side of her bowl and licking it clean. She grinned at me, "I can serenade you as we ride."

"Nimmet save me," I muttered, scowling into my mead.

Gwen stood suddenly, dropping the heel of her bread into her empty bowl and nudged her chair in with a knee. "I'm calling it a night. See you both in the morning." She turned and strode off without a backward glance at us.

Saoirse gave me a puzzled look, opening her mouth to call to her sister's retreating form. I—against my better judgement—shook my head subtly at her, pushing out of my chair to follow Gwen as she slipped through the milling people toward the stairs.

"Gwen." I caught her just before she got to them, catching her by the elbow.

She turned to me, looking flustered. "Go back and carry on flirting with Saoirse, Morgana. I'm exhausted and just want to lie down on an actual bed."

I was taken aback for a moment. She looked so damned beautiful; her cheeks flushed with what I assumed was anger as she glared at me. I tried to stop the amusement showing on my face, letting her go and holding my hands up in apology. "Don't let me stop you then, Princess."

She looked like she was going to say something, her teeth biting into her soft, full lower lip, as if it were the only way to silence the words about to spill out. Then she turned on her heel and disappeared up the steps, leaving me in a state of confusion at not only her reaction, but also at the guilt that was suddenly nipping at me.

I had been deliberately flirting with Saoirse. Not that it was unusual. Saoirse was probably the closest thing I had to a friend, and we had always had this harmless banter between us on the rare times we could relax in each other's company. But then Gwen had never been around the castle long enough to see it.

I went back to our table, Saoirse now reclining with her

feet up on another chair and talking animatedly to a blacksmith, holding one of her knives out to show him something. She caught my eye, not breaking her conversation, tipping her head toward where Gwen had gone. I nodded, letting her know she was fine as I picked up my cloak, suddenly not in the mood for talking. I murmured my goodnights before heading off to the peace of my own room, stopping to borrow a book from a small shelf in the hallway before stepping into the stillness of my room, and the first solitude I'd had in weeks.

12

MORGANA

I could hear the muffled noise from below as I idly flipped the fragile pages of the small book I had borrowed. It was poorly written; a tale of one of the old Gods and my mind kept drifting to the noise below. General chatter turned into off-tune music as some instruments were clearly pulled out, voices raising in bawdy songs, the mood so different from our last time here.

It sounded like hope, I realized, and my heart squeezed. Gwen had given them hope that they *could* make it through this winter.

I lay on my rumpled bed for what felt like hours, long after I had abandoned my book until the noises downstairs faded away and the voices outside headed back to their homes. I could almost feel the peace that settled over the inn, the odd creak and crack from the old building as if it were settling itself down for the night. And yet... I couldn't relax.

Feeling restless, I went to the dirty window and opened it, leaned on the sill and looked out over the darkness beyond. It was a still night, but the slightest of breezes caressed my skin, and I breathed in the icy air as my shadows began murmuring to me.

I closed my eyes, trying to focus on the words, the whisper of the voice that had seemed so distant recently… and then I felt it. Almost like a presence at my shoulder, beckoning me away from the window, toward the door at my back. I walked over to it, pulling it open before I even registered what I was doing.

Gwen stood behind it, arm raised to knock, a look of surprise on her face. She lowered her arm awkwardly, and wrapped both arms around her middle. "Can we talk?"

I stepped back, letting her walk into the room and silently closed the door behind her, my mind and heart clashing violently within me. One was yelling at me to make her leave, knowing that having her in my room alone, was in neither of our best interests. The other was begging her to stay.

"I wanted to apologize," she said softly, turning to look at me.

I cocked my head. "For accusing me of flirting with your sister? Or expecting me to play whore to your brother?"

She grimaced, dropping her gaze to the floor and I was immediately hit with a pang of remorse for the harshness of my words.

"For all of it."

I crossed my arms, needing to give them something to do to stop myself from reaching across and lifting her face, desperate to try and understand what she was thinking.

"I—" she broke off, looking around the room, as if looking for something to save her.

"I'm not oblivious, Gwen," I murmured, dragging her attention to me. "And if I were a better person, I would tell you to leave."

She looked at me pleadingly. "Morgana, I—" she cut off again with a sigh.

"What do you want, Guinevere?" I asked, my voice a low purr. "Stop worrying about what you think is expected of you."

She made a small sound of distress, looking as if she were about to turn and bolt out the door, but her hand reached across the space between us, the tips of her fingers trailing down the front of my shirt, sending shockwaves across my skin beneath at the slight touch.

Smiling a slow, wicked smile that had her breath catching, I stepped closer, searching her face. "Use those words you are so good at weaving."

"You." It was so quiet I almost missed it, had her eyes not been telling me everything I needed to know. She made to pull her hand back, the color rising in her cheeks, but I caught it in mine, watching her face intently as I guided it up to cup my breast, covering it with my own.

Her eyes widened and dropped to where she touched me.

"Is this what you want?" I purred, waiting for her to drag her eyes back to my face. I ran my fingertips up her arm slowly, noticing she didn't let go of me, but stepped forward hesitantly.

Trailing up her shoulder, I hooked a lock of her hair and played with it, admiring how the deep red strands glinted in the candlelight, unable to stop touching her now that I had given in to it.

She looked so unsure of herself that I took pity on her, my own desire smoldering steadily in my belly as I leaned in, brushing my lips across hers.

"Or is this what you want?" I murmured against her lips.

It snapped whatever had been holding her back and

suddenly her other hand was grasping my waist and tugging me against her as her lips crashed hungrily into mine.

Kissing her was more than I could possibly have dreamed and not enough at the same time. I ran a hand up to the soft skin of her neck, angling her so I could deepen the kiss, tasting her, stealing the breath from her.

The small groan she gave turned a smolder into a roaring flame and I broke the kiss, fighting to maintain a modicum of self-control as I realized her hand had slipped under my shirt, her thumb tracing absently across the smooth skin of my stomach, dangerously close to where my scars began.

I tensed, focusing on pulling back the whisp of darkness that had curled around her throat, small fingers of my power that had escaped my grasp as I was lost in her spell. Gripping her wrist, I slipped her hand out from under my shirt, bringing it to my mouth and nipping at the tips of her fingers.

"Oh Gods," she breathed as my tongue flicked against the tip of her pointer finger, and I looked up with a sly grin, sucking gently as I led her back toward my bed.

Her skin was so warm under my hands as I slipped them beneath her clothing to trace across her ribs before grasping the hem of her shirt and lifting it over her head. She crossed her arms protectively over her chest, looking at me pleadingly.

"I don't know what to do," she whispered, looking embarrassed. "I've never… with a woman I mean."

"Would you like me to show you?" I asked, slowly flicking the top button of her pants open. I watched the pulse in her neck pick up as the second button came loose, then the third. I paused to run a fingertip over the slight swell of her stomach and then ever so slowly, dragged it down.

She nodded, her breath catching as I ran that finger along the top of her loose pants, hooking a finger in them and tugging her closer to me. She was shaking, a slight tremor that was running through her body and I ran my hand back up her body to her hair, fisting a handful and tugging her head back to let me nip at her neck.

I kissed the racing pulse just below her ear, trailing my way up her jaw until I could claim her mouth, kissing her soundly until I felt her relax again.

Her hands buried in my hair as I pushed her pants lower around her hips, hearing them drop to the floor before she stepped out of them.

I broke the kiss to look down at her, tracing a finger around one perfect breast, her nipple hardening as I brushed a knuckle over it, watching her face with rapt attention.

My fingers continued their slow exploration of her body, my gaze locked on her and greedily devouring every reaction my touch elicited.

Her gaze dropped, brow furrowing as she took in my clothed state.

"Take this off," she said, her voice husky as she reached for the buttons of my shirt.

I smiled, slow and wicked at her as my hands replaced hers, slowly popping the buttons one by one, enjoying how her gaze lost focus as I slowly bared my body to her.

I took her hand, lifting it to my lips and kissed her palm before turning it and placing it on the rise of my breast, over my own hammering heart.

Gwen's mouth parted as she ran her hand slowly down, fingers trailing over my skin and making me shiver as they dropped to my waist... and then she stopped, her brow creasing.

She glanced down, hand brushing again and it was all I could do not to push her questioning touch away.

"Morgana," her voice was tight as she glanced up at me,

pushing the now undone shirt open with a gentle hand. "Are these burns?"

I grunted, looking down at her and running my fingers through her hair. "They are."

She froze, anger flooding her features. "Who did this to you?"

I huffed softly, running a hand down my ribs and over the tattoos that covered the vicious burn scars. "It doesn't matter."

"It matters to me," she murmured, and then leaned down, brushing a gentle kiss over my ribs.

I gasped, taken off guard as she kissed me again, her lips trailing down my ruined flesh as she lowered herself to kneel in front of me. She slowly undid the buttons of my pants, her eyes widening as she slipped them off my hips, seeing the extent of the tattoo-covered scars that reached all the way down to just past my knee.

I had never felt so bare in front of someone before, and closed my eyes, groaning softly as her lips brushed across the tattoos on my hip, then the outside of my thigh, her hair tickling my skin.

"Morgana—I—"

"I don't want to talk about that right now," I interrupted, grabbing her chin with my fingers and forcing her to look up at me. "I will tell you anything you want, but right now…" I trailed off as she rose to her feet again, hands settling on my hips.

She nodded and I rested a fingertip between her breasts, pushing her back toward my bed. She stopped when the back of her legs hit the mattress, and I flattened my hand against her, pushing until she sat, scooting backwards as I followed her.

I had lost control of some of my shadows, and they licked their way up her body to curl around her wrists, pulling them above her head as I began a slow perusal of her body.

"Morgana." My name was a prayer on her lips as I nipped at the soft underside of her breast.

She gasped as my lips closed around her nipple, her head kicking back against the mattress.

Her back arched as my hand slid down her stomach, teasing lower and lower until my fingers brushed a line of soft curls and... *fuck, she was drenched already.*

I groaned at how aroused she was, and she tensed.

"I—sorry, I—"

I cut her off with a fierce kiss, moving until I was kneeling between her legs and nudging them further apart.

"Don't you dare apologize for your body wanting me," I murmured, pulling back enough to look at her face. I ran a fingertip along slick skin, brushing ever so slightly against her clit, her breath catching as I did.

I did it again, giving her a bit more pressure and she gasped, her head falling back. Kissing her neck, her pulse thrumming against my lips I continued the slow tease, feeling as her hips began to roll, chasing my touch as I brushed against her.

"Gods Morgana, please," she whispered as I teased and played, enough to drive her wild, but not enough to give her the release her body craved.

"Do you want to come, Princess?" I murmured. *I could watch her like this for the rest of my existence and never grow tired of the sight.*

"Yes," she gasped, crying out as I circled her clit with firm pressure.

I was aching with my own need as I shuffled down, settling between her legs. I felt her tense again as I kissed one soft thigh, feeling the toned muscles in them flex as she shifted. I kissed the other, flicking my tongue along her skin, and licked the crease of her thigh, addicted to the sounds she was making as I did.

I hovered between her thighs, waiting for her to relax again and ever so slowly pushed a finger inside her.

Nimmet give me strength. The sight of her arching as I found that spot within her, the cry she let out would be ingrained in my mind for eternity. I felt my shadows release her wrists and she reached down blindly, fingers twining with my free hand as I slipped a second finger inside her, stroking in slow movements.

Her thighs relaxed and moved wider as I fucked her with my fingers, and I dipped my head, dragging my tongue across her clit.

She tasted better than I could have imagined, her cries becoming uncontrolled as I worked her with finger and tongue in tandem.

I kept her dancing along the edge of her climax until her thighs were shaking and her body writhing in uncontrolled spasms before I nudged her over the edge, sucking her clit gently as I flicked my tongue across it.

She came hard, drenching my hand with her climax, and Gods it was the most seductive thing I had ever witnessed.

I prowled back up her limp body, taking her mouth again so she could taste her climax on my tongue, and laughed softly at her dazed expression.

"Are you okay?" I murmured, resting on my elbow to watch her as I trailed a finger down the damp skin between her breasts.

She rolled toward me and gazed at me for a moment, reaching to brush her thumb against my lower lip, and then she was kissing me urgently, pushing me flat onto my back with one hand running to fist my hair.

"Show me how to make you feel like that," she murmured, her free hand moving to rest hesitantly against my stomach.

I was lost in sensation for a moment as her fingers traced the line where smooth skin met scarred, following it up to my where tendrils of burns bracketed my breast and reached across my chest. I groaned softly as her fingers brushed my nipple and she looked at me intently.

"You like that?"

She didn't give me a chance to answer before warm lips closed on it.

"Yes," I said, my voice husky, surprised to find I actually meant it. I usually hated my scars being touched, I hated them even being seen, choosing to wear clothing that hid them—but Gwen? I would let her touch me anywhere she wanted if it meant she would look at me like that, lust written plainly on her face.

She kissed me, and I took her hand, guiding it down my body and between my thighs, positioning her fingers where I needed them, to where I was aching for her touch.

She made a small sound as her fingers slipped against my wetness.

"Right there," I gasped, a jolt of pleasure running through me as she took over. "Just like that."

Her gaze dragged downward, her mouth falling slightly open as she began teasing me with more skill than most I had taken to bed.

Goosebumps rippled across my flesh as her long hair dragged across my skin, and then her lips were on me, trailing slowly down my body.

"Gwen, you don't have to do th—" My protest was cut off as she pushed inside me, dragging a primal sound I was nearly embarrassed of out of me.

"I'm not finished with you until I have you as undone as

you had me," she murmured against my skin, and Gods, it wasn't going to take long, not with whatever she was doing with her fingers. She changed her angle slightly and I cried out, a wave of pleasure rolling over me as my shadows skittered across the bed, loosed by my rapidly dissolving self-control.

She dropped a kiss below my belly button, another on my hip, my breathing becoming ragged as her warm breath whispered against my skin, lower and lower until…

"Gwen," I gasped.

And this time it was I who was praying.

13

MERLIN

"Arthur!" The rage in me was threatening to spill over, small arcs of light flickering across my skin as I stormed into the King's private chambers.

The sound of water splashing drew my attention to the bathhouse that was set off to the side.

"In here, Merlin." His voice was slightly slurred, and I heard a soft, feminine voice murmur to him.

I stalked into the room and was instantly enveloped in aromatic steam, just able to make out the outline of multiple figures in the large square bath that was set into the ground.

"I need to speak to the King," I snapped, a wave of my hand had a gust of wind clearing the steam in the room. The two women instantly shrank from me, but Arthur just gave me a smile that would freeze water, waving his hand toward the women. "Come, Merlin. You can have the blonde, come join us." A woman was currently perched in his lap, her full breasts bobbing in the water as he twirled a lock of her red hair in his fingers. He sighed. "Even a King needs a night off sometimes, it has been a long, tedious month."

The blonde he had so flippantly thrown my direction stared at me with wide eyes, offering me a hesitant smile.

"The Grotto," I said, ignoring her and fighting hard with my temper. "There was no need for that."

"Later, Merlin," Arthur said, waving a hand at me. "Whatever it is can wait." He turned the woman in his lap to face him, one arm disappearing beneath the water. "Be a good girl and show me how grateful you are to fuck the King, Sweetheart."

The redhead instantly went to work, her arms moving under the water, and Arthur groaned, resting his head back against the marble edge of the pool.

I crooked a finger at the blonde who was now looking uncertainly between myself and Arthur, and she came toward me with a faint look of fear. I grabbed a towel from a stack next to me, passing it to her as she neared and inclined my head to the door.

"Leave," I murmured to her, not taking the flash of relief I saw cross her face personally as she turned and fled, her wet feet pattering across the ground.

Arthur raised his head and huffed, arching a brow at me. "You are a wet blanket these days, Merlin." He sighed heavily, "Well if this isn't the biggest fucking turn-off. He patted the girl on the shoulder. "Go, wait in my room."

I waited, anger still boiling in my gut as he followed her out, water streaming from him and pooling on the floor as he strolled naked and half erect to a table laden with refreshments and poured himself a glass of wine.

"What is so important?" he asked, downing half the glass in one hit.

"There was no sickness," I bit out. "You ordered the Dragon guard to burn hundreds of homes—hundreds of lives needlessly taken."

He looked at me blankly, taking another swig of his wine. "What are you on about?"

"The Grotto. Tonight. The Dragon guard. The orders came directly from you, I was there."

Arthur frowned, raking his eyes over me, "Were you injured?"

"What?" I spluttered. "Of course not!"

"Then I don't see what the issue is?" Arthur said, leaning a hip against the table. "I was informed of sickness spreading fast through The Grotto. So I cut it off at the source before it spread." He downed the rest of his glass, the powerful muscles in his neck working as he drank. "You saw how fast the black death swept through last time."

"The well was poisoned," I said evenly, only the slight shake in my voice betraying how furious I was, hoping he took it for grief for the dead and not that I was envisioning plunging a dagger through his eye. "There was no sickness."

Arthur cocked his head, the empty glass hanging loosely in his fingers. "Well, that's unfortunate." He shrugged, making a non-committal noise. "Good thing it was only The Grotto then."

"They are *all* your subjects, Arthur!" I barely reeled in my temper before I said something that would jeopardize everything.

"They are citizens of The Grotto," he said, giving me an exasperated look. "Not to mention they were already dying if they had been poisoned. Half of them couldn't even afford burials anyway, I did them a favor. You know how fast humans breed—fifteen or twenty years and it will be teeming again." He tipped his cup toward me. "If you're not going to get your cock wet, how about a drink to ease those frayed nerves? You look like you need it." He gave me a calculating look, his eyes dropping lower. "Does it not work? Is that why you keep refusing the women I send to you?"

I barely bit my tongue in time, taking the glass he offered me purely to give my hand something to do before it wrapped around his neck and signed my death warrant.

"I prefer a woman's nails raking my back, not my face," I said through my teeth. "What happened to pulling humans into their rightful place in the world? Or is it only some of them you deem worthy? The rest you can exterminate like fleas?"

I was walking a fine line and I didn't miss the hardening of Arthurs eyes.

"I have done more for these people than any King in history," he said, his voice dropping to an ominous hum. "And I have done much for you, Merlin. Don't take my affection for you as the right to question my dedication. I have lived a long life, but even I cannot see everything."

I took a breath, tempering my features and tilting my head in apology.

"Forgive me. I spoke purely out of concern for your image."

Arthur gave me a long look, raising a brow, before reaching for a towel and slinging it around his hips. Even though he had the power of the Helix flowing in his blood, he hadn't let his body weaken, his muscles still as pronounced as they had been a century ago.

"I am your advisor," I said, "It is my job to advise you, and attacking your most vulnerable people is not a good way to ensure they trust you as King."

"They can trust me or not, it doesn't make any difference to me," Arthur replied. "Sometimes they cannot see what is best for them and I do what needs to be done, it is the curse of power, Merlin. With their fleeting lives, any transgressions they accuse me of will be forgotten in a blink of an eye for us. We are Gods to them, my friend."

A God. That is what he was coming to believe he was. He seemed to have forgotten that without the Helix, he was as human as the rest and his bones would have been dust in the earth many, many years ago. I hid my grimace. "A lone wolf is no threat to a bear," I warned. "But with its pack at its back, even a bear stands no chance. Turn your people against you and you will fall, my King."

Arthur chuckled softly. "So dramatic." He shook his head, reaching to pat my shoulder. "If the death of peasants troubles you *so* much, I will run it past you next time."

I inclined my head. "Thank you."

He huffed, raising his glass to me and turned, heading off toward his rooms but stopped as he got to the doorway. "Do you know who is responsible for this poison that you seem to think was the cause?"

A finger of ice traced down my spine, and I refused to let even a flicker of emotion cross my face. "Not yet."

"Hmm," he rolled his neck. "Find out, and then execute them. If my image is what you are concerned about, give the people their villain."

"Of course," I bowed my head to him.

The next attack came five days later, this time ten huge silos of grain went up in flames. Whispers of it being at The Black Rook's hand continued with the same sigil being painted on the only remaining silo. A huge blow to Irling as winter approached.

No word had come from Windhaven in response to the message I had sent, and this time Arthur was taking notice.

The Dragon guard had been sent to investigate the attack and had gotten there before I had, reporting the sigil's presence back to the King immediately. It was only a matter of time before someone made the connection, and I cursed myself for not thinking to scrub the Rook's name from the decoy notes I had handed over in the past.

I eyed the most recent note in my hand a moment longer, before throwing it into the fire.

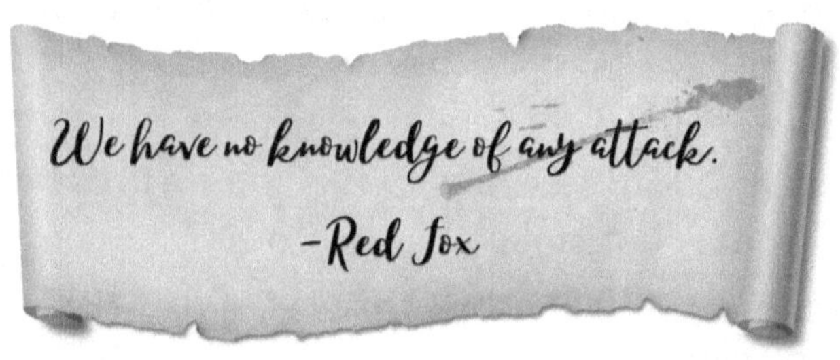

"You are backing me into a corner, Rook," I muttered under my breath, watching as the flames licked at the note. "Where are you and what the fuck are you playing at?"

I clicked my fingers at Sirin, and she flew to me, perching on my arm.

"Go make yourself useful," she said in a perfect copy of my voice.

I huffed, my fingers slipping into the feathers of her neck to scratch a particularly favorite spot of hers. "Yes, I need you to go back to Windhaven, my sweet. The one you listened to last time, Guinevere. I think she might be the Rook and I need to know what she intends to do next." I tapped her softly on her curved beak. "No hanging around the kitchens again."

She nipped at my fingers gently, clucking in a way she reserved only for me before taking a hopping step and launching herself from my arm, and flying neatly out her window. I watched her go, her white feathers disappearing quickly into the sunlight and murmured a prayer to Nimmet that she would keep my little friend safe.

14

MORGANA

I woke to fingers trailing my skin, wrapped in sheets that smelled like Gwen, the heat of her body nestled into mine. Stretching languidly against her, I cracked a reluctant eye to gauge where the sun was, shivering as her lips brushed the curve of my breast, right on the tendril of scarring that bracketed it.

Light was only just visible in the corner of the window, the sun beginning its slow ascent and the room still dark, and I peered down at her.

She was frowning slightly as her finger traced my tattoos, exploring them.

"Tell me," she murmured, throwing a pain-filled look at me. "How do I not know of you being hurt like this?"

I captured her hand and brought it to my lips as I tried to find the right words.

"You were dealing with your own pain while I was healing from mine," I said quietly.

I saw the moment she realized what I meant, her face

tightening. "The battle of Sirinelle," she said quietly. "When we lost Mother and Father."

I nodded.

"Your nightmares," she continued, her voice cracking slightly as her gaze fell back to my scars. "The Blood Traitor did this to you."

It wasn't a question, and anger hardened her words.

"He did worse to others," I replied, hating the agony on her face and wanting to wipe it away.

She sat up, the covers falling away from her naked body. "You were suffering, and you didn't tell us? Morgana, those burns are—"

"Hideous," I cut in.

"Horrific," she corrected, putting a warm hand across the scars. "Never hideous, they are scars that show you *survived*. You were what—eighteen during the battle of Sirinelle?" She frowned. "Who brought you back to Windhaven? I don't remember you coming back... you were just... there suddenly."

I cleared my throat, flashes of the agony of those days hitting me. "I walked. Crawled when I couldn't walk. I was delirious for a lot of it, so I have little memory of it. I just knew I had to get back and didn't know who I could trust so I stayed away from anyone I heard passing."

Gwen made a small sound of distress. "You were alone?"

"I was alone because I couldn't save those I should have been able to protect," I said, my tone sharper than I intended. "And I am fucking terrified that I am still not enough, and I will be the downfall of the Lowlands."

"It is not just on you," she said gently. "We are all responsible for keeping them safe."

"I am the only one that can keep that wall up," I argued. "And I don't know what I am doing. I barely have control of my power; when I have tried it gets away from me, I have just as much chance of killing myself or the people around me as I do protecting them."

"That is *not* your fault. I can't imagine how dangerous my gift would be had I not had the elders to help me," Gwen said. "You have had *nobody* to train you!" She paused a moment, her eyes boring into me. "That's what you meant wasn't it?" She asked. "When you said your nightmares were less than you deserve. Morgana, you were not responsible for that!"

"I hid in my tent like a coward," I said, guilt heavy at finally voicing those words. "While your *parents* died."

Gwen flinched but gripped my hand. "You were untrained. If you had tried you would be dead alongside them, you must know this, deep down. I do not hold you accountable for what happened. I know Tadgh and Saoirse wouldn't either."

I turned my face away, mortified as I felt the prick of tears behind my eyes.

"Don't," she breathed, turning my face back to her. "Don't ever feel you have to hide from me. I am not someone you have to be anything other than yourself with."

She leaned down and kissed me, and I gave into her, feeling a tear slide down my cheek.

Her hand cupped my cheek, thumb brushing it away as I flipped her, deepening the kiss with a low moan.

What was this woman doing to me?

"I should go back to my room," Gwen murmured a while later. She ran a hand across my stomach, nestling against my scarred shoulder with a sigh.

I didn't answer her, just ran my hand across hers, twined

our fingers together and tried to ignore how good it felt to do it.

She lay there for a moment, her thumb idly stroking my palm before sitting up with a groan and ruffling through the tousled sheets.

"If you are looking for your clothes, they are over there," I chuckled, waving my hand in the general direction of the far wall where I had thrown them.

I watched as she slipped out of bed, padding naked across the room, a slow smile tugging at my lips as she bent low to swipe them up and gave me a beautiful view of the backside that I had taken great pleasure in biting. I could still see the faint crescent of my teeth against the pale skin there, and a few faint scratches down her back that must have been from my nails.

Gwen did a double take as she turned back around, seeing me grinning at her and raised a brow in question.

"Want me to heal the marks I left on you?" I teased, raising a hand that swirled with whisps of inky tendrils. "Saoirse might have questions if she sees them."

She ran a hand over her rear, trying, and failing, to hide her own smile. "No. They can stay." She dressed quickly, then paused halfway to the door, giving me a seductive little smile. "Will I see you for breakfast?" She asked.

I slipped from the sheets, crossed the room and pulled her into my arms, kissing her soundly. "Just think," I murmured against her lips. "Every time you look at me today, know that I am going to be thinking about the taste of you on my tongue and what my name sounded like on your lips as you came."

Gwen groaned under her breath, her depthless blue eyes finding mine in the dim room.

"And every time you look at me, know that I'm going to be thinking about how you are the first thing I've ever chosen selfishly for myself, and that I can't find it in me to feel the least bit sorry for it. I've wanted you for years, and now that I have had you, I know it will not be enough. I'm not strong enough to deny myself anymore."

She kissed me once more and slipped out the door, leaving me blinking at the dark hallway beyond, utterly without words.

"If the sun stays behind the clouds and the snow underfoot doesn't melt this should be a relatively fast trip," Gwen said, peering up at the sun. We were at the crossroad between Windhaven and The Hollow, having eaten a quick breakfast and headed out early.

"Great," Saoirse said, her voice muffled from under the scarf that was wrapped tightly around the lower part of her face. "Now you have said *that* everything will go wrong."

Gwen laughed, the sound echoing off the trees around us.

The air was bitterly cold and all three of us were bundled against the wind that had come up through the pass, even the warmth of Gwen's body sitting in front of me on the horse couldn't penetrate the thick cloaks we were wrapped in.

It was easy travel through to The Hollow, the road flat and well-traveled in this part and the horses could relax, happily ambling along after each other.

Gwen's body swayed with the horse's gait, her hips rolling under my hands and the image of her naked body rolling against me flashed through my mind. She glanced back at me as I fumbled with the cloak between us, slipping my hand beneath it to run into the warmth beneath, sliding slowly over her hip.

"Morgana," she hissed, the color rising in her cheeks as she glanced furtively at Saoirse ahead of us.

"What?" I asked innocently. Touching her so easily like this was something I don't think I would ever get used to, nor the instant, hungry look in her eyes.

She pushed at my arm through the layers, which did absolutely nothing to stop me as I found the waistband of her riding trousers and slid my fingertips along the top of it.

"No one can see," I murmured in her ear, my eyes flicking to Saoirse's back. "Though you might need to work on your volume control if you don't want to scar your sister for life."

"Do you want to stop up here for lunch or push through?" Saoirse called, wheeling her horse around in a large circle.

"Let's push—" Gwen paused to clear her throat, sounding slightly strangled as my hand slipped slightly lower, fingertips brushing lightly against her, hidden under the layers of cloak. "Let's push through, if we make good time, we could make it to the Walsh farm and stay in their barn rather than the tents. It would be nice to check in on them since we are passing."

"Sounds good," Saoirse called, visibly brightening as she urged her mare forward again with a slightly longer look at her sister's face. I didn't miss the very quick glance she shot my way. "Hay sounds better than frozen ground."

I managed to get my other hand under the layers of Gwen's cloak and clothing, leaving a gap in my own cloak, the nip of the icy air seeping through it, but the breast I now cupped in my other hand made it worth the slight discomfort. I ran my thumb over the stiffened peak of Gwen's nipple, feeling her lean back slightly into me, the smallest sigh escaping her.

"Hush," I teased, speaking low enough so only she could hear as I slipped my other hand lower. "You can sing for me later when we don't have company." Her legs were splayed wide over the huge back of the gelding we rode, leaving her completely at my mercy as my fingers slid between her legs, instantly finding the swollen bud of her clit and running a fingertip gently over it.

Gwen spasmed, dropping the reigns and fumbling to grasp them again as I chuckled into her neck.

"Oh Gods, stop," she breathed, "What if Saoirse—" She trailed off as I slowly circled her clit again, groaning under my breath as I felt how wet she already was.

"I can stop if you want me to," I murmured, pinching her nipple and making her gasp. "Or…"

Gwen whimpered, turning her head and leaning her temple against my forehead.

I ran my other hand from her breast down her stomach, my hand splaying wide across it as I brushed a kiss across her jaw, one eye on Saoirse who was oblivious to the fact her sister was being corrupted behind her.

"Don't stop," Gwen whispered, her breath hitching as I added a bit more pressure.

I teased her with slow, lazy circles of my finger until Gwen's breaths began to become erratic, her hips moving not just with the rock of the horse's gait.

"Do you want more?" I whispered into her ear.

She nodded, her hand white-knuckled on the reins as I adjusted my angle and sank two fingers into her. My hand was crushed between her body and the saddle, the heel of my palm still pressed against her. I gripped her hip with my free hand, my own pulse a frantic song in my ear. "Ride my fingers, Gwen," I murmured, "Take your pleasure from me."

She groaned, the sound whipped away by the cold breeze as she rolled her hips, her head falling back to my shoulder.

I curled my fingers inside her, dragging another whimper from her as she rolled her hips again, grinding herself against my hand.

I was praying to Nimmet that Saoirse wouldn't turn

around, not as I felt the tell-tale flutter of Gwen's muscles around my fingers, the catch in her breath as she rode my hand toward her release. I bit her shoulder gently, my free hand pushing against her abdomen. "I am never going to get enough of your body, Princess," I murmured. "Tonight, I am going to ride you like this, and you can listen to what you do to me."

That's all it took to send her crashing over the edge. Gwen gasped, stiffening, one hand flying back to grasp my cloak-covered thigh and twist in the material as she came hard.

I smiled into her hair, as she shuddered through the waves of it, carefully withdrawing my crushed, numb hand. "That was fast," I chuckled as she regained her composure.

She eyed me over her shoulder, looking frazzled. "I can't help it if my daydreams had already done half the job for you."

15

MERLIN

I knew it was coming, but my stomach still felt like it was filled with lead when I got the summons from Arthur to the council chambers, and tonight was the worst possible night he could have chosen to do it.

I could tell the moment I entered the room that war was beckoning. The air crackled with his anger as the men threw furtive glances in my direction, as if I were the one who stood between them and the Kings wrath.

"I am done with the Lowland rebellion," he snapped at me the second he noticed my arrival. "Cerridwen's brats have strayed past my tolerance."

The comment surprised me, and I glanced around the room to see if others had picked up on it. It was the first time I had heard him utter Lady O'Mordha's name in decades.

"On the scale of threats, I still stand by what I said. If these attacks have truly come from Windhaven—which I am still dubious about—they are still nothing compared to what a hive of Drayyn would do if they decided to look to Kambria."

"Is that what you would tell the *hundreds* of dead that you were so upset about last week?" Arthur growled, his face thunderous. "Their worth is beginning to outweigh their cost."

I snapped my fingers at the men milling in the room. "Out."

There was a flurry of movement as they raced to comply, seeming only too happy to follow my order.

I waited until we had the room, my jaw clenched as I quickly filtered through the words threatening to spill over, cautious of the dangerous game I was playing.

"I am not a seer, my King. I give you my opinions based on what I see. I do not see how these attacks can have come from the Lowlands. Our men patrol these lands from here to Glenrock, and no one has reported any sightings of Sylvyn past the wall aside from the sporadic attempts at reclaiming their supply runs. Endreal is still not under your grasp and grows more powerful with each passing year, I still have no way beyond Windhaven's wall, and the heart of the Helix is still lost to us."

Arthur's face hardened at the mention of the heart of the Helix. It was a secret that only he and I knew about: the one thing that could potentially take back the power he had stolen was missing, and it killed him.

"Just because it has not been reported, does not mean it has not happened," he retorted.

"True," I tilted my head in surrender. "And I have sent men to look into it further."

Arthur glowered, striding to the map that had been carved into the stone wall and surveyed it.

"Adairn, Nareen, the outlying islands are all under my reign, yet Endreal is still a thorn in my side," he snapped, his finger trailing over lands that were mere outlines on this map, undiscovered yet.

I shook my head. "Send me to Endreal. I have said time

and time again that this is too important to only send the Dragon guard, especially with the alliances the Drayvn have made."

"I will be sending you once Endreal is in hand," he snapped. "I know you, Merlin. You will rush headfirst into that hive, and I need you alive for what is to come. And besides, if Windhaven has decided to grow a spine, I will need to move on them sooner than anticipated."

"The wall still stands, Arthur," I stated. I was walking a very fine line with my tone, though he didn't seem to notice.

"We have cut off every supply line, every exit," he said, his voice hard. "Starving them out has not worked for decades, and if they feel safe enough to venture out and attack Irling, then they are not suffering as bad as *you* assured me they would, and we will have to approach this differently. You yourself said you felt the wall weakening. Maybe with both of us, we can break it."

My stomach was about to drop out of my ass. *No, not yet. I was so close.*

"Give me a chance to find out who is behind the attacks first," I said. "We know from the intercepted messages that they are growing desperate. You have far more chance to bring them to heel if they think it's their idea. Attack them and you are only going to kill men that you will need in the long run, and unlike humans, Sylvyn do not repopulate as fast."

Arthur narrowed his eyes at me, then nodded, humming his agreement. "You make a point." He frowned at the table for a moment. "The Sylvyn in Endreal, what do you know of them?"

I shrugged. "Not much—most of the men that have come up against them haven't survived. From what I hear, they have a powerful young Wytchling by the name of Imogyn in their ranks. Why?"

"Chess, Merlin," he replied. If this Imogyn is Endreal's strongest player, then we need to neutralize her. This one has no wall to cower behind at least."

I raised a brow. "And how do you intend to kill a Wytchling who has murdered every one of your men that she has come up against, without sending me over there?"

Arthur chuckled, "I never said kill." He rapped his knuckles twice on the table. "The Drayvn may be powerful allies, but I doubt they are anyone's first choice. I would be interested to see if Morus is intelligent enough to consider new alliances. Ones that don't enjoy the taste of blood."

I could hear the twins bickering as I ascended the steps to my tower, mingled with the general clatter of their semi-consensual ransacking of my rooms.

They fell silent as I entered, looking slightly guilty.

"What did you do?" I asked, heading to the small chest I had at the foot of my bed and opened it. Light danced in patterns across the ceiling as the crystals in it shimmered and glowed where they peeked through the scraps of cloth they were wrapped in. I sighed, instantly noting the tell-tale signs that Una had been in here.

The girl had a fascination with these gems, and would sit and run her fingers over the flickering surfaces, always putting them back as she found them with the exception of leaving the cloths open to 'sparkle like stars' whenever the chest was opened.

"Nothin'!" they protested… too quickly.

I studied them for a moment, noticing they were both standing in front of my desk awkwardly. I narrowed my eyes at them before picking out a crystal that was the size of my fist, and hefting it in my hand as I felt the hum of my power within it. A bank of energy for when I needed it.

Standing, I closed on the two culprits, cocking my head at them. "What. Did. You. Do?"

To my absolute horror, Una's lip started wobbling, and she pulled out an envelope from behind her back.

"Please don't say yes, Da."

"For the love of Nimmet, I am not your damned D—" I broke off as I saw the handwriting on the note, the seal having been expertly popped from the paper without damaging it, just like I had taught her to do.

I scanned the letter quickly, my brows raising.

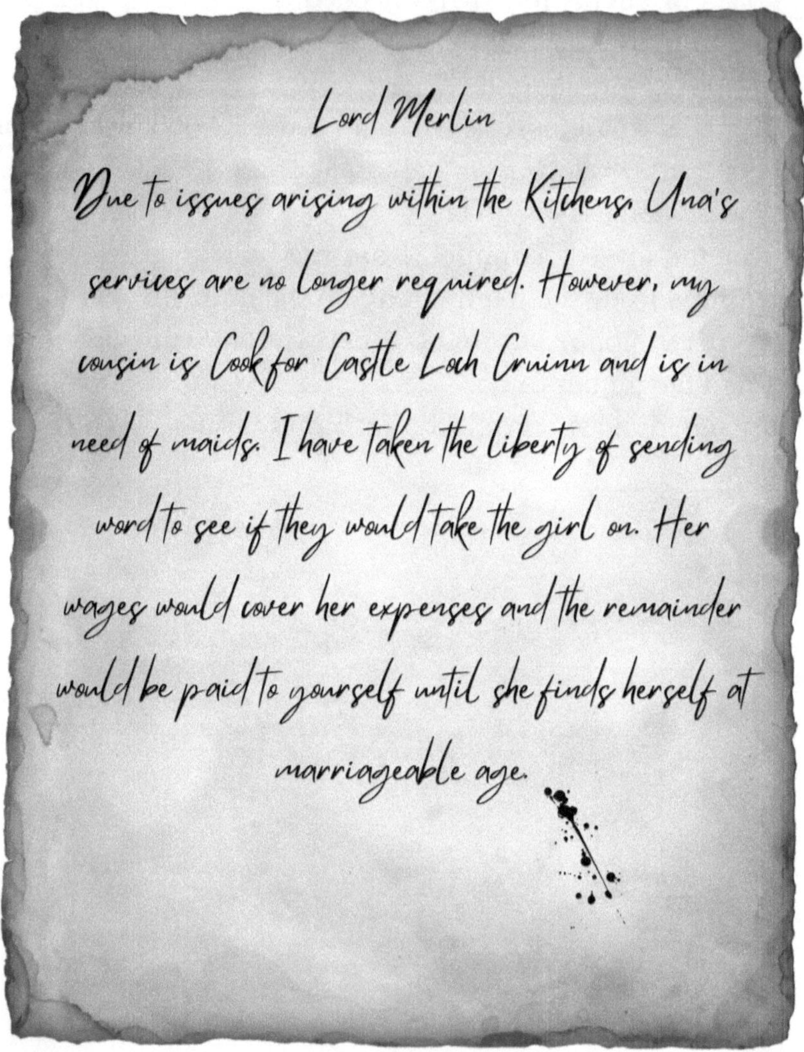

I frowned at the letter, reading it twice more.

"Explain?" I asked, eyeing them both in turn.

Otto scowled. "I told you, the girls been givin' her a hard

time. None of them like her and been settin' her up. Pourin' salt in her bakin' and blamed the burned stuff on her."

"Why?" I asked, nonplussed.

"They say we're bad luck," Una sniffed in a small voice.

I frowned between the pair of them, waiting for them to explain further.

"Because of how we look," Otto added. Patting the mismatched skin of his cheek.

A flash of anger rushed through me, the letter crunching into a ball in my hand. I tossed it into the fireplace, pointing to the small stack of papers on my desk. "Otto, transcribe a message for me."

Otto slid into my seat, looking anxious as I turned to my wardrobe, rummaging through it and pulling out a dark tunic and pants.

"I understand that there have been ongoing issues I was not aware of," I said, waiting for Otto to catch up as he began writing furiously. I was secretly quite proud of the boy's hand, I had taught them both to read and write myself, and his script was almost as elegant as my own.

Otto looked up at me expectantly and I carried on.

"I am less than impressed I did not know one of my twins were at the center of this issue, and please be assured, I have discussed this with them." I ducked behind a screen to change quickly, seeing Otto's solemn face as I came back out, quill poised over the message he had dutifully recorded. I gave him a small wink.

"I would advise you to reprimand your kitchen hands yourself because if I find you have let them treat one of mine in the way they have without consequence, I will personally come down there and they will not enjoy what follows next." I watched a slow smile spread across Otto's face, his hand flying to follow my words.

"Please cancel your thoughtful message to Loch Cruinn and shove it up your arse," I finished. Probably unnecessary, but after the events of this afternoon, that last part was highly satisfying. I let out an oomph as I was hit in the side by a low-flying projectile, skinny arms wrapping around my waist as a mass of curls tucked under my arm.

"Thank you," Una whispered, and the emotion in her voice tugged at my heart. I grunted, patting her on the shoulder. "I've spent far too long training you idiots to send you off to someone else", I said gruffly. I glanced at her brother as Una released me, taking the glistening gem from my hand to peer at it with an appreciative sigh.

"Are you good to take that down to the kitchens? I will deal with any issues when I return."

"Yup!" Otto said brightly, rolling the note in his hands and popping it in his tunic. "Where are you going?" He asked, frowning at me. "Can we come?"

"Sirinelle," I said, shaking my head, "and I can't take you. I'm going to flit there and it's hard enough doing that alone. I won't be long. If the King sends for me, you need to stall him. Tell him I am in the lower city and you will fetch me."

"And what do I say you are doing in the lower city?" he asked, putting his feet up on the desk.

I slapped them off, leaning over him to open a drawer and pull out a metal clasp to secure my cloak together. "I don't know, make something up."

"I'll say you are at the brothel," he said, a matter-of-factly.

I closed my eyes, sighing. "If you must."

"No man would bother another man at a brothel," he said, looking innocently at me. "If you were at an inn or playing cards there would be no reason not to leave immediately. At a brothel though yo——"

"Don't finish that sentence, Otto," I said, giving him a

warning look. "*You* might be beyond redemption, but I still have some hope for your sister."

Una frowned. "I'm not dumb, the kitchen girls talk all the time. I know a man goes in there to split a girl."

"Oh good Gods," I muttered, pinching the brow of my nose. I took a breath, shaking my head then eyed the pair of them. "I will be back by morning," I said wearily.

Otto nodded, jumping up and pulling open the cupboard I kept food in, emerging with a couple of apples and tossed one to Una. "Can we stay here? It's warmer than our room."

I snorted, as if they hadn't stayed in one of my adjoining rooms most nights for the past few years. It was always some excuse as to why they couldn't sleep in the perfectly good room that had been allotted to them by the kitchen staff. "I think it might be best if you stay here for the time being, until Cook has calmed down. And maybe order food to be supplied from the King's kitchen for now." I took the crystal from Una and hefted it in my palm. "Keep the fire going and stay off my bed," I frowned. "And ginger tea, fill a pot and put it over the fire, lots of it."

"Yes Da," Otto called, already pushing through the small door and into the room with the two pallets they slept on, neatly made and waiting.

I rolled my eyes, squeezing the crystal in my palm and I winced, already dreading what I was about to do. I *hated* flitting with a passion.

"Fuck," I muttered, taking a deep breath and holding it as I reached for the well of power within me. I closed my eyes, pulled up an image of where I needed to be… and stepped.

…

A woman screamed, backed up by a man's shout of alarm as my body slammed into hard—and somehow soggy —ground.

I took a moment to remember how to breathe, feeling like my spine had been ripped out of my arse and shoved back down my throat, groaning as I rolled onto my side—where I promptly fell off the table I had been lying on, and onto the *actual* floor in a shower of roasted vegetables and broken crockery.

"Merlin?" someone asked, sounding confused.

Probably not as confused as I was as I blinked at the three people looming above me. I pulled myself to my feet, swallowing hard as nausea washed over me.

"Who, the fuck, put a table there?" I demanded, then heaved, barely stopping myself from throwing up all over the floor at their feet.

"You ate before flittin' didn't you?" Kareen pushed passed her husband, hands on her stout hips as she frowned at me. "And I put that table there. Didn't think you would be appearin' on it in the middle of dinner, did I now?"

"It was an empty space when I was last here, that's why I aimed for it," I protested weakly, holding my sides and bending over. "Oh my Gods, that never gets any better."

"I'll get the tea," Kareen said, bustling off to her kitchen.

"Is everything ok, Milord?" The young man who had been eating with them asked.

"Don't *Milord* him," Kareen yelled from the kitchen. "Goes straight to his head it does." She came back, holding a cup of steaming tea, slices of ginger root floating around in it. "Drink this and you'll be right," she said, handing it over.

I took it gratefully, sipping at the scalding liquid. "The supply run headed through to The Spine, has it gone yet?"

Kareen raised a brow. "Of course not, heads out at darkest night, my Rupert was seeing it through after his dinner.

"Rupert, your son?" My gaze fell on the young man who was still standing, watching me with a concerned look, suddenly recognizing the child he had been the last time I had come through. "Oh,' I said, blinking.

"Oh indeed," Kareen huffed. "Been a right long time since you 'popped in' as you like to put it."

"What's wrong with the run?" Bain, Kareen's husband asked. He was a soft-spoken man in comparison to his firecracker of a wife, though I had known Kareen since she was a girl, and it was all bluster.

"Nothing, I need to talk to the Sylvyn who are hauling it through," I said, my stomach slowly settling as the tea hit it. I picked up the crystal that had rolled out of my hand during the collision with the table, checking it over. It had dulled substantially, but still flickered with life. Enough to see me back to Irling without needing to draw too much from my own power, which would otherwise leave me weak and sickly for a few days.

"Alright," Bain said, scratching his beard. "Though they don't like new folk—they might do a runner."

"I will take my chances," I said, sitting heavily on one of the rickety chairs.

I followed Bain and Rupert out as the moon was highest in the sky, watching in fascination as two other men and one woman joined us, all dressed in dark clothing and leading three wagons, their horse's hooves wrapped in sacks.

"We just take it as far as The Spine," Bain murmured to me, "Then they take it through the mountains to Kinconnal, and through the forest side to the wall."

I nodded, my ears straining for any noise. The Dragon guard patrolled these lands, and any one of them could identify me. I slipped my hand into my pocket, feeling for the crystal in case I needed to vanish.

The hours dragged by, and we walked in silence, The Spine looming ahead of us, until one of the women that led the procession held up a fist, motioning us to halt.

Only the creak and groan of the carts rolling to a stop broke the night air, my own breathing sounding loud in my ears as she let out a low whistle and waited.

After a moment she whistled again, this time slightly higher pitched and with a small trill at the end before it fell silent again.

This time the signal was answered in the distance, a two-toned melody that could easily have been a bird.

The woman waved her hand, altering our course slightly as she headed toward the noise.

I would have walked right past them, had I not sent a web of my power out, feeling ahead for the Sylvyn that lurked in the craggy mountainside. There were seven of them, seven souls flickering ahead in the darkness, and I made sure I was hidden in the recesses of my cloak as we drew closer.

"The Kelpie swims true," our leader called quietly into the darkness.

"And the Druka flies fair," a feminine voice called back. "Is that you Nora?"

"Aigh, it is, Eileen," she called back.

More voices murmured to each other as dark figures met, some greeting each other warmly, others more reserved.

Bain touched my elbow, guiding me toward a tall figure who was as hidden in his cloak as I was, only the outline of his body visible.

"I have someone who wants to speak to you," Bain said quietly. "Ye can trust him, known him as long as I've known mi' wife."

The figure stiffened, turning toward me slowly.

"I come as a friend," I said quietly.

"What do I call you then, *friend?*" a male voice asked, sarcasm lacing the last word.

I hesitated a moment. "Wolf, and yourself?"

"Donal," he said, shifting on his feet.

"Does the Rook travel with you?" I asked, trying to search every part of their posture for any information he might be hiding from me.

"She does not, nor has she ever attended one of these trips," he replied quietly.

I made sure I kept my posture loose, and didn't show the flash of surprise at the revelation of the Rook being a woman, which all but confirmed my growing suspicion that it was Guinevere I had been conversing with all these years. "Do you know where the Rook is at the moment?" I pushed.

"It is not my place to enquire where the Rook goes, nor is it yours, Wolf." He said, his tone tightening.

"Irling has been attacked twice," I said, keeping my voice low enough to not let the others hear. "The Rook's sigil was left behind on both occasions. This needs to cease immediately before the King sets his sights on the wall—that is what is coming if there is another attack. Can I speak to her myself?"

Donal laughed softly from under his hood. "So like a human to blame the Sylvyn when they begin to reap what they have sewn." He shook his head. "The Rook is busy, though I will be sure to pass on your message to Fox and he can do with it as he wishes."

Fox. That must be the young Lord O' Mordha then. I shook my head, frustrated. "Is there another attack ordered? Hundreds of innocents died in our slums."

Donal stiffened. "Even if I knew what you were talking about," he growled, "What makes you think I give a single fuck about you humans dying after me and mine have been living like this for decades?" He was inches from my face, and I could see the glint in his eyes from deep within his hood, the pale grey of them glowing softly. "You dare cry about the lives of the free who have turned a blind eye to our plight, while I am here trying to get basic necessities to our children and elderly so they make it through the winter without freezing to death or dying of hunger?"

"I am doing what I can to prevent that," I hissed.

"Well try harder," he said flatly.

"Get her in line," I replied quietly. "Or get Fox to rein her in. If this continues, my hands will be tied, and she will have undermined decades of planning."

He was silent for a moment. "I will inform them. That is the best I can do. I do not stay long in Windhaven."

I nodded, hoping it was enough as he turned abruptly, leaving me standing alone. The handover finished quickly, the carts hitched to horses brought by the Sylvyn and led away into the darkness.

"Will you be returning with us?' Bain asked quietly.

"No," I replied, watching as Bain's people led the unburdened horses away. "I have heard what I needed to." I patted him on the shoulder. "Stay safe, my friend. Tell Kareen I won't leave it so long next time."

I waited until they were far enough away that the flash of light from flitting wouldn't draw their attention before pulling the crystal out of my pocket and rolling it in my palm, taking a few deep breaths.

Groaning slightly, I shut my eyes and stepped into the gut-wrenching stillness.

16

MORGANA

The sun was still high by the time the small farm came into sight. Saoirse called out a greeting to some young men who were working in the unnervingly bare fields, tilling the soil in long lines as a few children ran along behind with baskets of seeds.

A couple of them called out to Gwen in delight, one girl squealing and dropping her basket altogether.

By the time we rode up to the main house, a small group of people were following us, and Gwen had slipped off the horse to walk with them, holding a young boy's hand and swinging his arm as a girl who looked to be no older than fifteen spoke animatedly to her.

"Lady Guinevere, Lady Saoirse," an older woman with slightly greying hair and long pointed ears greeted us warmly, touching her hand to her heart. Her gaze rested on me, and she gave me a wide smile, her fingers brushing her forehead. "Sorry love, I don't know your name?"

"Lady Morgana," Gwen offered, beaming at a group of

young men who had emerged from one of the sheds. "My, you three have grown a foot since I was here last!"

All three boys looked identical with sandy blond hair and a heavy dose of freckles, and all three touched their hearts to her in unison as they nodded their heads in greeting.

"They have all been practicing what you taught 'em too, Lady," the woman said. "They been going through to the 'ollow and showing the younger ones too, and they been no end of help keeping those damned bánánach away. Dreadful creatures have been getting into the last of my chickens!"

Gwen slung an arm over one of the youth's shoulders, no easy feat as he was nearly taller than she was, and smiled up at him. "I would expect nothing less from my star students," she teased.

The poor boy flushed bright red under the brilliance of Gwen's attention. Mumbling something that sounded like "it was nuffin' really," before Gwen turned to greet some men who had come up from the fields.

A broad-shouldered man with dark hair and fair skin that was tanned from long days in the sun punched Saoirse gently on the arm, giving her a warm smile. "Hey there, old girl. Haven't seen you for a while."

"Call me old again Rian, and it will be the last time I grace you with my presence," Saoirse shot back good-naturedly, smiling sweetly up at him.

"Rian le Fay!" the woman scolded, flapping her hand at the men. "Leave off. Poor women have only just arrived and you're flirtin' with 'em already. No wonder they ain't been back here in years." She gave the closest one a shove. "I will call you when supper is done."

"Alright, alright," Rian chuckled, and he gave Saoirse a wink. "Give you a game of knives tonight?"

"Because that went so well for you last time?" Saoirse shot back, a wicked grin on her face. She stuck a thumb in her belt. "Last time you walked away with loose slacks and your pride in tatters, what do you want to wager this time, le Fay?"

Two of the other men howled with laughter as the group of them moved away, hauling the younger ones with them.

Rian blew a kiss to Saoirse, nodded respectfully at Gwen, and I saw the very slight flush in Saoirse's cheeks as she turned to her horse to unsaddle it.

Le Fay. No one had batted an eye at the name reserved for fatherless bastards. In Windhaven it was a slur, a few muttered it when they thought they were out of earshot, but here… I watched the men walk away, jostling each other in good-natured playfighting before gingerly swinging my leg over my mount and slithering ungracefully to the ground.

I heard Saoirse snort as I stiffly handed the rains to a waiting boy and surreptitiously tried to stretch my back out.

"Oh, deary me," the woman said, eyeing me over. She looked like she was trying not to laugh as she beckoned me toward the house. "Come in, love. We ain't got much but we do have some hot tea, and I know just the herbs to help take some of those riding pains away."

"Oh! Wait!" Saoirse said, whistling to the children who were leading the horses away. She trotted off toward the horses, coming back a moment later with a couple of fat hares she had shot on the way in.

"We come with gifts," she said, smiling as the woman gasped in delight.

I sat in front of the fire on the pillow Gwen had surreptitiously handed to me with an amused, pointed look at my *incredibly*

tender ass—no matter how much riding I seemed to do, I still hurt badly at the end of each day—and listened to Saoirse chatting to the woman who had introduced herself as Cara Walsh, the current overseer of her family's farm, as the pair of them skinned and butchered the hares. They were added to the thin-looking cauldron of stew that bubbled over the fireplace as Gwen kneaded some dough off to the side.

She had a streak of flour across one cheek, red hair piled in a messy bun atop her head, and she was wearing Cara's threadbare apron as she worked.

I don't think she had ever looked more beautiful. There was an ease to her in this environment that seemed to bring out a side of her I hadn't seen. She was laughing easily, flashing her brilliant smiles to anyone who approached her, not seeming to think about how she held herself or appeared to others. *This* was the Gwen that the Lowlands had fallen in love with, I realized.

Cara's house didn't have much, but the warmth that exuded—not just from her, but the home itself—was so different from the atmosphere at Windhaven. She had a sharp tongue, scolding the men for not removing their boots or washing their hands as they trailed into the large living space and found a spot to recline, but she did it with a sparkle in her eye and a smile behind the stern words.

Not even Cerridwen had been this warm when she had lived. She had been fair and reasonable compared to Kerrich's stern demeanor. But never warm like this woman, and I realized how utterly alluring it was, wondering how different I might have been had I grown up in a home like this.

A call that the fire was lit had everyone heading back outside. Gwen pushed the last of the small balls of dough she had been rolling into the huge iron pot that was hanging over the flames next to the stew, and beckoned me to follow her to where everyone had gathered around the small bonfire away from the house.

Saoirse was already out there, sitting close to Rian, their heads close together as they spoke to each other, sharing a blanket for warmth.

I raised a brow at her as I passed, and she flipped her middle finger up at me without even looking in my direction as if sensing my teasing gaze.

We found a spot on a log that had flat seats carved into it and settled ourselves amidst the general chatter and laughter. There were about thirty people in all that resided here, children included, and the noise was something I'm not sure I could get used to. It wasn't unpleasant, just a lot to take in when I was accustomed to quiet solitude.

Gwen appeared to be in her element, chatting and laughing at something one of the men had said to her while seemingly oblivious to the moon-eyed looks the triplets were throwing her way as they demonstrated their prowess with the gifts she had a hand in teaching them in. Two of them were gifted with fire, the same as her. The other was wielding wind, sending his brother's little arcs of fire upwards into roaring spirals of flame, pulling a delighted laugh from Gwen.

A couple of people tried including me in their conversation and I was polite but content to just listen. The fire in front of me popped and crackled, the odd spark shooting out too close for me to be able to relax entirely, the heat touching my face making me slightly clammy in a way that was nothing to do with the heat of it.

I was grateful when two of the men lifted the huge pot of stew out outside and Cara dished out bowls of it to everyone, the children handing out steaming bannocks and giving me something else to concentrate on.

Conversation buzzed and I let myself be distracted by it,

eating until my stomach was comfortably full. A few logs were thrown onto the fire, sending it roaring, the heat hitting my skin and making me flinch.

"I'm getting a bit hot here, let's move back," Gwen murmured, and I turned to see her watching me intently.

I nodded, relieved at the excuse and I held her cup as she stood, working to keep her blanket from touching the cold ground as we moved to a bench further back. Gwen opened her blanket and extended it around my shoulders as we sat, then took her cup back before launching into animated conversation with a few of the men.

She edged closer after a while, tucking a cold hand into the crook of my arm beneath the cover of the blanket. A very cold hand. She had definitely *not* been too warm by the fire, and I realized belatedly that she had noticed my discomfort and given me an out.

She kept talking to one of the men, her attention on him, but her finger brushed absently against my skin and I covered it in my own, warming it with a whisper of my power until all the coldness had left her skin, mulling over feelings that I was not sure how to deal with. Feelings that were deepening far, *far* too fast.

We stayed like that for a while, watching as Saoirse and a handful of the men began a game of knives, throwing them at a hide-covered target set upon a log, while Gwen slowly seduced my hand with hers.

Rian won after an obnoxiously bad throw from Saoirse, which I was sure had been purposeful on her part, and she made a great show of offering him the belt back that they had been wagering on.

Rian took it with a bow, cracking it once against his palm with a wink at Saoirse before slipping it back around his hips.

"Are they…" I trailed off, looking at Gwen in question.

"I absolutely don't want to know," Gwen muttered, looking at me with a crooked smile. The firelight shone in her eyes, setting the blue of them dancing, the red of her hair glowing as if from the embers themselves. Her eyes dipped to my mouth, lingering there a moment.

"What are you thinking right now Princess?" I murmured, trying to stop the smile that was tugging at my own lips.

"I'm trying to think of a valid reason why I shouldn't kiss you in front of all of these people," she murmured back.

"I can think of three blond-haired reasons that would be *terribly* upset if their crush stuck her tongue down someone else's throat," I teased softly, flicking my eyes over her shoulder to one of the triplets who was again watching Gwen with a moony expression.

Gwen laughed softly, dipping her head so the blanket muffled her words. "They are harmless. It is cute, though terribly inappropriate. I was here teaching some of the older ones when they were still in cloots." She cocked her head, narrowing her eyes playfully. "Are you jealous, Morgana?"

"Do you want me to be jealous?" I asked. "It's not in my nature but I could easily make an exception for you."

She huffed a laugh, her hand sliding out of mine where it had been making a slow perusal of my fingers and onto my leg instead.

I had to bite the inside of my lip hard to keep from groaning.

Clara took this moment to come over with an armload of blankets, her face flushed and hair escaping her bun. "Can I not tempt you to stay in the house?" she asked, looking concerned. "Plenty of room on the floor around the fireplace, or I can send the boys out to the barn for the night, and you can have their room?"

"We will be fine, honestly," Gwen laughed, taking the

blankets from her, leaving me bereft of her touch. "And I told you we had all our own blankets; you didn't need to go out of your way."

"Oh, hush now," Clara scoffed, "I won't sleep if I'm worried you three are not warm enough." She put her hands on her ample hips. "The boys laid some bedrolls out in the loft for you when you are ready for bed. I'm going to settle the youngins and head to bed me'self. Will I see you in the morning?"

"We are going to head off at first light," Saoirse said, moving up next to Clara and resting a familiar arm on the woman's shoulder. "If we sleep in the house, we might wake the children as we leave, and a warm barn is a hundred times better than our tents, we will be fine."

"Hmmph," Clara said skeptically, peering up at Saoirse. "I'll leave the door unlatched in case you change your mind."

She bustled off, and the next few minutes were spent with children coming to kiss Gwen on the cheek and nodding shyly to Saoirse and myself before scuttling off to bed.

The fire was burning low by the time everyone else started melting off to find their beds. Some to the big house and others to the ramshackle little cottages that were just across the clearing. A group of the men seemed to be living in one of these and all moved off together, Rian among them, after he and Saoirse had lingered on the outskirts of the fire, murmuring to each other.

We excused ourselves and said our goodbyes, making our way across the darkness to the barn that loomed by the tree line, and I couldn't help but throw my shadows out ahead of us, feeling for anything that could be lurking in the trees beyond. Aside from the odd, small life that moved through the underbrush or nestled in the trees above I could feel nothing, and I relaxed, reeling them back in and letting one brush against Gwen as it passed her. A teasing caress against her neck, just disturbing the curtain of her hair and making her throw me a small smile that was laden with promises over her shoulder.

The barn smelled strangely nice; the sweet alfalfa hay letting off a gentle scent as we climbed the ladder and found the bedrolls that had been laid out for us.

Saoirse flopped onto hers, yanking her pants off with a dramatic sigh and stretching out on the far side roll in only a shirt and underwear.

"My feet hurt," she moaned as she extended a long, slender leg. "Someone rub them for me."

"Gross," Gwen snorted, slapping her foot away. "I'm sure Rian will rub them if you ask him nicely."

"I'm sure Rian would rub more than her feet if she asked him to," I said, chuckling at the dark look Saoirse gave me. I chose the bedroll on the other side leaving the middle free for Gwen, and pulled a blanket over myself, still fully clothed.

"You're going to be uncomfortable sleeping in those," Saoirse warned as I listened to the sounds of Gwen getting undressed and straightening her bed.

"Better than you staring at my arse all night," I mumbled into my pillow and then grunted as something hit my back and bounced off. A rolled sock from the feel of it.

"If I'm staring it's because I'm wondering how you manage to walk around with that stick lodged so firmly up it," Saoirse shot back, the last of her words lost in an enormous yawn that had her jaw cracking.

"It's not a stick, it's the fucking saddle," I muttered, shifting my hip into a comfortable position and stretching with a contented sigh. "If anything needs rubbing it's my arse."

Saoirse chuckled darkly. "Want me to ru—"

"Shut up Saoirse," Gwen said darkly, groaning as she lowered herself to her bed, close enough that her intoxicating scent wafted to me, mingling with the alfalfa we lay on.

17

MORGANA

Sleep has never been my friend. Even here, with only the sounds of breathing coming from the two women beside me, I couldn't slip away into oblivion. Gwen turned in her sleep, sighing softly and murmured something, caught in the middle of a dream. I reached out before I realized what I was doing, running a soothing hand down her back and she settled into stillness.

A bird called in the night, it's low whistle breaking the eerie silence, and it was only after the third call, when Saoirse stirred, slowly slipping from her bed, bending to pick up her clothing and stepping across Gwen's prone body, that I realized it wasn't a bird at all.

"You had better use that throat trick of yours," I whispered as she stepped over me. "Because if you aren't back here soon, I'm going to fill your boots with manure."

Saoirse jumped, swearing under her breath. "I highly dislike you sometimes," she hissed as she mounted the steps and began climbing down.

I grunted into my pillow, shifting against the hay to find a better position. "You will dislike me more if I have to come and find you."

Saoirse murmured to someone in the darkness, a low voice answering as the sound of soft footsteps moved away.

I sent a whisper of a shadow after her, trailing her as she moved away from the barn toward the tree line as I slipped an arm under Gwen's covers. She stirred, murmuring my name and turning toward me to nestle against my neck as I tugged her toward me in a rustle of hay.

Of all the lovers I had taken over the years, I had never wanted this kind of affection from them, always throwing them out of my rooms after I had taken what I needed and given them pleasure that had always had them coming back for more.

I ran my fingers into Gwen's hair, letting the long, silky strands flow through my fingers as I tried to unpick what I was feeling. Understand why I was feeling at all. Man or woman, I had never felt this drawn to anyone, and it unnerved me a little.

No, that was a lie. It unnerved me a lot.

"Did my sister just leave to go and have sex in the woods?" Gwen asked, her voice husky from sleep.

I laughed softly, dragging my fingers across her scalp and drawing a soft moan from her that had me repeating the movement just to hear it again. "I'm afraid so."

"Would I be a hypocrite if I called her a hussy?" she asked, and I could hear the smile in her words.

"Yes," I said, my fingers moving to the back of her neck and kneading it. She moaned again, louder this time and I realized that I was totally content with this small touch.

Gwen drifted back to sleep again after a while, one arm draped over my stomach, her breath soft against my shoulder as I listened out for the sound of Saoirse returning, already regretting the moment I would have to roll Gwen gently away from me.

Sleep was beginning to beckon to me as the faintest whisper of a shadow brushed past my ear, pulling me back into consciousness. I stilled, my ears straining into the darkness as I felt the hairs along my arms beginning to rise.

"Gwen," I whispered, pulling my arm carefully from beneath her and sitting up.

"Hmmm?" she hummed muzzily. "What's wrong?"

"I don—" I cut off as a shadow hit me with a force that shook my whole body, urgent whispers merging in a blur of sound. I pushed the heels of my palms into my eyes, trying to pick the voices apart as I felt Gwen sit up next to me.

Saoirse.

The name solidified in my mind in that young, yet ancient voice as I was already moving from bed.

"Morgana?" Gwen called from behind me.

"Stay here," I ordered, and opened the floodgate of my power, throwing myself off the loft and into the darkness of the night.

I shadow walked through the darkness, throwing a net of my power out as far as I could reach, feeling for where she was. A faint flicker ahead had me turning slightly, barely disturbing the leaves around me as I flowed through the darkness.

I could hear her now… and Rian, his voice raised in anger, and it spurred me on faster, ready to rip his spine from his body if he had laid one fucking finger on her if she hadn't wished him to.

The rage that had risen in me almost made me miss the other lives flickering into my consciousness around me, and it wasn't until I reached a small glen, solidifying in a cloud of inky shadows in front of Saoirse and hearing her stifled scream, that I registered the pack of bánánach that had cornered them against a tree. I whirled around, taking everything in, the ring of Saoirse's flames keeping the bánánach at bay as they snarled at the edges.

"What in the name of the Gods?!" I heard Rian blurt. I saw him briefly in my peripherals, he had pushed Saoirse behind him, a large stick held aloft as he faced the pack that was far too large for either of them to take on.

I hissed a warning at the bánánach that seemed the boldest, it's sleek black and grey dappled fur almost invisible in the moonlight as it snarled at me. It seemed almost ethereal, its edges blurring slightly into the shadows it lurked in as it flashed wickedly sharp fangs. Its long, tufted ears were flat to its head on either side of its small, viciously pointed horns. These were larger than the lone bánánach I usually saw. They should be no bigger than an average-sized dog, but these were nearly to my waist, their long tails flicking as they prowled around the ring of fire on silent paws, claws unsheathed and ready to rip into us. Their eyes reflected the firelight, making them glow as if they were burning coals, like something sent straight from the depths of Ankii's underworld as legend said they were.

Movement to my right drew my eye as a bánánach tried to leap a low point in the flames and was sent skittering back as a spear of Saoirse's fire shot out at it, hissing and spitting its anger at the woman as Rian hauled her behind him again.

"You have *no* weapons," I heard him snarl. They will take you down in seconds."

"Drop the flames Saoirse," I said, eyeing the largest bánánach that seemed oddly intent on me, it's focus unwavering.

"Are you mad?" she yelped. "They will be on us in seconds!"

"Drop the fucking flames, Saoirse!" I snarled, grappling with the power that was all too eager to come out. Whisps of shadows were floating from my skin, like black ash floating in the air around me. The tips of my fingers began staining black as my power pooled there waiting for me to unleash it, summoned from the adrenaline that had flowed in me just moments before, and I knew from the look of utter fear on Rian's face, that my eyes were as black as ink.

This was the side of me I let no one see. The side of me that even I feared, that Gallin had warned Cerridwen about, and the reason she had finally relented and let me train.

Because no one had yet seen a Child of Nimmet with the level of power that lurked within my veins, except maybe The Blood Traitor himself. And he had caused the destruction of an entire race when he had given The Pendragon the power of the Gods.

Saoirse swore under her breath and dropped the flames as I reached into that secret chasm within me. The one I never touched, never dared to even acknowledge, and ripped it wide open.

There must have been thirty of them—*was* thirty of them—I corrected myself, as I looked at the ground around me that was littered with corpses. Some were cut clean in half; others were missing limbs and heads. Every one of them was dead. As was the grass at their feet, the plants that had populated the dense underbrush... even the surrounding trees had all turned the muted black and brown of death.

I had crossed my arms like a shield in front of my body, pooling that dark power in the space of a breath before flinging them out in a lethal wave that had taken the bánánach and everything around them down in a blink. The only thing that had moved in the silence that had followed were the dozen trees in front of me that had been caught in the wave I had unleashed. Their trunks withered as if the life was sucked from them, and they had slowly toppled before crashing to the ground with a force that shook the forest, taking the surrounding trees down with them.

And then I turned, my head spinning wildly from the sheer volume of power that had been ripped from my body and faced Saoirse.

She was pale, her eyes wide as she surveyed the carnage around us. But it was Rian who spoke first. "Child of Nimmet," he breathed. And then I watched as he dropped to his knees and bowed to me, pressing his forehead to the ground.

"Don't," I tried to say. But my tongue felt thick in my mouth. I blinked and tried again, reaching out a hand to pull him up. I heard my name called out, and turned to see Gwen stumbling into the glen, faltering as she saw the blood that covered everything, the blackened, dead plant life that stretched far, *far* too wide and the bánánach lying motionless within it. And then my heart dropped as she looked at me with the one thing that I had never wanted to see in her eyes.

Horror.

She was looking at me with absolute horror, and I deserved it.

"I told you that you should stay away from me," I murmured, and then my vision went black.

18

MERLIN

The crystal I was concentrating on glowed softly as I repositioned it on the delicate metal bracket, squinting at it until I was happy.

Pricking my finger on my letter opener, I hovered my hand over the crystal until a drop of crimson fell on its surface before sucking on the small hurt, my nose wrinkling at the copper taste of it.

I picked up a vial with my free hand, pouring a drop of its contents to splash across my own, a darker, nearly brown splash of blood that ran slowly down the face of it.

Placing both hands over the crystal, I focused on it, light raining from my hands in a sheet that absorbed into it, setting its heart glowing like an ember in flames.

The door crashed open, my candle guttered and flared and papers flew across my table to scatter on the floor to the sounds of Una's cheery voice.

"Sirin is back!"

I pinched the bridge of my nose, my eyes closed. "Una,

why have I taken to coming down here, rather than working in my rooms?"

I grunted as she leaned across my back, peering over my shoulder.

"Oh, that's a pretty one!"

"Una…" I growled.

"Because it's quiet?"

I slid my eyes from the crystal—its heart flickering softly and marred with cracks, not the brilliant light it should have— to Una, her eyes reflecting the glowing light. I gave her a dark look that she ignored.

"Did you hear that Sirin is back?"

"I did."

She pushed off me, rounding the table to lean her elbows on it, her chin in her hands as she gazed at the crystal. "Is this to replace the one that you took the other night?"

I sighed, plucking it up and surveying it closely. "No, I was trying something else."

"Hmmm," her attention turned to the scattered papers on the ground, bending to retrieve them and set them back in a neat pile next to me. "Oh, and Otto set the hearth rug on fire."

"WHAT?" I stood up. "Why didn't you lead with that?"

She frowned at me. "He put it out!"

"Nimmet save me," I muttered, pointing at the door. "Come on then."

I could hear Sirin before I had even started up the steps to my rooms, her cackling crones laugh that she loved to mock people with.

"*I'll leave you in the stocks next time,*" my own voice filtered down the stairs, followed by an angry grunt and the flap of wings. More cackling.

"Shut *up* Sirin. You nearly got me caught as it is."

"Naughty boy!"

"I will shove a stick up your arse and use you as a duster!"

"Naughty, Naughty boy!"

More angry grunting and I rounded the corner to see Otto, curly hair plastered to his forehead and damp with sweat, wrestling with a rolled rug that was half on his bony shoulder, half dragging on the steps.

He dropped it with a thump, both he and Sirin, who was perched on his shoulder looking at me in silence. He turned accusatory eyes on Una. "You filthy snitch!"

"What did you do?" I sighed.

His mismatched brows came down in a scowl. "It was an accident."

"I have no doubt," I said, leaning to pick up the rug under one arm and gesturing for him to go ahead.

He scurried up the steps, opening the door for me to lumber through with my burden before I dropped it on the floor in front of the bare hearth, a small black patch on the stone below.

"Was settin' you some tea to boil and I kicked a log, and it rolled out," he said sullenly. "You been sayin' you been feelin' sick since you went to Sirinelle."

Snorting under my breath, I hid the smile that had kicked up the corner of my mouth. "Idiot," I muttered, but ruffled his hair as I passed, gesturing to the rug. "Roll it out then."

I held my hand out to Sirin as Otto bent to the task, and she hopped to my arm, fluffing her feathers up for a scratch. "Oh no, you were complicit in that," I scolded.

She tilted her head, eyeing me reproachfully.

"What have you heard?"

I had half an eye on the twins as they rolled out the heavy rug, puffing and panting between them as Sirin began to rattle off a few unimportant things that seemed of no value.

"Send rooks, I need her back here immediately."

I sat up. "The Fox? What else of him?"

"They have been gone for over a month and not a word from them. She knew I worried about the danger involved. Find her and tell her it's time to return home."

My heart fell. If Rook was still away from Windhaven, we were still at risk. Short of combing the land for her myself, hoping to pick up some trace of her power, I was at a complete loss as to what to do.

Running my hand over my face I rapidly ran through my options.

Time. I needed more time.

I was still so far away from what I had been working toward, the answers at the tip of my fingers and just beyond my reach with the heart of the Helix still missing. I was no closer to my goal than I had been decades ago, and it was eating me up from the inside.

I had been so fucking close. Just before the battle of Sirinelle, I had almost gathered all of the pieces of my plan together, and then the heart had been stolen from under my nose. The group of radicals that had stolen it thought they could take from it what was already lost and become like Arthur, not realizing the Helix was already dead. Arthur had blamed the Sylvyn, not listening to me when I told him the betrayal had come from inside his own walls, and the result had been the battle of Sirinelle that had killed so many and burned bridges for me that I still hadn't restored.

By the time we had tracked where the heart had been taken, they had run into Drayvn lands and the heart was lost to us... and now with the Sylvyns who had allied with them, getting it back had gone from a difficult task to a damned near impossible one.

Sirin helped herself to the box of nuts on my desk, mumbling to herself as she found one of her favorites and balanced on one foot, her treasure in the other as she cracked the hard shell.

The twins had successfully rolled out the new mat, both lying stretched out on it in front of the fire. The color of it caught my eye, the emerald green and gold trim of the King's guard.

"Where did you get that?

Otto lifted his head and grinned at me over his filthy feet. "Sir Calgorn hasn't taken over his new Captains of the Guard quarters yet, so won't know it's missin' anyways."

"Oh, for fucks sake," I muttered.

19

MORGANA

I woke to voices and daylight. Neither of which I was particularly enamored with as the tiny slither of light that had forced its way through the crack in my eyelids sent a bolt of pain through my skull. I swore under my breath, groggily covering my eyes with my hands and praying to Nimmet for a quick death. There was no way a head could hurt this much without it being fatal.

The voices around me hushed and a cool hand rested on my brow, another behind my neck, the coldness of them instantly soothing the intense pounding in my head.

"There now," I heard Cara say, as another warm hand touched my arm.

"Can you drink this?" It was Gwen's voice, and I opened my eyes only to suck in a breath and shut them again as another stab of pain jolted through my head.

"Erin, draw the curtains," Cara called to someone, followed by the sounds of light feet pattering through the room and curtains being drawn.

"Ye silly wee thing," Cara scolded, and I risked opening an

eye a crack to see who it was she was talking about. Then I gingerly opened the other eye as I realized she was staring directly at me with a worried frown on her face.

"Excuse me?" I asked, then paused, shocked at the waver in my voice.

"Ai," she said, nodding at me. "Near killed yerself ye did. Then what would I be tellin' everyone? First Child of Nimmet we have seen 'round these parts in decades, and I go and let her die in me backyard. Went and put your body into shock, love!"

I blinked at her, wondering if I had ruptured something in my brain and wasn't understanding her.

She still had her hand on both my forehead and the back of my neck, though she let go of my forehead briefly to wave her hand at someone. "That's cool enough for her to sip now, bring it over."

I glimpsed the glimmer of ice across her fingers as she did, which explained the blessed coolness of her hands.

She caught the direction I was looking in and wiggled her fingers in front of my face before placing it back on my forehead. "Cold is the best thing for a headache," she said, as if having a grown woman stretched out on what I assumed was her own bed after decimating an entire pack of bánánach and a good section of forest, was the most normal thing ever. "Cools the blood and draws it away from the head," she went on, reaching for the cup Gwen was holding and put it carefully to my lips. "Drink this, it will have you right as rain soon enough."

I was too taken aback to refuse and swallowed a mouthful of the sweet liquid without complaint, my eyes finding Gwen's as anxiety flooded through me.

How she had looked at me in that glen…

Even now she was looking at me with uncertainty, which

was making the hollow feeling in my stomach grow by the second, and I looked away from her, not wanting to see what else I would find in her eyes. I couldn't stand it if she feared me.

"Cara, can I have a moment with Morgana?" Gwen asked softly.

Cara made a noncommittal noise as I took another swallow of the liquid, then she took the cup from me and glanced into it before nodding. "Well done," she said, getting up with a groan. "You will start feeling better in a moment love, no gettin' up, mind."

Both of us were silent as she walked from the room, ordering some people that I couldn't see from my prone position out with her, and it was only when the door snicked shut that Gwen sat carefully on the bed next to me and reached for my hand.

"Is Saoirse—"

"She's fine," Gwen interrupted, her eyes searching mine.

The warmth of her hand was distracting me from what I knew was coming, the distance she was about to put between us, and I couldn't fault her for it.

"You nearly died, you fool," she breathed.

It was the second time I had been taken aback in less than five minutes, and I frowned at her, confused as to why her eyes were suddenly brimming with tears.

"I just fainted," I protested weakly.

"You stopped breathing!" she said, her voice raising slightly. "You stopped fucking breathing, Morgana!" She reached for the covers that were across my chest, pulling them down to show my bare breasts, a dark purple bruise between them. "I had to force your heart to start beating again, breathe air back into your lungs. It was only after Erin was dragged out of bed and brought to you that we were able to get your heart beating on its own again!"

"Erin?" I asked, confused.

"She has the healing gift. Barely anything, enough to heal cuts and scrapes. But what she did have was enough to save you, you… you—"

"Fool?" I supplied.

"Do not mock me!" she snapped, her eyes flashing.

"Are you angry at me?" I asked, trying to sit up and realizing that my chest hurt nearly as bad as my head.

"Yes, I am angry!" she hissed, then faltered as I groaned in pain, my hand going to my chest.

"I'm sorry," she said, her voice tight. "I'm so sorry, I think I cracked one your ribs, I felt something crunch and… I …" her voice caught in what sounded like a sob as I gingerly laid back down and peered up at her.

"Gwen, everything hurts too much right now to figure out if you are angry or upset," I said, wincing as I took a deep, careful breath.

"You nearly died, Morgana," she repeated, grabbing my hand and bringing it to her lips. I felt the hot splash of a tear against the back of my hand and stilled.

"And all I could think about was how much time I had wasted trying to stay away from you. I was so scared that I was never going to get the time with you that I should have had when I was too much of a coward to just *tell* you what I have always known."

I must have looked like the fool she was accusing me of being, just lying there blinking at her.

"But I saw how you looked at me in that clearing," I protested weakly. "You were horrified."

"You were grey!" she whisper-shouted. "You looked as if you had already passed over. I have seen one other person that color and they were *dead,* Morgana! Then you looked at me, with eyes as black as night and fainted at my feet, *not breathing.* Do you know what it felt like to put my hand on your chest and feel your heart stop? Yes, I was horrified, but not by you!"

I stared at her. "I—I'm sor—"

A soft knock at the door interrupted us, and we both looked to see Saoirse peering in.

I tried to pull my hand subtly out of Gwen's grasp, but she was having none of it.

"I know," Saoirse said, a small, very lopsided smile tugging at her lips as her eyes went to where Gwen held my hand. "To be honest, you are both terrible at hiding things. I'm actually disgusted by how long it took the pair of you to do…" she waved a hand in our general direction, "this."

Saoirse rounded the bed to lay on my other side. "Thank you… and sorry."

"So much shit is going in your boots," I groused, trying to pull my thoughts together as they swirled with Gwen's words.

She grinned. "Does that mean you forgive me?"

"I hope the dick was worth it," I retorted, flapping at her to move back as her weight pulled the blankets tight over my *very* sore chest.

"Would it make you feel better if I said I came *at least* three times?"

"Before or after I died? That will be the decider for me."

Gwen made a disgusted sound, shaking her head at her sister. "Why are you like this?"

"Well," Saoirse said, shuffling the blankets out from under her to loosen them over me. "When Mother and Father had a moment of not disliking each other as fiercely as they usually did, they did something disgusting that we will never talk about again, and you were born. Then a year later they decided it usually takes three tries to make something perfect and, ta-da—me."

"There was definitely a lot of wine involved with your conception," I muttered.

"Get out," Gwen said, giving her sister a dark look and pointing at the door.

"No, wait!" Saoirse protested, "I do have one very important question."

Gwen raised a brow.

"What's Morgana like in bed?" she said, waggling her eyebrows at her sister. "I've heard rumors and I'm *dying* to know if she started them herself."

I choked on a laugh, yelping as pain flared in my chest, and then again as Saoirse leaped off the bed to escape Gwen who had violence in her eyes as she made a grab for her.

I caught sight of some deep scratches down the back of Saoirse's arm as she fled toward the door, cackling.

"Wait, Saoirse."

She turned, leaning back through the doorway.

"Are you ok though—the scratches?"

Some of the laughter dimmed from her eyes and she nodded. "I'm fine, Rian is too. Thanks to you. I'm sorry I put you in that position."

She was gone before I could answer her.

20

MERLIN

"The extra soldiers have reached Endreal," Arthur said, scanning a scroll he had pinned to the table under his large hand. "I've ordered them to make contact with the Sylvyn there. I doubt we will have any more news until the spring now."

I hummed my acknowledgment, frowning at the ledgers I had been given to look over. I eyed Sir Eckbert, the Master of Coin over the top of it. He was sipping his wine, his face too relaxed, surveying his wine with too much interest amidst the chattering clamor of the room.

I let the paper fall from my fingers to the table, picked up my ale and leaned back in my seat, a finger stroking Sirin's foot. She leaned down, her head next to my cheek and I scratched her, turning my head to murmur instructions.

"Tell Una I require her services."

She rubbed her head once against my cheek before taking off, swooping out one of the high open windows.

Arthur rapped his knuckles twice on the table, making Sir Eckbert jump in his seat slightly, sloshing his wine on his shirt.

"I have now conquered more land than any King in history," he said, the room falling into a hushed silence. "Adairn and Nareen have been taken from the Drayvn. Spring should see Endreal come under my reign as well. Once our men return, I plan to move on Rhaore. It will be the next step toward enlarging our great Kingdom. They have rich lands that will be a boon to our trade."

Murmurs filled the room.

"Rhaore is heading toward the Sylvyn lands," one of the men said. "Our men would be fighting Sylvyn warriors."

"They would," Arthur said. "Though that is not something you need to worry about now. The reason I bring this up, is I need strongholds set up within the lands I have taken. Already we have had Nareen try to retake what they lost, the *humans* we liberated from the Drayvn thought to repay my kindness by trying to overthrow my banners."

More murmuring as Arthur gave them a moment to mull this over. "My hand advised that I select men from amongst my advisors to become the heads of these strongholds."

Silence fell over the room as the leeches that were his advisors tensed.

"I need men that I can trust. Men that will ensure the citizens of these countries remain loyal to the crown… and understand what happens to those who are not." His eyes flicked to mine, a silent command to take over.

"Sir Eckbert," I said softly. "I suggested your name to take Adairn."

Eckbert inhaled his wine, choking on it, his already reddened face becoming redder.

"Me, Milord?"

I tilted my head, giving him a slow smile. "Loyalty is always rewarded, Eckbert."

"I-I am most grateful," he stammered, dabbing at his shirt. "I would be most honored. I live to serve the K—"

"And the other name I suggested," I interrupted, raising a dismissive hand to Eckbert, "was yours, Sir Bastian. For Nareen."

Bastian's eyes flared wide. "But my age, Merlin. I am well past my best years."

"You hold respect with the men, and you are a good man," I said. "That is all you need. Nareen needs a firm, fair hand, and they will have that in you. I have personally selected the men that will become your Dragon guard there and the stronghold is suitable for you to take your family."

Old Bastian inclined his head to me, then stood, bowing deeply to the King.

"It is settled," Arthur said, rapping his knuckles again before dismissing the room with a wave of his hand.

"Not you, Merlin," Arthur said to me as I made to rise.

I inclined my head, moving to refill my drink and waited for the room to clear, trying to gauge the King's mood through subtle glances.

He looked relaxed as he reclined in his chair, scanning over some papers.

"The Dragon guard intercepted an attempted shipment to be smuggled through the wall the other night," he said, glancing at me over the paper. "Apologies, I forgot to tell you. It seems this Rook you are concerned about wasn't with them, however, they are indeed desperate enough to be leaving the wall."

It took everything in me to keep my face in its bored, neutral mask as I forced my cup to my lips, taking a long swallow.

"Ah, good," Arthur said, looking up as guards appeared in the doorway, a figure held between them in chains. Arthur stood, beckoning them in. "I have been working on something I wanted to show you."

I tried to keep a look of interest plastered on my face, while inside, I could feel the cold fingers of fear running along my spine. Not for me, but for the woman that sagged between the guards. She was filthy, with dried blood and burns covering both her and her clothing.

Arthur strode to her, holding a finger under her chin and raised it. "Hello again, Eileen."

She spat in his face.

Eileen. The woman who had been leading the band the other night.

One of the guards backhanded her, a solid blow that had me clenching my fist beneath the table.

"Eileen here is a Wytchling. She ripped the air from the lungs of three men before she was taken down," Arthur said, pulling a handkerchief from a pocket to wipe his face. He patted the side of her cheek. "She has been most helpful," he took her arm from a guard, holding it up. "I think this is our answer. This little bit of metal confines her power within her body unless *I* will it." He turned to her. "Demonstrate for us, darling."

She ignored him.

One of the guards raised a hand to strike her and Arthur stopped him with a raised hand. "I've lifted the confine on your gift, Eileen."

She didn't move, just stared at him, the slightest breeze disturbing her hair, as if testing his words.

Suddenly she turned, not to attack Arthur, but to the guard on her right, her face twisted in rage.

"I told you I would make you pay, you fucking monster," she hissed at him.

The guard clutched at his throat as wind lashed him, gasping, before falling to his knees. The other guard let her go, backing away looking terrified as the struggling guard fell forward, still clutching at his throat, his lips turning blue.

"Enough," Arthur said quietly. Eileen froze, the air stilling around her. Her hand flew to her own throat, gasping for a moment before she sagged again, taking deep lungful's of air.

"Thank you for your help," Arthur said softly, before taking a step forward and slicing his dagger across her neck.

The breath caught in my throat as her body hit the floor, her blood spilling onto the ground next to the unmoving guard at Arthur's feet.

Arthur turned to me, a victorious look on his face. "I have the Sylvyn's leash, now I just need the key to their cage."

Una was waiting for me as I came out of the meeting rooms, lurking in the shadows.

"Sirin said you wanted me?" she asked, falling into step beside me.

My mind was reeling, and I struggled to string a coherent thought together. Eileen's face as she had fallen was burned into my mind. It was relief that had passed over her features, and it tore at me. The terror she must have been feeling, not knowing if she was going to be used against her own. Her family.

"You have your pins on you?" I asked quietly.

"Of course," she frowned at me. "Where do you want to go?"

"Eckbert has been stealing coin from the treasury for a while now, I just checked the ledgers to confirm it," I said. "And he visits his family tomb far more than his horrible mother deserved. Be a darling and go and check his mother's grave, will you?" Take Otto, you might need his… muscles. I will be in Eckbert's suite."

She grinned, slipping away silently.

Eckbert's suite was in the lower section of the castle, a small set of rooms that he shared with his family. I took a moment to compose myself, trying to shake off the horror that I had just witnessed before I rapped on his door, leaning against the frame until he opened it, his face paling as he caught sight of me.

"Merlin," he said, his voice rising an octave. "Is something amiss?"

"You tell me, Eckbert," I said, forcing a wolfish smile onto my face. I pushed into his rooms, inclining my head to his young wife. "Ma'am."

"My lord." She dipped me a curtsy. "Can I get you something to drink?"

"That would be lovely. Some tea, possibly?"

I waited for her to scurry away before casting my eyes around Eckbert's suite. "This is lovely."

Eckbert swallowed. "What can I do for you?"

"You can start by telling me what you plan to do with nearly two thousand gold marks." I dragged my gaze back to him, tutting. "Naughty boy, Eckbert."

"I-I don't know what you mean," he stammered. "You went over my ledgers. It is all there. You can check my numbers."

"You think I don't know how much it costs to feed the people that inhabit this castle?" I said, huffing. "You don't think I know the cost of feed for the stables, the cost of iron for their shoes?" I gave him a disappointed look. "Eckbert. You wound me."

He blanched, going quiet as I raised a hand, letting arcs of snapping light dance between my fingers.

"I will say, you made a better attempt than others I have seen. You raised the cost slowly over the years. Any other man, who hadn't studied decades of those ledgers. wouldn't have noticed."

"What do you want?" he asked.

"Straight down to business, I like it," I said, pulling a chair out and sitting, motioning him to do the same.

He sat slowly, watching me cautiously. His wife came in with a steaming pot of tea and poured one for me, and I gave her a wide, warm smile. "Thank you."

She blushed, moving to her husband and poured one for him too.

"Merlin and I need to discuss business, Love," Eckbert said, casting an eye over his wife. "Give us a moment, would you?"

She nodded, bustling back out of the room.

"Lovely wife you have there," I said, blowing the steam off my tea. "Such a shame if she were to be widowed, though I'm sure I could find it within me to... console her for you." I waggled my brows at him over the brim of my cup, watching his face darken.

"What do you want?" he asked again, fear shortening his tone.

"You were the prison warden before you took this position were you not?" I asked.

He rocked back in his chair, frowning. "I was."

"I need the services of some men. The lowest of the low. Murderers, rapists, you get my drift."

His brows raised. "For what?"

"I need them to cause a bit of harmless damage. Start some fights, maybe set the odd fire or two."

"Where?"

"The town square, tomorrow night. I want them to paint a

black Rook on whatever damage they create, and when you hire these men, tell them it was in the name of the crown."

He frowned at me. "Why?"

"So many questions that you just don't need to know the answers to," I said, tutting.

He went utterly silent. "It's you. You're the Grey Wolf."

I smiled at him. "The one and only."

He flung himself out of his seat. "The King will know of this."

I had him immobilized in bands of crackling light in seconds, his breath cut off. "I can snap your neck right here," I warned. "Or you can sit down and listen to what I have to say."

He flailed, clawing at his neck.

"Oh, sorry," I loosened my grip on him. "What was that?"

"Alright," he rasped, his eyes bugging.

"Much better," I pointed at his seat. "Sit."

He sat heavily, sweat sheening on his forehead.

"Now," I said, taking another sip of my tea. "You can do as I ask, keep what you know to yourself and skip away none the wiser to Adairn with your lovely wife and the money you have accrued to live well as the lord of the territory," I winked at him. "So many opportunities might come your way if I see you are being a fair, reasonable man over there."

The door slipped open behind him, and Una slipped in.

I flashed a questioning look her way and she flipped a gold coin in her fingers, catching it deftly and slipping it into her pocket.

"Or," I continued. You attempt to tell the King about who I am. See how far you get. I may or may not kill you before you manage to get to him, but either way he will know you have stolen from his treasury… and you know how much he despises betrayal."

"You put yourself at my mercy telling me this," he said, his eyes glittering with contempt.

"Not really," I said. "You *could* run, but it would be as a destitute beggar with no name or title. How is your late mother by the way? Have you visited her recently?"

Eckbert lost whatever color he had left.

"So, what will it be Eckbert?" I asked, draining my cup. "Will you do as I ask and live a good life away from Kambria and what is to come… or will you throw your life away?"

He was silent for a moment, the only movement from him the slow rise and fall of his chest. "How many men do you need?"

I winked at him. "Surprise me."

21

MORGANA

It took three days of Erin's small, incremental healings before I was able to sit up without help, and another two before I could breathe without pain.

Neither Gwen nor Saoirse would even contemplate the idea of me going near the horses before I was moving easily again, a fact that had irked me, as now the inhabitants of Walsh farm knew what I was, they had begun to treat me differently. Wherever I went, I would catch them looking at me with wonder and a little fear, my skin prickling with the weight of so many eyes on me.

"Tomorrow," Saoirse agreed as I moodily flapped my arms up and down above my head, proving that I was perfectly capable of getting on the damned horse again.

Gwen, who was cross-legged on the floor of the loft we had moved back into as she folded our freshly cleaned clothes into packs, smirked up at me. "You will be begging to come back after a day on horseback."

"I don't beg for anything," I snapped, then narrowed my

eyes at Saoirse as a sly grin spread over her face. "Whatever you are about to say, don't."

"Pretty sure I overheard something of the sort last night when I came in, but maybe I was hearing things?" she blew me a kiss, hopping nimbly onto the ladder and disappearing over the edge.

Gwen chuckled under her breath, and I glared at her. "Don't encourage her."

She laughed softly, stuffing the last of the clothing in her bag and crooking a finger at me. "She wasn't wrong though," she teased. "You did beg."

I arched a brow at her. "That hasn't happened to me before, and it isn't going to happen again."

She gave me a wicked grin. "Is that a challenge?"

A memory of the night before flashed through my mind, and I had to give myself a moment to compose myself. The woman was a *very* fast learner.

Gwen's eyes slowly roved down my body. "Saoirse is heading out hunting," she murmured, the hay rustling as she rose to her knees and pulled her shirt over her head. "Why don't you prove to me how healed you claim to be? Then we can discuss leaving tomorrow. I think it's my turn to beg."

I absolutely hated riding horses.

The sun was at its peak, I had put on enough layers to slowly cook myself, and sweat was slowly trickling down my spine. To make matters worse, my chest was aching fiercely, and I desperately needed to relieve myself, yet the idea of peeling off all the layers that I had struggled into that morning was more painful than my bladder was.

We had spent a cold night in a shallow valley at the

beginning of the mountain ranges, waking up to fresh snow covering the two small tents we had pitched. Saoirse, tired from using her gift to keep herself warm all night alone in her own tent, had been irritable all day and it was doing nothing to help my mood.

"Finally," Gwen sighed, shielding her eyes against the sun.

"The Hollow?" I asked, squinting in the direction she was looking.

Gwen grunted, urging our horse forward. "We will reach it by nightfall if we don't stop for lunch," she answered, holding back as Saoirse's mare pushed past us with its sullen rider.

I frowned, glancing at the sky. "It's barely midday?"

"It takes hours to skirt the basin," Gwen said, pointing to a spot in the distance. We moved toward it, and my brows flew to my hairline as we came up to the edge of a ravine, a path winding its way around the edges.

"Holy Gods," I breathed, peering over the edge of the horse and feeling my stomach lurch at the sight. It was a huge, circular basin, the bottom of it hidden in shadow.

"Some say it is the door to Ankii's Kingdom," Saoirse said quietly. "Others say it is where the first Drayvn crawled from, thrown up from the bowels of the earth."

Gwen huffed softly. "And then the ones with reason say it once was a crater of fire, gone dormant. The molten rock it once spewed from its depths created the mountains that surround us, and the jagged pillars of stone under the sea on this side rip through the hulls of ships and sink them.

There were so many things I had not seen out here, as closeted as I had been. I had always believed the Lowlands to be dull. Full of unhappy Sylvyns that I could not help but feel I had let down with my limited training. But it was richer than anything I had imagined, the people I had met so full of life.

"I wonder if Mads is here?" Saoirse called over her shoulder.

Gwen groaned. "Let's hope not," she muttered.

"Do I want to know who Mads is?" I asked, wincing as our horse stumbled over a root, my chest flaring in pain.

Gwen twisted, eyeing me over her shoulder. "I felt that, are you in pain?"

I raised a brow. "Are you avoiding the question?" I asked, a smile tugging at my lips.

"Mads is the formidable old goat that runs the school Gwen started when she is not visiting her daughter in Nairn," Saoirse chimed in, grinning at whatever look Gwen was giving her sister. She cast me an innocent look. "When she is in Nairn, it is her son Faolán who manages it."

Gwen muttered something I didn't quite catch under her breath.

"Past lover of yours, Gwen?" I asked, amusement rising as I saw her ears, which had just begun to hint at Sylvyn tips, begin to blush.

She ignored me.

Saoirse laughed, twisted in her saddle and groaned as she kneaded her lower back, throwing a wink at us. "The last time we were here, Gwen was still Faolán's betrothed."

The Hollow was spread out, the city itself nestled into the foothills of the great mountains behind it. Rambling stone cottages peppered the countryside from the edge of the basin through to the town in various stages of disrepair.

"They spend so much time foraging and hunting what little game there is here that they have no time to mill wood and prepare stone for the houses," Gwen said, noticing where my attention had gone as we passed yet another house with crumbled stone fencing and patched roofs. "Even the children work, it took me so long to convince the parents here to allow the children a few hours a day to learn their gift and receive a simple education. I think as winter sets in, and food is harder to find, a lot of the children will be pulled from school entirely."

She waved at a girl who had emerged in a doorway, a pail on her hip, then laughed as the girl dropped the pail in a splash of water with a small squeal, running back into the house and calling for someone.

It didn't take long for word to spread of our arrival, and by the time we had arrived on the outskirts of the town we had amassed a small crowd of people eager to see Gwen.

She had slipped from the horse, walking at its head with a young boy on her hip, his arms slung around her neck with a bright smile on his small face. Two girls were chattering animatedly to her, their voices grating against my ears as others shrieked and skipped around her.

Saoirse looked almost as unamused as I felt, murmuring to her horse who was fidgeting and prancing at the noise.

"Guinevere!" an older man called, his large frame eating up the ground as he strode toward us with an adoring look at her.

I glanced at Saoirse. "Faolán?"

She barked a laugh, startling her horse and making it shy, and was still chuckling as she brought him back around beside me again.

Gwen looked at us questioningly before turning back to the man with a warm smile of her own. "It's good to see you, Darragh."

I tried not to show the relief I felt, though I could hear Saoirse's muffled cackling from behind her scarf as she once again wrestled with her anxious horse. She gave up after a moment, jumping down and taking the animal's head and touching her forehead to Darragh.

"Saoirse," he said, his tone markedly stiffer.

"Don't tell me you still hold a grudge after all these years," Saoirse chuckled, patting the large cheek of her horse absently.

"Of course not," he said politely, though there was a slight edge to his tone. "We always welcome any O'Mordha here."

"Hmmm," Saoirse said, looking amused. "I feel *very* welcome," she winked at me, busying herself with pushing her scarf into one of her travel packs as Gwen introduced me to Darragh and a dozen others who had come out as well. None of whom I would remember.

I dismounted, following Gwen as she headed toward a large building, a small courtyard and well in front of it with a small stable off to the side. Some of the children took the horses from us, squabbling between themselves over who would tend Gwen's horse as they led them off to the stables.

"Is that my Guinevere?" a voice called over the noise of everything.

Gwen stiffened next to me and I heard—to my great amusement—the curse she muttered under her breath. She threw what looked like a look of apology at me, before turning, a smile that I had come to recognize as her courtiers smile on her face.

"It's been a long time, Madraigh," she said, opening her arms to hug the woman who had rushed out to greet her. Madraigh seemed to pause for a moment, her hands going to Gwen's arms and pulling back enough to look over her face, a slight frown creasing her brow. A look passed over her features as she pulled Gwen back in for another hug. So fast that I nearly missed it—masked as quickly as it had slipped from her grip—was a look of grief that made a pool of ice settle in my stomach.

Madraigh was a beauty, with dark hair that hung in ringlets down her back and the tips of her pointed ears peeking through them. She had beautiful sun-kissed tawny skin and rich brown eyes that seemed to see through you, and I stiffened as she turned them on me, a flash of intrigue crossing her features. I felt my power surge in response to that questioning look, and for a moment I wondered if she was Nimmet touched.

"Morgana," she said. Not a question, as if she already knew me. "I have seen your face many times. I wondered when the Gods would send you my way." She looked slightly shaken, and I couldn't tell if it was from what she had seen in Gwen's eyes, or from my presence.

"Have we met?' I asked, studying her face and trying not to sound as unnerved as I was.

She smiled, transforming her attractive face into absolute, stunning beauty. "Many times, but only within my dreams. It is only in the last few years I have learned your name though."

"Madraigh is a seer," Saoirse said dryly. "And she doesn't know how creepy she sounds sometimes," she smiled sweetly at the woman. "Please tell me you saw us coming and have some sort of tea over the fire?"

Madraigh huffed a laugh. "It doesn't work like that, but yes, tea is on. Come in and warm yourselves and tell me what has brought about this visit."

We followed her through the heavy wooden doors, past a few large, open rooms, some filled with desks and what looked like a kitchen, and through into a cluster of smaller rooms toward the back of the building.

Saoirse went straight to the fire, a wave of her hand enticing the flames higher as she turned, warming her back.

"How has the school been?" Gwen asked, gazing out the window toward the mountains that loomed behind.

"Attendance has been getting worse, but that is to be expected," Madraigh said, pulling a battered-looking pot from over the flames and sniffing the contents. "Do you still like honey in your tea? Faolán found a hive last month."

I saw a muscle tick in Gwen's jaw, the only outward tell she had when she was irritated, and it only intrigued me more.

"I do," she murmured. "How… is… Faolán?"

I hid a smile at the reluctant question, taking a cup of steaming tea and moving slightly closer to the fire, enough to feel its warmth but not close enough that it would make my skin crawl.

Saoirse gave me an amused look, sipping on her own tea as we pretended not to notice how uncomfortable Gwen was.

Madraigh's bookcase drew my attention away, and I sipped the scalding tea that tasted like wild mint. It pooled pleasantly, warming me from the inside as I ran a finger over the titles, only half listening to the conversation that started up between the three women. There were so many books I would love to study. Drayvn lore and lineage, tales of the Gods I had not yet read, and lands I had only heard of in passing.

A book of creation, so old its cover looked as if it would crumble if I attempted to open it, sat on a high shelf, my shadows reaching to brush its cover as if they were as curious as I was. Next to it was a black book with 'Ankii' scrawled on the spine in wobbly script.

"We lost a child recently." The words dragged my attention back to the conversation, and I turned to see the pain on Madraigh's face. "A young girl from the outer cottages was dragged into the forest, and by the time her brother had run back to tell his mother, she was gone," she said sadly. "We sent out a search party for the child, but there was no sign of her, and bánánach tracks everywhere."

"We ran into them by Walsh farm," Gwen said, her eyes flicking to mine for a moment, the echo of fear in them as she must have been visualizing the scene she had walked into. Bodies littering the ground, and me… dying at her feet. "Those were hunting in a pack as well—it could have been the same ones? If so, all are dead already," she offered Madraigh a half smile. "I would hope it's not a behavior they are all taking on or it is going to be a rough winter."

"I will go tonight," I said. "See if I can find traces of them in the area."

"No one takes to the woods here at night," Madraigh warned, her eyes wary. "My son can accompany you in the day, it is no place for anyone to be alone."

As if her words had summoned him, footsteps sounded through the corridor in long, unhurried strides. I didn't bother arguing about the woods, it would be easy for me to slip away later.

Gwen squared herself, looking resigned, her fingers tightening ever so slightly around her mug, and she seemed to be intent on looking anywhere except at me. I hid my smile behind my own mug and turned to greet the man who walked through the doors.

"Morgana," Madraigh said, smiling warmly. "This is Faolán, my son. Faolán, look who dropped in!"

Holy fucking Gods.

22

MERLIN

Otto was sitting on a small trunk on the floor when Una and I returned to my rooms, crumbs on his shirt as he tucked into a pasty.

"Good work," I said, nodding to the trunk. "Did you count it?"

"Just shy of two thousand gold marks," he replied, cheeks bulging.

I grunted, quietly pleased my calculations were correct.

Una swiped the second half of her brother's pasty, ignoring his look of outrage. "Will he do what you asked of him?"

"Oh yes," I muttered, motioning him off so I could flip the lid open. "One thing you can always count on is human greed, once it has its claws in someone's soul."

"Then why does your face look like that?" Otto asked.

I gave him a dark look. "Like what?"

"Like you just flitted and there is no ginger tea."

"Because I just stamped out an ember only to have a bonfire roar to life," I said, huffing under my breath as I eyed the pile of gold marks. "The King surprised me today, and it has been a long time since that happened."

I was half-heartedly watching the dancers that were weaving and gyrating in the center of the dining hall the following night when two of the Dragon guard approached Arthur. I looked across to see Eckbert watching me from across the room and winked at him.

Arthur seemed to be irritated at the intrusion, motioning the men to leave with a swipe of his hand before his eyes scanned the room for me. I met his gaze with a raised brow, tilting my head in question and he motioned me over.

"It seems there has been another attack, this time on the town square," he muttered when I neared his table. "See to it will you?"

"Of course," I murmured, turning to follow the guards.

They led me through to the lower levels of the castle that the guard inhabited, leading me into a large stone room lit by oil lamps that hung on the walls. Countless grated doors lined every wall, some leading down to the cells a level below, others to rooms that were reserved for unspeakable acts of violence. The air was colder down here, the stone darker, as if the pain and suffering had leeched into the stone itself, tainting it.

In the center of the room stood seven men, some with the brand of convicted murderers.

"These are the men?" I asked, my gaze passing over them, the sneer that curled my lips real as I looked upon the faces of some of the worst of humanity.

"Aye. Caught that one painting a Rook on a shop that was aflame red-handed," one of the guards said, pointing to a grubby man with long, greasy brown hair. He had the branded

M on his face that singled him out as a murderer, one side of it smeared and misshapen, the edge of his eye dragging down as if he had fought it, nearly blinding himself in the process.

I felt no guilt implicating these men in my deception. There would be seven fewer men to inflict pain on a world already brimming with it.

"Who is your master?" I asked, my tone a low growl.

"Couldn't tell ya," the greasy-haired man replied, snorting through his nose before spitting phlegm at his feet. "Was let out of my cell, told I had a visitor, and then next thing had coin pushed into my hand and told to go set fire to some buildings in the square. To make sure I did a wee bit of art before we made a run for it. Guess I got a bit too into watching those pretty flames," he laughed, a cold sound that was edged with a hint of madness. "Such a pretty sight. The flames speak to you, you know, they sound so beautiful when they consume the souls of those they capture."

"Did any of you see what the man who hired you looked like?' It was one of the Dragon guard who spoke up.

I clicked my fingers, sparks of light bursting to life on them as I turned back to the men, some of them shrinking away from me. "Anything at all would be helpful."

"N-no," one of the men stammered. "Though I did hear him curse the Sylvyn. Don't think he knew I could hear him."

"Hmmm," I glanced at the guard, my heart racing. That could have been my name that slipped from this man's mouth.

"You think it's the same group?"

"Looks to be," the guard said. "What do you want me to do with them? We have already questioned them, there is nothing else they have of use. Whoever hired them covered their tracks."

"Such a shame," I murmured, turning my gaze back on the waiting men. "Throw them in the cells for now, in case they remember anything else, and let the King know the culprits have been located."

"Yes, Milord," the guard bowed low, his emerald cloak glinting in the light. "And I will allocate men to search for their employer."

I grunted, dismissing him with a wave.

Ember snuffed out, now to deal with the bonfire and pray to all the Gods that The Rook had listened to my warning.

23

MORGANA

Faolán was a fucking giant. He brushed his fingers to his forehead, inclining his head to me in greeting, then touched his chest, over his heart to both Saoirse and Gwen.

"Three beautiful women visiting—it seems the Gods decided to bless me this day," he rumbled, his voice a low purr that no doubt made most women wet just listening to him.

Fantastic.

He turned his attention to his mother, patting her on the head affectionately. "And of course, you, Ma."

She swatted at him, chuckling softly and busied herself refilling the pot over the fire.

He had his mother's dark, lightly curled hair, cut short. Strong features that were made even more striking with rich brown skin and eyes as green as moss—that were currently focused on Gwen with an intensity I recognized.

"How fares Windhaven, Guinevere?"

Gwen shifted under his gaze, her eyes flashing to mine briefly. "Much the same as it always has, hanging on by the skin of its teeth and our only line of defense," she tipped her face up as Faolán crossed to her and bent to brush a kiss against her cheek, his hand resting on her upper arm as he did, and it was that possessive gesture that made an unexpected surge of jealousy rush through me.

I was still grappling with the foreign emotion, calming the shadows that had been ready to spear across the room and wrap around the hand that rested on her and snap every one of his fingers, when he stepped away, turning his intense gaze on me instead.

"Yours is a face I have not yet seen," he said. "And one I would have remembered."

Saoirse snorted softly. "Don't even bother," she chuckled, "she has a sharper tongue than your axe."

He gave me a wicked smile, tucking his thumbs into the waist of his pants. "Do you now?"

I immediately hated him.

"How long will you be staying for?" Madraigh interrupted, an odd look on her face as she watched me warily. "Shall I light the fire in the back room for you?"

"We can stay at the inn," Gwen began saying, but Faolán cut her off with a wave of his hand.

"The inn isn't fit for guests currently, and they have been struggling to feed themselves, let alone others. Stay here, I took down a goat last week and we have enough to share. I was going out tomorrow to hunt again anyway."

"I don't want to be in your way," Gwen said.

"You are never in the way," he insisted. "Please stay, both of us would enjoy the company."

"With such a shortage, Faolán has been hunting most days to supply enough meat to offer the children who attend the school a hot meal," Madraigh said, flashing a warm smile at her son. "It encourages them to keep attending. We have enough food to share."

My dislike of the man deepened. Tall, way too handsome, and great with children. That shouldn't irk me as much as it did, and yet I wanted to scratch his beautiful Gods-damned eyes out.

What the fuck was wrong with me?

Gwen looked at Saoirse, who shrugged. "I really don't care where I sleep as long as it isn't as cold as last night."

"Good," Faolán said, including me in the warm smile he gave Gwen. "It's settled. I will go and bring your bags in."

The evening dragged on for what felt like an eternity. Saoirse and Madraigh retired early, leaving Faolán, Gwen and I in front of the fire, talking in hushed voices about moments of Gwen's life I had missed entirely.

She had spent years here before her return to Windhaven. An entire life lived away from the influence of her family, working to improve the lives of her people, while I had been hidden behind walls of stone. Guilt nipped at me as I listened to them laugh softly together.

The coals had reached a dull glow by the time Faolán stood, stretching with a soft groan. "It is late," he said, his eyes holding a question as he gazed at Gwen.

I stood as well, not looking at Gwen as I tidied the cushions I had been sitting on. "I need some fresh air before I sleep," I murmured, feeling her gaze rest on me as I turned to him. "Have a good night, Faolán."

His smile was warm and genuine. "I hunt after breakfast if you want to join Saoirse and I."

I nodded, my eyes finding Gwen's, who was looking at me warily. "Goodnight, Princess." I ignored the amused chuckle from Faolán, making my way through the silent building and out to the small porch that served as a private courtyard for the back living quarters.

I had no claim on her. She wasn't mine, regardless of how

much she had turned into an addiction for me. If she wanted to go to Faolán's bed, as he so clearly had been asking, I was not going to stop her. Not when he looked at her with the adoration she deserved.

The night felt like it was holding its breath as I sat on the steps, watching my own breath mist in the frozen air. A few of my shadows slipped from me to dance with it, twining through the air to melt into the darkness. It was as if leaving the confines of the castle had released something in me. My power had always been a flickering black flame within me, but I could feel it growing stronger, pushing at the hold I had on it, eager to be set free.

I felt Madraigh before my shadows whispered to me, her presence at my back sending the fine hairs of my neck rising, and I turned silently to look at her.

"What are you, seer?" I asked quietly. "You are not like me."

There was no point in hiding what I was, I could tell she had known the moment she set eyes on me.

"No," she said, padding across the cold deck with bare feet and sinking gracefully down next to me. "Though I am not like the others either," she slid her gaze to me, the edges of her full mouth quirking up in a small smile. "Nimmet is not the only God to occasionally take an interest in our world, Morgana."

One of my shadows flowed toward her in the air, and she reached out a fingertip, letting it curl around her, slipping through her fingers as she studied it curiously.

She frowned, her attention drifting back out to the gloom as if she were focused on something far away. "You know you are going to bring her great pain," she said sadly, her face tensing as her eyes turned as dark as night.

I stiffened, staring at her. I could see so many similarities between us, yet the feel of her power was so different. "What have you seen?"

She cocked her head as if listening. "There were three paths that could have been walked," she said softly. "One was already lost when she decided to return to Windhaven. I tried to stop her, tried to urge her toward the life I could see for her and my son, yet something stronger was calling her away," she turned her head to me, her eyes a swirling haze of black mist. "You."

"I didn't—"

"Your soul called to her, and hers answered," she said, disregarding my protest with a small flick of her hand. "Both paths remaining hold suffering that she may not survive, the cost of both are high, yet…" she trailed off with a small shake of her head.

My blood ran cold in my veins. "What do you mean I will bring her pain?" I asked, fear making my words come out clipped.

Madraigh looked at me, the black in her eyes clearing away like mist in the wind, and some of the color seemed to leach from the light brown of her skin. "You will be her salvation or her doom, but your fate is tied to hers now. I cannot see which path she will take, but it is not your will that will decide what is to come. It is hers," she leaned into me, close enough that I could see the fine lines that barely creased the skin around her eyes. "Do not underestimate her. The fire in her veins is something few have seen the true depths of. Her power is her control, not only over herself but over what she turns her attention to. Death is the only answer to her losing that control, and I cannot see if it is her death, or the death of those around her."

She reached out a hand, her fingers grazing my chin, frowning at me slightly. "Death still lingers around you too, you—" she cut off in surprise. "You have not learned how to wield the power that lurks within you?"

I tensed. "My tutor was murdered when I had only learned the basics. Everything I have learned since has been what I have discovered alone."

That seemed to unnerve her more, and her dark eyes studied mine for a moment, though… seemed to look right through me.

"Do not touch that darkness again. Not until you have learned how to control it," she warned. "Even I am loath to touch it, with the toll it takes on me. You should not have survived what you did at that farm."

I huffed under my breath. "I didn't, apparently." Madriagh's words sunk into me though, and I snapped my gaze to look at her. "What do you mean? Do you have it too?"

Her face tightened. "I do. I would offer to teach you what I know, but that is a path not offered to us. Time is not on our side, nor Gwen's."

"And if I walk away?" I asked, my tone rough. "Right now, I disappear… make her hate me. If I do that, will she be safe? Can I push her back toward the path you first saw?"

Madraigh shook her head sadly, reaching to brush a finger across my cheek. "It doesn't work like that," she murmured. "If it did, I would be sitting here holding my grandchildren with fire-colored hair and emerald eyes," she huffed a laugh. "This is why I do not call my power a gift. Sometimes it shows me things that shimmer just outside of my reach, and when I grasp for them, they disappear and all I am left with is empty hands and the echo of what could have been. I broke my own rules and tried with Guinevere and Faolán," she frowned. "I can't help but wonder if it would have come to pass, had I stayed out of it. I will not do it again, not when there are lives already in this world at stake."

She gave me a look and I couldn't tell if it was pity or disappointment. "I will be seeing you again, Morgana. I just hope when I do, it is still as friends."

She left me then, sitting on the step and the cold that chilled my body had nothing to do with the icy bite in the air as my shadows began whispering to me. One word slowly formed in their murmurings.

Pendragon.

It was long past darkest night when I made my way to the room we were to share. The door to Faolán's room was shut and no sound came from behind it, and for that I was grateful. Images of Gwen's slender legs wrapped around Faolán's muscled waist came unwanted to my mind.

I padded through the living quarters and into our room, trying not to bump the half-open door and set the rusted hinges creaking as I slipped through it.

Saoirse was splayed on a small pallet in front of the fire, the soft glow of it illuminating her peaceful features, her hair strewn about her, the strands glowing golden in the soft light.

I made myself look at the bed Gwen and I were to share, expecting to see it empty, and paused as I saw her curled form in the middle of it. I tried to ignore the wave of relief that flooded me as I silently undressed and slipped in next to her.

Gwen stirred, her hand reaching for me between the sheets and running over my arm.

"It's late," she whispered sleepily.

"I didn't realize you were waiting for me," I murmured, reaching out and tugging her warm body against mine.

She laughed softly under her breath, melting back into me until her form aligned perfectly with mine, our legs entwined, and my arm draped across her middle. "Where else would I be?" she asked dryly, and I could tell from her tone that she knew why I had left them by the fire.

I brushed my lips over the delicate shell of her ear as her fingers traced over my arm, drawing idle patterns across my skin.

"I didn't want you to think that I believe I have the right to lay claim to you," I said finally, keeping my voice low.

"You wouldn't have minded if I had taken up Faolán's offer of spending the night in his bed and not yours?" she asked.

"I didn't say that," I muttered, and she laughed quietly again. "I could see what he was about to ask, and I wanted you to have the freedom to follow your desires."

"Well," Gwen said, and I could feel the laugh she was suppressing. "He asked for both of us. He wanted to know if you would join us if he invited you as well."

"Hmmm," I murmured, frowning into the darkness. "I don't know if the idea of watching him fuck you makes me want to kill him or turns me on."

She wiggled in my arms, turning until she could look at me, her features barely visible in the dim light. She looked amused. "I'm where I want to be, Morgana."

I brushed my lips against her neck, drawing a small sigh from her.

"You are where I want you to be too," I said against her skin as Madraigh's words echoed in my mind.

"Your soul called to hers, and hers answered."

"Am I going to have to fight him for you tomorrow?" I teased, nuzzling her neck. "Claim my woman for everyone to know?"

"I'm already yours," she murmured as she turned her head and kissed me. I kissed her hungrily, her tongue flicking against mine, her scent filling my senses. She was slightly breathless as she pulled away, her eyes finding mine in the darkness. "I think I always was."

I couldn't speak for a moment, a tumble of emotions vying for space within me, kissing her to give myself time to compose my thoughts. She moaned softly as a shadow slipped from my grasp, its inky tendrils closing around her throat like a shadowed hand, tipping her head back for me to deepen the kiss.

"I swear to the Gods if you two start fucking, I'm setting your blankets on fire," Saoirse muttered from across the room.

I felt Gwen's lips curl into a smile against mine before she turned in my arms again, settling back into me and relaxing. She was asleep again in minutes, Saoirse too by her deep, even breathing, yet oblivion took a long time to find me, my heart heavy.

Cerridwen's voice called to me from my memories, a soft plea to keep her children safe as I had sworn to do so many years ago. Now my selfishness, my lack of self-control when it came to this woman who could make even the blackest of souls fall for her, might be the cause of something unimaginable. A world she did not exist in was one I didn't have the strength to face, and I swore to myself in that moment that if it came down to a choice between myself and her, it was always going to be her.

24

MERLIN

I woke from dreams of a husky, seductive voice.

"Enjoy your night, Princess."

Those four words had echoed in my mind, again and again over the past months and it was driving me mad. One sentence was all it had taken to be ensnared by this infernal woman, and I knew how ridiculous that was. I had been tossing up whether to send Sirin back just to find her and learn more about who she was, but with the unrest in Irling, I needed the rook closer to home.

Running my hand down the sheets, I gripped my cock, running my fingers along the underside and tracing the ladder of piercings that ran along it. A smile kicked up the corner of my lips at the distant memory of Ameena in her twenties; all curly hair and delicious curves as she had perched naked on my thighs, tongue between her teeth, needle in hand and a wicked smile on her face as she had given me the first of these piercings… and then promptly scolded me for my inability to remain stoic as she happily committed acts of only barely consensual torture on me.

A vicious little thing she had been back then.

What followed—after she had finished—had been one of the most painful and erotic experiences I have had to date. That had been nearly sixty years ago. Ameena was just one of many reminders of how fleeting human lives were.

I let my mind wander to Vivian who—for all her flaws—really did possess the most glorious breasts, as I stroked my hardening cock.

"Enjoy your night."

I groaned, tightening my fist, imagining that voice whispering in my ear.

"Ugh, it's so cold my cock has disappeared up me arsecrack."

My eyes flew open as I was ripped violently from my fantasies by the gruff male voice, flailing in the bed sheets as Sirin's crone's cackle filled the room.

"When the fuck did you get back?" I snapped, spotting her in the dim light on the perch that had been *very* empty when I went to sleep.

She let out a hearty snore, blinking innocently.

I glared at her. "I do not snore."

The door to where the twins had taken up residence opened and Una padded out, blinking blearily at me as she made her way out of the main door to the corridor that led to the lavatory, followed moments later by a sleep-tousled Otto.

"Mornin', Da," he grumbled.

I ran a hand over my face, trying to remember which exact life choice had led me to this moment. Mocked by a bird, cock in hand, never given a moment of solitude by children that were not even the fruit of my barren ball sack.

"Morning D—"

"I swear to the Gods I will roast you if you finish that sentence," I warned Sirin, glaring at her from between my fingers.

She cackled again, flying to my desk and helped herself to the box of nuts.

Accepting that I was not in any way going to finish the train of thought I had woken with, I got up, washed and dressed before making my way down to breakfast. I was nearly at the base of the stairs when Una flew into me, her face pale.

"You need to come quick," she hissed, grabbing my arm and dragging me along.

"What is going on?" I asked, realizing she was dragging me toward the great hall.

Una shook her head. "It's bad. They have already gone for the King. I couldn't stop them."

"Couldn't stop wh—" I broke off as we rounded the large wooden doors to hushed whispers.

"Oh Fuck," I breathed. Across the wall at the end of the hall, in dripping blood red letters were the words:

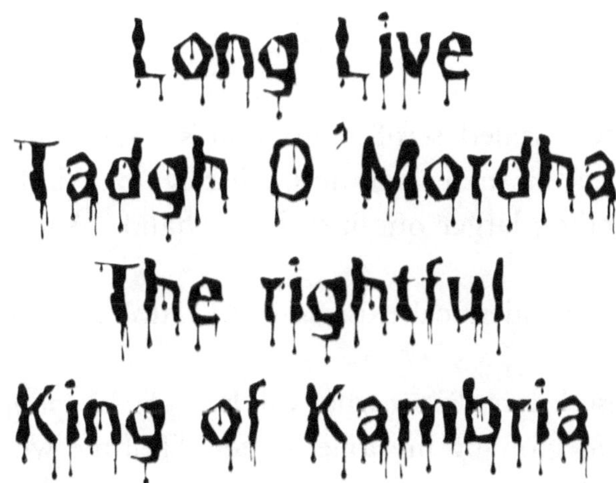

Under it, a bloody Rook was painted, with the butchered body of Arthur's prized hunting dog slumped on the floor.

I stared at it. There was no coming back from this, and no time to hide the evidence. This was a direct challenge to the King, and he was not going to let this pass.

Silence fell around me and I turned to see Arthur, his steely gaze fixed on the words written in the blood of one of the only creatures I had ever seen him treat with genuine affection.

I saw his fingers rap once… twice on his leg before he turned his attention to me. "I want every guard who was on duty last night hung. I want my captains in my chambers within the hour and I want The Rook found and brought to me immediately. I am done, Merlin. We march on that wall today, and you had better figure out how the fuck to bring it down because I am not leaving until the Lowlands are mine. There is only one King, and I am going to make sure they know it."

I pushed two sealed scrolls into Otto's hands, ignoring his glower. "I need these sent immediately to Windhaven." I pushed another, larger one into Una's hand. "And this is for Emmie."

She had an identical expression to Otto's. "Why can't we stay here?"

"Because I don't know what will happen," I snapped, then took a breath, forcing my tone lighter. "Tell me what I want you to do if I do not return."

Otto's scowl deepened. "Stay with Emmie and Ameena."

"And?"

"Get to Sirinelle," they both said, sounding less than

amused. "Kareen and Bain are on the corner of Chestnut and Gabe with the thatched roof."

"Good," I said, straightening. "Sirin will go there. You make sure you take her with you if it came to it," I said, eyeing them both in turn.

Otto nodded, his floppy hair cascading over his forehead. "Yes, Da."

"Good lad," I patted him on the shoulder.

"Will the King bring the wall down?" Una asked, her eyes wide.

"I don't know," I said, sighing. "He has always had the power to do so." I looked at them. "I may have to turn against him, openly. If I do…"

Una's chin wobbled. "Can we come with you?"

"If I cannot return here," I said gently, "it will not be safe for you with me. Kareen knows what I expect of her. She will get you, Otto, and Henry out of Kambria. Nareen will be safe enough for you, Sir Bastian is a good man, and he is leaving for his new position there in the spring. Emmie and Ameena will be with you, and they will look after you both. You don't need to worry." I pointed at the chest they had stolen from Eckbert. "You can use that. There is more than enough in there to keep all of you for the rest of your lives."

I put a hand over both of their bracelets, pouring my power into them until the crystals in them gleamed before pulling their sleeves down to cover them. "Do not take them off under *any* circumstances, do you understand?"

More sullen nods.

"Good." A minute part of the worry that had been weighing heavily on me eased. Kareen and Emmie between them would look after my small band of irritants.

Two days. Two days was all it took for Arthur to summon his men and begin the march toward the Lowlands. Two days for the fate of an entire race in Kambria to be put in jeopardy. I had once again failed.

He had taken it as a sign that the Sylvyn were rising against him, and nothing I could say or do was going to change his mind. I don't know if I am strong enough to stop him if it comes to it.

Every fucking step feels like a lead weight to my heart. Every beat mocking me that I should have had the answers I was seeking by now. I could have done more. I could have been better. And now it is the Sylvyn that will pay, once again, for my mistakes.

The snow ahead of us is untouched. Pristine white against the stunning scenery around us as we skirt through the side of The Spine. Behind us lies churned, muddy ground. The bleak symbolism is not lost on me.

"Why so sullen, Merlin?" Arthur asked, his horse falling into step beside me. He didn't wear a speck of armor, just a tunic of deep, forest green with a rearing golden dragon, the same sigil that fluttered from the bannermen that flanked us.

"You know I dislike travel, my King," I huffed, forcing my face into a smile.

"Have I let you get soft over the years?" he chuckled, his leg bumping mine as his horse sidestepped around a rock. "There is going to be a lot of travel in your future if we can bend the Sylvyn gifted to my uses."

I laughed softly. "The next land you conquer, can I suggest one with less snow?"

"I will keep your request in mind," he replied, eyes on the

land ahead. "Your birthland is one I have had my eye on for a long time and should be arid enough to keep you happy. Calibyre has sand and sun as far as the eye can see. It is still Sylvyn held though. One of the last rooks William sent described it. He scouted it on his way to dispose of his part of the Helix. It is much larger than Kambria. It will take a lot to claim it, and travel that far to the east will take its toll."

"Sun you say?" I slid my gaze to him, feeling a flicker of possessive anger at his mentioning the lands my family emigrated from, so many years ago now. "To think I could have spent all these years actually feeling all of my extremities at once."

"Fate clearly had a plan for us when it guided you to Sirinelle," he mused.

"Hmmm," I hummed half-heartedly, tracking Sirin's flight back to me as she circled through the air. She came into land lightly on my shoulder, her cold beak pushing against my neck, settling herself against me for the ride. I slipped into memories of my parents, so distant now I could barely remember more than the faintest outline of what they had looked like. Both were long gone, dead at the hands of Drayvn. I have no memory of how they had died… I just somehow knew.

It was as if my mind blocked out that particularly painful memory, and in truth, I did not want to dig further into that darkness. I was picked up by a fishing boat at just seven years old from the shores of Endreal, trying to feed myself out of the rock pools there, and Kareen's great, great grandmother had found me on the docks in Sirinelle, scared and alone.

She had worked in the castle at the time, and I had accompanied her on occasion. Arthur had been only four years older than me at the time, and I had not known it was the young prince that had approached me that day to play a game of knucklebones in the dirt behind the kitchens.

The friendship we struck up over those years, the trust he came to put in me, was the only thing that saved me from the massacre of the Nimmet blessed. Something I will forever feel a deep guilt for.

"We march to victory, Merlin," Arthur said, inhaling a deep breath of the cold air and pulling me out of my memories. "I can feel it in my bones."

25

MORGANA

Saoirse woke me as dawn was breaking, and I reluctantly untangled myself from Gwen, already missing her warmth as I pulled on layers of clothing and padded into the main living quarters with a scowl at the obnoxiously bright woman.

She ignored me, pushing a hot cup of tea into my hands as she sipped on her own.

Faolán strolled in moments later as I was looking out over the mist-shrouded forest through the window, the steam from my tea fogging the window.

"Good morning ladies," he rumbled, stooping to pour himself some tea and kiss his mother on the temple as she blearily stirred porridge in a blackened pot over the flames. Madraigh seemed to be as much of a morning person as I was.

Saoirse beamed at him, kicking a chair out for him to sit with her at the table while I turned, giving him a slight tilt of my head in greeting.

"I trust you slept well?" he asked me, a slight curve to his lips.

"Well enough, thank you," I replied politely, refusing to rise to the bait.

He lay a large hand on Saoirse's head, ruffling her hair as he passed her, and there was no animosity in his gaze as he moved to join me by the window, his shoulder near touching mine as he stopped to peer out into the gloomy morning.

"It's going to rain," he murmured, frowning up at the sky. "If we leave soon, we should get in a few hours of hunting before it sets in." He scratched his cheek, his fingers rasping against the slight stubble there. "Are you sure you want to go after the bánánach? They tend to stay in their dens when bad weather approaches. What weapons did you bring?"

"Gwen is worried about the danger they pose to the town and wants them dealt with," I replied, my eyes tracking a bead of condensation as it dripped slowly down my glass. I slid my gaze to his, noting the frank curiosity he appraised me with. "Her wish is my desire."

He inclined his head, hearing my unspoken message. "As it is mine," he said softly. He winked, walked over to Madraigh and hauled the pot off the flames, setting it down on the table for her. Madraigh followed with an armful of wooden bowls and a weighted look in my direction.

"Where are your weapons?" Faolán asked, frowning as he surveyed me, hefting his own axe over his shoulder and securing it with a clip. Saoirse huffed a laugh, checking over the bandolier of knives that were strapped across her chest, and short sword belted at her hip. "Don't worry about her, she doesn't need them."

"Gifted?" he asked, looking slightly less worried.

"Something like that," I muttered, taking the coat he offered me and ending the conversation. I was eager to get moving, I had felt restless all morning, my shadows murmuring to me, but not loud enough to decipher what they were saying. It put me on edge, feeling as if I should be looking over my shoulder every moment, and making me anxious about leaving Gwen behind. She was still sleeping, and I knew she wanted to stay back to see the students at the school, or I would have insisted she join us if only to keep her within my sight. Madraigh had already disappeared to make breakfast for a few young ones who had arrived at the school early, looking for food that they did not have at home.

Saoirse bounced on her toes, puffing into her cupped hands with cheeks that were flushed from the cold air. "Let's go, it's far too cold to be standing still."

I nodded, motioning for Faolán to lead the way, falling into step behind him as he moved off. I had barely made it to the edge of the property when the murmuring that had been plaguing me all morning grew louder, an urgent edge to it now that made me pause.

Saoirse nearly walked into me, resting her hand on my back. "What are you doing?" she asked, as I turned back to the house, frowning as I strained to hear the faint whispers.

Behind me, Faolán had paused as well. "Morgana?"

I held up a hand to silence them both, closing my eyes as the voices murmured just past my senses.

"I don't—" I trailed off, frustrated. Had it been night I could have thrown a net of my power through the dark, feeling for what they were trying to tell me. In the day, with the sun chasing the shadows away, I was muted. It felt like someone had placed hands over my ears and muffled my hearing.

I stepped back toward the school, seeing Madraigh appear

on the small side porch, her body as tense as mine, but she wasn't looking at us, instead her focus was back down the route to Windhaven.

Faolán brushed past me, a hand going to the hilt of his dagger, head cocked to the side. "I hear hoofbeats."

I strained my eyes in the direction he was looking, catching movement coming around a copse of trees in the distance.

"It's a lone rider," Saoirse said, shielding her eyes from the glare of the sun as she came up beside me.

Faolán hummed in agreement. "They are in a hurry and heading straight for the school by the look of them."

Thundering hooves began to echo in the still air as the rider drew close enough to make out and Saoirse stiffened, taking a halting step forward.

"Rian?"

It was only moments until he was on us, his horse blowing and lathered in sweat, Rian himself looking grave.

"I bring word from Lallymoore. Rooks have been sent through to Nairn and Vinkirk. The Pendragon advances on Windhaven and Lord O'Mordha calls every able-bodied person to arms." His gaze rested on me. "And you are needed back at the wall immediately."

My stomach went cold, my gaze sliding to Madraigh who had gone pale, her eyes that black sheen again as she stared off toward Windhaven. I pushed away from the group, stalking toward her.

"What do you see?"

She didn't answer me, her fingers clutching the baluster of the deck.

"What is wrong?" Gwen appeared behind her, taking in Rian and then my expression. She rounded Madraigh until she could peer into her face. "Mads?"

Madraigh turned to her slowly, raising her hand to cup

Gwen's cheek as her eyes cleared back into their natural color. "Your brother needs you, my love." She turned to me, her face devoid of emotion. "He needs all of you."

"The Pendragon?" Gwen breathed, looking over my head to Saoirse.

"It's at least a week's ride back to Windhaven," Saoirse said, joining us. "Longer, since you are riding double. The horses can't travel faster than that in the snow." She lowered her voice, looking at me. "You need to go back ahead of us, you can get back in half the time we can."

I shook my head. "I'm not leaving you both on the road without me. Not with the possibility there are more bánánach still hunting."

"If The Pendragon is moving on Windhaven, Tadgh needs you more than we do," Gwen said, her tone holding no option of argument.

Indecision ripped me in two and I shook my head again, looking from Gwen to Saoirse.

"I will accompany them back," Faolán said, drawing my attention to him. "I assure you they will both be safe." He was looking at me with interest, as if trying to assess why my presence was so urgently needed back at Windhaven.

"I will stay with them too," Rian chimed in, tilting his head to me. "I know that probably means little to you, given... our history. But I won't be caught off guard again."

I swore under my breath, looking to Gwen. "I will be days away."

"Don't act like I haven't been out here my entire life without your protection," she said, raising a brow at me. "I am perfectly capable of looking after myself, even with the bánánach, please trust me on this."

She had a look on her face that I couldn't discern. As if she were trying to tell me something I was missing entirely. "I wasn't insinuating you weren't," I said, though I clearly was and kicked myself that I had been so transparent. It was the conversation with Madraigh that had rattled me to the point I could barely stand the thought of letting her out of my sight.

"What are you?" Faolán asked suddenly. "Given what I am about to ride into, I feel like it's not too blunt of a question."

At this point, I don't think it mattered if the whole of the Lowlands knew what I was, my life would be as forfeit as the rest of theirs with what was heading our way. And I turned to him, letting the power that seemed to be swelling with every passing day slip slightly.

His eyes widened as he looked into eyes that I knew had become as dark as night, as dark as his mother's.

"I am the only one who is going to be able to keep the wall up when The Blood Traitor and Pendragon attack," I said quietly. "Yet I will not leave Gwen's side without your word that both she and Saoirse will get back to Windhaven safely."

He swallowed, though to his credit, he didn't grovel like most did when they realized what I was. Maybe it was due to a life raised by a woman whose power was an echo of my own. I hated that it made my respect for him rise, even if it remained the merest fraction above dislike.

"You have my word, Morgana." He looked to Rian. "I need the day to spread the word through The Hollow and gather every able-bodied man and woman that can be spared."

"I will come with you," Saoirse said, holding Rian's mare's head as he dismounted. "We can be out of here by first light tomorrow."

The rest of the day was spent in a flurry of anxiety-riddled movement. There was no point to me going with them as they broke the news to people they had known their entire lives that they would need to say goodbye to their families—perhaps never to see them again—and come to Windhaven. I was a stranger to them, and trust was something I had not yet earned. Instead, I spent the day uselessly packing the meager possessions we had arrived with, checking and rechecking bags and wrapping small parcels of food that would keep Gwen and Saoirse fed on their return journey. I should have left already, but in her haste to get into town that morning, I hadn't said goodbye to Gwen, and I couldn't bring myself to leave without doing so.

Madraigh had dismissed the school, keeping back only a handful of teens and together they were going over maps of the mountains in case they would be needed to lead their people into them. A last desperate attempt at survival while they waited to be saved. It was a small kernel of hope that might be something to cling to, should our defenses fall, yet I could see as well as they could that it was a fool's hope. Who would come to their rescue? If the wall fell, there would be no one left.

Dusk had fallen by the time they returned, exhausted and quiet, Saoirse clasping me on the shoulder as she passed and trailed into the school after the two men.

Gwen paused on the steps with me, her eyes hollow. "I was worried you would have already left."

I brushed a lock of her hair back. "Not without saying goodbye. How did today go?"

She grimaced, leaning into my hand. "They will do what they must, but they have little choice. I just had to tell hundreds of people they may be spending their last night with their loved ones." She closed her eyes, sighing. "I want to go back to last night."

"There will be more nights like last night," I murmured, tipping her chin up to make her look at me. "I promise that was not the last night you will fall asleep in my arms."

"Don't make promises you can't keep," she said, holding my gaze. "You know as well as I do what war brings. I lost so much the last time The Pendragon turned his eyes on us."

I bared my teeth. "I will fucking end him if he tries to take what is mine."

There was a slight tug at the corners of her lips, a warmth returning to her haunted eyes. "Say that again," she whispered. "The last part."

"Mine," I said, dipping my head to brush my lips across hers. "For better or worse, Princess. I am not strong enough to stay away from you, and for that, I am so sorry."

"Shut up and kiss me again," she huffed, giving me a wry smile.

I did, pushing her against the wall and kissing her deeply enough that we were both breathless when I pulled away.

"See you in a week?" I said, taking a step back.

"Tell Tadgh we are coming," she replied, pressing her fingers to her lips, as if trying to retain the feel of me on them.

I winked at her, and took another step back into the shadows, releasing my hold on my power and throwing myself forward. It was almost a relief as my body melted into the darkness, streaking forward across the frostbitten land toward Windhaven.

26

MORGANA

Dawn was just beginning to creep across the horizon as I reached the wall protecting Windhaven, testing its power as I skittered up the looming face like a ghost and flowed along its turreted top. I was relieved to feel steady strength humming from deep within its center, as steadfast as it has always been. The grey stone was nearly as black as the surrounding rocky mountains after the rain had sluiced the land overnight, the skies opening as if it knew what was to come and wept for us.

No one saw me, though even if they had looked hard, all they would have seen was a wraith of darkness, not even disturbing the air around them as I moved through the night.

I followed the edge of the wall, moving along to the tiled roofs and gliding around turrets, keeping out of the rays of sunlight that had begun to break through, straight into the open window of Tadgh's offices in a billow of ink-colored ash that dissipated into nothing as I forced my body back into its normal form.

I was met with a chorus of alarmed shouts, the high-pitched scream of a woman, followed by a roar from Tadgh for silence.

It took a moment for my vision to clear as I stepped into the light of the room, my gaze immediately finding Tadgh's. "How long do we have?"

He looked slightly taken aback, his hand still raised to silence the others in the room who were staring at me in a mixture of fear and wonder. His brows came down, his face darkening in a storm that I knew was his temper about to be unleashed.

"Where the fuck were you?" he snarled at me. "I have sent rook after rook for you, with not one word back."

My own temper was too close to the surface, fueled by my power that wasn't quite back under my grasp yet. "You dare ask me where I have been *Lord O'Mordha?*" I snarled at him. "I have been scrabbling through forest and snow for our people, doing what you should have done, and now I am here to guard the wall that protects them. I regret the fact that I have stayed here for so long, listening to you when I could have been out there doing more to help. Now, how *fucking* long do we have?"

He shook his head, rage a flicking fire behind his eyes. "Two weeks at best. I don't know exactly when The Pendragon moved." He ran a hand over his face, then beckoned for a man I recognized as one of his advisors. He took a scroll from him, holding it out to me. "Tell me you did not have a hand in this?" His face was drawn as he waved a slip of paper in my direction.

"In what?" I asked, taking the scroll and squinting at the small letters.

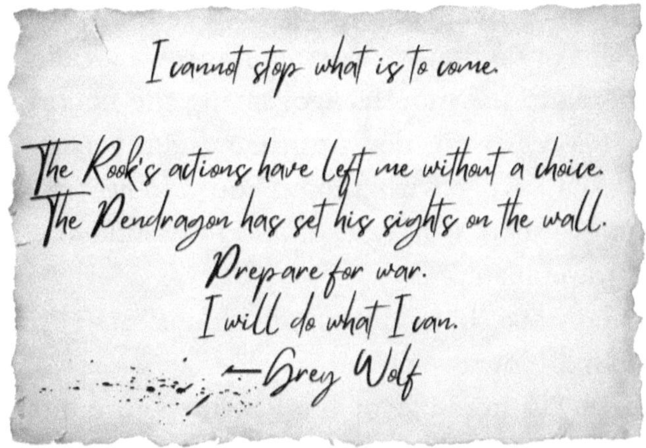

I stared at the note. Utterly nonplussed. "What is this about?"

"Wolf has been sending rooks for weeks," he muttered, pouring himself a glass of wine and drinking deeply. "I sent word to Vinkirk, thinking you were there, but word came back that you had already left. I thought your next location would be Nairn, so I sent riders and they must have missed you on the road. There have been attacks on Irling, I don't know what, just that hundreds died from it, and they are saying it is the Rook who has led these attacks." He leveled an accusatory eye on me. "Did you have anything to do with it? To push my hand into war?"

"Why in the name of Nimmet would I do that?" I snapped. "We would be fighting with starving soldiers... We *are* going to be fighting with starving soldiers. Half of them are not even armed, you fool!"

"Because you yourself said we were going to struggle to get

through this winter. Now we have no choice but to strike back."

"With what?" I exploded, throwing the note at him. "You know as well as I do that we won't win this war, Tadgh!"

"You came to me months ago, saying the majority of The Pendragon's forces were tied up in Endreal, according to the Wolf. *If* we can truly trust them. You *told me* we should be making a move then, I disagreed, and now suddenly I have no choice but to retaliate."

"A move to take back the supply chains!" I yelled. "Not to launch into full-blown war!"

"Then why is there talk of the Rook—your damned calling card—in Irling?" Tadgh roared.

"How the fuck would I know?" I snapped back, grappling to maintain control of myself. The tips of my fingers had begun to stain black, itching to be unleashed, and I had to take a breath to gather myself. "This is the first time I have heard of this," I said, forcing my tone gentler. "Have you replied to the Wolf?"

"Of course I have," he hissed. "Which no doubt was an empty plea of innocence since he was expecting a reply from the Rook and didn't get one. It's only going to make it more suspicious that I'm claiming your innocence here in Windhaven while you are clearly absent!"

"What if I attack them first, shadow walk beyond the wall and try to hit The Blood Traitor before he even gets here?"

I was cut off with a scornful huff from Tadgh. "You are untrained. They would know you were there and kill you before you had a chance to do anything, and then we would be left utterly defenseless. Remaining behind the wall offers you a shield that you can strengthen."

"There has to be something we can do other than waiting here like a sitting target?" I paced along the edge of the room, a breeze flowing in from the open window that smelled faintly of pine.

"There is nothing to do now other than heed the Wolf's warning," Tadgh said, looking suddenly exhausted. "We prepare for war and hope for a miracle. Where are Saoirse and Gwen?"

"Coming from The Hollow with as many men and women as they can muster," I said, still reeling. "Who would implicate me in these attacks?"

Tadgh huffed. "If you truly had nothing to do with this, then it's someone who hates the Sylvyn enough to force war… So, take your pick."

A woman came forward, her eyes round as she handed me a stack of rolled papers, bobbing a curtsy to me as I took them from her. It was a woman I had seen hundreds of times, though she had never paid much attention to me, nor me to her.

"Don't do that," I muttered, waving her off with an irritated flick of my wrist.

"Sorry, Child of Nimmet," she murmured, bobbing again, then paused with a look of uncertainty… then bobbed a third time as if in apology.

I sighed, pressing a finger to my temple which was beginning to throb before glaring at the room at large. "I am no different from the woman most of you have ignored for years now. Just because you can now see the power I possess, doesn't mean you should lose your spine. We need strength right now, not pups cowering at my feet. If that is all you have to offer, get out." I pointed a black-tipped finger at the door, some closest to me shrinking away.

Three of them fled, four more stayed, though one looked as if they were about to pass out or wet themselves. I would wager coin on them being the next to fold.

"Mim, I need them," Tadgh sighed from behind me, and I heard the creak of his chair as he sat down.

I turned to see him leaning over his desk, his head in his hands. "You don't need *them*. There are men on their way that will serve you better than those cowering fools, best weed out the weak now before your life is in their hands."

He didn't answer me for a moment, just ran his hands through his hair. "Are you ready to face what is to come?" he asked quietly. He raised his head to regard me with his whiskey-colored eyes.

I felt my spine lock, though I refused to let the fear that laced cold fingers into my gut show on my face. "Are any of us?"

"The Blood Traitor doesn't take prisoners."

My hand moved to my side, running down the scars beneath my clothing. The scars The Blood Traitor had given me a child. But I was no longer a child, and trained or not, I was more than he had faced before. "Neither do I."

"Scouts say the army has reached the coast above Sirinelle and is moving slowly," Tadgh said, eyeing the map spread out over the huge table that now dominated his office.

Four days had passed and from the dark circles under his eyes, he had slept as little as I had. Men and women had arrived from Lallymoore, more from some of the smaller outposts and cottages from the surrounding area, none of them looking ready for war.

Every smith in the Lowlands had been summoned to make any weapons they could, melting down every spare bit of metal they could get their hands on. Even the carts hadn't made it through their frantic search for materials, the axles being melted down even though the metal was barely fit to make crude hammers.

Every gifted Sylvyn who arrived had been given priority rations, trying to strengthen their reserves, even the mules were put to slaughter to feed them. It was a blow that we had to absorb, their use as food far outweighed their use in the war coming.

I stared at the map, my eyes following the path of the approaching army as Tadgh pointed to a spot further up.

"They bottleneck near Glenrock," he said, pointing to a spot between The Spine and Glenrock. "They will have to thin out to pass through there, and with that terrain, they will be slow moving and have to camp at least once."

I shook my head. "If you are thinking of attacking there, don't. You yourself said we couldn't face The Pendragon in open combat. War is the fallback plan if the wall falls. Windhaven is a bottleneck to the Lowlands, if they hit us, we will have the same advantage here."

"No, we wouldn't stand a chance meeting them in open war beyond the wall, but..." he paused, his eyes regaining a slight shine to them. "They won't anticipate a night attack from The Spine. They think that they march on the wall while we cower behind it, they will have no reason to look to the mountains."

"What?" I frowned at him. "Have you slept at all these last few days?"

He glared at me across the map before turning to one of the men that I had taken to calling Frog in my head, for his wide mouth and the gormless look that was always plastered on his face.

"How many ungifted soldiers do we have right now?"

Frog peered at him with his usual dead-eyed stare. "Ungifted, Milord?"

I tilted my head, brow raised at Tadgh, waiting for him to explain.

"How many ungifted soldiers are here right now, Merrick?"

Ah, so Frog was called Merrick. Whatever.

"Uh," Frog fumbled around with a stack of papers, dropping a few on the floor. "Maybe two hundred at a push?"

"What are you thinking?" I asked as Tadgh turned his attention back to the map.

"I was thinking about what you said the other day," he muttered, frowning at the map. "About hitting The Blood Traitor before he hits us."

"With ungifted Sylvyn?" I asked incredulously. "You would just be throwing lives away."

"The Blood Traitor *and* The Pendragon can sense power, that is why I couldn't risk you going in alone," Tadgh said, in a tone that made it sound as if I were a stupid child. "In that stretch, their army will be drawn out and at their weakest."

I caught what he was intending immediately and shook my head. "There is no way our men are getting within a sniff of that army undetected, unsuspected or not. And they would be as good as defenseless against them. Tadgh, The Blood Traitor butchered your parents, and they were some of the most powerful Sylvyn we have had—sending ungifted in is a suicide mission. If you are sending anyone in, it's me. I at least have a chance."

"You are too valuable," he said flatly.

"Any life is valuable!" I hissed.

"Why do you think I'm risking their lives then?" he snapped back. "Do you think I want to send them into that mess? I have thousands of lives on my shoulders, Morgana. I am trying to find a way to keep them alive! This could be our chance to get to The Blood Traitor. Our only chance," he waved a hand at the others in the room. "Out."

They quickly dispersed, leaving Tadgh and I alone in the room.

"I can't do this with you fighting me at every turn," he said, leaning his weight on his hands. "It makes me look weak in front of those I am trying to lead."

"Then stop making foolish decisions," I said, glaring at him.

He hung his head between his arms. "I am doing the best I can do, with no fucking support."

"That is entirely of your own doing," I retorted. "Gwen and Saoirse have backed you from day one. You have been too proud to return that respect."

"And you?" he said, straightening and rounding the table to me. "Do I have your support or are you something else I have to fight?"

"I'm here," I said. "Isn't that proof enough?"

"Who are you here for?" he asked. "Because I know it isn't me."

I bristled. "I'm here for the Sylvyn, as I have always been."

He gave me a long look. "That wasn't what I meant, and you know it."

I didn't break his stare, raising my chin in defiance. "Don't ask questions you don't want answers for."

He was inches from me, his breath tickling my face. Close enough that I could see a muscle feather in his jaw.

"Then you shouldn't care that I will lead those men out of the gates myself. You have told me enough times I could have done more. I'm doing it now."

"What?" I stared at him. "Tadgh, they will sense you a mile off!"

"I don't have to be in the camp to lead them. I can stay in

The Spine and be there if they need to run." He held a hand up as I moved to argue with him again. "And before you try to throw yourself on the pyre again, I am not the one who is needed to keep the wall standing. You are not going, Mim. There is one man leading the approaching army, and if he falls, this will end. If it goes wrong, I can at least hold The Blood Traitor off so they can get back to you and you can keep everyone here safe."

"No," I shook my head. "Absolutely not."

"Every life is valuable," he said, giving me a wry look. "You said it yourself."

"I didn't mean for you to lead our soldiers to their deaths and then martyr yourself on their corpses! You don't think The Pendragon has a full guard day and night?"

"I don't plan to die, let's try not to get too morbid."

"Tadgh," I grabbed his arm as he moved to push past me. "At least wait until Gwen and Saoirse arrive with reinforcements. Give Nairn and Vinkirk time to get here as well. This is ludicrous."

He shook his head, straightening. "Any closer and we will lose the advantage in The Spine. My mind is set, I will wait one more day for the men to prepare and then I am going. You wanted me to be a leader, get out of my way so I can be."

He shook me off, striding across the room to bark orders at some men outside the door.

"Please, do not do this." Desperation was beginning to leech into me.

He gave me a loaded look, before laughing softly under his breath, the sound devoid of humor. "If I had known that all I had to do to make you look at me like that was put my life on the line, I would have done it a thousand times over already." He ran a knuckle down the side of my cheek, and it took everything in me not to step away from the touch.

"Look at you like what?"

"Like you give a shit about me," he said sadly, before pushing past me and out the door.

Anxiety was a pent-up ball in my chest as I tried to sleep later that night. I tossed and turned for hours before giving up and donning my gown. I found myself outside without realizing where I had been heading, walking to the wall and peering up to where it stretched toward the night sky, its solid presence reassuring. I ran my hand over the cold stone of its face, feeling the familiar hum of power within it. It was as if the wall breathed against my hand, a pulse of life within the rock itself. Gallin was within this wall, his power having fed it for decades before his death, a small piece of him still here with the rest of the souls that had poured their power into protecting the Sylvyn.

Flattening my hand as I had done so many times before, I pushed some of my own dark power into the rock, melding it to my will and feeling it take for only a moment before it drifted away. Gallin had never had the chance to teach me how to make my power stick, how to embed it into the wall and strengthen it. It was only while I touched it that I could reinforce it. Sometimes a trace of my power lingered, but never for long.

"Can't sleep either?"

I whirled to see Tadgh wander up behind me, looking at me with trepidation, as if not sure how I would receive him.

"No," I huffed softly. "I feel like I'm never going to sleep soundly again."

He gave me a wry look. "Mim, I'm sorry. I feel like all we

do is argue and that is not how I want it to be between us. Not after everything we have been through."

My lips pressed together, forcing down the harsh words that always seemed to rise when I talked to Tadgh and nodded grudgingly.

"I am equally to blame for that."

He hummed softly, falling into step with me as we continued our slow stroll down the wall.

"I want to go back to the days when my greatest concern was how dull lessons were," he murmured into the still air. "And whatever trick you were trying to pull on me that day."

I laughed, the sound surprising me as images of the past flashed before my eyes.

"The ink was a particularly cruel one," he chuckled, sliding his gaze to mine.

I had replaced his inkpot during one of our long lessons together with ink that would disappear after a while. We had both left our papers on Lord Kerrich's desk and gone to supper, only to have him turn up wild-eyed and furious, waving the blank sheets under Tadgh's nose.

"I couldn't sit down for three days," he muttered. 'I still have a belt buckle scar across my arse from that punishment."

I bit my lip to keep myself from laughing again. He had gotten me back, sneaking into my room when I was asleep, opening my window wide and lighting little balls of flame to hang just inside of it. By the time I had woken in the morning, my room was swarming with insects drawn to the light, and I was covered head to toe in itchy bites that had driven me mad.

"We grew up, and the weight of Windhaven fell on your shoulders. The weight of the wall on mine," I said quietly.

"And that is why I have to go out there tomorrow," Tadgh said. "These people have been my burden from the moment my parents fell, and I have not done enough. I am not doing this recklessly, Mim. If we can put an end to this before it starts, I have to try."

"Then let me come with you," I said, turning to look at him. "You know how dangerous this is, at least with me there you have a better chance."

"No," he said flatly, leaving no room for argument. "My job is to protect my people. Your job is and always has been to keep that wall standing. So guard the wall, Morgana, and pray to the Gods that Arthur falls tomorrow because if I fail, you are it." He tilted his head, looking up at the wall. "From our greatest weaknesses, can come our greatest triumphs," he said softly. "And I am done being weak."

27

MORGANA

"Open the gates!"

I grunted in frustration, slapping the stone with my palm, the sting of it against my skin a balm to my fractured nerves and a distraction I sorely needed as I heard the hooves of the riders I was about to let through approach me.

I turned, looking up at Tadgh as his horse ambled toward me. He wore simple clothes, no armor that could catch the moonlight or make noise, a dark cloak around his shoulders and his hair was tousled from his old habit of repeatedly running his hands through it when thinking.

"Save your breath," he said, giving me a tired look as he caught sight of my expression.

My mouth thinned with the effort of holding back the words I wanted to scream at him, casting one final look toward the Lowlands, hoping I would see Gwen coming through the gates.

"The smiths have pulled down a line of iron fencing from the back gardens," he said, his horse fidgeting beneath him while more mounted men began to gather around him, looking grim. "The swords they have been making are worthless, so tell them to use the new metal for arrows and put any spare hands to work fletching them. We may have no way to retrieve them if The Pendragon gets to the wall, so I want a surplus. More than our archers could need."

I nodded. "As you wish."

He leaned down in his saddle, so only I could hear his next words. "Do not step foot beyond those walls, Morgana. That is a fucking order, do you understand?"

I scowled at him. "You have made that crystal clear, Tadgh."

"Good." He waved a hand at the men. "Ride out!"

I placed both of my hands on the huge wooden gates of the wall, pushing my power into it. I could feel its question to my command, its reluctance to crack open the gates. "Open," I hissed to it, forcing it to my will until I felt it give. There was a hollow boom, the creak of heavy hinges, and then the gates shuddered and swung slowly open. Only the O'Mordha's or a Child of Nimmet could open these gates, the power running within the rock coded to their blood and to the power that flooded mine. Should all of us fall, so would the wall, leaving the Lowlands to be ravaged like the rest of Kambria.

I kept my focus on the wall as it pushed back against me, the decades of power in it screaming to close the gap, feeling the shudder of the ground as the horses passed at my back. Only when the last horse had passed did I risk a look out at the barren ground beyond. Tadgh had turned his horse, looking back at me, and I felt an inky tendril of my power run an ice-cold finger up my spine as he turned and spurred his horse after his men.

"Nimmet watch over them," I murmured, letting the gates close back into place. Not a prayer, nor a request. It was an order.

The day dragged, every one of my frayed nerves on edge as I oversaw the smiths start work on the arrowheads, organized a work unit to begin fletching them, and gave the order for the last of the geese to be slaughtered, their feathers plucked and bagged, ready for use. Even with the cold bite to the air, I was sweaty and flushed by the time I reluctantly retired to my rooms. I couldn't bear the thought of the food that had been left out for me, my stomach twisting into knots as I perched on the edge of my sill and looked out beyond the wall, hoping I would hear a whisper from my shadows telling me what I should do.

They were silent, leaving me completely alone in my torment.

The night stretched on in strained silence, and I must have grabbed the latches to my window a dozen times, ready to throw myself out of it and into the darkness, following Tadgh's path. Every time I resolved to throw caution to the wind, something would hold me back. Not the guiding whispers of my shadows, but something else. I couldn't tell if it was just indecision, or something deeper, and I could feel a sort of madness begin to settle in as those hours slipped by.

"Fuck this," I muttered to myself after I had nearly paced a hole in the threadbare carpet in front of my window. I changed into fresh clothing, resigned to the fact I was not going to be getting any sleep even if I tried, and pulled my hair back, knotting it at the back of my head before heading to Tadgh's offices. If I was going to be stuck in Windhaven, I was at least going to use the time to help us.

Tadgh's office was eerily quiet, the moonlight shining through the louver windows lighting the room in a soft glow as

I waved a hand, setting a fire roaring in the large fireplace at the end of the room. Another wave of my hand had the candles that lined the desk burning as well, years of melted wax forming stalactites that dripped from the edges of the sturdy desk. Grabbing the closest ledger, I sat down and began.

By the time the useless array of men that Tadgh called his advisors began to gather in his offices, I was already compiling the lists of names that had arrived overnight, allocating them to workforces or moving them into units where their skills would be most useful.

I was mortified by how little organization there was to this effect already. I could remember the records Kerrich had kept of the people in the Lowlands, how many gifted we had, how many smiths and farriers, soldiers and men and women capable of defending us if necessary. The stack of papers I found amongst the piles on Tadgh's desk were nearly useless. What the fuck had Tadgh been doing all these years?

Frog came and stood nervously in front of me as I was squinting at Tadgh's spidery handwriting on a document detailing the population in Nairn.

"Milady, if you would excuse us to go and break our fast, we will retu—"

I cut him off with a black look over the top of the paper. "None of your people out there get to break their fast, so neither do you," I muttered, waving the paper at him. "When were these lists last updated?"

He had the balls to look affronted. "I—uh," he frowned at the paper. "I am unsure."

I let the paper dangle from my fingers, glaring at the group gathered in the room before standing slowly. "Every man, woman, and child out there has been limited to one meal a day." I pointed to a stiff-backed man at the back of the room. "You, go down to the kitchens and inform them that every person in Windhaven is to receive the same rations. Any extra is to go to the soldiers that will be defending us, they are the ones who will need it."

"My lady," Frog began to protest.

I turned on him. "One word, Frog, and I will feed you your own tongue, do I make myself clear?"

His mouth snapped shut, his eyes widening as he nodded at me.

"You have all taken advantage of a life inside these walls, as have I," I said. "This changes today." I waved the useless bit of paper in my hand. "I want up-to-date lists of every member of the Lowlands as they arrive. I want to know how many gifted we have, how many are trained, and I want to know this before you even think about your next meal."

There was a low murmur as they dispersed, throwing nervous glances in my direction. I waited until they had left before I ran a tired hand over my face, scrubbing at my eyes. "Tadgh, you have fucked us," I murmured to no one in particular.

This is what Gwen had meant. Why she had pushed me so hard to take a place at Tadgh's side. She had seen this coming a mile off and I had been blind to it. I had let myself be complacent while Gwen had been out doing everything she could, fighting against her brother's pride.

Now we were scrambling when we should have been ready.

It didn't take long before the first reports hit Tadgh's desk. Detailed numbers of who was on hand and who was yet to come. It was less than I had hoped for and better than I had expected. I sent these records to the kitchens, letting them know how many were expected to help them ration accordingly, before heading out.

My first stop to the smiths showed a healthy pile of weapons growing, carts of arrowheads being taken to the nearby barns where men and women sat fletching them amongst sacks of grey goose feathers and baskets of shafts. Some of them raised their heads in greeting to me as I passed, and I was surprised to see a few even touch their foreheads in respect before going back to their work.

Frog caught up to me as I was talking to a group of young soldiers, directing them to relieve the lookouts along the wall.

"Milady, Nairn is approaching, I have numbers from the riders ahead of them." I murmured my thanks, scanning the lists he held out to me.

"Send the gifted through when they arrive. I want a barricade of our strongest ready to defend the wall at a moment's notice." I pointed to a column on the left. "These are fire Elementyls?"

Frog nodded.

"Split them in two, the more experienced to the wall, the lesser through to the camps and tell them to make sure the fires stay burning. Keep our people warm, there is a cold front coming through tonight, and tents alone will not be sufficient."

"Of course," he scurried away again, only to be replaced by another man I vaguely recognized.

"You asked me for a report of healers at our disposal?"

I nodded for him to continue, grimacing as he showed me a list that was far too short.

"Thirteen," I sighed. "Give them priority rations."

"There are more coming in from the Lowlands," he offered. "The list is not complete, but growing."

Shouting off in the distance dragged my attention away from him, and a wave of relief washed over me at the sight of movement to the west of the camp that was steadily growing beneath Windhaven.

"The Hollow arrives," the man in front of me said, shielding his eyes. "And from the looks of it, Vinkirk with them, I can see the grey of their banners."

I waited, feeling the weight of the world descend over me as a horse broke away from the group, cantering toward us through the rows of tents. Even from this distance, I could see Saoirse's hair whipping around her in the cold air as she guided her horse around the camp and up the rocky path to the plateau Windhaven sat on.

"Miss me?" she asked as she got within hearing range. She threw a leg over her horse and slid off, passing the reins to a waiting groom with a wink.

My stomach hollowed out, trying to find the words to tell her how I had failed them yet again.

"Gwen is coming through with Vinkirk," she carried on, her cheeks flushed. "We met them coming in, along with the stragglers of Nairn, and she is leading them through. They all answered, every one of them has come." Her eyes shuttered slightly as she glanced toward the wall. "No sign of The Pendragon yet?"

I shook my head. "Not yet. I have lookouts posted on the wall."

She cocked her head slightly, a small frown creasing her brows. "What aren't you telling me?" her eyes drifted back to the wall, falling on the men I had stationed along its top. "Why have you posted them? Where is Tadgh?"

I braced myself. "Come inside. I need to fill you in on everything that has happened, and I need Gwen to be part of this."

Saoirse's eyes snapped back to mine, alarm flaring on her face. "Tell me right now, Morgana."

At my moment of hesitation, she grabbed my arm. "What the fuck has happened?"

I swallowed the guilt that was threatening to choke me. "I tried to stop him. He's taken men past the wall."

"What? When?" her eyes snapped back to the gates as if she were about to go after him.

"Yesterday morning," I said, hearing the defeat in my voice.

"To scout? Gods, why would he go himself?" Saoirse asked, her voice rising.

I shook my head. "Not to scout. He's leading a group of men to assassinate The Pendragon before he reaches the wall."

Saoirse dropped my arm, her own falling limply at her side as she stepped back, her face draining of color. She stared at me for a moment, looking as if she were struggling to breathe.

"And you let him?" she whispered finally.

My heart broke at the betrayal that crept across her face.

"You just let my brother walk out of those gates to his death? How *could* you?"

28

MERLIN

War changes you. Sometimes it is glaringly obvious, other times it is subtle. There has always been a side to Arthur that terrified me. Combined with the power that he has flowing in his veins, it is the shackle that I have worn for a century now. I do not fear for myself. I fear for what he could be, what he could do if unchecked.

It would have been so easy to turn my back on Kambria and leave it to implode. Maybe if I hadn't been here to undermine Arthur at every turn, his reign would have spread faster, become more destructive, and the Sylvyn that dwell in other lands would have taken notice. Maybe they would have risen to face him. It's a war I'm not sure he would have won, and maybe in my attempt to right my wrong, I have just made everything worse.

Maybe.

I am no seer. All I do know is that with every passing year, I begin to question whether I have sunk too far into the grey area of necessity to be redeemed, and the promises of what could have been now sit heavier on my shoulders.

Arthur's true power is something I cannot comprehend. I don't even know if *he* knows. It's as if he is reluctant to explore its limits, and for that I am grateful, but desperation, desire... I fear it could push him to unlock something within that would be unstoppable. War could change him into something I cannot control, and I am beginning to see glimmers of it already.

The frozen ground has melted from the heat of the fires where we camp alongside The Spine, turning the ground to mud. Arthur has slowly become quieter the closer we have gotten to Windhaven, which is never a good thing.

Bawdy laughter drags my attention to a group of men reclining by one of the fires, Arthur at the center, picking meat off a boar carcass that had been spit-roasted over the flames. Some of the men were flirting with a young woman who was moving through them, topping up mugs of ale from a barrel that was sitting off to the side, and valiantly slapping away groping hands and ignoring lewd comments.

I shook my head in disgust, leaning back against the boulder I was sitting by and pulled the deep hood of my cloak higher.

Sirin, nestled against the crook of my neck, grumbled under her breath as the cloak pulled tight around her as well, her cold foot flexing against my skin where it had slipped under the neck of my tunic.

"You can go and sleep in a tree if you are going to whine," I murmured.

She muttered something less than complimentary back, shifting her small body until she was comfortable again.

There was a yelp, drawing my attention back to see the young woman sprawled face-down on the ground, her jug rolling along the ground in front of her and the contents splashed over the ground and—I groaned—halfway up Arthur's leg.

"I'm s-sorry, my King," the woman stammered, ripping off the apron that was tied around her waist and lunging to mop at him.

I watched, on edge as Arthur's lip curled in a salacious smile, eyeing her.

"Accidents happen," he murmured.

Accidents. I could see the soldier who had tripped her smirking, his foot still jutting out unapologetically, and my ire rose.

The woman was frantically trying to clean the ale from Arthur's clothing, hesitating as she reached his thigh, her gaze flicking to him.

"All of it," Arthur said quietly, his tone changing.

She dropped her head and made quick work of the rest, before making to rise and pulling up short as Arthur put a hand on her shoulder and shoved her back down.

"I said all of it."

Her eyes dropped to his leg in confusion. "I did, my King."

Arthur's lip twitched in disdain as he lifted his booted foot with splatters of ale amongst the mud. "You expect your King to lead an army covered in ale, girl?"

"N-no," she replied quickly, reaching to mop at it.

"Not with that," Arthur said, and she froze, her whole body beginning to shake. With the intensity of his gaze and the terror on her face, I could tell he was speaking directly into her mind.

I was grateful he did not use that particular gift often. It wasn't a two-way door, thankfully, or my life would have been forfeit decades ago, but it only took one look at the woman's face to remember what it was like to feel him slip into your mind. It felt like a violation.

I watched the silent, one-way conversation and saw the woman blanch then lean down toward the offending boot, the tip of her pink tongue slipping out.

"Arthur," I said, forcing my voice into a jesting tone.

Arthur looked at me, raising a brow. "Merlin?"

"I have a mind to take that one to my bed later," I drawled, ignoring the helpless look she threw toward another woman who was watching on. "I would much rather her mouth wasn't filled with mud."

Arthur snorted, and I realized then that he was slightly drunk as he gave the girl a shove that sent her tumbling backward on the muddy ground.

"All yours. Clumsy thing isn't going to be good for much though."

"Good enough to keep my bed warmer than it was last night," I chortled, feeling my skin crawl at my own words.

Fuck.

"Go," I ordered, snapping my fingers at her and grinning at some of the men who jeered at her reluctantly departing form, silently praying none of the other women would find themselves on Arthur's bad side tonight.

I stayed by the fire until it had died down to embers and Arthur had stumbled to his own tent, my thoughts running wild with what would happen once we reached Windhaven. It was Sirin who eventually dragged me out of my musing, her sleepy mumble as she stroked her beak down the side of my face making me huff in amusement, and I stood, groaning as I stretched out my back.

It was as I turned to go to my tent that felt a prickle up my spine, making me pause, my eyes searching the darkness beyond the camp. I threw a net of my power out when I couldn't find any movement in the gloom, forcing it to pierce the darkness with no little effort, feeling for what could have made me so uneasy suddenly. But I felt nothing, nor could I hear anything, my ears straining for any noise separate from the sounds of a sleeping camp.

Sirin murmured softly on my shoulder, but her little body was relaxed against my neck, and I began to relax again too, turning back toward my tent with one last, long look into the darkness.

The woman was on her side on my bed as I pushed into my tent, though from how still she was, I could tell she was awake. Setting Sirin down on the back of a chair off to the side, I sighed, my eyes lingering wistfully on the bed before I stooped and grabbed an unused blanket and spread it out on the floor. A quick rummage through my packs found another cloak, which I wrapped around my body before resigning myself to the makeshift bed on the floor and closed my eyes.

There was a rustle of blankets and the woman's breathing took up a staccato rhythm in the silence.

"I am not going to touch you," I said quietly into the stillness. "Though for both of our sakes, in the morning I would strongly advise acting like I am the monster everyone believes me to be."

There was a long silence, and I wondered for a moment if I had been mistaken and she was asleep after all, until her reply came, so quiet I almost missed it.

"Thank you."

29

MORGANA

"I will go after him and bring him back," Saoirse said, her voice rough from all the yelling she had just been doing, most of it directed at me.

Gwen threw an exhausted look at her sister. "I'm not risking your life too."

"He's our brother, Gwen!" Saoirse said, her tone rising.

"And he made his decision," Gwen retorted, meeting Saoirse glare for glare. "As much as it kills me that he is out there, I cannot justify sending any more lives on a fool's errand."

"He should have returned by now," Saoirse pushed.

"What would you have me do, Saoirse?" Gwen snapped. It was the first time I had seen her crack under the stress. "None of us can get close enough to do anything to help without The Pendragon sensing us. Sending ungifted could draw attention to the men already out there and get them all killed. Tadgh has put us in an impossible position—he has tied our hands. Not even Morgana can get within a mile of that camp without them hunting her down. You know what happens if any gifted is caught by them, let alone a Child of Nimmet."

Saoirse's mouth thinned into a hard line, but she said nothing.

I gripped the back of the chair I had been leaning on, nails digging into the wood as power surged in my veins, getting stronger every moment. I was struggling to hold it at bay, whisps of shadow flickering across my fingers in the moments I took my attention from it, and the rage that was gathering in my core was making it harder. Rage at myself, rage at Tadgh, rage at the fucking treacherous prick that called himself the King's hand. If he hid not stand with The Pendragon, we may have had a chance.

I felt Gwen's gaze on me and opened my eyes to meet hers.

"I'm sorry," I said. It was all I had for her at this moment, though I did not expect her forgiveness.

She looked away from me, so I couldn't see the reproach I knew would be in her eyes. "It is done, we need to focus on our defense."

"Lady Gwen?" Frog appeared in the doorway. "I have a Faolán requesting to be seen."

"Send him in," Gwen said, sounding as if the weight of the world were on her shoulders.

She had barely gotten the words out before Faolán entered, ducking his head through the doorway. He looked even larger here without the high, arched ceilings of the school. He nodded a greeting to me before turning to Gwen.

"Vinkirk, The Hollow and Nairn are in position. I followed the direction Morgana had already implemented; it seems to have been working well."

Gwen glanced at me, her brows raised. "I'm sorry, I haven't had a chance to catch up on those details yet."

"I placed our strongest gifted at the wall, archers with

them. Weaker fire Elementyls to the camp to ensure fires stay lit through the night. Inexperienced soldiers are helping to fletch arrows and gather whatever armor we can source."

I held my hand out for the book Frog clutched as he hovered in the doorway. "And there are now updated records of what our numbers are… and who we still have coming in from the Lowlands."

Faolán whistled softly, raising a dark brow. "Not bad, Morgana."

Gwen took the book, glancing over the numbers. "Tadgh had these numbers taken?"

"No." It was Frog that spoke up. "The numbers haven't been properly recorded since your father was in command, my Lady. This was the Lady Morgana. This was all her."

I blinked at him, and he ducked his head at me.

Gwen swallowed hard. "Thank you," she said to me, her voice thick.

There was an angry grunt, and I looked up in time to see Saoirse stalking from the room. I went to follow her, but Gwen stopped me with a raised hand.

"You following her right now is only going to result in you both hurting each other unnecessarily," she said quietly. "Let her work her temper out in the sparring ring."

"She can take it out on me," Faolán said, throwing us a wink. "It's been a while since I brushed off the old sword." He turned on his heel, disappearing in the direction Saoirse had vanished.

Gwen turned her attention on the rest of the room, running through orders with a quiet authority. You could almost see the calm energy that exuded from her as it flowed into the people she addressed, confidant in their trust of her.

A maid arrived with a steaming pot of tea as the last of the others swept from the room, and I took it from her with a murmur of thanks and tucked the two mugs under my arm.

I turned to see Gwen staring out of the window, her body drawn as tense as a bowstring. "Have you eaten anything today?" I asked gently. "Or yesterday?"

She didn't answer me.

I silently poured a cup of the tea, the scent of chamomile and mint drifting up to me on the scented steam. Rounding on her, I ran a cautious hand down her arm, noticing how cool her skin felt under my touch. "Please drink this," I murmured, lifting her hand and cupping it around the warm, pewter rim, trying to lend her its heat.

Her hand was trembling slightly in mine, and I squeezed it carefully. "Gwen?"

She made a small, distressed sound, her breath catching in a near silent sob as she swayed suddenly, as if whatever force had been keeping her together had suddenly fallen away.

The cup slipped between her hands, and I barely caught it before it slipped to the floor, setting it on the table before I grasped her face gently in my hands, making her look at me.

"Gwen, talk to me."

"I can't do this," she whispered, and the look of ravaged pain in her eyes nearly sent me to my knees. "My brother is out there, and I have to act like I'm ok."

I didn't know what to say, feeling as if a rock had settled against my chest, crushing me in guilt.

"I'm so sorry, this is all my fault," I choked out, my voice cracking.

She shook her head, pulling out of my grip. "I know what he is like. When his mind is made there is no stopping him." She frowned, her breath becoming short as pushed a hand to her chest. "They are all relying on me, Morgana. If I were to go after him, I would need to send our strongest gifted to even stand a chance. I would need to send you—" she broke off with a jerky shake of her head, pacing to the window to look out, bracing herself against the stone sill, her fingers white with the force of her grip. "He's made me choose between him and our people, and I can't choose him, no matter how much I want to." Those last words came out as merely a whisper, laced with an agony so thick that I could almost feel it myself as her words hung in the air between us. She hung her head, a sob breaking from her.

I crossed the room, unable to bear the sight of her standing there alone. I didn't say anything, just grasped her arm, pulling her around to face me until I could enfold her in my arms as she broke.

Sobs wracked her body, her hands wrapping into the fabric of my dress as she clung to me. I desperately wanted to say something… anything to take some of this burden from her, but I was at a loss. Stroking her hair gently, I murmured nonsensical nothings to her as she wept.

I heard footsteps approaching down the hall and Gwen stiffened, pulling back as she wiped at her face and took great, gulping breaths of air.

A wave of my hand had the door slamming closed, the bolts snapping across to seal us off from everyone.

Gwen was still breathing hard, her face pale and blotched and her hand pressed against the base of her throat.

"Let—let them in. What i—if they—" she broke off with a gasp, panting heavily as another sob wracked through her, her body bending as she began to spiral into the rising panic.

"They can survive on their own for a moment," I said, grasping her hands and pulling her upright. "Gwen, look at me."

She had her eyes closed, her breath becoming more and

more erratic, and I grasped her chin with my free hand. "Look at me, Princess."

She opened her eyes, the faintest echo of a spark shining from deep in the pit of despair she was drowning in.

"Take a moment, it's ok," I murmured.

"I can't breathe," she gasped, and I could feel her pulse racing under my fingers where they brushed her neck. Her hollow eyes went over my shoulder to the window.

She was moaning softly with each tortured breath, and I could see her eyes beginning to glaze.

"You are letting the panic take over." I tightened my grip on her chin, forcing her to look at me again. "I need you to slow your breathing, Gwen."

I lost her to the window again, and I swore softly under my breath as she began to crumble. I closed my own eyes, feeling for the flickering mass of power within me and gripped it, throwing it out like a net through the room. It was barely a wisp of what I held inside me, but I felt Gwen stiffen in my grasp and opened my eyes to utter darkness.

Half a thought had a black flame flicker to life above us, bathing Gwen in a dim light, just enough that I could see her wide, panic filled eyes.

"It's just you and me," I soothed, letting go of her face to run my hands down her arms, capturing her fingers in my own and twining them together.

"Just you and me," I repeated, as her eyes locked onto mine, her breathing slowing. "Not the Lady of Windhaven and Child of Nimmet. Just Gwen and Morgana, and we can be just that, right now, for as long as you need, okay?"

Her fingers twitched against mine, her breathing slowing slightly.

"They are all looking to me," she said, her voice strained. "And I am breaking."

"They are looking to you, because you are worthy, Gwen" I said gently, my thumb stroking her fingers. "You are their strength, and I will be yours. I will find you in the dark and stay with you while you break, and then I will piece you back together, do you hear me?"

Her hand curled around mine, squeezing. "Yes." She untwined our hands, stepping forward into my arms again, and I held her as she calmed, feeling her heart slow until it matched the rhythm of mine again. I don't know how long we stood there, in our small patch of flickering light, surrounded by a blanket of inky power, until Gwen sighed softly, straightening.

"I'm ready," she murmured.

Light seeped back in as my power dispersed like mist on a breeze, night turning to day in an instant.

Gwen blinked, her eyes adjusting. She was pale, and looked slightly ruffled, but a few passes of her fingers through her hair and a cloth soaked in cool chamomile tea quickly fixed that. It was like watching a soldier don armor as she straightened herself and checked her appearance over in a small mirror before nodding to me.

I passed a subtle eye over her one last time before waving my hand at the door, the bolt sliding back with a rasp, followed by the creak of the door swinging open.

Moments later three men filed in, looking cautiously at me, before their eyes fell to Gwen, now sitting at the desk, her eyes scanning a pile of papers. She looked up, beckoning them to enter.

"How can I help, gentlemen?"

I stayed as close as I could to Gwen for the rest of the day, without it being obvious, but she remained outwardly as solid as she had been before. She seemed to ease the tension that was building slowly in the air as the day stretched on, as if she took the burdens of others eased their worries. It worried me, knowing how badly she was hurting, but only once did I see her eyes go to the window and linger there.

Dusk was beginning to descend as Gwen and I made our way back to the castle, catching sight of Faolán supervising a group of men who were weaving nets together that could be thrown from the walls. I didn't want to think about what it would mean if it came to that, and Tadgh still hadn't returned. It was a heaviness that was weighing down my heart with each moment the sun inched across the sky.

I subtly slipped away as Gwen was talking to a group of women, sidling up to Faolán.

He flashed me his normal, wide smile. "Morgana."

"Where is Saoirse?" I asked, too tired to bother with small talk.

"Last I saw, she was beating the shit out of one of the sparring dummies," he said, frowning at a knot he had just made in a mess of ropes. He handed me a coil of it, gesturing to hold it between my hands as he unraveled another section, taking the knot in his white teeth to work it loose.

"Have you seen Rian?" I pushed. "He will know where she is."

"I don't think talking to her is the best option right now, not until she has calmed down and is seeing things with a clear head," he mouthed around the rope, tugging it sharply and grunting with satisfaction as it came loose, the two pieces in either hand. He deftly retied it in the right spot before taking the coil from me. "You know what her temper is like, she will say things she doesn't mean… things that are not deserved."

He pinned me with a frank look. "And then she will feel even worse than she already does."

I clenched my jaw, nodding before turning to walk away.

"Morgana."

I looked over my shoulder, brow raised in question.

"It's him she's angry at. You just happen to be the only one she can take it out on. She knows the weight on Guinevere right now, and how close she is to breaking. They say you show your feelings to the people you feel the safest with. She will come around."

I took a moment to let his words sink in, hating that they made a small fraction of the weight on my heart lift. "Thank you," I said reluctantly.

He grinned again. "That almost sounded sincere."

I rolled my eyes as I walked away, catching up to Gwen as she made her way back to the castle. "You are coming to my room and taking a bath while I get you something to eat," I murmured as I reached her, running my hand across the small of her back. She opened her mouth as if to argue and I cut her off with a glare. "Don't even try arguing, you will not win."

30

MORGANA

A desperate murmuring in my ear woke me as the first glimmer of dawn began to creep through my window. It had been a long night, Gwen tossing and turning next to me in a fitful sleep as nightmares had plagued her.

My heart instantly kicked into a staccato beat as I struggled from the fog of sleep, straining to hear what the shadows were warning me about, and loathe to wake Gwen from a moment of peace. She was curled against my side, her hands clasping one of mine to her naked chest as her breath warmed my shoulder.

Sundered threads weave a path, wake now, a ghrà mo chroì.

I frowned into the dim room, wishing I could reach out and throttle the shadows and their cryptic whispers.

One of their inky threads curled through the air, having escaped from my grasp while I slept, and I raised a finger to it, coaxing it back to me and watched as it rested against my finger, wrapping itself around me like a cat before melting back into my skin. And then came the noise that turned my blood to ice. Horns.

It felt like the air had suddenly been ripped from my lungs, and beside me, Gwen had gone still as death. Horns could only mean one thing. The Pendragon had arrived. If Tadgh was still in The Spine, he was cut off from getting back to us.

"No." Gwen's whispered words were an echo of what was currently screaming in my head, both of us lurching out of bed at the same time, Gwen dragging discarded clothing on while I went to the window and peered out across the murky landscape, straining to see. It was so tempting to cast a net of my power across the land, feeling ahead for what my eyes couldn't yet see, but The Pendragon would know what it was instantly.

I spun as the door creaked open, in time to see Gwen bolting through it, and paused only long enough to grab a robe to throw around my shoulders before hurrying after her.

Soldiers met us halfway to Tadgh's office, their faces grim.

"The army has been sighted," one man said, a dull metal helmet in his hands. "Runners from the wall said they must have come in and camped during the night. They are still a good half day away and don't appear to be moving yet."

Gwen nodded somberly. "No sign of Tadgh and his men?"

"No Milady," he said, looking nervously at me. "Though there is a chance he could have come down The Spine on the Kinconnal side and is skirting the coast to come back."

Gwen was silent for a moment, appearing to think. Even dressed in rumpled clothing, her hair loose around her shoulders, she commanded the respect of these men. They watched her in silence, waiting with bated breath for her command.

"We need to proceed as if Tadgh is not returning before The Pendragon reaches us," she said after a moments pause, only the slightest hint of strain in her voice. "Gather my captains together, I need to speak to them immediately. Have the healers brought into the castle and order the kitchens to serve meals in the morning, rather than night. I want every soldier and gifted at full strength should we need them. And send out all the rooks—let our people know The Pendragon has reached us and we are officially at war."

The soldier who had addressed her bowed deeply before shoving his helmet on his head and striding out.

"Where is Saoirse?" Gwen asked, frowning at Rian who had just appeared, bleary-eyed in the doorway.

He frowned back at her. "I've come from her room, she left last night to get dinner and speak to you and never returned. I assumed she stayed with you?"

A cold knot of dread formed in my stomach, and I snapped my fingers at a young woman who had been lighting the candles in the room.

"You, go to Lady Gwen's rooms and see if Lady Saoirse is there."

Gwen looked at me, her face devoid of color. "You don't think she—"

"She may have just needed some time to herself, she would have known your rooms would be empty." I didn't care about the curious looks we were now getting.

"She would be here," Gwen said quietly. "You know she would."

Rian made a choked sound, turning desperate eyes to Gwen. "Tell me you don't think she went after Tadgh."

Gwen cleared her throat, ignoring the question and looking as if she were struggling to stand upright as she addressed one of the men standing at attention by the door. "Send for Faolán, he is in the barracks with the soldiers."

"What are you going to do?" Rian asked.

"I'm going to prepare my people for war, Rian," Gwen said, her voice shaking. "I don't have the luxury of being able to lose my mind." She turned to me, her eyes saying more to me than her words could.

"I will find her," I promised, reading everything I needed to in that desperate look. I had only made it to the end of the first corridor when the young woman I had sent to Gwen's rooms hurtled around a corner, crashing into me. We both teetered for a moment, off balance, before I grabbed her upper arms, setting her on her feet, and saw the scroll she clutched in her hand.

She thrust it under my nose before I had a chance to ask for it. "It was on the Lady Gwen's bed, Milady," she said nervously. "It's in the Lady Saoirse's hand."

I felt like a hand of ice had hit my heart as I ripped off the scrap of leather that bound it, my eyes frantically scanning the small, neat words.

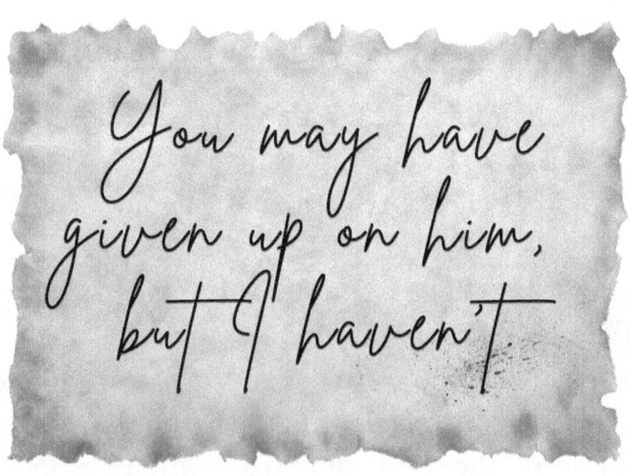

"Fuck." I read that handful of words over and over again,

but each time I did, the crack that formed in my chest grew larger.

She had gone beyond the wall, and this was going to break Gwen.

The walk back was the hardest walk of my life. My head was utterly silent as I pushed past the milling people who had gathered, the noise in the room rising to a dull hum as voices rose and fell.

Gwen's eyes locked onto mine the second I entered the room, her whole body going stiff before her gaze fell to the note in my hand.

She didn't even reach for it, just waited until I had reached her before she whispered, "She's gone after him."

I nodded, seeing her eyes shutter, a slight catch in her breath. Outside, she kept her calm composure, but I could feel her soul screaming. The howl of a broken heart, hidden under the armor of a Queen.

"Let me go for her," I murmured, low enough that only she could hear. "Let me go for both of them."

"You can't," she said, and there were broken things in her voice. "Without you, the wall..." she trailed off, shaking herself slightly.

She turned to address the room. "You all have your orders. Take a moment if you need it to prepare yourself, and then to your posts. The Pendragon is at our gates, lets show him why he should have stayed away."

There was a flurry of movement that I lost her in momentarily, only when the room cleared slightly did I see her leaning close to Rian, talking to him as his face dropped into pained lines.

Faolán appeared at my side, silent for all of his size. His touch on my elbow startled me and I peered up into concerned eyes.

"You are both needed at the wall. The Pendragon's forces are on the move."

I subconsciously reached inwards, running a mental hand across the well of power simmering inside me, checking it was still there, that it was enough for what was to come.

I cleared my throat, drawing back his attention that had strayed to Gwen. "I need you to make me a promise," I said quietly. "I know you owe me nothing, and you don't have to like me, but I need you to do this."

He cocked his head, waiting for me to continue.

"If the wall falls. If anything happens that means I am not able to protect her. I need you to protect her from herself."

His eyes slid to Gwen again as I continued, my head turned slightly so he could hear my words that were barely a whisper.

"Saoirse has gone beyond the wall after Tadgh. If I—" my voice faltered, and I had to clear my throat again. "If I am not here either—she puts the Lowlands before herself every time. She needs someone left in the world that will put her needs first."

His nod was subtle, but it was all the confirmation I needed, lifting a weight from my shoulders I hadn't realized had been crushing me.

We left in silence, all of us deep in our own thoughts. Gwen left me at the door of my rooms to change out of her sleep-rumpled clothes while I quickly did the same. I pulled on the soft, tan pants I had become accustomed to riding in so I could move freely, along with a thick tunic that would protect me from the bitter winds that lashed the wall, before hurriedly heading to join Faolán and Rian who were waiting in the courtyard.

The atmosphere was bleak outside the castle, an eerie

silence spreading across the landscape as everyone seemed to hold their breath.

Gwen caught up to us as we reached one of the many steps that climbed the wall, and it was as we crested the top of them that I got my first, clear view of The Pendragon's legions.

"One of our gifted can take down fifty of their soldiers," Rian muttered as we all stared out at the army that doggedly approached.

"Maybe," Faolán said, his eyes sweeping across them. "But they outnumber us a hundred to one."

"I don't want to hear that talk," Gwen said, her eyes not looking to the army, but to the edge of The Spine that stretched off to the left of it. "Where the fuck are they?" she murmured.

We remained on the wall, keeping out of the way of a convoy of men and women bringing up basket upon basket of arrows as archers took their places along the turrets, their gazes fixed to the oncoming threat inching toward us. They were close enough for us to make out the outlines of the soldiers, their armor glinting in the sun that was doing nothing to warm the cold air around us.

The sun had reached its peak when I rested both my hands on the cool stone of the wall, feeling the hum of the power within it and looked out over the army that had come to a halt in front of us. A rippling wave of men that stretched across the desolate landscape in front of the wall.

Faolán stood to my left, an unwavering, steady presence. Gwen to my right, a bow slung loosely over her shoulder as she surveyed the lines of soldiers with a stony expression.

Every nerve ending was firing within me, waiting for the first strike, not knowing what to expect. Half of my concentration was fixed on what lay in front of me, the other half was murmuring to the wall, coaxing it out of its slumber. I felt age-old power awaken in it at the threat that gathered at its feet, tendrils of power reaching to brush against mine in a silent greeting that snapped and bit at me like small electric shocks.

At our back, our people waited. Sylvyn ready to put their lives on the line to defend their families should The Pendragon breach our defenses. Gwen moved suddenly, striding past us to brace herself on the low edge of the wall on our side, looking down at the solemn masses.

"My people!" she called suddenly, her voice carrying across and echoing down the valley, funneled on the harsh wind that whipped at us. "I have always belonged to the Lowlands. You have taken me in as one of your own, shaped who I am. You are my friends, my peers, and my family." She raised her chin, defiant to the danger at her back. "I may not be the leader you deserve, but I swear to you I will do everything in my power to see you through this. We are so much more than what has become of us, and we are going to show The Pendragon that he can hunt us, he can take our land and make us bleed, but he will not break us!"

There was a roar as our people raised their weapons in salute.

"The Pendragon can come and knock on our doors," Gwen yelled. "Let's show him that these are your lands, and he is not welcome here!"

An even louder roar echoed through the valley, moving like a wave down into the distance as her words were passed down.

Gwen unslung her bow, snatching up an arrow from one of the baskets as she passed before jumping nimbly onto the wide edge of the other wall. Faolán jerked, as if he were about to grab for her, but stopped as he saw the tendrils of black power I had thrown out to wrap around her waist, holding her secure.

She glared down at the rows of soldiers forming neat lines. "Archers!" she yelled, and there was a rippled line of movement down the wall, as archers moved into the gaps in the stone along the walls ridge, taking aim. I saw Gwen close her eyes from my vantage point to her side, and moments later her arrow burst into flame and passed from archer to archer in a wall of fire that spread all the way from mountain ridge to mountain ridge. Gwen opened her eyes and fired, her arrow flying swift and true. It arced through the air, followed by a hundred others, all burning fiercely, to embed themselves in the frozen ground in front of the soldiers. A burning line. Gwen's warning to them that we were not going to be taken without a fight.

Our enemy faltered, a few of The Pendragon's legions stepping backward and out of formation as the burning arrows lodged into the ground mere feet from them.

It was then I felt the first brush of power on the wall, as if a hand touched its surface, questioning what lay beneath.

"The Traitor is here," I hissed, laying both of my hands flat on the stone and sending a wave of my power to stalk his like a wolf watching from the shadows. I felt it retreat and then surge forward again, trying to find a weak point, and I was there every time, snapping at it.

I closed my eyes to concentrate on what was an invisible war of wills. On my side, ancient stored power, guided by my own raw magic. On his side, decades of honed skill.

It changed suddenly, the small jabs and exploratory pushes suddenly became a blanket that shimmered in my mind's eye, smothering the face of the wall. I barely had time to question it before I was rocked by the force of an attack that hit directly over the gates below. This bite was different, a stinging blow like a sword slicing across its surface, and I gasped, opening myself a little more to the well of power in the wall and feeding it with my own.

"Morgana?" I heard Gwen's worried question from just above me and threw her a quick look.

"The Pendragon has arrived."

Another two attacks came one after the other, spearing for the same spot as the first, both deflected harmlessly away, followed by more querying pushes from The Traitor.

Movement from below pulled my attention to a knot of soldiers who moved forward bearing the trunk of a thick tree as a battering ram between them, headed for the gates.

Faolán barked an order and arrows flew for them, dropping the front men as soon as they were within range of our archers. They were hauled out of the way only to be replaced with others that kept on coming.

"Fire!" Faolán roared again, and this time, the arrows flew only to be burned out of the air above the incoming battering ram, others lodging into the ground harmlessly around them.

And then I saw *him*. The Blood Traitor. He stood slightly in front of the soldiers, appearing as if out of thin air, his focus not even on the men he guarded, but upwards. His eyes raked the lines of our archers, searching.

Searching for me, I realized, as I felt another questioning nudge. I pushed back, and when my gaze returned to him, our eyes met for a moment. It was a split second, the same as when we had last locked eyes so many years ago, but it hit me like a physical blow, a jolt of energy that crackled down my spine. I couldn't look away from him, hatred simmering in my veins, and it took every shred of my willpower not to shadow walk the small distance between us and throw every last piece of myself into his destruction.

"Our archers can't get through that shield," Rian called,

drawing my attention away as a third volley of arrows burned away to nothing.

"I can take it down," I hissed, removing one of my hands from the wall, raw energy already gathering at my blackened fingertips, begging to be unleashed on The Traitor.

"No." Gwen's fingers gripped mine, pulling my hand down behind the protection of the wall. "You do that, he will know exactly what you are. A ram won't get through the wall anyway, he is trying to draw a response from u—" she cut off mid-sentence, her eyes fixing and locking on a point in the middle of the lines of soldiers.

My eyes followed her line of sight down as a voice carried up to us.

"Lady O'Mordha, I will accept your surrender at any time."

Gwen bared her teeth, her eyes flashing as she glared at Arthur Pendragon. The man who had taken everything from us. She didn't answer him, just notched another arrow, looking down the shaft at him with pure contempt before letting it fly. It would have been an arrow to the heart had it made it to him, the distance further than any our archers had let fly, but it too burned to ash in the air before it came close to him.

He cocked his head, and suddenly his voice was in my head, speaking as if he were standing in front of us. "That was rude."

From how everyone suddenly stilled around us, I knew they had also heard.

"You have my answer," Gwen spat at him, her face pale as she notched another arrow. "I will not open my gates."

"Your brother said that too." His deep voice echoed in my mind, though fainter this time, as if it were an effort to keep the connection open. "Right before I took his head."

The world went still around me, an odd ringing starting in

my ears, my head snapping away from where I had been watching The Traitor, to The Pendragon.

The battering ram hit the gates with a dull boom, barely a speck against its solid shield.

"What?" I said, my voice sounding distant.

The battering ram hit again, but this time it came with another blow of energy, blunt force and magic hitting the gates together, ripping my attention back, my mind swirling in a riot as I slammed my hand down on the wall and speared dark energy toward the gates that had shuddered with the blow.

"You lie!" It was Faolán's voice that rang out this time, and I spared a brief glance to see he had hold of Gwen by the arm, bracing her. She was frozen in place, looking as if every last drop of blood had seeped from her body.

"I am many things, but a liar is not one of them," The Pendragon retorted.

And then Gwen began screaming. A sound so full of anger and grief, so broken that it will remain etched into my memories until the day I depart this world.

I wrenched my eyes back to The Pendragon and the world stood still.

He held an empty sack in one hand, the brown fabric loose in his hands, the bottom half of it stained brown. In his other hand, his fingers wrapped in blonde locks I knew so well, was Tadgh's head, eyes still open and staring at us.

31

MORGANA

I must have made some sort of sound as Rian was suddenly there, hands clasping my upper arms and holding me back as I lurched toward a gap, as if he were worried I would throw myself from the wall.

I didn't care. I could see nothing but the horror of what was in front of me, my eyes fixed on what had been the Lord of Windhaven.

"No," I choked, grief spearing into my heart like a physical blow. Dark, crackling energy gathered in my fingers along with a black rage as I saw Gwen buckle against Faolán, only his arm holding her upright. I reached down deep, gathering myself, brushing a hand across that deeper well that terrified me. The darkness that Madraigh had warned me to stay away from.

I drew back, ready to unleash everything I had. To rend and tear. To rip the life away from The Pendragon's unworthy body and take his soul to the depths of Ankii's underworld if that's what it took.

"No!" Rian suddenly had my wrist in his grip, panic in his

voice as he shook it, trying to get my attention. "Morgana, no! You will kill Saoirse too! He has Saoirse!"

Through the black fog that had taken over my mind, I slowly registered his words, rage turning to terror as I saw where he was pointing. To the man who dragged a small figure forward and thrust her into The Pendragon's grip. His hand closed around the back of her neck, and he pushed her forward, leaning close to whisper something in her ear that made her thrash and buck against him.

He shook her, and I could hear her small cry of distress as he thrust Tadgh's head into her arms.

She didn't look down, but her arms came around him, cradling her brother to her chest as if she could keep him safe.

"Lower your arrows." The cracked, broken order came from Gwen as she seemed to drag herself back under some sort of control. She was shaking from head to foot, her eyes fixed on her sister.

Below, another blow came from the battering ram, along with another spear of power, but I was too focused on Saoirse, too lost in agony to care. Even from here I could see her injuries, the way she was bent slightly, arm pressed against her side. Blood was smeared across her and her clothes were ripped in a dozen places.

Another wave of The Pendragon's arm brought forward more figures. Tadgh's men, their arms chained behind them. There were a cluster of them being shoved through the men, unflinching as they were jeered at and spat on, their heads held high.

He motioned for one to be brought forward, a young soldier I recognized. He was forced to his knees, facing Saoirse, and I saw her lips move as she murmured something to him, his nod back to her.

I jerked, as in one clean movement The Pendragon

unsheathed his sword and drew it across the man's neck, his body falling to the side.

Saoirse cried out, blood splattering her face as the man fell, and she lurched, arm out as if she would catch him, only to be pulled up short.

"Either you open your gates, or I slaughter every one of your men here," The Pendragon's voice echoed in my mind again, as he tilted his head to look up at us. "And when I run out of men to kill, I will give your sister to my men, and you can watch as they defile her." He wrapped his free arm around Saoirse, grasping her breast through her torn tunic. "She's a strong one. Took down far too many of my men before I had her in hand, which means we should be in for hours of entertainment at least. My men will be *very* happy."

"Get your fucking hands off her!" Rian roared, only to be pulled back by two of our men, struggling and yelling words that were lost to me through the dull pulsing in my head.

Gwen's tortured gaze fell on me, and it was if it sliced a blade through the fog that I had been lost in. Noise came rushing back in, my senses beginning to fire again as my head focused into sharp clarity and I covered the distance between us, taking the hand that was hovering in the air between us... reaching for me.

"Open the fucking gates, Gwen. Let me out there," Rian snarled from where he was struggling against the hands that restrained him.

Gwen made a small sound of distress, her fingers clutching mine so hard the bones creaked, as if she were drawing whatever strength from them that she could.

Boom.

I winced this time as the ram hit the gates again, the ground shuddering with the blast that accompanied it, feeling the foreign power ripple along the outside of the wall.

"An O'Mordha must always be behind the wall," she breathed. "Morgana… I …"

I felt my lip quiver as Saoirse's voice drifted up to us.

"Don't you fucking *dare* open those ga—" she cut off and Faolán snarled from his post.

Refusing to hide from the horror of what was unfolding, I looked to see Saoirse doubled over, one hand pushed to her stomach as a soldier stepped back, shaking his fist out.

"I've seen children throw stronger hits than that," Saoirse taunted, her voice weak and thready as she straightened again, still clutching Tadgh.

She screamed suddenly, her head thrown back and body arched, Tadgh's head falling from her stiffened arms with a sickening thud as she reached back, fingers clawing where The Pendragon still gripped the back of her neck.

"Stop!" Gwen screamed, running to the edge of the wall.

Still Saoirse screamed, writhing in his grip as his power ripped through her mind.

"Stop!" Gwen screamed again, and this time she threw her hands out, a ball of flame erupting from her. It speared toward The Pendragon, Saoirse going limp and falling to a knee as his attention was taken from her long enough to wave a hand, the flames hissing out before the heat even disturbed the air around him.

"Last chance," he called, hauling Saoirse to her feet again.

She reached for Tadgh, straining to get to him, but was yanked upright and pushed roughly toward three soldiers. The one who was stupid enough to make a grab for her first met with her fist, dropping like a stone as she landed a solid blow to his temple, the other two having to leap on her together to restrain her. She fought them, cursing and biting at them as her arms were wrenched behind her back.

"Fuck you, you ignorant son of a whore!" she screamed at

The Pendragon. "The Sylvyn should have buried you years ago like the worthless piece of shit you are. You are not worthy of a crown."

"Saoirse," Gwen moaned, desperation in her voice. "What are you doing?"

I watched with dread as he stepped toward Saoirse menacingly, only to stop as The Blood Traitor appeared at his side, a hand on his chest as he leaned in to say something to his King.

"She's trying to get him to kill her…" I said, the words like a frozen shard of ice in my throat. My eyes searched for any stretch of shadow, wishing the sun to disappear and give me the chance to shadow walk. Anything that could get me down there fast enough to grab her.

Boom.

This time no spear of power came with it, the blow barely registering.

"End it, Morgana!" Saoirse screamed, lashing out with her foot at a man who was trying to advance on her. He slapped her, and her head snapped to the side.

My throat caved in as I stared at Gwen, knowing what Saoirse was asking. Knowing why it was me she was asking. She couldn't ask her sister to do it, knew it would break her beyond anything she could return from.

She was asking me to kill her because it would be a mercy.

My brows bunched, a sob ripping from me as I took a step back from Gwen. Knowing she was never going to forgive me. Knowing I would never forgive myself. I raised a hand, power creeping from my blackened fingertips up my flesh and past my wrist, pooling into what would be a quick, lethal blow.

"Do it!" Saoirse screamed again.

Gwen's eyes widened as she saw my intent, her mouth

opening to scream at me, fire curling around her fingers as she raised it, not toward the threat below, but toward me.

BOOM.

I faltered as the wall shook with the attack. The combined power of both The Blood Traitor and The Pendragon hit it with such force that the wall shuddered beneath my feet.

I swore, slamming my hand down on the rock, the killing blow I had aimed at Saoirse's heart hitting the rock instead, pushing back the fingers sinking into the wall.

Voices were yelling around me as all of my attention was suddenly locked on the wall, footsteps clattering along rock and light flaring, as around me our gifted lit up the air, their power spearing for the soldiers below.

BOOM.

They were targeting the gates now, both throwing their power in time with the battering ram, and I heard the distant splinter of wood, terror lacing through me.

I needed to get to those gates and center myself behind them. All around me, people were moving, running to fill the gaps in the walls under barked commands from Faolán, who stood head and shoulders above most. The time it would take me to push through the throng would break my connection with the wall for too long.

In two steps I raced for the low wall and threw myself over it, shadow walking through the thin slip of shade that had just formed on our side of the wall as the noon sun had begun to descend.

I landed in a billow of inky ash in front of the gates. "*Move.*" I snarled at the wide-eyed Sylvyn who were standing guard, weapons in hand.

They scattered and I lunged, thrusting both hands against the rough wood as I unleashed everything I had into it, trying not to think about what was happening on the other side.

I screamed as raw energy ripped through me and into the wall, leading the old magic in its wake to rip and tear at the power that was trying to force its way through. Wave after wave hit me, broken only by the dull boom of the battering ram that seemed to be getting stronger with every blow.

My shadows were swirling around me, particles floating like ash in the air as I strained to keep the enemy back. The gates buckled under my hands, threatening to cave in and I screamed my rage at them for daring to disobey me, the wood buckling and bending, light shining through the warped edge as I forced them back... back. But it was breaking. *I was breaking.*

Men hit the wall on either side of me, trying to use their physical strength to help me, and I felt my foot slip back as another vicious blow connected.

I could feel my body start to wane at the sheer volume of energy that the wall was ripping from me, and I reached down deeper to that blackness at the base of my soul, brushing a hand against it.

It cracked an eye, whispering to me.

Nach bhfuil tú réidh, a ghrà mo chroì.

Baring my teeth, I forced it to my will, beckoning it forth, drawing whisps from it with the rest of the energy leaving my body, and forced it into the stone as I screamed my rage.

Movement around my ankles made me glance down, and I saw a young Sylvyn slip between me and the door, reaching through the twisted gap as fire flared from his fingers.

Screams erupted from the other side, and there was a blessed break in the battering ram for a moment as they battled the flames.

A familiar hand grasped my wrist, squeezing. "Let me through."

If I had thought I was terrified before, nothing could

prepare me for those three words. I ripped my eyes to Gwen's, seeing the defiant glint in them.

"No."

The brief reprieve we had been granted let Saoirse's scream rise above the noise of the army, dragging knives of ice through my heart.

Gwen slammed her palm on the gates, and my power pushed back.

"Now!"

"No!" I gritted out, sweat trickling down my spine. "I will not let you throw your life away."

"They are killing her, and our men!" she roared. "I know what I have to do, you just have to trust me that I can do this!"

"He will kill you *both*!" I snapped, desperation starting to take over as I felt myself falter, pain lacing through my body as black spots began to shimmer at the edges of my vision.

No, it was too soon. I was stronger than this. I had to be stronger than this.

I dug deep as the attacks lashed against me, a deep ache forming in my bones as I gripped more of that terrifying blackness within me, ripping it up and feeling as it raked its claws along my soul in protest.

"Let me through, Morgana!" She pummeled her fist against the buckled wooden doors that flickered with the black threads of my power.

Pain was ravaging my body as I pushed past my limits, it felt as though knives were being dragged up my bones, my muscles quivering and cramping as sweat slicked every part of my body. I cried out as the shield I was barely clinging to was hit with another onslaught, feeling the needle-like pricks of The Blood Traitor's white power linger where my hands were pressed against the wall. I felt a new rush of energy and pulled on it, throwing everything I had back.

I felt my heart crack as I heard Saoirse cry out again on the far side of the wall, tears beginning to roll down my cheeks as my breath caught in a sob.

"Morgana!" Gwen's voice was cracking in panic, and I felt the bite of her flames as she erupted against my shield, trying to force her way through to Saoirse.

"Gwen, I can't save her," I choked, the words bitter on my tongue as I felt something irrevocably break inside me. Not from the power I was expending. It was my heart, a rending of what was left of my already bleeding soul. "I can't," I sobbed. I couldn't even let go of this shield to give her the quick, painless death she had begged me for. The second I let go they would break through, and it wasn't just Gwen's death I would be responsible for, it would be the thousands of defenseless Sylvyn at my back as well.

I screamed a guttural, tearing sound as I reached deeper and threw more power into the wall. I couldn't save Saoirse. I had failed Tadgh. I had broken my promise to Cerridwen, but Ankii damn me, I would *not* fail the Sylvyn.

"Let. Me. Through."

Gwen's hand gripped my arm, my sleeve singed by the flames that were flickering across her skin. I felt the sting of it, but it was inconsequential. I wasn't going to live past this anyway and I would gladly go to the underworld with Gwen's mark on my skin. I dragged my eyes to meet hers, the blue depths of them flickering with smoldering flames and brimming with tears. And then I saw the blade she held to her own throat, the point of it digging into the pale, soot-smeared skin of her neck.

Blood dribbled from the small wound she had made, and I felt myself buckle as my heart plunged into frozen fear.

"No," I choked. I forgot how to breathe for a moment, my heart going wild. "Gwen, No!"

"Let me out, Morgana," she said flatly. Her fingers squeezed my arm to keep my focus. "Let me out or I die right here in front of you, because I will not stand here and watch Saoirse be tortured to death. I am the expendable one, not her."

"You die if I let you out there," I sobbed. "I will lose you both."

"I need to try." There was no shake in her voice, no ounce of uncertainty, just cold rage. "He will not take another one of my family from me, Morgana." She dug the blade slightly deeper, and blood began to run freely down her neck.

"Stop!" I begged, just as Saoirse's voice cried out, screaming at someone in a long stream of curses beyond the wall.

"Morgana!" Gwen roared.

I screamed my own curse, damning the Gods for letting this happen, and twisted one of my hands against the wall, ripping a small opening where the gate was buckled and pushed in, enough to let Gwen pass.

I saw her body sag in relief, turning toward it with a determined look, but then she stopped, whirled, and threw herself onto me. It took everything in me to keep my hands on that wall, not to wrap my power around her and cocoon her in it, safe. But it was her or everyone behind these walls, and she would never forgive me if I chose what my heart was pleading for me to do.

Her lips crashed to mine in a desperate kiss, her tears wetting my face. I kept my eyes open, committing every curve of her face to memory in case this was the last time I saw her.

"I love you," she whispered against my lips. Words that I had dreamed of hearing and might never again. Then she was gone, slipping through that rip in the wall before I had a chance to say it back.

I dragged a breath into lungs that were screaming in pain, the taste of her still on my lips.

"I love you too," I sobbed, feeling the last of my heart shatter.

Above me, shouts from the archers rippled down the walls to cease fire, as a wave of heat erupted from behind the wall, screams cut off abruptly in the face of Gwen's fury. All through Windhaven an eerie quiet descended, as if everyone held their breath, their focus on the lone woman who had put herself between the enemy and her people.

I could just see them through the gap I left open, hoping above all else that it would be for Saoirse and Gwen to come back through. My shadows strained toward that gap trying to follow her, while beyond, silhouetted against the setting sun, were The Pendragon's legions.

The endless attack on the walls stopped the moment Gwen had stepped beyond them, an eerie silence settling over both sides. Even the archers on the walls seemed to be frozen in place, only the slight movement of their bows tracking Gwen across the scorched field let me know they had not turned to stone.

Pain was pulsing from my entire body, stretched beyond what I thought myself capable of. My nails were bloody and torn where I had pushed them into the stone, using the pain to anchor myself to consciousness. Even my shadows were silent, not a whisper came from them. I wondered if Nimmet had abandoned me… and then I realized I no longer cared. The woman who held my heart was beyond my protection, and as spent as I was, I could do nothing to stop what was about to come.

I wanted to die before I was forced to witness it.

I wrenched my hands from the wall. Every breath in burned my torn throat, hoarse from my own screaming, and I tried to take a step toward the opening, Gwen now a small figure in front of the hoards.

My legs gave way uselessly beneath me. My head spun as violently as it had in the woods after the bánánach attack; a day that seemed so long ago now.

I welcomed it, the death that was surely looming. The last thing I saw as darkness descended was the ground rising to meet me, and I hoped I wouldn't wake up again.

32

MERLIN

Utter terror lanced through me as the slight figure of a woman ran toward us and away from the smoldering ruins at the base of the gates. I had been distracted, seconds away from going into the O'Mordha girl's mind and taking everything away so she didn't have to feel any part of the torture Arthur had just ordered on her. I couldn't save her body, but I could save her soul. Take it from her before it was irrevocably damaged.

A flare had ripped my attention away, seeing the base of the wall erupt into flames, and seconds later as the cloud of smoke cleared, she walked out of it, through the ashes of what had been Arthur's men, with no sign of their battering ram. She had incinerated it all.

The blonde girl—Saoirse was the name she had spat at Arthur—had frozen in place from where she had been struggling in the grasp of Arthur's men, the tear on her face an echo of my own. The head of her brother, the young Lord O'Mordha was in the dirt at her feet, lolling obscenely to the side, and she had fought with an intensity that put many of our best soldiers to shame.

Three men were dead, their throats cut from a hidden blade that had emerged from her sleeve, another burned viciously by her gift, before Arthur had again gripped her flames in his power and smothered them.

It had taken four men to finally subdue her after the wall had erupted into movement at her screamed order to whomever Morgana was, and still she fought them, snarling and spitting as the shredded remains of her tunic was torn from her, exposing her to the cold air as they leered at her. One had a small dagger in his hand, the tip of it paused from where he had been slowly dragging it across her stomach in a long, shallow cut.

"Halt," Arthur yelled, holding up a hand and eyeing the lone figure running toward us with an expression I couldn't decipher.

The man holding the blonde girl swiped a finger through the scratch, smearing the blood that was seeping from it across her pale skin and drew an agonized cry from her, obvious disappointment on his face as he sheathed his blade.

"Go back," Saoirse screamed. "Gwen, no! Go back!" Her voice broke, the first real fear I had heard from her, and it confirmed my worst nightmare. The last of the O'Mordha siblings was here, where I could not protect them.

"Gwen—" her words were a sob now as she jerked against the men's grip.

"Shut up," I heard one snarl at her, wrenching her arm higher up her back and kicking her hard in the back of her leg. She went down hard on her knee onto the frozen ground next to her brother's head, glancing at it briefly before wrenching her eyes away with another choked sob.

Guinevere was close enough to make out her features now

and see the terror in her eyes that were fixed on her sister. No flames burned around her hands that were held out to us in surrender, yet I knew what lurked beneath that beautiful exterior, and I watched her cautiously. *Surely, she knew she walked to her death. What the fuck was she thinking?*

She stopped only feet from us, the terror morphing to relief as she saw her sister was still breathing. Then she turned her gaze on us, and that relief turned to burning rage.

"Take me, let my sister go," she said, her voice unwavering.

Arthur laughed, a cold sound that set my teeth on edge. "Why the fuck would I do that, when I now have both the remaining O'Mordha's?"

I opened my mouth to order a soldier to stand down as he moved to grab her, but he stiffened before he had even made contact, a silent scream coming from his open mouth before he collapsed, skin cracked and grey as a whisp of smoke escaped his mouth with his last, dying breath. Guinevere hadn't moved, not even lifted a finger as she had burned the man to death from the inside, and there was not one flicker of emotion from her as she surveyed his body at her feet.

"I am not defenseless, though I am not fool enough to think I could stand up to your strength, Pendragon." Her lip curled in distaste as she said his name. "Or yours, Traitor." Her gaze landed on mine with a ferocity that I had to admire.

She turned back to Arthur. "What is it you want from the Sylvyn, Pendragon? Our lives? You have already taken my parents and my brother from me. If it is just blood you want you can kill me now, kill the Sylvyn you hold here and do what you want to our bodies, but those gates at my back will never open. We have ancient magic pooled beneath the wall that is yet to be touched, yet to be drawn on, and you will not get through it."

Lies. I could feel the wall give under every blow. If I hadn't been feeding it my own power, it would have fallen already. Though something… someone had been fighting me with every breath behind it, making it nearly impossible to meld my power with the stone to assist. I was impressed, she told the lie with such conviction.

Gwen glared at Arthur. "They are under my orders that unless my sister and our remaining men walk back through the gates, they stay shut, they will survive, and those lands will never be yours."

"You think your screams won't be enough to make them open those gates, Lady Guinevere?" Arthur said, a lupine smile curving his lips. "You think the screams of your sister and your men won't make them abandon their orders? It has already drawn you out here."

"I know it won't," Gwen snarled softly. "Though I will make sure my sister dies cleanly by my hand before you defile her body. I don't care what you do with me. I will know my people are safe from you."

"Brave words, but would you *actually* follow through with it," Arthur murmured. He tilted his head, surveying her with a predatory look. "What is your point, Guinevere? I assume you have one."

"My sister returns behind the wall. My men return to their homes, and the supply chains that have long since fallen are reinstated to allow food and resources back into the Lowlands. My people will eat, and thrive as you all have for decades, and in return… I will kneel to you." She raised her chin defiantly, giving the words a moment to sink in. "The Lowlands will bow to your reign. You will have Kambria, all of it, as you have coveted since your rise, but not at the cost of more innocent lives."

I couldn't believe it. She was giving him exactly what he

wanted and it fucking terrified me, it could all go wrong in seconds and rip away everything I had been working toward.

"You want me to believe promises of a girl?" Arthur asked. "What proof do I have that the second I do as you ask, you will not disappear behind those walls again and leave me in the same position?"

"Because you will have me," Guinevere said, her voice straining for the first time.

"No, Gwen!" her sister choked and was quickly silenced by a sharp kick to the side, her breath exploding from her in a sharp groan.

Guinevere jerked, as if she were about to lurch toward her, but caught herself, glaring at the man who had kicked her.

"Enough," Arthur hissed, swiping his hand. The man was wrenched backward as if by an invisible fist, his body thrown back until he hit a rocky outcrop with a sickening thud. Arthur didn't even look in his direction.

"You would lay the Lowlands at my feet for the life of one girl and a group of wretched men you call soldiers?" he said, sounding amused. "How interesting, yet I still do not believe that if I release her, you can deliver on these grand promises. The Sylvyn have always been a proud race."

Guinevere looked down her nose at the King, quite the feat as he stood a foot taller than she did, before throwing a pointed look to the side of us.

I glanced warily in the direction she had indicated, nervous to take my attention from her after the demonstration of how lethal her gift was, then looked again, feeling my face slacken in surprise and having to force it back into neutrality.

Every man in the Sylvyn group had silently kneeled as she had been speaking, their heads bowed and a hand covering their hearts.

Not in surrender, for they had fought with everything they had, and would keep fighting if she had asked them to.

Not to the King, whose face had gone blank as he watched the lines of men.

But to their Queen. This fierce woman who stood between them and death and offered her life for theirs.

Arthur surveyed the lines of kneeling men with a look I couldn't decipher before he turned and stepped toward Guinevere, one slow step at a time.

I tensed. If she was going to attack him, it would be now, but she merely raised her chin, looking up at him with defiance as he drew close enough for them to share breath.

He took her chin in his hand, and I saw the slight shudder that rippled through her at the contact. "So, you offer yourself, for your people, Lady Guinevere," he murmured, as he ran a thumb over her full lower lip, sneering. "To do with as I will. You know I could stow you away in my dungeons or put you to work in the fields for the rest of your *very* long life?"

"It's worth it," she bit out. "They are worth it." She wrenched her face from his grip, taking a step back. "But my sister leaves, now. So do the men. As long as I live, my sister will ensure the Lowlands stay under your rule."

"So demanding," Arthur crooned, tilting his head as his eyes raked down her body. He glanced over his shoulder to me. "What do you think, advisor. Should I take this deal?"

I swallowed the hope that was slowly growing in me that we could walk away from this with minimal bloodshed, keeping my face in a slight sneer as I looked her over, needing this lie to be the most convincing I had ever told.

"She tells the truth, the Gods magic is still too strong for me to penetrate. If you do not think we can convince them to open the gates with her blood, then it is a logical option." I crossed my arms, eyeing her sister who looked as if she was going to start crying. "How highly do you value your sister's life, girl? Do you know what will happen to her if you do not uphold this agreement?"

Saoirse curled her lip in a snarl as she glared at me. "If you harm her—" she began.

"Saoirse," Guinevere warned under her breath.

Arthur turned back to Guinevere, picking up a strand of her long, red hair and rubbed it between his fingers. She turned her face away from him, the tip of a slightly pointed ear poking out of her hair, and I saw Arthur's gaze go to it. "A woman that stays young and beautiful and commands the respect of the Lowlands," he murmured, the tip of his finger brushing that pointed curve. It was as if he couldn't help but touch her. He let the glistening strand slide through his fingers. "I accept your offer, Lady Guinevere. What fun we shall have together. I cannot think of a more fitting end to the Sylvyn rebellion than to have its *Queen* as my pet."

Guinevere was frozen in place. I could almost see the despondency shutter down over her eyes. She had just signed the rest of her life away, tied to a man she despised to save her people. I knew what that was like, and I wouldn't wish it on my worst enemy.

"Send the other girl beyond the wall," Arthur said, waving a hand at some of the nearest men. They recoiled from the movement, eyes flaring in fright. "My new pet and I will discuss the terms of the Lowlands surrender."

Saoirse was protesting, her snarled worlds lost in a hum of voices as people began moving with a snap of Arthurs fingers as I cautiously moved toward Guinevere, keeping every one of my senses open for the first lick of her gift spearing for me.

Men strode forward to grab Guinevere, and I waved them back, my attention drawn toward her sister who was struggling in the grasp of two men.

"Release her," I ordered, watching Arthur from the corner of my eye as he made his way back to the ranks of our men and the tents beyond, seemingly confident I would navigate the handover.

The men let Saoirse go immediately and she fell forward into the dirt, scrabbling back up and crossing her arms over her body to cover herself. She lurched forward, throwing herself onto Guinevere. I could hear the quiet pleading she was doing to change her mind and saw the white-knuckled grip Guinevere had on her sister, crushing her in a hug.

"I wasn't returning through those gates the second I left them," Guinevere whispered, the words so quiet I barely heard them. "And I have already made peace with that. You need to be strong for me, Saoirse. I can't do this without knowing you are going to be ok. And… the rest of them. You need to look after them all, you hear me? Don't let *anyone* make foolish decisions."

They made eye contact for a moment, a silent conversation flickering between them on that weighted look, until Saoirse choked back a sob as tears began to fall freely down her face.

"I can't leave you out here," she whispered.

"You must," Guinevere whispered as she pulled her in for another hug, turning a hard look on me over her sister's shoulder. "The men?"

I nodded, waving my hand at the soldiers guarding them. "Let them go," I called. "Return their weapons and leave them unharmed."

I watched as the battered men were set free, but none of them turned and fled back to the walls like I had anticipated. Instead, they approached where Guinevere still held her sister, the two women clinging to each other, each man brushing a touch over her arm, her hair. Bowing to her or touching his heart in a gesture I recognized as old Sylvyn for respect. One removed his cloak, draping it over Saoirse, and Gwen was quick to pull the edges closed around her sister's battered body.

No words were spoken, but they were not needed. They were paying homage to their savior.

I turned back to see Arthur had stopped, watching the men with an expression I hadn't seen in a century. Not since he had gazed upon the glowing surface of the Helix.

Greed.

The need to covet what was not his, and I couldn't tell if it was for the woman that had stood fearlessly in front of an enemy army and given up her life for those she loved, or if it was for the respect her people gave her of their own free will.

Guinevere suddenly stooped, and I realized she had her own cloak in her shaking hands as she wrapped her brothers head in it, her face pale as she handed it to her Saoirse.

"Bury him next to Mother and Father," she said, her voice shaking. "Go with the men, I will send word with what the—" she faltered, swallowing hard. "With what the King's terms are."

"He will never be my King," Saoirse hissed.

"He already is," Guinevere answered, her voice hollow.

33

MERLIN

"Get your hand off me," Guinevere hissed under her breath as I led her toward the tent that was being rapidly erected. It was a splash of red against the barren terrain, Arthur's banner already fluttering above it, his claim staked on this newly acquired victory.

I tightened my grip on her elbow, not letting her pull her arm free. "Believe me when I say I'm the better option for you right now," I muttered out the side of my mouth, flashing a quelling look at her. "There is an army of men surrounding you that have been deprived of the blood they were promised. Don't be a fool."

I shoved her through the flap of the tent, the sides still shuddering as men hammered pegs into the frozen ground outside it, and followed her through. I pointed to the ground, ignoring the flash of anger sparking in her eyes. "Stay here."

"I am not a dog," she said darkly.

"You have about as many rights as one currently," I said back, glancing back over my shoulder to the men I had just left with her sister. I didn't want to risk leaving her any longer than

I had to, the need to get her back beyond those walls to some semblance of safety chafing at me. "If you want your sister to get back behind your wall with no further harm you will do what I fucking tell you to, woman."

My frayed nerves were making me sharper than I intended to be, and I rolled my neck, forcing myself to take a breath.

"This is *my* tent. No one except the King can step one foot in here and he is currently busy, so in here and in here alone you are safe, Guinevere. I need to go and return your sister to Windhaven because *she* is currently *not* safe. Do you understand what I am telling you?"

Unspoken questions flashed across her face, but she clenched her jaw and nodded. The smallest of acknowledgments. There was a fluttering at the entrance and Sirin burst through the flap, muttering under her breath as she landed on my shoulder.

"Hello," Sirin said, picking one of her random assortment of voices as she cocked her head, looking at Guinevere. I was slightly surprised, the damned rook hadn't been that polite to someone in years, the last woman she had seen in my rooms she had called a dirty whore.

Guinevere blinked, looking taken aback. "Hello… bird," she said haltingly. She turned her gaze back to me, her eyes hardening. "Go then. Those gates staying open relies on my sister getting back in one piece." She bit out the last words as if she knew my thoughts instantly drifted to her brother. "She is The Pendragon's ticket to the Lowlands."

I reached up, unhooking a small wooden pole attached to the roof of the tent on either end by two lengths of chain, letting it hang down at head height. Sirin hopped onto it, stretching a wing out as she fluffed her feathers up.

I leveled an eye on Guinevere, one hand resting on Sirin's

back. "Harm a feather on Sirin while I return your sister, and the King will be the least of your concerns."

Indignation washed over her face. "I am not the monster here, Traitor."

I was relieved to see the blonde O'Mordha standing ramrod straight, flanked by two soldiers who were eying her warily. Her arms were wrapped around her gruesome bundle, her eyes pools of hatred.

"Where have you taken her?" she asked as soon as I was in earshot.

"She is in my personal tent," I said, gesturing her to walk. Ahead of us the Sylvyn soldiers were already moving, some being aided by others, their injuries slowing them down.

Her footsteps were reluctant, as if every step pained her, and I knew it wasn't the physical pain that was tearing at her the worst.

We walked silently across the barren ground. Nothing grew here, just frozen rock and scorched earth, as if the magic in the wall had seeped out, bleeding into the ground and stopping life from forming. Even the snow didn't settle here, melting away to nothing.

She stumbled and I automatically reached out to catch her, pulling my hand back when she reared away from me and I held it up in silent apology.

The ground was blackened as we reached the gates, and I tried not to look disgusted as I stepped through the ash of burned bodies. Nothing remained of the men that had stood here except the scattered, hardened pools of melted metal that had once been their armor.

The men ahead of us waited, milling at the gates, their ranks opening to let us through as we reached them.

I looked up at the huge wooden behemoths, their surface scarred and bleached by time, marred with dents lower down from the ram. The wood was buckled in places, a lower edge bent in enough for a small body to pass through. Or a red-haired Queen, I realized, surveying the small gap.

From how close I was now; I could feel its power. Felt its tendrils reach for me, scented with my own power that now lingered in its depths. It had a curiosity that was almost alive, and I reached back, stroking a mental hand down its surface, letting it feel my intent.

Saoirse placed a hand on it, closing her eyes for a moment before murmuring something under her breath. There was a moment of silence, and then with a rush of air that sent her blonde hair flying, it groaned, and the huge gates opened.

"Open them wide and hook them back," I ordered, as I caught sight of my first view of the Lowlands. Movement from all angles as men and women hurried about in well organized pandemonium. A wall of Sylvyn suddenly appeared in front of us, hands up in warning, some swirling with fire, others holding weapons of ice as two more stood behind, winds whipping around them.

"Stand down," Saoirse said, taking a faltering step forward. She swallowed, once, twice as if struggling to get the next words out. "We have yielded to The Pendragon. Gwen —" she faltered again as a tall man appeared at her side, slipping an arm around her and holding her steady. I saw her sag against him slightly, letting him take some of her weight. "The Lady O'Mordha has negotiated a truce for the Lowlands," she called across the waiting crowds.

"The Pendragon does not negotiate with anyone," someone called from the silence that followed.

"It is true," I said. "I am the King's hand, and I accompany the Lady O'Mordha back as the first part of this agreement."

Hushed whispers broke out as men and women alike drew

back from me, and I saw a flurry of hands reach for weapons as if assuring themselves of their presence. As if steel could stop me should I wish harm on these people.

"You have done what you said you would, Traitor," the man who held Saoirse said, his tone icy. "Now get the fuck out."

I gave him a bored look, turning my eyes to Saoirse who looked as if she were about to collapse. "You can send three guards to accompany your sister to Irling. Three *ungifted* guards. Send them out under a white banner when you have made your decision." I nodded politely, taking one long look at the mountain ranges beyond and turned on my heel, striding out of the now wide open gates and back toward the settling army.

Arthur pushed into my tent not long after I had returned, his eyes instantly going to Guinevere who was sitting on a mat in the corner of the tent, her arms curled around her knees. She looked so small like that, barely anything left of the fierce woman who had raged across the battlefield to defend her people.

She pulled herself to her feet as he came in, arms wrapping around her waist defensively, but her eyes regained some of that defiant glint.

"Pet," he said, giving her a shallow, mocking bow.

He turned to me, a smile hooking the corners of his mouth. "The gates are open I see."

I nodded, helping myself to the ale that had been put in my tent upon my departure, offering one to Arthur. "The gates are open, and the girl has been returned. There will be three men arriving to accompany Lady Guinevere to Irling."

He scowled at me. "Pardon?"

"Good faith in what is to become a truce between the Sylvyn and Humans," I said, taking a deep swig of my own ale and sinking into a chair. "It shows we are committed to this working. They have no reason to believe our word that the Lady will remain alive, but they will believe the word of their own people."

Arthur grunted. His gaze slid back to Guinevere. "So, *Pet.*" The word was an insult, meant to degrade her. "I have the Lowlands, and I have ordered my men not to touch a soul that dwells there. I believe you said you would kneel for me."

I saw her body stiffen, but she said nothing, merely lowered herself very slowly until her knees hit the hard ground below.

"The supply chains?" she asked, her voice stiff.

He leaned back in his chair, the wood creaking under his large frame. "Come." He pointed to the ground at his feet, summoning her like he would one of his hounds.

My teeth clenched, shame washing over me at being in the room to witness Guinevere's degradation. Even Sirin was thankfully quiet from her perch over by the door.

Guinevere remained silent, but her eyes flashed in barely concealed rage.

"I guess the death of your parents at such a young age meant they didn't have a chance to teach you what a negotiation is," Arthur said, giving her a viper's smile. "I give you something, you give me something in return. That's how this works, Pet."

Very slowly, Gwen lifted a leg, ready to stand and walk toward him.

"No," Arthur admonished. "For making me wait, you can crawl to me. I need you to understand that your life, every action you now take, is mine to decide."

Her eyes flashed to mine ever so briefly, before I lowered

mine to the mug in my hands, feigning indifference. It was the only privacy I could give her.

"That's better," Arthur crooned as I heard something brush across the rough, woven mat on the floor. "I can allow shipments through Sirinelle. They are to be checked before entering the Lowlands. No weapons, no steel, and if I find this rule broken, *you* will be punished. A public flogging that will be reported back to your sister, so they all know the cost of not following my rules. And in return, in the spring, your gifted will join my army. I have use of them. They will be treated as well as any of my own men and will be permitted to return to their homes between service."

"If you want soldiers that are worth their place on your ships, there needs to be supplies enough to help feed my people through the winter. And livestock to widen the bloodlines we have left." Her voice was closer now.

"That can be arranged. We have plenty of livestock and food," he huffed. "I will have men left behind. They are to be given full access to the Lowlands and reside in Windhaven. If you want men in Irling, I will have mine there.

"And Tadgh's body?" Her voice was clipped.

"What of it?" Arthur said, sounding bored.

"Where is it?" The question was so quiet I had to strain to hear her.

"In a shallow grave along The Spine along with four or so of his men," Arthur replied. "Do you want to see it? Though I warn you, he lost more than just his head."

I cringed inwardly at the callous words. The young lord's body had been hacked to pieces before being thrown into that grave, but that had come after. His death had been mercifully quick.

"I would like one of the men permitted to accompany me to be shown the graves so they can be taken home and buried with their… with our family." It sounded like she was barely holding herself together.

"As you wish," Arthur said.

"When do we leave?" Guinevere asked, her tone stiff. She made a small noise, and I looked up to see Arthur had leaned forward, her chin caught between his fingers.

"I believe the words you are looking for are 'Thank you, my King'."

I admired the moment of silence she took, her eyes boring into Arthur's.

"Thank you, my King," she repeated back.

"You are most welcome, Pet," he murmured, releasing her jaw to pat her cheek.

"My King, the smith is here," a voice came from outside the tent.

"Enter," Arthur called, picking up his cup and drinking deeply.

A small, wiry man entered holding something in his hands, and Arthur gestured for it.

"I'm sorry, my King. With such short notice, it's just a rough job made with the tang of a spare dagger I had."

Arthur grunted, surveying the object. It was a metal cuff in the shape of a bracelet, glinting softly in the dim light.

"I can make a clasp for it when we return to Irling and I have my tools, Sire," the smith said, wringing his hands. "And I can give it a cleaner finish."

"No need," Arthur said, "this will do fine. You are dismissed."

The smith nearly bolted from the tent, relief etched into his face.

"Give me your wrist," Arthur said, holding a hand out to Guinevere.

"Why?" She looked ready to bolt out of the tent after the smith.

"You don't think I'm going to let you into Irling, around my people with that gift simmering in your veins, do you?" he scoffed. "What King would I be, putting my subjects at risk, especially after seeing what you did to the men at my gates." His tone lowered to a menacing rumble. "I won't ask again, Pet. Give me your fucking wrist."

She reached her arm out and he grasped it, pulling it across his lap as he slipped the cuff over her delicate wrist. Tugged as she was, Guinevere overbalanced and caught herself with her other hand on his leg and quickly whipped it back, as if the touch scalded her flesh.

Arthur snorted softly, his hand closing over the cuff and squeezing until the ends touched before turning her wrist over, the metal of the cuff so out of place against her pale, lovely skin.

He wrapped a hand around the cuff again and light flared, Guinevere jolting suddenly and crying out as the faint smell of burned flesh filled the air and Arthur peered at the join that had now melted together. "You try to use your little fire tricks on anyone, and this cuff will deflect all of that fire back into your own skin," he said, lifting her arm and waving it in front of her face. "You will burn your own arm off before you harm me or anyone else in my lands, understand, Pet?"

Guinevere nodded, a sheen of sweat breaking out on her forehead.

"How do you answer me?" Arthur growled, his fingers going white from the grip he had on her wrist.

"Yes, my King," Guinevere said, her voice tight.

"Better." Arthur stood up, glancing to me. "I need men organized to remain behind, meet me in my tent. And set guards on the tent for her. I won't have her slipping away under my nose."

"Of course," I raised my cup, swilling the contents. "I will be right there."

He left without another glance at her, where she was still kneeling and cradling her wrist. I waited until he had gone before I turned to her.

"Let me look at that."

She glared up at me. "Why?"

I sighed. "Because I can heal it."

"Why do you care, Traitor?"

Fuck this, I didn't have the time or the mental capacity to fight her at every step, so I bent, grasped her wrist and yanked it up, drawing a pained gasp from her.

"Fucking arseh—"

"Shut up Sirin," I snapped at the rook, "I do not need your smart mouth at the moment." I peered under the cuff, seeing her skin was blistered and raw beneath the now welded ends, and covered it with my hand. Her eyes dropped from where they had been burning into me, to my hand, brows raised as she watched the little flickers of light that danced over her skin, working under the cuff to heal her hurts.

"It's not dark?" she asked.

"What isn't dark?" I asked, lowering a brow.

"It doesn't matter." She twisted her wrist out of my grip, peering underneath it, and before I could stop her, a flicker of flame winked into life at her fingers. The cuff began to glow red, and she quickly flicked her hand, extinguishing the flames and the glow together, hissing under her breath.

"Don't try that again," I warned. "He does not bluff." I studied her bent head, her hair glinting in the candlelight from the table. "Keep hold of that fire, Red. You are going to need it."

"How can I do that when it is just another thing that he has taken from me?"

"Not these flames," I said, tapping her hand. I pointed to her heart. "Those. No shackle is strong enough to smother that. Not unless you let it."

Her brows lowered, wariness exuding from her.

"We are not on the same side, Traitor. If there is nothing else you want from me, go run after your master like a good little dog."

Sirin cackled from her perch, and I gave the rook a dark look. "Have fun with this one," I muttered.

"At least the bird has the balls to say what it really thinks," Guinevere said from behind me as I strode out.

I don't think Arthur has any idea what he's gotten himself into. Fire like that, it decimates. And what it might consume was yet to be seen.

34

MORGANA

Pain.

That was all there was. Pain and darkness. It was flooding into me now, every muscle and bone aching with an intensity that stole my breath. There was pain in the afterworld? I would need to have a chat with Nimmet about this. About a lot of things.

A wave of nausea washed over me and I barely rolled in time to throw up over the side of my bed that I now realized I lay on, as the world came into focus.

There was a small noise of alarm somewhere from my right where I glimpsed movement before the sound of running feet faded away.

I think I may have passed out again, because the next thing I knew, hands were on my face, my name being repeated urgently in a voice I recognized.

"Saoirse?" I croaked, my voice cracked and husky to the point of being unrecognizable. I cracked my eyes open, bracing myself against the pain it caused and choked on a sob

359

when Saoirse's face sharpened into view in front of me. "You're here? How is tha—" I cut myself off as I got a better look at her. She had more bruises and cuts than clear skin, and the dark rings under her eyes stood out starkly against her pale skin. But she was alive.

"Oh my Gods," I hauled myself up and dragged her to me. "I'm sorry," I choked, repeating the words over and over. "I tried… I couldn't…"

Saoirse shuddered in my arms but said nothing as she clung to me, burying her face in my neck.

"Gwen?" I asked, suddenly rearing back as the gravity of everything slammed back into me. I didn't need to ask though. I didn't need to see the haunted look in Saoirse's eyes, my shadows were already whispering to me that Gwen was gone.

"Is she dead?" I asked, making myself meet Saoirse's eyes as the shredded pieces of my heart turned to ice.

"No," Saoirse whispered, her voice shaking. "But she may as well be. The Pendragon has her."

It took a second for her words to filter in, and the horror of what she was saying settled, unwanted in my stomach.

Saoirse made a sound of distress as I pushed the covers back, heaving myself out of bed. I couldn't even muster enough dignity to be ashamed of the whimper that tore from my throat as my body protested violently at the movement.

"You shouldn't be moving yet," Saoirse said, grabbing my arm as I swayed. "What are you doing?"

"I'm going to get her back," I snapped, pulling my arm from her grip and blinking rapidly to clear my head. I saw some clothing draped over the back of a chair and snatched it up, nearly toppling over as I tried to raise the shirt over my head to pull it on. I growled in frustration as Saoirse once again had to steady me. "Help me," I said, shoving the shirt into her hands.

"Morgana," Saoirse pleaded, kneading the fabric in her hands.

"There isn't time for this!" I snapped, "Help me, or get someone who will."

"She's *gone*, Morgana!" Saoirse snapped back at me. "The army left three days ago. You have been unconscious for four. Gwen is gone." Her voice broke on the last part, and she dropped to end of my bed, burying her face in the shirt she had been holding as her shoulders shook.

I just blinked at her, uncomprehending. I ran a hand over my face, trying to control the panic that was threatening to take over. I reached out a hesitant hand, laying it on her shoulder.

"I tried to make them kill me," she whispered through her hands. "I told her to turn back, I begged her to go back behind the walls, but she wouldn't listen."

Her eyes were hollow as she raised them to look at me. "I'm sorry. It should be me out there, not her."

Saoirse told me everything that had happened. Her words hurt more than the pain of my magic ravaged body. I made her keep going, no matter how much I didn't want to hear it.

We paused only while a maid was called to deliver me some food, Saoirse refusing to go on until I began to eat the stew that tasted like ash in my mouth.

Between the food and the tea that I had been sipping, filled with herbs and honey, I was beginning to feel stronger, though with that came a burning rage deep within me.

"The wall?" I asked after Saoirse had gone silent.

"The gates are open," she said quietly. "The Blood Traitor ordered the excess resources from the army to be left behind.

It's already been sent through to the Lowlands and there is a delivery set to arrive in two weeks through Sirinelle."

"Bartered for with Gwen's life," I snapped, then instantly regretted it as I saw Saoirse's face stiffen.

"I'm sorry," I said, forcing the anger from my voice. "If Tadgh had stayed behind the wall… I could have kept them all at bay. At least I could have tried, and Gwen wouldn't be alone and in the hands of our enemies."

"Tadgh paid for his decision with his life," Saoirse said, her tone stiff. "And I may have failed to stop Gwen from throwing her freedom away, Morgana, but I did not let her go alone."

"What?" I asked. "Who?"

"Rian," Saoirse said. She looked away from me, swallowing hard. "Twenty men volunteered to be part of her personal escort. Rian was one of them. When The Blood Traitor escorted me back to the wall, he informed me that The Pendragon had permitted three ungifted Sylvyn to remain with Gwen. I'm not sure if they will allow her to converse with us directly, and there is no one I would trust with her life more than Rian out of the options I had."

I shook my head, swearing under my breath. "It should have been me," I said. "I should have been one of them."

"He would have sensed your power and killed you on the spot," Saoirse said flatly. "I felt his power, he snuffed out my gift in my veins without any effort."

"Who else did you send?" I asked.

"Two of our best warriors," she replied wearily. "Both can hold their own against a group of men if needed, but they are nothing against The Pendragon and The Traitor."

"Any maids?" I asked, quickly.

"She refused them. A few volunteered."

I nodded, an idea slowly forming in my mind. "Do you still have the key to your father's study?"

Saoirse looked at me warily. "I know where Tadgh kept it, why?"

35

MORGANA

Kerrich's office hadn't been opened in over two decades, the hinges on the old wooden door rusty with disuse, so it took both of us to push it open. It gave with a forlorn creak, musty air greeting us in a cold rush.

I coughed as dust swirled in the dim air, waving my hand in front of my face to clear the cobwebs that decorated the corner of the arched doorway, and stepped into a room where I had spent a lot of my childhood.

The little desk I had learned to read and write at still sat in the corner of the room, the inkwell and quills still arranged neatly at the top of it as Kerrich had preferred. All of us had been taught at Kerrich's hand, though it was Tadgh and I that had spent the most time in here—Tadgh going through the history of the Sylvyn while I had been the recipient of books upon books about the Gods. Not that any of it had been of much use to me once Gallin had passed. It was all just words on a page, the meaning of it lost to me, and I had been too nervous of Kerrich's quick temper to question him on it.

I glanced across the room to the other desk, the twin to

mine, my stomach twisting as I made out the faint impression in the corner—T.O. in lopsided letters—scratched into it with the knife Tadgh's mother had given him for his thirteenth birthday. That little act of rebellion had landed him a cuff around the ears and a week scrubbing out the kitchens.

I looked away, the ghost of the boy I had once known still sitting in that chair, sticking his tongue out at me across the room.

"I'm sorry," I whispered.

Saoirse was surveying the huge bookcases that stretched along the back wall behind Kerrich's desk, running her finger along the spines and craning her neck to read them.

I turned my attention to the huge desk that dominated the room, and the object that rested at its head nestled in a carved groove of the table, its surface blacker than any moonless night. I ran a finger down the smooth surface of the Helix stone that had been Kerrich's prized possession, remembering how Tadgh and I had dared each other to touch it, trying to outlast each other as it had sucked greedily at the power in our blood. My lips twitched at the memory of how Tadgh had fainted twice in his efforts to try to outlast me.

"From our greatest weaknesses, can come our biggest triumphs," I recited, the phrase burned into my memory from how often Kerrich had said it to us as children.

The Helix pulled at me, eager for the power that was slowly accumulating inside me again, and I shivered at the age-old feel of it. I bent, grasping the edge of the cloak I wore and ripped off a strip of the fabric, using it to pick up the stone that was no bigger than my fist and bundled it well.

Saoirse spun at the noise, her eyes growing wary as she saw what I was doing. "What do you want that for?" she asked.

"You're right," I said, checking to make sure all parts of the stone were covered before tucking it under my arm. "I can't get into Irling without detection as a Child of Nimmet. So I will become nothing."

"What?" Saoirse asked, frowning at me. "What are you on about?"

I patted the stone, giving her a lopsided smile. "They won't know what I am, if there is no power in my blood to detect."

Saoirse jolted, her eyes flying to the Helix and then back to me. "No." She rounded the desk, holding out her hand. "Give it to me."

I walked past her, heading for the door.

"You can't!" she protested, grabbing my shoulder and pulling me back. "You think Gwen is just going to follow you out of Irling when it means death for our people? Even if you get back here before The Blood Traitor does, we would have to slaughter the men he's left behind to guard the gates and condemn our people to a life of hunger. You know her better than that, you are just going to get yourself killed."

"You're right, I do know her better than that," I hissed. "If I thought she would come willingly, without hating me for the rest of her days I would go in there and burn Irling to the ground to get her back. If I thought begging her on my knees to save herself would work, I would do it. But she won't, not now she knows the Lowlands has a chance of not just surviving but *living*."

"Then what the fuck do you think you are doing?" Saoirse snapped. "Because if you have a way of saving my sister, tell me and I will do it!"

"I'm going to kill The Pendragon," I said calmly, then stalked from the room, leaving her gaping in my wake.

The smith looked at me blankly. "You want… what, Milady?"

I held the Helix out to him. "Can you do it or not?"

He scratched his cheek, frowning at me. "Crushin' the half you want done is easy, a few whacks of my hammer should see that done fine. The chips aren't gonna be a problem neither, but I haven't made a blade like that before."

I passed him the drawing I had sketched out, pointing to the spine of the blade. "It's a normal blade, all except for the spine. It needs to have cavities to hold the Helix chips.."

"I can see that," he muttered. "It's not the idea of it that's the issue, it's mighty fine work to be putting into a blade so small. And having the cavities in it is going to weaken the dagger."

"It only needs to be used once," I assured him. "As long as it can do the job once, it will work."

He eyed me suspiciously, his beard bristling as he chewed on his lips. "Who you plannin' on stickin' it in?"

"Nobody you know," I replied, raising a brow.

He grunted, eyeing the picture again. "Give me four days."

"Tomorrow," I said, ignoring his protests. "Whatever you are doing, put it to the side, this is more important."

He grumbled, shaking his head. "I will do me best but I'm not promisin' anythin'. I will send me boy for ye when it's done."

I nodded my thanks and left him to it, going to the seamstress next and giving her the dress and cloak that I had taken from a maid, and showed her the pockets and hidden linings I wanted sewn into the hems. Enough to easily hide the Helix dust in without it coming into contact with my body, and dispersed through the clothing so it wouldn't be found easily.

Then I went back to face Saoirse, who hadn't spoken to me since I had told her my intention.

I found her in Tadgh's study, her face drawn as she talked to a group of guards. She saw me come in and dismissed them, waiting silently as they brushed fingers against their brows in respect and headed off.

She looked tired, made worse by the injuries that covered her body, still unhealed as she had refused a healer's help until all the injured soldiers had been seen to.

"Have you changed your mind?" she asked wearily.

"No," I said quietly.

"Then we have nothing to talk about," she said, leaning her head on her hands.

I hesitated, unsure of what to say before cautiously rounding the desk and squatting next to her, making her look at me.

"I can save her," I said. "I might be the only one who can."

"You don't think I want to save her?" she whispered, her eyes rimmed with silver. "Every moment of every day I think about what she must be going through."

I shook my head. "Then why are you so against me going?"

"Because I've lost everyone," she said, a tear tracking down her cheek. "You want to walk into The Pendragon's lair. To face him and The Traitor, completely defenseless, and expect me to believe you are going to come out alive?" She huffed a mirthless laugh. "I wish he had just killed me. Better than having to live through this."

I grasped her hand, swallowing hard. "I made a promise to your mother when I was a child. She gave me a life I shouldn't have lived to see. A childhood, in exchange for protecting her children when I could do so. I've already failed Tadgh, I have to at least try."

"And what about me?" Saoirse said. "If you die, I have no one left."

I made myself grin at her, though it felt like a lie. "Have a little faith in me, Saoirse. I've already died once, I will just tell death to go fuck itself again."

She made a sound that I wasn't quite sure was a laugh or a sob, but her fingers tightened around mine. "If you die, I will find you in the land of the Gods and kill you again myself. I can't do this alone. I wasn't the one meant for this."

I gave her a sad smile. "No one ever is, but the Lowlands trust you. *I* trust you, and I promise I'm going to do everything I can to get them back to you. Gwen *and* Rian. But I need you to promise me you will stay here, behind the wall. The Lowlands need an O'Mordha protecting the wall if I am not here to do it. Only you will be able to seal those gates again, and if I send word to close them, you do it without a moment's hesitation."

She met my gaze, conflict warring behind her eyes.

"Trust me," I said softly.

She nodded slowly, looking slightly defeated. "Okay," she said at last.

I slept poorly that night, my mind racing. Dreams of The Traitor swirled through nightmares of Gwen screaming in fear and I woke drenched in sweat. I bathed before heading out to collect the clothing from the seamstress and then called on the smith. The dagger was simple at first glance, but at closer inspection it was a thing of beauty. He looked slightly smug as he held up the rippled blade, pointing out the small cavities down its centre meant to hold the Helix.

"Some of me best work, that," he said proudly, pushing the dagger back into the leather sheath he had made to fit it and passed it over with the two pouches that contained the Helix dust and chips. "Mind, you swing it around too wildly and you might lose the chips. Shove em in nice and tight."

I murmured my thanks, instructing him to collect his payment from Saoirse later in the week—the chickens he had asked for were not something we had readily available—and I took my items back to Saoirse's rooms where we spent the next few hours laboriously funneling the dust into the little pockets the seamstress had made and stowed the chips into others.

Night had descended by the time we both stood, groaning as we stretched out our aching backs. Saoirse had a hand pressed to her stomach, wincing slightly as she bent to collect the needle she had been using.

"Can I heal you before I go?" I asked.

"You should save your strength," she said, rolling her neck to loosen it.

"I don't need it," I corrected, holding up the Helix-stuffed dress.

She eyed the dress and sighed, nodding slightly, then stood still while I ran light fingers across the deep bruising across her face and shoulders. She lifted her top and I sucked in a breath, fury and grief warring in me as I took in the long, shallow slice that ran across her stomach, the reddened edges crusted with blood. The shadows that flowed from my fingers disappeared immediately under her skin, and I could feel them working on bone, melding a crack together and drawing out deep bruising as more stitched together the flesh wounds.

Saoirse took the first deep breath I had seen her take since I had woken, her shoulders relaxing slightly.

"You should have let me do that sooner," I murmured, patting her hip for her to loosen her pants and let me get to the scratches that looked like nail marks that I could see peeking out the top. I was going to kill them all. Every man that had laid a hand on her.

"Why should I be the only one not suffering," she replied, her eyes fixed out the window as I worked.

I gave her a dark look and shook my head, trying not to notice just how many fingerprints my shadows were easing away from her pale skin, but I knew exactly how she felt, and I couldn't find the words to argue with her.

When I was done, she helped me to dress, strapping the dagger to my thigh and lacing the garment up tight. It was a snug fit, the bodice tight around my ribs and the cut lower than I would have chosen, but the grey fabric was practical and in the style the maids around Windhaven tended to wear.

Saoirse stepped back and eyed me over, then gave the laces under my chest one last tug, making me grunt uncomfortably.

"If nothing else, you can distract them with those," she said, raising a brow and looking pointedly at my breasts that were so tightly confined they puffed out over the low collar.

"They can look all they like if it gets me close enough to The Pendragon to get the dagger in him."

Saoirse looked anxious again, but said nothing, just handed me the dark red cloak that had pockets of Helix chips in the hem.

"I hate this," she whispered.

"Me too," I said, and then she was hugging me, and I was hugging her back, hoping this wasn't the last time I saw her.

I stepped through the open gates of Windhaven alone, having poured all but the barest trace of the power I had accrued again into the wall. I felt slightly shaky again, my body still recovering as it was, but I ignored it, focusing instead on the miles I would have to cover by sunrise. Armies moved slowly but they still had five days on me, even with the speed I could move through the night.

I patted the little pocked under my right breast, feeling the tiny swell of powder trapped there, ready to use when I was within sight of the army, refusing to let myself think past that point.

My shadows were urging me forward, whispering for me to hurry.

"*Nimmet,*" I murmured into the darkness. "*You chose me, now give me the strength I will need to see this through. You chose wrong with The Traitor. You owe us this.*"

I waited for a moment, listening, but not even the faintest whisper passed my ear. Just the urge to go, to melt into the darkness toward the woman whose soul called to me, fainter and fainter as she was taken further away.

I took one last glance at Windhaven, looming behind me, its gates flung wide for the first time in decades, and stepped into the darkness.

Time felt different when I gave myself the freedom to move like this. I traveled faster than I ever had before, barely disturbing the snow that was falling in light swirls, or the leaves that still clung on to winter tipped trees as I soared across the land. There was no melting from shadow to shadow—in the dark I was limitless—the only thing slowing me down was the need to track the path of the army, and that wasn't hard.

I had never tested the boundaries of my shadow form in its natural element. What usually took days of travel to Glenrock by horseback, I covered in hours, pausing in a cloud of soot-colored shadows to get my bearings. If anyone had peered outside the dark windows of Glenrock's cottages, they would have seen me there, half merged with the darkness and as I gazed up at the houses now inhabited by humans.

These homes had been full of Sylvyn's once, their children playing happily in the streets and a bustling marketplace where Gallin had taken me for food on many occasions.

I threw myself back into the night, following the path the army had left. Muddy snow and broken trees were littered in their wake, hacked down to provide warmth for their campfires against the bitter nights. Snow had been trampled into sludge, their progress slowed as they had fanned out over the difficult terrain, passing by Sirinelle and then skirting the forest beneath The Spine.

It was as I drew closer to the coast that I began to see I was gaining on them. Tracks were fresher, a camp was left with the smell of smoke still clinging to the trees and my shadows began murmuring to me. A warning that I was closing in on them.

I skirted the coastline, the smell of the sea air mingling with the sound of crashing waves that were hidden under a moonless sky, and I began to slow, throwing out a net of my shadows ahead of me as I went, cautious not to send them close enough for The Pendragon to feel me coming.

It was when I began to feel the faintest inkling of lives ahead of me that I slowed, pulling back into myself. I stepped out of the darkness when I saw the fires of the camp in the distance, taking a moment to center myself back into this form, swaying slightly as my body struggled to adjust.

I took long, deep breaths, sinking to a knee and pressing my fingers into the cold snow, feeling as everything slowly aligned back into place within me, then I ran my hands over myself to check I had not lost my treasures on the journey.

The dagger was still firmly strapped to my inner thigh, the small bumps of Helix still in their pockets, and I heaved a sigh of relief before gingerly picking at the seam I had chosen out for tonight.

It only took a moment to pull it loose, leaning forward to pour a tiny amount of the Helix dust into my palm. I shivered as it hit my skin, the tingling pull of it instantly unnerving me as I eyed the small amount, hoping it wasn't too much.

I glanced once at the fires ahead, then tipped the dust into my mouth and swallowed.

I instantly choked, the dust coating my tongue and throat in a horrible, bitter taste. I scooped up two handfuls of snow, sending power into my hands to melt it, only to feel it struggle and whither in my veins. It had barely gotten half of the snow melted to water before it flickered out entirely, and I gulped down what I could, trying to wash away the taste.

I felt the water go down, dragging the Helix with it like fingers of ice. I groaned, falling to my knees again as I was suddenly cut off from a part of me that I wasn't sure I could survive without.

I dragged breaths down, not entirely convinced I wasn't suffocating as a hollowness grew in my stomach and spread through my entire body. And then the worst of it came, when the whispers stopped. Those little voices that I was so used to kept me company, guiding me when I didn't even realize it. I hadn't realized how quiet the world was until they were shut off, as if a hand had been put to their throat and squeezed.

I swore as I hauled myself to my feet, fighting the urge to curl up in a ball in the snow, but without my power, I was in very real danger of freezing to death. I had no way of keeping myself warm, other than the clothes on my back, and I could already feel the bitterly cold air creeping through them.

Focusing my watering eyes on the firelights in the distance, I began to walk…

EPILOGUE
GWEN

An O'Mordha must always be in the Lowlands.

Those words had been drilled into me since I was a babe. An O'Mordha *must* always be in the Lowlands, Guinevere.

Without an O'Mordha, the wall would fall. Our people would be left with no protection. Even Morgana couldn't hold it up forever, with the magic in the wall tied to the legacies of the Sylvyn royalty left in Kambria.

My knees ached against the cold ground, my arms shaking from holding the plate laden with food in front of me. I ignored the pain, latching my eyes onto the shackle circling my wrist instead.

"Hungry, Pet?"

I raised my eyes slowly to meet his, hoping my stomach wouldn't growl and betray me as he held out a thick chunk of meat, its juices dripping down his hand. My mouth watered. I hadn't eaten in three days and my head was starting to spin every time I moved.

Tightening one hand on the plate, I cautiously reached, hating every inch of space I relented.

He pulled his hand back, tutting softly and I dropped my hand in defeat, grasping the plate in both hands again as it began to tremble in my one-handed grip.

"You know you want this," he murmured, his attention fixed on me, oblivious to the raucous behavior from the camp around us.

I jumped as a scuffle broke out, men's voices jeering and catcalling as two men wrestled, nearly upending into the fire.

"Eyes on me, Pet."

Fuck.

You.

I wanted to scream it at him, jump on him and dig my thumbs into his eyes until I was covered in his blood, but I kept my face blank as I slid my gaze back, that morsel of food once again hovering just inches from my mouth.

Power. That is what he wanted. What he got off on, and I could either break myself fighting against it, or play him at his own game.

I opened my mouth, feeling another part of my soul wither and die at the triumphant gleam in his eye.

He leaned forward, hesitating for a moment, the meat just touching the tip of my tongue, a reminder that he could take it away, before he delicately placed it in my mouth.

"See what happens when you do what you are told?" he said, eyes watching my mouth as I ate the small morsel.

Flavor exploded in my mouth, seasoned by hunger as my stomach cramped at the promise of more.

"Thank you, my King." I met his gaze, running my tongue over my lower lip to catch the faint glaze the meat had left, his eyes following it as his own tongue mimicked mine.

He speared a slice of peach on his knife, holding it to me, and I took it, the juice dripping down my chin.

It was meant to break me, but there was nothing of worth left in me to break. My pride was in tatters, lost somewhere back on the muddy, frozen path we had traveled, and my heart was safely back in Windhaven, held in the hands of the first thing I had ever chosen for myself.

Morgana.

My life has never been solely mine. It was always destined to belong to the Sylvyn. They have always come first for me. I have dedicated my life to trying to better theirs, using the power in my blood as an example to teach, to nurture, to guide those I can.

And then I let myself want something for the first time in my life.

She was meant to be his, I had known from a girl that Morgana was meant to be my brother's wife. Mother had talked so often of how the pair of them would lead the Sylvyn's back into the light.

I had tried so hard to ignore what I felt for her, it had been one of the reasons I had first left Windhaven, trying to put distance between us, trying to sever the hold she had on me.

Then I had returned after trying to find a life in the Lowlands. It had only taken one look to know that the years I had spent trying to forget her had been in vain.

She was my addiction, and for the first time in my life I was selfish. I let myself give in to what my heart had been screaming for. Those weeks I spent in her arms were more than I could have dreamed of, and not enough. It was the promise of what life could have been.

"Good girl." His words dragged me back from my memories, his thumb brushing the line of juice that dripped from my chin. He followed the line of it up, hovering it over the seam of my lips, and I only hesitated for a moment before dipping my head to lick the juice from it.

The corners of his mouth curled, and he took the plate from my stiff fingers.

"We have a long day of travel tomorrow, and you look as if you are about to fall asleep on your feet. Go and rest, Pet."

Forcing my legs to move, I stood, my feet numb and feeling clumsy beneath me. *Don't you dare stumble.*

I inclined my head to the monster that had just ripped my life apart, fantasizing about what it would feel like to rake my nails down his face, feel his blood coat my hands. But that would only get me killed, the tenuous truce I had clawed out, over before it had begun.

The Blood Traitor caught my gaze as I turned, his mismatched eyes roaming over me with a bored expression, and I gave him the same back. Of everyone here, he was the one that confused me the most.

Arthur was simple. I had already worked out what twisted fantasies possessed him.

The men we traveled with were inconsequential.

The Traitor I couldn't yet work out, and reading people was a gift of mine.

I walked toward my tent, Rian and Donal waiting at the entrance as they always were, their presence nothing more than a symbolic gesture of false security. They were mere witnesses to my degradation, and I was trying not to hate them for it.

"Gwen." Rian stopped me with a light touch to my arm as I passed him, and I paused, turning my head the slightest fraction, not wanting to look at him.

"Are you ok?' he asked. "Can I... get you anything?"

"I just want to sleep," I said, my voice cracking with exhaustion.

His hand brushed over my arm, squeezing gently.

"There is nothing you can do, Rian," I murmured, making myself meet his gaze.

Pity and anger is all I saw.

"I chose this," I said quietly. "So stop looking at me like that."

Rian let his hand slip from my arm, his gaze full of hatred moving toward the men behind us.

It was true, I had chosen this willingly, and I would do it a thousand times over, because my people lay at my back. Families, children, innocents that didn't deserve their fate. Beautiful, strong, loving people who had been left to rot in lands that could not support them.

But an O'Mordha must always be in the Lowlands. So I did the only thing I could do, I offered myself up instead. Bartered Saoirse's life with the respect I had gathered over the years. The trust the Sylvyn had given me without a second thought.

Because I am no O'Mordha. I am le Fay, my mother's dirty little secret. A bastard daughter who only carried the O'Mordha name to save Kerrich the disgrace of people knowing his wife had strayed.

I am Guinevere le Fay, and I will not be broken.

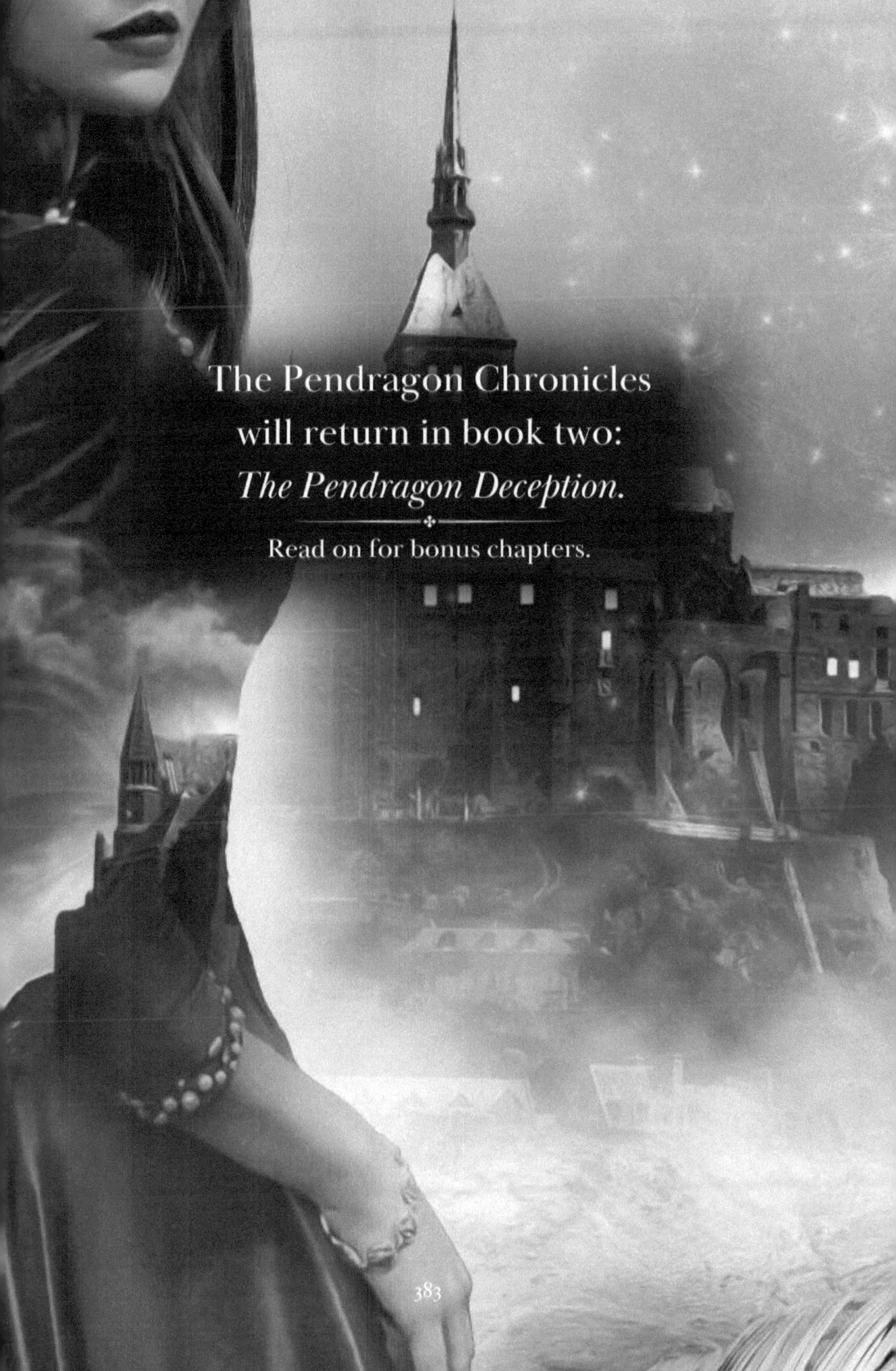

The Pendragon Chronicles
will return in book two:
The Pendragon Deception.

Read on for bonus chapters.

THE BELT

Seven years prior

I hate the cold, and I hate the rain. And right now, I am both frozen *and* soggy.

The rain began pelting me the day after I left Windhaven, and my mood has been about as black as the stormy sky.

Dearg, my mare, is almost as dark about life as I am, ears flat to her head and mane plastered to her neck.

There are still days of travel ahead before I reach The Hollow. The promise of Madraigh's stew, a warm fire, and a hug from my sister are the only things keeping me from scuttling back to Windhaven. That and the fact that I haven't seen Gwen in months now, and I miss her bitterly.

I let a tendril of my gift crackle to life around me, warming my drenched clothing, but I can't keep it up if this miserable weather continues.

A crack of thunder above me has Dearg flinching, but she stands her ground, whickering softly as I pat her withers. My hand came away covered in hair, stuck to my wet skin, and I grimaced, wiping it on my pants.

Up ahead was a marker, a boulder with smaller rocks piled above it in a haphazard design, and I recognized it as the one to the Walsh farm that we had stopped at once before. Gwen knew them and had mentioned Cara—the owner—to me before.

With a last, long look at the sky, I turned Dearg toward it.

"Hellooo the house!" I called as I approached the small farm. It was well kept but showed the wear The Lowlands have suffered these past years. No one has much anymore.

There were a few animals in pens, some goats blatting at me from the shelter of their makeshift sheds, and a single cow that looked as if she were getting on in years. Some bedraggled chickens peered out at me from under the deck of the house, and a cat squatted by the front door, glaring at my approach.

The door pushed open, and an older woman stepped out that I recognized as Cara. She was short, and had slightly greying hair, her long Sylvyn ears showing how many winters she had seen, and was wearing simple, clean, but worn clothing.

Drying her hands on her apron she peered up at me with concern.

"Blessed Nimmet, lass! Weathers too rough to be travelin' in—you will catch your death of cold! Are you in need of shelter?"

"Yes, if you have the room," I said, brushing my fingers to my sodden forehead in greeting. "Your barn will do fine. We met a while back, my name is Saoirse O'Mordha."

Cara startled, looking at me closer. "Lady Gwen's sister?"

I didn't get a chance to answer before she leaned back in the doorway, hollering something I couldn't catch.

A moment later a young boy trotted out.

"Settle the Lady's mare, darlin'," Cara ordered the boy, beckoning me down. "Come in, come in. Good grief, I didn't even recognize you, all blue around the edges!"

It took me a moment to get my packs unbuckled, the leather swollen and hard to undo, but then I was trailing her into the house and its welcoming wall of heat.

I stood just inside the entrance in a slowly spreading pool of water, feeling more and more like a drowned rat with every passing moment as multiple pairs of eyes landed on me.

Cara whipped away my saddle bags, my drenched clothing from within them laid out and steaming in front of the fire in moments, then she gave me a long assessing look. "I might have some old clothes you can borrow while we dry those that yer' wearin'? Nothin' special mind, but I have a few dresses I haven't fit for a while now."

A broad-shouldered man with dark hair and fair skin tanned from days working in the sun, laughed from where he was reclining by the large fireplace. "Cara, your dresses will come to her knees!" He turned his attention to me. "You can borrow some of my clothes if you'd like?"

I glanced at him, flashing him a grateful smile, then looked closer, trying to be subtle about it. He had soft brown eyes and a wide smile that kept my eyes lingering on him longer than they should have.

He sauntered toward me, his grin holding more than just friendliness as his eyes swept over me... and then I realized how terrible I must look, travel-stained, and half-drowned in yesterday's clothes.

"I have a room out the back," he said, winking. "You can change in there too if you'd like."

I mumbled my appreciation, following him through the house and out the back door. There were smaller rooms tacked onto the back of the house, and he disappeared into one, leaving the door open for me.

The room was simple, but tidy. A narrow cot took up one side of the room, a modest table with a rickety chair under a small window that let light into the room on the other side. The man began rummaging through a set of draws by the window while I took in the small carvings that littered the room. They were exquisitely detailed, and I peered closely at a small badger, looking as if it were walking along his window ledge.

"You like that one?" he asked, crossing to me with some folded clothes over his arm.

"It's beautifully made," I admitted. There were all kinds of animals, from rooks to hares, but it was that little badger that held my attention.

He picked it up, turning it over in his hand as he studied me thoughtfully. "It suits you."

I raised a brow at him. "Pardon?"

He chuckled softly, holding it out and I took it, squinting at the fine designs that made it look as if it had been captured in motion, the wind rustling its hair.

"Badgers keep to themselves mostly. They are intelligent and tend not to start trouble… but corner them, and they are vicious wee beasties." He shook his head as I went to hand it back to him.

"People tend to be drawn to the ones that represent who they are inside. Keep it, it's yours."

I gave him a dry look but couldn't help my fingers curling around the small carving. "Did you just call me a vicious beastie?"

He smirked, handing me the clothes. "If the boot fits…"

I narrowed my eyes at him. "You don't even know me... and I didn't catch your name?"

"Rian. I was here the last time you came through with the Lady Gwen," he said, with that slow smile that was doing strange things to my stomach. "Though I didn't get a chance to introduce myself back then. And no, I don't know you... yet."

"That's bold of you, Rian."

"I believe 'thank you' were the words you were looking for," he said, dropping his eyes to where I was gripping the carving. "And you are most welcome, Saoirse." He winked at me, and strode out of the room, shutting the door behind him and leaving me blinking in the middle of the room.

The Walsh farm had an air of welcoming about it that I fell in love with very quickly. By night, the rain had stopped, a fire had been built and we ate supper around it under the stars.

Even though food was scarce and they barely had enough for themselves, not one person begrudged me for sharing their food and Cara wouldn't hear of me eating the dried travel rations I had brought with me for the trip.

I vowed to myself then and there I would never come here again without something to offer them.

There were more people here than I had imagined. A small group of men worked on the farm, two of whom had wives. Cara, her three daughters, and a gaggle of children that belonged to various members of the farm and were impossible to tell who they belonged to.

I got on well with the men, which wasn't unusual, I tended to prefer the company of men in general. Morgana was the exception, but then... she wasn't like most women I knew. I chuckled under my breath as I imagined her face if she had to sit with the groups of women that tended to congregate together in the castle, talking about the latest dress they had made, or a man they were lusting after. It would end in tears, and none would be hers.

"What are you thinking about, wee beastie?" A deep voice came from next to me, and I looked up to see Rian, holding a mug of ale out to me, his back to the fire.

I stood, one hand holding the pants I was wearing that were far too loose and threatening to drop to my ankles, and took the ale with my free hand, wincing as I took a sip of the bitter liquid.

"Yeaaah, it's not the best," he chucked. "But the harvest was poor and we made do.".

"I wasn't complaining," I rasped, choking it down.

"Your face did it for you," he snorted. "And you didn't answer my question."

I raised a brow.

"You were smiling," he said softly. "Thinking about anyone in particular?"

I gave him a flat look. "I was thinking about a friend."

His face fell ever so slightly, but I caught it before he managed to hide it. I don't know why I felt the need to clarify but I went on. "We grew up together. She lives in the castle and is like a sister to me."

He slid his gaze to mine, the firelight catching in his eyes. "What is she like?"

"She's a complete bitch," I huffed. "But that's why I love her. I like it when people speak their minds, and she does it enough for all of us."

Rian choked on his ale, and I moved to his side to thump him heartily on the back. This resulted in the pants slipping lower down my hips and I hastily pulled them back up.

Rian snickered. "They fit well."

I glared at him. "The chivalrous thing to do would be to offer me your belt before I accidentally bare my arse to the entire farm."

I felt his eyes on me and turned to see him running his eyes ever so slowly down my body.

"I can assure you, they would appreciate yours more than mine." He stuck a thumb in his belt. "This is my only one."

I sucked on a tooth, studying him. "I will play you for it."

We were standing far enough away from the others that they couldn't hear our conversation, the fire warming our backs nicely, but he still lowered his voice as he leaned into me. "What do I get if I win?"

Nimmet burn me, this man was trouble.

"What would you like?" I asked, my words far bolder than I felt.

He thought for a moment, his eyes lingering on my lips long enough that his answer took me by surprise. "A favor, to be collected at a time of my choosing."

"A favor?" I asked dubiously, my brows raised.

"Aye." He smirked at me. "With how often I come to Windhaven, it's a wise bet for its Lady to owe me a favor. Do you know how hard it is to find a decent meal there?"

I chuckled, studying him a moment longer and seeing nothing behind his eyes but frank honesty. It was refreshing.

"Done," I said, holding my hand over my heart. "Cards or knives?"

"Knives," he said. Prepare to lose, beastie."

I handed his arse to him. Twice.

We had gathered an audience of almost all of the inhabitants of the farm by the time we were done.

I bested his throws every time, my blades hitting their mark with near perfect aim, even if his throws were nearly as good.

I even ended on a perfect bullseye, my second blade lodging into the hilt of my first and earning appreciative whistles from the gathered crowd, and there wasn't a hint of reproach as Rian unbuckled his belt and whipped it off, passing it to me with a wink.

"Well, send me running back to my room with my tail between my legs and pants round my ankles why don't you," he teased good naturedly.

"You throw well," I offered.

"Don't mock me," he laughed.

"I throw *better*. But that doesn't mean you aren't impressive yourself," I chuckled.

"I'll take it," he muttered under his breath, nodding his head at some men as they called their goodnights, his hand gripping the waistband of his—now dangerously loose—pants.

Cara bustled over to us, a young child tucked on her hip. "I'm turnin' in now, love," she said warmly. There is a bedroll set up for you by the fireplace inside."

"Honestly, the barn is perfectly oka—" I cut off as she flapped a hand at me.

"Nonsense! The barn roof has a leak and there is plenty of room inside." She gave me a warm smile, before turning her gaze on Rian. "The lads asked if you would attend the hunt in the morning, they saw some deer deep in the wood and they will need help carryin' it back if they find them again."

"Of course," Rian said, inclining his head to her. "Those fences down in the lower fields need fixing, but they can wait until I get back."

We both watched Cara scurry away, calling children to her as she did, and I couldn't help but smile once again at the homely feel of this place.

I turned to see Rian watching me in the dim light.

"I should turn in too," he said, giving me a wry smile. "Those lads are awake before the roosters crow."

I was surprised by how much I didn't want him to go, content to stand by the fire with him, but I hid my disappointment in my mug, taking another swallow of the vile stuff.

"Did you want to join the hunt?" he asked, and I could hear the faint glimmer of hope in his voice.

"I need to keep moving tomorrow. If I take too much longer, Gwen will send half of The Hollow out looking for me… but, maybe next time?"

He nodded, a sparkle in his eye that had nothing to do with the flickering flames behind us.

"I will practice then. Maybe next time you will be the one to lose the belt."

I smirked at him. "Maybe. Or perhaps I will find something else of yours I want."

His smile was wicked as he touched his hand to his heart.

"Goodnight, beastie. Sleep well."

I touched my own hand to my heart. "Goodnight, Rian."

THE HAYLOFT

BONUS CHAPTER | BEST READ AFTER
CHAPTER 21

"I did tell you it was too much too soon."

I gave Gwen a dark look from the tree that I leaned against, trying in vain to catch my breath with the shallow gulps of air my cracked ribs would allow. My wet hair was cold against my neck, a damp patch spreading across my chest where the end of my braid rested, and my skin was still pink from the scrubbing I had just given it in the achingly cold water of the nearby river.

She put her hands on her hips, a ruddy brow raised at me. "Did I not?"

"There is only so much laying down I can take," I replied, pushing off the tree and trying to keep my back as rigid as possible as I walked. "And I was starting to smell like a goat."

I stepped on uneven ground and jarred my ribs, sucking in a subtle breath as I waited for the spike of pain to subside.

Gwen's hand flattened against my back, steadying me.

Clearly not subtle enough.

"I offered to bring water to you to wash," she said, resigned.

"I managed perfectly fine," I said.

It was a lie of course. This short trip to the river had taken the best part of two hours and I had used every filthy word I knew in the process, my dignity left somewhere back on the river's edge after I had admitted defeat and allowed Gwen to help me wash.

Gwen muttered something under her breath that sounded suspiciously like "stubborn wretch" but I was too focused on trying to breathe through another wave of pain to defend myself.

In truth, I had just wanted out of that damned cabin.

I was tired of being stared at. Tired of the way voices would hush whenever I looked in anyone's direction. Tired of more food being offered to me than anyone else, and the fluffing over me that Cara had been doing. But what had set me on edge the most, were the glances of anxious hope that I was starting to see from all of them. Like I was some promised miracle that could change their fates. The only one who treated me no differently was Rian, and I had a feeling Saoirse was behind that.

"There ya are!" Cara called as she caught sight of our slow progress back to that infernal cabin. "Erin was looking for you."

As if on cue, the girl skipped around the corner, faltering as she caught sight of me and skidded to a halt. She bobbed her head and lowered her eyes to the ground.

"I'm ready for your healin', Child of Nimmet."

"Thank you, sweetheart," Gwen said gently, squeezing my arm in warning as though she could sense my irritation at the title. "Where do you want her?"

"Lyin' down please," Erin said, giving Gwen a hesitant smile that dropped as soon as she looked back my way. "Follow me."

"Be nice," Gwen murmured to me as I tackled the porch steps one by agonizing one.

"This *is* me being nice," I shot back.

My black mood improved slightly as Erin's small hands across my torso melted away the pain that had been biting at me with every breath. I even managed a small smile as she stepped back afterward.

"Thank you," I said.

"It's my pleasure," she replied before skipping away, albeit with a bit less gusto than she had before. The child had a weak healing gift, enough to have saved my life and encouraged my heart to pick up the sluggish beat Gwen had forced it to maintain, but not enough that these healings drained too much from her. For that I was grateful, I was already feeling the deep pang of guilt harshly enough.

I ran a hand over my chest, pressing slightly against it and welcoming the pain that flared under my fingers. It was a reminder of what she had done. Gwen had fought for me, ripped me back from Ankii's beckoning fingers by sheer willpower alone and refused to let me go, even after my body had given up.

Something had changed in her after that night. I could see it in the way she looked at me, a final wall she had been keeping between us had shattered and she had lain herself bare.

It terrified me.

She had seen the blackness in my soul and did not run from it.

I reached a mental finger down to that darkness now

slumbering once again within me, and brushed across it, feeling it crack an eye.

Chan e, mo fhear dorcha.

The shadowed words that brushed my ear sounded like a warning, even if I could not understand their meaning. My heart skipped a beat, as if reminding me of what happened the last time I ignored those whispered messages, and I drew away from that darkness, my gaze sliding to Gwen.

She was leaning against the countertop, chatting to one of the men who had come in to have a small wound on his hand patched. He smiled at her, his eyes lingering too long on her lips, his injured hand held out between them as he waited for Cara to come with a bandage.

"That looks sore," I said dryly, pushing off the bed with a small groan.

His eyes snapped to mine, then lowered to my feet as I crossed the space to them.

"Oh, it's nothin', Child of Nimmet," he said quickly. "Just need a scrap of cloth to cover it so it don't get infected none."

I grunted, grasping his wrist and pulling it to me so he had to turn away from Gwen, ignoring the ache of my ribs from the movement. I sent my shadows into the small wound and knitted it together in moments.

He yelped as it stitched faster than it should have, stepping back from me only to gawk at the unmarred skin, a smear of blood the only proof it had been there at all.

"Th-thank you," he stammered, ducking his head at me, then touched his heart to Gwen. "Milady." Then he was gone, scurrying back out the door.

I turned to see Gwen, surveying me with a raised brow.

"What?" I asked, widening my eyes and trying to look innocent.

"You have no people skills, have I ever told you that?"

I winked at her, giving her a slow, heated smile. "I beg to differ."

Her cheeks stained pink, the only sign of how flustered she felt as I stepped closer, tilting my head to the side. "Want me to remind you of exactly what those skills are, Princess?"

"I take it your ribs are feeling better?" she asked.

"Much," I replied softly.

"Hmmm," she hummed, sounding less than convinced, leaning in until her lips were almost brushing mine.

I ran the tip of my tongue along her lower lip. The same lip that man had been eyeing, my breath catching as the movement pained my ribs, before kissing her deeply, her hands resting on my hips.

"Liar," she whispered against my lips, the corners of her own mouth kicking up. "Come sit by the fire and prove to me how nicely you can play with others."

I have never felt so personally offended by an inanimate object than I have been by the ladder to that God's forsaken hayloft. Fuck that ladder. Fuck it hard.

I refused to spend one more night in that cabin, so the ladder it was, and I realized I had made an egregious mistake roughly twelve steps into the twenty—fucking—seven it took to get to the upper level.

Had Gwen not been softly laughing to herself at the bottom, I would have quietly slunk back to the cabin.

By the time I had reached the top, there were stars flickering in the corners of my vision, and I was silently committing myself to living out the rest of my days up here because there was no way I was getting back down.

I lowered myself gingerly to my bedroll, catching my breath as Gwen followed me up.

"Would it have been easier to shadow walk up here?" she asked.

"No less painful," I muttered, leaning my head back against the crackle of the hay.

"Cara was more than happy for you to stay in the cabin," she teased, and I heard her moving around the loft, straightening her roll before moving to the bags and rummaging through them.

I rolled my head, watching her as she unlaced her dress and pushed it off her shoulders, her back to me, and the loose fabric caught at her hips.

She had two dimples at her hipbones, and I had taken great delight in kissing them when I last had my hands on her, before running the tip of my nose up the concavity of her spine. The memory of how soft her skin had been was still fresh in my mind.

"Come here," I murmured.

She peered over her shoulder at me before shrugging the loose shirt she slept in over her head and shimmied out of the rest of her dress, then turned and picked her way across the loft before stooping to grab her bedroll and dragging it into place beside mine.

I ran a hand down her back as she settled next to me, my fingers tracing the curve of her waist, and tugged gently, whisps of my shadows skittering up her back and melting into the fabric of her shirt, seeming as eager to be against her skin as I was.

Gwen leaned on her elbow next to me, her hands tucked against her chest as if she were too scared to touch me in my injured state.

"You need rest," she murmured.

A shadowed hand gripped her throat, and she gasped as it drew her down until her lips hovered over mine, right where I wanted them.

"I *am* resting."

She braced an arm across my torso, careful not to lean against me, but I could see the arguments dying on her lips as I reached to run my fingers into her hair, the shadowed hand at her throat dissipating as I ran my lips along her jaw.

"You are not playing fair," she whispered, closing her eyes.

"I will never play fair when it comes to you," I murmured back, reaching her lips and kissing her softly.

She melted against me, her kiss turning urgent. Her tongue flicked across mine as power danced in my blood, set aflame by her touch.

I felt a tug at my shirt where it was tucked into the borrowed pants I wore, my own clothes still too snug around my chest for comfort, and then her warm hand was moving up my side, over my scars to cup my breast, a low hum of contentment coming from her as she deepened the kiss.

Suddenly the ladder didn't seem so bad after all, not as Gwen's hand left my breast and she slowly slid a leg over me until she was straddling my thighs and began to deftly unbutton my pants. I slid my leg up, pressing my thigh between her legs, smirking as her fingers fumbled on the last button.

Her hands curled around the waistband of my pants, and I lifted my hips enough for her to slide them off, clenching my jaw against the flare of pain in my chest as I did.

Gwen prowled up my body, settling her weight on my hips, and I groaned as I felt her bare against me under her shirt.

She froze. "Did I hurt you?"

"No," I said, my voice husky. I made to sit up and gasped as pain gripped me for a moment.

"Stop," Gwen murmured, pushing me gently back, her hands on my shoulders. "It's too soon for this, you are still too injured. She moved to swing her leg off me, and I gripped her hips, stilling her.

"I don't need to move to have you moaning my name, Princess. I can feel exactly how much you want me right now." I slid my hand from her hip, across her thigh, dipping between her legs.

Her face slackened as I brushed my fingers over her, covering my fingers in her arousal before bringing it back up to the space between us, her eyes falling to my glistening fingers then widening as I brought them to my lips and licked them clean. A blush crept up her neck, momentarily entranced as she watched my tongue glide up the side of my finger and her hand ran slowly up her thigh as she watched me, gliding between her legs and disappearing beneath the oversized shirt.

I could feel what she was doing, pressed against me as she was, and I couldn't help the sound I made as I felt her begin to touch herself.

Her eyes sharpened on me at the noise, those beautiful lips of hers kicking up at the sides.

"Oh." Her fingers moved again as she watched me for a reaction. "I can see why you enjoy teasing *me* so much." She rocked her hips against her hand once, her smile turning wicked as I felt my mouth fall open slightly, my attention honed on where her hand disappeared under that damned shirt.

She sighed softly, rolling her hips, her fingers moving slowly against herself and then gave a *very* deliberate moan.

"Keep going," I murmured, running my hand up her leg as she peered down at me like the queen she was sitting on her throne.

She smirked at me, finally grasping the hem of her shirt, drawing it up and over her head before tossing it to the side.

Gods she was beautiful.

"Maybe I want you moaning for me."

With the ache that had flared between my thighs, that wasn't going to be hard. I would do it now if it meant she kept touching herself like that.

I made a sound of protest as she lifted herself off me and she laughed softly, leaning down to tease me with the promise of a kiss before lowering herself beside me, her lips moving to my neck, my collar, her deft fingers beginning to undo my shirt.

I ran the backs of my knuckles along her breast, but she caught it, pushing it down and trapping it between our bodies.

Anxiety ran its claw down my mind as my shirt parted then was removed entirely, my scars now visible to her. Gwen's face held nothing but desire as she traced a finger down the edge of them, and it eased something within me. The deep blues and purples of the bruising across my chest were stark against the paleness of my skin and hers as she ran her fingers over the upper curve of my breast, pausing over my heart to feel it's steady thump for a moment.

I swallowed, unprepared for the wave of emotion that hit me as similar feelings crossed her own face, and then she was bending to drop a kiss there, her breath warm against my skin. Her lips trailed a line of scar that bracketed my breast, her hair trailing across my sensitive nipple and making me suck in a breath.

"Hurting?" she murmured.

"No," I breathed. "Not at all."

She hummed under her breath, her tongue trailing warm and wet across the heavy underside of my breast before coming up to capture a nipple, and I gasped, her hand catching my leg and pulling it across her hip. She moaned softly as her fingers trailed down my thigh, her tongue flicking against my nipple in a way I desperately wanted between my legs instead, the ache that was building there surprising me with its ferocity.

I didn't know what to do with this. This need that took over like a wildfire and set my skin ablaze in a way that I craved. Fire was my enemy, except when she wielded it, and I would gladly burn for her.

"I love you like this," Gwen murmured, pulling my rapidly evaporating self-control back from the clouds as she moved fluidly to straddle my hips.

"Like what?" I asked, as she twined our fingers together and pushed my hands flat to the hay beneath us.

She leaned down, trailing the tip of her nose along my ribs, moving down my body.

"Mine," she said quietly. "It's a side no one else sees. You let yourself be vulnerable."

I definitely felt vulnerable as she brushed kisses over a particularly scarred patch on my hip, although the hand that trailed lower and nudged at my thigh quickly distracted me.

I slid my leg to the side, letting her settle between them, but she gripped under my knee and pushed it wider still.

"Gwen," I gasped, feeling her edge lower.

"Hmm?" She had moved down to my belly button and was peering up at me through her lashes, a devious smile on her face. "Yes, Morgana?"

I would have given *anything* right then, for my ribs to have been fully healed. She would have been on her back in moments with her thighs around my neck and *Gods* I wouldn't stop until she was screaming loud enough that the entire Lowlands would know she was mine.

"This isn't fair, I'm not very… capable right now."

She chuckled darkly. "I will never play fair when it comes to you, Morgana."

Nimmet save me. If my soul wasn't already twining itself around her like an enraptured cat, it would be after hearing her echo my own words back to me, full of wicked intent that made the darkness in me sit up and listen.

Hay crackled as I sunk my fingers into the blankets and her breath warmed my thighs. But she only kissed it. First my scarred thigh, then the other.

Her tongue flicked across my skin, hand pushing my other leg wide until I was completely bared to her. I had allowed past lovers to touch me. I enjoyed using their hands and fingers to reach my pleasure, but not like this, this was too intimate… too… *oh my Gods.*

There was a flash of pain as she bit my thigh, then eased away the small hurt with her tongue, and I moaned softly as her breath fanned over me as she moved to the other thigh, nipping at it too.

"Tell me what makes you feel good," she murmured, nipping her way up to the crease of my thigh and then running her tongue along it.

"This," I gasped, my breathing beginning to come faster as all my attention focused on the path her tongue was taking along my skin.

"No. Tell me the things you haven't asked for from others," she said softly as she moved to the crease of my other thigh and gave it the same attention. "The things you do to yourself when you are alone."

I was aching for her to stop teasing me, the throb of it becoming more intense as she brushed a fingertip through my folds, the light touch worsening the ache. It took a moment before I could trust my voice.

"What you did with your tongue, back in Lallymoore. It was perfect," I breathed, my heart pounding.

Another teasingly light pass with her fingertip had a whimper escaping from me, and she rewarded the sound with a slightly firmer pass, slowing over my clit as she did.

"Just my tongue?" she asked, her own voice husky as her finger dropped lower, slipping through my wetness and pressing against my entrance.

"No, give me your fingers," I breathed, not caring that I had lost all composure.

I moaned low in my throat as she did what I asked, my eyes rolling back in my head as she crooked one finger inside me, massaging in just the right place. I could hear how wet I was around her finger, the sound lewd in the silence of the barn, only the wind outside breaking the peace.

"Just one?" she whispered, and then I felt a featherlight pass of her tongue that had me clenching around her. She cursed under her breath, and I glanced down my body to see her attention locked on what her hand was doing before she looked up at me with hooded eyes.

"Just. One?" she repeated, and I shook my head, watching her face as she withdrew her hand then added a second finger, her own breath becoming short.

I couldn't help the sound that came out of me as I felt my body grip her.

"Can you come just like this?" she asked, her fingers working that spot inside me that was sending waves of pleasure through me.

My head fell back, a small cry ripping from me. "No," I said when I could speak again. Her hand withdrew, and then I felt her add a third finger, easing them very slowly back inside me.

"Fuck," I moaned, hands twisting in the fabric beneath me

as the stretch of my body around hers almost tipped me over the edge. "Like that, but deeper."

She slowly began working her fingers in and out, pushing deep and crooking them until I could do nothing but pant and moan.

She edged me like that for what felt like hours, pleasure and frustration fighting each other as my thighs began to shake, dancing on the edge of my orgasm.

"Gwen, please," I whispered, not sure if I could take much more of her exquisite torture.

She rolled her fingers in answer, pressing the heel of her hand against me as she did and I rocked my hips, trying to grind against it and give me what I needed to crest this wave she kept me on, but she pulled it away, and I moaned in defeat.

She thrust harder with her fingers and my spine bowed, head kicking back into the hay, ignoring the pain in my chest as I felt my muscles quiver around her fingers, so close, yet maddeningly out of reach.

"I need your tongue," I gasped, every roll of her fingers sending pleasure pulsing through me.

I felt the heat of her tongue graze lightly over me.

"Like that?" she teased.

She got to her knees between my legs, pushing my leg up and angling my hips in a way that had her hitting places within me that I didn't realize I had.

"Gwen, please!" I begged again, reaching down and brushing my fingers over my clit. It sent shockwaves through me, and I felt the start of my release begin as I desperately worked myself toward it. She entertained it only for a moment before she pushed my hand away.

"Tell me what you need," she urged.

"Your tongue, let me come on your tongue," I pleaded, stars flickering in my vision as she worked her fingers harder.

She dipped her head, and my breath exploded from me in a wail as she ran her tongue firmly over my clit, her fingers massaging within me.

It took an embarrassingly short amount of time before my entire body locked up and an orgasm hit me so hard I couldn't even breathe as it wracked my entire body.

She worked me through it with long swipes of her tongue, each one drawing another wail from me as I contracted around her, slowly coming down from the stars she had thrown me into.

It was only as I felt her prowl over me, her weight on her arms that I could find the energy to crack an eye open and stare at her in wonder.

"I think you are going to need to restart my heart again," I whispered, my voice cracked and hoarse.

She grinned at me, then leaned in, kissing me deeply and I tasted myself on her tongue.

"I will restart it as many times as I need to, to keep you here with me," she replied softly.

I fell asleep faster than I had in decades, my body completely sated, as Gwen trailed her fingers up and down my back… and that night… there were no nightmares.

ACKNOWLEDGMENTS

This book had so much love from so many different, wonderful people, that it belongs in part to them too.

A village baby, if you will.

Shelly—You took my manuscript and polished it into a gem, working with you is a wonderful experience and I can't wait to see what we can achieve together for the rest of this series.

Haus of Fables—Sam, Shelly, and Celeste, for not only the undying support in all aspects of my author journey, but for putting together the truly spectacular ARC boxes and managing the release of this book into the world.

My team—You have all played a part in different ways. Thank you. It doesn't ever go unnoticed. #bestteamever

My ADHD—You really are a pain in my ass but holy Gods you are the bomb at hyper-focusing out books. Well done, couldn't have done it without you. But like… Could you chill out please?

Much obliged.

ALSO BY C. C. DAVIE

Heliacle Rising | The Wytchling Chronicles

The Shadow of Wings | The Wytchling Chronicles

The Heir of Vasilica | The Wytchling Chronicles